JILTING
The DUKE

BOOK YOUR PLACE ON OUR WEBSITE AND MAKE THE READING CONNECTION!

We've created a customized website just for our very special readers, where you can get the inside scoop on everything that's going on with Zebra, Pinnacle and Kensington books.

When you come online, you'll have the exciting opportunity to:
- View covers of upcoming books
- Read sample chapters
- Learn about our future publishing schedule
  (listed by publication month and author)
- Find out when your favorite authors will be visiting
  a city near you
- Search for and order backlist books from our
  online catalog
- Check out author bios and background information
- Send e-mail to your favorite authors
- Meet the Kensington staff online
- Join us in weekly chats with authors, readers and
  other guests
- Get writing guidelines
- AND MUCH MORE!

**Visit our website at
http://www.kensingtonbooks.com**

JILTING
the DUKE

RACHAEL MILES

ZEBRA BOOKS
KENSINGTON PUBLISHING CORP.
http://www.kensingtonbooks.com

ZEBRA BOOKS are published by

Kensington Publishing Corp.
119 West 40th Street
New York, NY 10018

All Kensington titles, imprints, and distributed lines are available at special quantity discounts for bulk purchases for sales promotion, premiums, fund-raising, educational, or institutional use.

Special book excerpts or customized printings can also be created to fit specific needs. For details, write or phone the office of the Kensington Sales Manager. Attn.: Sales Department. Kensington Publishing Corp., 119 West 40th Street, New York, NY 10018. Phone: 1-800-221-2647.

Zebra and the Z logo Reg. U.S. Pat. & TM Off.

First Printing: February 2016
ISBN-13: 978-1-4201-4086-6
ISBN-10: 1-4201-4086-8

eISBN-13: 978-1-4201-4087-3
eISBN-10: 1-4201-4087-6

10 9 8 7 6 5 4 3 2 1

Printed in the United States of America

To Ted Dotts (1934–2015),
for the grace of your company.

To Jodi Thomas,
for sharing your time, expertise, and knowledge with
generosity, kindness, and good humor.
I could not have had a better mentor.

ACKNOWLEDGMENTS

No book makes its way to readers without the kindness of many people, so many that I fear I will miss someone.

I'm especially grateful to the following: my agent, Courtney Miller-Callihan, for her instincts, patience, and general good sense, and Ingrid Powell, for her generous and insightful critique.

At Kensington, I've been lucky to have a great cover designed by Janice Rossi and illustrated by Anthony Russo as well as engaging cover blurbs written by Erin Nelsen Parekh. But most of all, I've been tremendously lucky in my editor, Esi Sogah, for her advocacy, her articulate and perceptive commentary, and her questionable sense of humor.

I benefited as well from a gracious and attentive group of readers: Cathy Blackwell, Celia Bonaduce, Leigh Bonds, Michelle Carlin, Ann Donahue, Stephanie Eckroth, Jean Kimball, Jeff Kinman, Veronica Rice, Lynn Rushton, Brandon Shuler, Tony Walker, and especially Lowell Rice.

Finally, I would like to acknowledge my family who never questioned that I could do it and, as always, Miles, who reads everything well.

Chapter One

July 1819, London

Who murders a dying man?

Aidan Somerville, Duke of Forster, pulled loose the tight knot of his cravat. News of Tom Gardiner, Lord Wilmot's death had arrived in London the preceding fall. But even after a year, Aidan had no answers, just suspicions. He only knew that he had failed his old friend—and continued to fail him—in not avenging his death.

The streets were dark, illuminated at intervals by the dim light of street lamps low on oil. It was reckless to walk London streets alone after midnight. But the walk was short—no more than half an hour if he took the path across the park—and it couldn't be helped. He'd sent Fletcher and his coach home hours ago.

From the darkened alleyway ahead of him, Aidan heard muffled sounds of movement, and he stepped into the shadows. Waiting to see what trouble emerged, he wished—not for the first time—that he hadn't gone to Lady Belmont's salon. Her invitation included more than witty repartee, but he had felt nothing, not even male pride, when she'd let her hand linger too openly on his. And nothing later, when at dinner—during a rancorous debate on currency and the bank question—she had slipped a nimble foot up the inside of his thigh, then asked coyly whether he took pleasure in "the increased movement . . . of foreign markets." Lady Belmont would have laughed if he had confessed that a dead man haunted his dreams. She would have turned it into a provocative game: *"Ah, then, let us undress each other, my pet, and we will chase away the night until it is day."*

Listening, he moved his hand midway down his walking stick; the solid brass knob on the strong ebony made an elegant weapon. Another sound, closer. He would feel foolish to come up dead after living through the worst campaigns of the Peninsular War. But perhaps his grave would be quiet, quieter at least than Tom's. Aidan tightened his grip. Another low sound, just beyond the entrance to the alley. He tensed, a seasoned soldier ready for battle.

From the alley, a large red fox trotted into the light. Aidan caught back a laugh. An old soldier alarmed by a fox. As the animal disappeared into the dark on the other side of the street, Aidan continued past the alley toward the park, his thoughts returning to Tom, a man so ill no one had expected him to live out the year. Others might think it a natural death, but Aidan knew it had been murder, just as surely as he knew who had done it.

Tom's wife. Sophia.

The thought of her name twisted like steel in his chest. Even now, after the separation of a decade, her name still evoked desire and the memory of the supple warmth of her body taking him in. He felt her betrayal as a cold mass below his diaphragm, impeding his breath. If he could discover proof of Sophia's treachery, he could avenge them both, himself and Tom. Yet despite Aidan's inquiries, he knew no more than he had a year ago. He quickened his pace, as if exertion could exorcise his guilt, then crossed into the park.

The night was beautiful, cool, with a hint of the evening rain still in the air. But the scent of-something else, something heavy and florid, drew him into a section of the park lit only by intermittent moonlight. He knew the path well, for he often walked it when sleep wouldn't come. It undulated gently along the side of the park, curving against the open iron fence separating the park from the street in front of his house. Each bank of shrubs concealed the next section of the path, and he always liked the surprise of reaching the end of one bank to suddenly gain the vista of the next.

In the first section, banks of flowers, blooming white in the night, escaped their beds and crowded the path. *Ipomoea.* Without thinking, he remembered the flower's proper name, and—without wanting to—Sophia's hand warm in his, teaching him the names of the night-blooming flowers as they walked through her uncle's gardens.

Name it right, and I'll give you a kiss.

Will you not kiss me if I name it wrong?

You'll have to name it and see. But I'll tell you a secret: If you drink in the scent when it blooms, like now, you'll have visions and dreams while you sleep. And they always come true.

I don't need dreams. I already have you.

Then he had kissed her, naming all the flowers by their botanical names in a line from her lips, down her neck, and to her breasts, and back to her mouth, until her kisses, sweet against his lips, turned mad with longing. In his youth and inexperience, he'd mistaken her fervor for love.

He pushed the memory away. Had he taken her advice and slept, not in her arms but in the scent of the flowers, he might have known she would betray him. Instead, the wound she'd struck festered still, leaving him a future as bleak as his past.

The moonflower's scent was delicate, familiar, but not the source of the heady hyacinth-like perfume that pulled him deeper into the garden. Along the next curve of the path, the moonlight fell on a bank of tall flowers covered with whorls of white and pink blossoms. Their scent was so rich that its sweetness echoed on his tongue. He did not know their name, and he found their anonymity comforting.

As he stood, he sensed the presence of someone, or something. At the opposite end of a long bed of flowers, a figure emerged out of the darkness into a pool of moonlight. The figure turned slowly toward him, revealing a woman in a long hooded cloak that fell almost to the ground.

Her face came fully into the moonlight. He would have known her—the shape of her face, the contours of her cheeks—even if it had been pure dark. When her eyes met his, he felt trapped, paralyzed, as the body does at the end of dreams when not fully awake. He didn't attempt to speak. She wasn't real. Instead, he stood, fists clenched, his heart beating fast, waiting for her to disappear.

She seemed unsurprised to see him, as if she had been waiting for his arrival. In one hand, she held a cutting of the plant, its white blooms still open. She lifted the other hand slightly, palm up. To welcome him or ask for forgiveness, he didn't know. She paused, watching his face. Then she stepped back into the darkness.

He knew not to follow.

In the pool of light, a white blossom lay on the ground.

Sophia Gardiner, Lady Wilmot, kept to the darkest parts of the path, cursing. He hadn't recognized her, she consoled herself. He couldn't have. It had been too long, and she was much changed. Her face had lost the winsome fullness of youth, her lips had thinned with worry and determination, and her eyes carried the sadness of one who had long lived with death. But what if she were wrong?

At the end of the park, her hands struggled against the

latch of the iron gate, tearing the skin at her knuckles. She ignored the pain, looking over her shoulder into the darkness. Only darkness. The gate pulled free, but she forced herself to close it quietly behind her, lest the sound betray her escape.

Past the gate, she needed only to reach the corner, then a turn would protect her from sight. His sight.

She'd risked the night to see the Nottingham Catchfly— *Silene nutans*, she could hear her father correcting. They only flowered for three nights. That afternoon, her son Ian had brought her a spent white flower, asking her to name it. And she had been unable to resist the pull to smell its richness once more. The last time, she had been seven, her mother still alive. On each night of its blossoming, she, her mother, and her father had walked through the fields, until they reached the spot where the scent overwhelmed their senses. Afterward, they celebrated with savory biscuits flavored with rosemary and candied lemon peel.

She turned the corner and leaned back against the cold wall, listening for the sound of his pursuit. But she heard only the hard beat of her heart.

She had planned to propagate the cutting in her hothouse, then show Ian how the burgeoning buds heralded which nights the plant would bloom. She'd hoped the pleasure of the flowers blooming white and sweet might dispel some of the lingering sadness in Ian's serious blue eyes.

Had she imagined Aidan would find her in the park, at that hour, she would have stayed home for another year, or twelve. It wasn't solely for mourning that she hadn't ventured out; no, she'd stayed home to avoid the risk of seeing him again. Now her efforts had gone for naught, and at what cost? What would he do now that he knew she was back in London? She pulled away from the wall and walked swiftly to the alley that led to the mews behind her home. Before she turned in, she looked back. The street was empty.

When she had seen him standing at the end of the row,

she'd known immediately who he was. She felt the pull of his presence, tight in the depths of her stomach. How could she not know him? Memories of his lips, warm on her neck and shoulders, had never left her. Even on her wedding day, her thoughts had turned to him.

She wiped unbidden tears with the back of her hand, then cursed herself for crying. But he'd been so beautiful, even with his face in the half-light, the shadows forming smooth planes below his cheekbones.

He hadn't spoken, only looked at her as if he saw through her. She wondered what he had seen in that long gaze: her guilt? her fears? her desire? But as he'd watched her, she'd known—if she hadn't known before—that she would never be free of loving him.

She would never risk visiting the night-blooming flowers again. Even though she'd promised Tom, she wasn't yet ready to share her secrets with Aidan.

Chapter Two

Perkins dug in his shovel, loosening the dirt of the garden beds. "M'lady, which plants were ye wanting as a border for this bed? There's plenty of boxwood."

Sophia looked from her plans to the plants from her country estate. "I want box as a border for the outer beds, but for these inner beds, I want a different texture. Lavender, perhaps?"

Perkins wiped his brow with the back of his hat, leaving a smudge of dirt on one temple. "We've enough for this bed, and there's more at the manor house." At the wagon, he chose similarly sized lavenders to form an even border.

Turning her attention back to her plans, Sophia saw the torn skin at her knuckles. She bent her fingers, the dull ache a reminder of her recklessness. There would be no consequences, she promised herself for the twentieth time. Aidan had not followed. He had not known her.

For more than a year, she'd been plagued by a sense of foreboding. She had left London a bride not yet twenty and returned a widow not yet thirty. Buffeted by the salt wind as the ship approached the white cliffs of Dover, she'd knelt beside her watchful young son, drawing his shoulders into her side and whispering comfortingly, "This is England, Ian. This is home." But she knew it wasn't true. After the deaths of her parents, she'd never had a true home in England, only the unstable generosity of her father's relatives. And the loss of Tom's protective presence left her feeling hollow along her spine.

But if England were not her home, she could make it a home for Ian, and home for both of them meant a garden. Each night after she kissed her dark-haired boy good night, she sat at her easel, drawing and redrawing the garden beds, then watercoloring each one to see how the plants would complement one another. Her estate manager, Seth Somerville, had sent so many plants from the estate that she wondered if he had been pleased to see her setting aside her mourning.

Perkins, a laughing Cotswold plantsman with a gift for "growin things," returned from the wagon and began setting the lavender in the bed.

Sophia watched him work. She loved the planting. Seeing the flat paper of her watercolor designs transform into the depth and height of the plants gave her a sense of purpose. For too long she had felt like a tree struck by lightning, not dead, but never putting out new growth. She was afraid of disturbing that precarious stability, but perhaps—despite her encounter with Aidan in the park—she would find a way to take root and thrive here.

"What goes inside the lavender, m'lady?" Perkins interrupted her reverie, his wheelbarrow empty. He stood, tucking the spade into the side of his belt.

"My son asked for forget-me-nots, petunias, and marigolds . . . all in a jumble together." She tucked a lock of walnut-brown hair back under the confines of her bonnet. "They were my husband's favorites, and tomorrow is the anniversary of his death. I'd like to have this bed ready as a remembrance."

"Happy plants, those are. I will have the bed planted this afternoon." Perkins pushed his wheelbarrow back to the wagon.

As she watched Perkins move the marigolds, already blooming, into the wheelbarrow, Sophia recalled a long-forgotten memory. Ian, holding out marigolds in both hands, toddled toward her, with Tom, ever watchful, walking closely behind. Tom's eyes had met hers, and they had both smiled. Struck by the sweetness and the sorrow of the memory, she felt her throat tighten.

Perkins returned from the wagon, then looked past her toward the house. "Mr. Dodsley needs your attention, my lady."

Sophia turned to find her butler, all smooth propriety, approaching with a small silver tray. "M'lady, a note from Mr. Aldine. His messenger is waiting for your reply."

She recognized the plain, concise hand of her solicitor as she took the note, a single sheet folded to make its own envelope.

"Also," Dodsley continued, "Mr. Murray has sent another packet. I took the liberty of placing it on your desk in the library."

"Thank you, Dodsley. I'll write my reply in my dressing room and ring when I am finished." Sophia took her leave from Perkins, who was setting Ian's garden into an orderly chaos. As she walked back to the house, she broke the seal and unfolded the note.

"If her ladyship would be so kind, some pressing business requires her attention. I could visit her ladyship two hours hence, if she will be at home. Your most humble, sincere, and obedient servant, Mr. H. William Aldine."

In the warm sunlight of the garden, Sophia felt the chill of foreboding return.

Sophia stood in front of her wardrobe, trying to choose a dress for her afternoon meeting with her solicitor. She had already removed her garden frock and apron, and washed her arms, chest, hands, and face in the basin. Now she stood in her chemise, staring at her choices. It should be easy: one black mourning dress looks much like another. What, she wondered, did one wear to accompany a sense of impending disaster?

In a way, the problem of the dresses was rather funny. There were only three, and, by now, the ever-observant Aldine had probably catalogued her entire afternoon wardrobe in one of his precisely ruled notebooks. The only thing he had never seen her in was her chemise. There, that's a decision: wear your undergarments downstairs and see if Aldine blinks or just takes out his notebook and makes another entry.

With a sigh, she chose the unassuming black silk that buttoned from the bodice to the floor. The practical choice, she thought. It required no help from her maid, allowing Sally to remain in the nursery with Ian. As Sophia pulled the dress on, she felt the wear on its covered buttons. It was no longer a dress even a widow in mourning would wear, but the thought of venturing out, of buying new clothes, overwhelmed her.

To calm her nerves, she stood at the open doors of her balcony. Below her, the pale green grass darkened into deep shadows below the oaks, yews, and alders, and past her yard, several houses over, a statue of Flora, goddess of flowers, stood on top of a conservatory of iron and glass. Hers had become a circumscribed life, and one Tom would not praise. The house, the garden, the park with Ian, the vista from her window, they had become the whole of her world. It was a stark contrast to their life in Italy, filled with laughter and sparkling conversation. But Tom's death had stolen her ability to talk brightly about nothings with near strangers. She had no idea how to broaden her circles, or even if she wished to. Just as with the dress, she was caught in limbo. She didn't know how to change, or even if she could.

She touched the small key worn on a ribbon around her neck, a reminder of her unfulfilled promises to Tom that weighed increasingly heavy on her heart. Breathing in slowly, she turned and left her room.

As she walked down the back staircase to the library, she tried to imagine the reason for Aldine's visit. The newspapers were filled with parliamentary debates on the stability of the Bank of England and its monetary policies, alongside stories of how vast family fortunes had been lost in a single day to volatile investments.

What if their money were gone?

The idea knocked the breath from her chest. She pressed her hand against the cool plaster wall. Would she lose the house and the estate? The London house was her refuge, Tom's gift, allowing her to live in town rather than on his country estate, with her uncle and his prim wife for neighbors. But if it were a choice, she'd keep the estate. It was Ian's future.

But both? What if there were *nothing* left? To be reliant on the narrow kindness of relatives was something she'd sworn she would never do again. But for Ian, she would reconcile with the Devil . . . or her brother Phineas. She preferred the Devil.

The image of Aidan standing in moonlight rose before her. She shook it off. She would do what she had to do. She always had.

If the problem weren't their finances, then had someone learned their secret? But why take the information to Aldine,

and not to her? To know, they would have to have the
papers. . . .

She had to know. She entered the library and pulled the
key from beneath her chemise. Kneeling behind the partner
desk she had shared with Tom, she pressed a latch hidden in
the elaborately carved paneling. A panel moved to the side,
revealing the door to a hidden compartment. She unlocked
the door, holding her breath. The papers—and the hair she
had placed over them—appeared untouched.

Suddenly tired to her bones, Sophia spoke to Tom's portrait, hanging above the fireplace, "You promised me all
would be well. But after last night . . . after seeing him . . .
I don't know how it can be."

When her solicitor arrived, he handed her a letter in Tom's
hand, and she found that she had been completely wrong
about how bad the possibilities could be. The truth was
much, much worse.

Aidan stepped from his bath and rubbed a towel over his
chest and upper arms.

"You'd enjoy rake's hours more if you spent them on the
town, your grace." Barlow smiled at Aidan's scowl. "I'm sure
Cook would be delighted to concoct another sleeping posset.
She says she knows what went wrong last time. Her newest
recipe, she promises, will have you sleeping like a condemned man."

"If I risk Cook's remedies, I will *be* a condemned man.
I prefer to lie awake until morning, then sleep until noon. I
find it less damaging to my bowels than Cook's remedies."

"I think, your grace, you have simply lost your nerve."
Barlow chuckled.

Aidan threw the towel at the back of Barlow's head. But
his old sergeant turned and caught it. "You won't be catching me out," Barlow said. "I've been wise to your ways since

you convinced me that the adjutant general's daughter fancied me."

"I thought your midnight serenade at her window quite affecting." Aidan laughed. "I only wish the musicians had shown more talent."

"As I remember, your grace, you hired the musicians. Promised me they were the best in town." Barlow folded the towel in two brisk motions.

"But I didn't say *which* town. The madam of the brothel assured me she hired only the highest caliber of musician." Aidan smiled. "But I think you more than repaid me with the frog in my pack."

"I still feel for that frog. I never expected you to carry him croaking for five miles," Barlow said as he selected clothes from the wardrobe.

"It would hardly have been fair to leave him to find his own way to a good pond." Aidan watched Barlow's choices. "Am I entertaining visitors?"

"A Mr. H. W. Aldine." Stout and sturdy, Barlow had the face and the manner of a man other men trusted. Given fifteen minutes, Barlow could take any recruit's full measure, knowing his hopes, dreams, fears, and most important, whether he cheated at cards. When Aidan left the regiment, he had taken Barlow with him, and on their missions, Barlow's instincts had more than once saved their lives.

"How does he look?"

"Like a solicitor."

"Not another creditor trying to recover my brother Aaron's debts?" Aidan asked as he pulled on his trousers, shrugged into the suspenders, and buttoned the fall front on each side.

"No, your grace. Too careful with words. And he carries a portfolio of papers. . . . I placed his card on your desk." Barlow helped Aidan into his shirt.

"So if he *is* a creditor, he has the good sense to pretend to be something else." Aidan allowed Barlow to tie his cravat. "Well, show the *solicitor* into my study. I'll be down presently."

Aidan walked into his study five minutes later, having run a comb through his wet, unruly hair. His dress was casual enough to signal a lack of concern, even contempt for the business at hand. Creditors were like wolves. Any sign of weakness translated into deep losses for the ducal estate. Five minutes of polite attention could lead to months of negotiation. No, Aidan had learned quickly after his eldest brother's and then his father's deaths: a dismissive nonchalance produced the best resolutions.

A stolid man, Aldine stood behind one of the more comfortable chairs, his worn leather portfolio open in the seat before him. Aidan sized up the solicitor as he had a row of army recruits or his contacts in the more perilous world of intelligence gathering. Barlow was right: this man was no creditor. Inked at the fingers, but meticulous in his clothing, Aldine held himself with a grace that belied his sturdy frame. A man to have beside you in a fight, Aidan realized. He reconsidered Aldine's fingers: a man who wished to be underestimated. How, he wondered, would Aldine respond to a frog in his portfolio?

"Well, Mr. Aldine, what business is so urgent that you must come without warning?" Aidan used the brisk tone he found most effective at limiting unwanted interactions.

The solicitor looked from Aidan to his study. Aidan watched with interested satisfaction, knowing the room revealed little. The furniture was well-appointed, the objets d'art fine, but not extravagant. The pieces revealed no particular preference as to period or style: an ancient Grecian urn on a carved mahogany pedestal stood before a contemporary painting by a little-known artist. Aidan wondered whether Aldine saw a rake, unkempt from a night of carousing, or the former officer known for his ruthless detachment. The men's eyes met, both having taken the other's measure.

The solicitor folded his hands behind his back. "I come on behalf of Thomas Gardiner, the late Lord Wilmot. I'm to deliver a letter his lordship wrote you shortly before his death. If you agree to the proposition he outlines, I have brought papers for your signature."

At Tom's name, Aidan stiffened with complicated emotions: fondness, regret, anger, betrayal. "Wilmot has been dead a year, yet the delivery of these papers is urgent?"

"Lord Wilmot was very specific. Your letter—and one to his widow—were to be delivered within a day of the first anniversary of his death."

"Then it is convenient I am in town." Aidan leaned against the edge of his desk.

Aldine held out a letter, its seal unbroken. "His lordship instructed I am to remain while you read."

Aidan nodded acquiescence, and Aldine began laying out papers on the desk.

Tom's handwriting, though still legible, had grown less controlled.

My dear old friend,

Knowing one is dying gives a perspective to the past. Besides time and distance, only one thing stands between us, an act I cannot regret, except that it separated us. Had I lived, we would have talked and embraced again as brothers, but that conversation and the sight of your dear face has been denied me. These lines—poor substitutes— must stand in their stead.

Look beyond our present silence to our years of brotherhood when your father took a fatherless boy into his home and reared him as his own. His sons I cherished as brothers, but none more than you. Since

*I must leave my son fatherless, I ask you to serve as
his guardian. Take him into your home and heart.
Shelter him and guide him into manhood, for the
sake of our old friendship.*

*In this guardianship, I give you a partner: his
devoted mother. Do not separate the mother from
her child. Ian would adapt, as children must do, but
Sophia would suffer immeasurably. Find some way to
live near one another, forgetting the past, for my dear
child's sake.*

Love my son, protect him, rear him as your own.

Yours ever most affectionately and sincerely, Tom

Had Aidan been alone, he would have cursed out loud.
Tom's letter was unwelcome, as unwelcome as Aidan's
father's summons five years ago to return from the wars to
care for the ducal estates.

Aidan turned to the guardianship papers, noting several
contradictions between them and Tom's letter. "Let me make
sure that I understand. Wilmot's son is to live with me part of
the year?"

"If you wish. My firm disperses funds for the boy's maintenance, supported by the approval of both guardians, or one
guardian and our firm."

Aidan raised one eyebrow. "What is the rationale there?"

"If one guardian is unavailable or if you and Lady Wilmot
cannot agree, the firm adjudicates on the child's behalf."
Aldine offered a long pause. "It is a right we prefer not to
exercise."

"Ah, money is tied up in this arrangement." Aidan leaned
forward toward Aldine. "Did Wilmot believe his wife would
run through the funds?"

"No. His lordship valued his wife's judgment. She's an
able manager."

"He valued her judgment, but removed the boy's estate from her control?" Aidan let his voice convey disbelief.

"No, the estate remains under her ladyship's control until the boy's majority. This guardianship administers a trust for the boy's maintenance. Wilmot wished to provide the boy with a male mentor, but you can refuse the guardianship." Aldine pulled another document from his portfolio. "Your signature on this makes Lady Wilmot sole guardian."

"So it's me or no male guardian." Suddenly, Aidan remembered Tom as a boy, playing King Arthur and his knights with Aidan and his brothers. He cursed inwardly: Tom had known honor would not allow Aidan to refuse. "Then I will accept."

Aldine returned the refusal to his portfolio. "My clerk can witness your signature, unless you prefer someone of your household."

Aidan rang the bell. "I always prefer someone of my household."

Aldine moved Aidan's copy of the legal papers to the side and produced the official contract, a large piece of vellum, carefully lettered, with six signatures and seals already in place. Three signatures dated from shortly after Wilmot's marriage: Wilmot's own, large, flourished, and confident, and those of two witnesses. Wilmot's seal—a dragon's head—drew Aidan's attention. Something tugged at his memory, but wouldn't come clear. Lady Wilmot's hand was firm, but restrained; her witness, an Italian with a neat Continental script. Aidan read over the official document to ensure it was consistent with his copy.

When Barlow arrived, Aidan signed in his best, most official hand, adding flourishes to the tail of the *S* in Somerville, the curve of the *D* in Duke, and the *F* in Forster to mirror those in the ducal seal. An expansive signature to suggest full and willing consent. Barlow signed in a competent school hand, then slipped from the room.

"While the ink dries, have you any questions?" Aldine offered.

"I would like a sense of Wilmot's intentions beyond this." Aidan waved his hand over the documents. "I leave London in three weeks. May I take the boy with me to my estate?"

"The guardianship papers stipulate you may, but it might be wise to delay exercising that provision. Though his lordship established the guardianship a decade ago, her ladyship appeared surprised it had been called into effect."

"What you do mean?" Aidan knew Tom never kept secrets without a reason.

"Lord Wilmot sent the instructions related to the guardianship in three letters, to me, to you, and to her ladyship. All were folded together in a cover addressed to my firm, signed and sealed by Lord Wilmot and carried to England by her ladyship." Aldine tested the edge of the ink for dryness. "It seemed rather like the scene in *Hamlet* where Rosencrantz and Guildenstern act as couriers of the papers that lead to their executions."

"An interest in drama, Aldine?" Aidan quizzed.

"A student of human nature, your grace." Aldine folded the contract until it formed a tall narrow book with a title already carefully lettered on its spine.

"Why do you think her ladyship was unaware of the guardianship?" Aidan asked, interested in Aldine's observations.

"Her ladyship rarely shows emotion. But her shoulders stiffened when she read the letter."

"Then her ladyship is unhappy with this 'partnership'?" Aidan replied, pleased at the news.

The solicitor returned the documents to his portfolio. "I simply report her response to the letter." Aldine withdrew a slip of paper and held it out. "Lord Wilmot purchased a house for her ladyship quite close to your own. If you do not wish to meet at her ladyship's, my office is also available."

Aidan looked at the address—Queen Anne Street, just around the corner. Near the park. The implications settled slowly. Aidan could likely look out his bedroom window and see her yard. "No, I will call on her."

"Those copies are yours." Aldine indicated the papers remaining on Aidan's desk.

Aidan extended his hand in parting. The solicitor's handshake was firm and confident.

Aidan waited until the solicitor reached the door. "Wilmot's letter claims that her ladyship is devoted to the boy. Is that correct? Women in the *ton* often find children merely an obligation to be fulfilled."

Aldine paused. "Then her ladyship is unusual. Observe the mother and the son together to determine the depth of her ladyship's affection for her child."

"Why do you say that?"

"You will charge me once more with a fondness for drama." Aldine placed his hand on the doorknob.

"I'll refrain."

"Then I'll answer. Only with her son does Lady Wilmot seem to be a woman, rather than a beautiful statue carved in marble." With those words, Aldine, ignoring the requirements of rank, wished Aidan a good day and left.

From the window, Aidan watched as Aldine and his clerk, a thin, limping man in rumpled clothes, parted ways on the sidewalk. Aldine's walk was all efficiency, long strides in a fluid gait. The solicitor was more interesting than he ought to be, and all the more interesting because he tried to hide it. Perhaps Aidan should inquire at the Home Office about Mr. H. William Aldine of Leverill and Cort, 19 Cateaton Street.

Aidan had waited a long time for his revenge. To have it fall so neatly into his lap seemed a sign of Fate's approval. Tom had placed Sophia in Aidan's power. A shared guardianship required a devoted mother to remain in his good graces, to be civil, even courteous, lest she lose the ability to make decisions regarding her child. Perhaps, given how quickly Sophia had exchanged Aidan's bed for Tom's, she might even offer her body as a bargaining chip. That would be rich.

At his desk, Aidan reached not for his standard notepaper, but for the fine foolscap sheets he used for correspondence or when, as now, he wished to impress his reader with his wealth and rank. He wrote one sentence in the middle of the sheet, then folded and sealed it, pressing his ring into the soft wax until his signet came clear. He held the letter, feeling the same exhilaration and anticipation as he did before a boxing match or a horse race—or even a battle. Then he called decisively for his footman to deliver his first correspondence in a decade with the woman who had once been his fiancée.

Chapter Three

Charters twisted his spyglass. Lady Wilmot was in her library, reading. He could observe her so easily. Yet she had no idea he existed, much less that they had business together.

From his rooms, he could see her garden and her library. Well, the rooms weren't really his—just an empty house with insufficient locks and heirs abroad.

He had his own house in London, the one that came with his earldom. But if he used it, he'd have to resume his real identity as well, and he'd grown to like playing Charters. The disguise was simple, but a complete deception once in place: a pair of tinted spectacles, a wig of long brown hair pulled back in a pigtail, and thick-soled shoes with variable heels to make him limp. As he'd learned in the wars, he was more *himself* as Charters than as "his lordship."

No, before the *ton* knew "his lordship" had returned, this business needed to be settled. Unresolved for too long, it put all his plans at risk.

He hadn't expected Lady Wilmot to return to England so quickly after her husband's death. But one could turn events into opportunities. She'd left so few servants behind at her villa that it had been easy to search. But the papers were not there. Wilmot had always sent his coded documents home in duplicate, each set carried separately by whatever unsuspecting fool he could conscript. Wilmot would send the key to decode the documents by a third method, equally inscrutable. Charters had acquired one copy of the document when he intercepted the courier, but the second copy and the code key had eluded him. After months spent waiting for the second set to arrive at its destination, Charters had decided to find the papers himself.

Back in London, anticipating that Wilmot might have sent the papers to his solicitor, Charters had found employment as a clerk with Leverill and Cort. It hadn't been luck that the firm had needed help. Rubbing the thick, raised scar on the back of his left hand, Charters thought of the clerk he'd replaced, a callow country youth lonely for home and willing to see traitors in Aldine's wealthy clients. Charters had intended simply to pay the clerk for information. But the boy had grown suspicious. Even so, the clerk had not expected Charters to throw him over the bridge into the Thames. The boy had even held out a hand as he fell, as if Charters would reach out and save him. At the water, the body had broken against a floating log. The log tipped and rolled with the weight, and the body had disappeared into the dark waters below. Another opportunity.

But even at Aldine's, Charters had still failed to find the papers.

Charters took one more look through his spyglass at Lady Wilmot. These were his favorite moments, setting traps as his quarry remained unaware. By the time Lady Wilmot realized she was in danger, she would not be able to escape. Did she know she had the papers, and what they meant? Or was she simply unfortunate? Either way, he would enjoy watching her play the game.

Chapter Four

With trembling hands, Sophia picked up Tom's letter to read it again.

My dearest Sophia,

On the anniversary of my death, I write from beyond the grave to remind you of my love—and your promises.

If you have not already set aside your mourning, it is time. It does not honor my memory to bury yourself away. Cast off your sadness and live, if not for yourself, then for our son.

You have promised to return to society. When you do, men will vie for your hand, whether to gain your beauty or your wealth. Naturally you will consider Ian's interests when you choose a husband, but I enjoin you: only marry a man who respects you, your education, and your intelligence.

You have promised to provide Ian with a male guardian, a surrogate father to aid him as he grows to manhood. You know my choice. No one will take his obligations more seriously than Aidan. His very name as guardian will offer Ian the protection I cannot; it will provide Ian with alliances and connections he will need in manhood. At the same time, I know this guardianship raises specters you are unready to face. So, I have lifted the burden of your promise and invoked the guardianship myself. Unless Aidan refuses—and he will not refuse—he will share our son's care until Ian reaches his majority. You may not forgive me for this decision, but I hope with time you will see its wisdom.

Your other promises I leave to your heart and conscience to fulfill.

I would like to believe that I could protect you and Ian from beyond the grave as I have done in life. But that is likely the wishful thinking of a man who has valued you, and your friendship, more than almost any other relationship in his life.

All will be well. Remember this, and that I have loved you and our son.

Tom

Sophia turned her head toward the garden, toward the bed of pansies, marigolds, and forget-me-nots, and wept.

Some time later, Dodsley brought her a note on a silver tray. Breaking the dark wax seal, she found one sentence in the middle of a large expanse of white paper. An expensive use of paper, she thought, before the words registered.

"I shall call upon her Ladyship tomorrow at two. Forster."

Perfectly appropriate, with an ease of command suitable to his rank. The note a superior would send to a subordinate.

There was no suggestion of their past intimacy and no hint of future amicability. No suggestion he'd seen her only hours before. With one signature, Forster—as Sophia steeled herself to think of him—established the limits of their relationship.

But he also prompted her to action.

Within fifteen minutes, she had called for her carriage, sent a message to Ian's tutor that she would return by dinner, and changed into appropriate dress for the forty-five-minute carriage ride to the home of her sister-in-law.

Ophelia Mason lived in the rural village of Kensington, some six miles away. Sophia wished she had someone to confide in other than Tom's unrufflable sister. Sophia needed a friend who hadn't loved Tom deeply and who wouldn't care that she had sometimes resented her husband for ignoring her wishes. But she couldn't think of any woman outside of Tom's sisters whom she knew well enough to burden with her troubles.

As she climbed into the carriage, musty from lack of use, she wished that she could take a horse instead, but full mourning disallowed it. On a horse, she could feel the wind in her face. Her first horse, a Spanish gray mare named Cob, had been a present from her uncle. Though too old for the hunt, Cob had loved to run, and Sophia, riding astride like her cousins, would let the horse run long and fast. Suddenly, she remembered Aidan racing beside her. She had held Cob back enough to let Aidan think he'd won, then she'd spurred the horse forward to victory. At their goal, she hadn't known to play coy, to wait until he helped her down. On dismounting she found him already beside her, laughing, calling her his "self-sufficient Sophia" and claiming the victor's kiss, even though he'd lost.

She opened the curtains of the coach to watch the town slip into countryside, her thoughts turning back to Tom's guardianship plan and how she'd only agreed because she had no choice.

Three weeks before his death, Tom had handed her tickets to take her and Ian back to England. She'd refused. "We can't leave you, Tom, not when . . ."

"Not when I'm dying." Tom never had any trouble speaking the truth. Placing his hands on her upper arms, he'd made her look into his eyes. "The Carbonari talk revolution and nationalism all around us. As long as I am alive, my friendships with the Bourbon ministers protect us. But support for the Italian nationalists grows each day, as does sentiment against Ferdinand's British and Austrian allies. You and Ian must go home."

"No." She'd held her hands up in refusal. "Revolution is years away. Our friends will warn us when it's time to leave. And Ian will not understand. Both you and I know the pain of losing a father so young, how we would have traded anything for another year, or another day. . . ." She'd let the words drift off. Watching Tom slip away had taken all her strength.

"Death is never easy." Tom had spoken softly. "Ian must learn his own country, not this mongrel society we have created for him."

Sophia bristled. "Our life here is a hybrid, like our roses. From our Italian friends, he has learned to live joyfully; from our English friends, he has learned to be circumspect."

"Then we will go together." He'd pulled out a third packet of travel papers. "In six-week's time, we will have the best weather and the quickest winds; we should be in England within ten days."

"If the trip doesn't kill you, the climate in England will. Either way you cut short our time. Propose some other plan." Her hands tightened behind her back.

He'd watched her silently, then explained his four requirements. Each one, a promise she had to make.

Be established in London within a month of my death.
Live in London for at least part of each "season."
Take up your place in the bon ton.

At the third requirement, she'd objected. "I was an orphaned parson's daughter; I don't have a place in society to take."

"Yet Ian will need you to know and be known. In London, you were admired for your poise and your bearing. Here, invitations to your dinners were much prized. Set your mind to this, and you will create a community—perhaps form another salon. Besides, you will not be alone: my sisters and your cousins will ease the way. Finally, within a year, you must call upon Aidan and ask him to serve as Ian's surrogate father." His hand lay on the tickets, his blackmail. He'd sat so still that she should have realized that he would not survive another year.

"No." She'd turned away, hiding her face. "We've heard the rumors even here: he's grown hard, unforgiving, more like Aaron than Benjamin. If you want Ian to be guided by someone from your boyhood, Colin is well respected for his amiability, and Seth already manages your estate. Of my relations, Malcolm is devoted to his new wife's boys. Any would be more suitable."

Tom had shaken his head in firm refusal. "Of my Somerville cousins, none were closer than Aidan and I. He must have felt our marriage a betrayal. We must, if that is true, try to undo the damage."

"Sometimes the damage of the past cannot be undone. And you will not be there. Only I will." She had met Tom's eyes. "You don't know what you are asking, or what it will cost."

"I do know, but it will be worth the cost, for Ian as well as for you."

The soft Italian breeze had carried the scent of rain

through the open doorways facing the loggia. Sophia had suddenly realized that Italian rain smelled nothing like rain in England. The rain in Naples always had a hint of spice, of the dust that sometimes rained from nearby Vesuvius and fertilized the cultivated land. Rain in England smelled fertile, like field upon field of pasture, of crops not yet come in for the harvest, of waiting in the summerhouse with Aidan for a storm to end. She preferred the Italian rain: it held no memories and offered no secrets.

She'd looked at the set of botanical illustrations she'd just finished. "What about your book? If you die before it is finished, should I promise to see it through the press?"

"That needs no promise, for you will do it whether I ask or not." Tom had smiled. "The others are burdens. But, Sophia, knowing I have your promises will allow me to die easy."

"Then I promise." There was nothing else to say.

And then Tom was dead.

"What was Tom thinking, Ophelia?" Sophia embraced her sister-in-law. "Aidan isn't a knight in shining armor. In fact if the rumors are true, he's far from honorable. I'm not sure that Tom was entirely himself when he put Ian under Aidan's control."

"My dear, Tom didn't give Ian over to Aidan. You are also his guardian. But I'm afraid this partnership might be my fault." Ophelia patted the open space next to her on the couch, and Sophia sat beside her. "When we were in Italy, Tom asked me all the latest news about Aidan, and I must admit I glossed over his more scandalous moments. Had I known Tom's intentions, I would have been less generous."

"It wouldn't have mattered." Sophia wiped away angry tears with the back of her hand. "Tom would have believed the good, justified away the bad, and ignored the middle.

Most of the time, I found that endearing. Now . . . if he weren't dead, I'd kill him myself."

Ophelia drew several handkerchiefs from her sewing stand and tucked one into Sophia's hand. For a moment, the women sat in silence, Ophelia's hand placed comfortingly on Sophia's.

"You must admit, my dear, this arrangement offers advantages," Ophelia reasoned. "If anything were to happen to you, your brother would catch the scent of money and appeal to Chancery to serve as Ian's guardian over whomever you might have chosen. But Phineas will not cross Aidan. Since he has become duke, Aidan's natural magnetism has grown into an ease of command."

Sophia wiped her eyes with the corner of the linen. "I wasn't thinking of it that way, but yes, you are right. As for Aidan's 'ease of command,' you should have seen his note. One can't call it a summons, since he's coming to me. But he expects compliance all the same." She rubbed the handkerchief between her fingers, distracting herself with the ornate curves of monogrammed initials. An *A* was obvious and an *F*, then with an artist's eye, she followed the line of the intertwined *S*. In shock she realized the shape of the pattern. "Oh, my word . . . Phee! Aidan has been to visit you!?"

"Oh, dear, forgive me." Ophelia swept the soiled handkerchief from Sophia's hand and tucked it out of sight. "When Aidan came to us after Tom's death, I cried on his linen. I keep forgetting to return it." Ophelia handed Sophia a new handkerchief. "After our parents died, we girls didn't live only in London with Aunt Millicent. We spent summers with Tom and our Somerville cousins. Even now, Aidan often acts as our brother. He escorts us to balls when Sidney is obligated at Whitehall, and he always dances with Kate and Ariel in the second half."

"Of course, I should have realized. Forgive me, I'm simply . . ." Sophia searched for the right word.

"Overwrought, my dear. You've had an unwelcome surprise," Ophelia offered with characteristic good sense. "But how do you intend to convince Aidan to reject Tom's plan?"

"I thought I'd appeal to his bachelor instincts, ask him to be Ian's guardian in name only, visiting as he sees fit when he is in town, advising me on whatever matters he finds important, but leaving the day-to-day oversight to me." Sophia watched Ophelia's face hopefully. "If that fails, I would suggest that, given his reputation, his brothers or my cousins would more suitably fill the role of mentor for a young boy."

Ophelia looked pensive, her straight auburn hair, unencumbered by a cap, twisted into a high bun. The gray ribbon banding her head was the only trace of half-mourning. "Aidan's reputation as a rake aside, he takes responsibilities seriously. He's never failed when we've called on his help. In fact, I was unable to say anything against Aidan when Tom asked because . . ." Phee shifted in her chair. "I suppose it won't hurt to tell you."

Phee looked for assent from Sophia, who nodded.

"We arrived in Naples so unexpectedly because we left London in haste. Ariel's season had been lovely until she confided in that foolish gossip Susan Flanders the news of Tom's settlements on her and Kate. Suddenly every penniless scoundrel found my sisters the most attractive morsels on the market. One, George Winthrop, decided to convince Ariel to marry him by abducting her from Lady Mallory's ball."

"Abducting?"

"If Aidan hadn't noticed Ariel was gone, well, she would have been ruined, or worse, married to a wastrel and a reprobate. Aidan found me, just as a footman delivered a message that Ariel, feeling ill, had caught a ride home with Lady Balmoral. When I tried to ask questions, the footman turned away without answering. Aidan pulled the footman into a withdrawing room and sent me to find Malcolm.

"By the time we returned, Aidan had the full of Winthrop's plan. Aidan and Malcolm caught up with Winthrop's carriage not too many miles out of town, with Ariel, still unconscious from a bump on her head. We feared that Winthrop might try to force the marriage, claiming he'd compromised her. We'd already received your letter urging us to visit, so we came to Naples."

Sophia shook her head, refusing Ophelia's positive view of Aidan's character. "In Ariel's case, a young woman he cared for was endangered. But Aidan doesn't know Ian. If he wished to act as father to a young boy, he would have married by now and begun a family."

"Yet Ian needs someone he can ask all those pesky questions boys come up with," Ophelia suggested gently.

"And what will Aidan teach him? The best brothels in town? Isn't that what all aristocratic men teach each other at their clubs?"

"I don't think Aidan frequents brothels," Ophelia offered lightly. "He usually has a mistress."

"Of course, that's better," Sophia said with some bitterness. "Ian can learn that gentlemen aren't expected to regard their wives with the same attention they give their light o' loves."

"Well, a mistress disobliges no one if the man is unmarried." Ophelia nodded to the footman who had come to the door with a tea service. He placed it on the tray before her. "Bentley, would you call my sisters to tea?"

"From what I've heard"—Ophelia lowered her voice until the footman had pulled the door shut behind him—"the demimonde have been waiting for months to see who would gain his patronage. In fact, we have a pool going on who will be his next liaison. I believe Lady Belmont is a favorite, but

Sidney thinks . . ." Ophelia stopped at Sophia's silence. "Oh, dear, this doesn't help, does it? To know that people speculate over which woman he will next take to his bed."

"Who tells you such things?" Sophia felt her face turn warm.

Ophelia grinned. "You'd be surprised the information one can pick up over cards at a ball. And Sidney listens at his club. Thank goodness, he isn't a prude about sharing details! I dare say he enjoys the chatter more than I do. He always quizzes me about what we ladies have discussed at tea!"

Sophia found this information about her brother-in-law surprising; he had always appeared to be a middling sort of man with middling sorts of interests.

Ophelia's teasing turned more sober. "If you are to be in such close contact with Aidan over the guardianship, you might consider . . . You are a widow, and he's known to be quite obliging. Perhaps you could seduce him into relinquishing the guardianship."

"Ophelia! I expected you to encourage a life of celibate devotion to your brother's memory. But instead . . ." Sophia searched for words.

"Sophie, Tom is dead." Ophelia's voice turned stern and firm. "Despite his wishes, you continue to wear full mourning. If you will not remarry, at least embark on a discreet liaison. No man in the *ton* is reputed to be more attentive during an affair or as well-tempered after as Aidan. And certainly no man is more tight-lipped than Aidan about his liaisons."

"Then how do you know so much about them?" Sophia accused.

"It's the women, dear, the women. They can't keep quiet that they've been in his bed. Nor would I, if half the things they say are true!" Ophelia laughed at the look of horror on Sophia's face. "Oh, I don't mean it—it would be like kissing a brother. But if you aren't going to take Aidan to your bed and seduce him out of the guardianship, you'll need to come up with some compelling argument for him to relinquish it. And his own questionable reputation isn't likely to work."

At that moment, Kate and Ariel flung open the door and ran to embrace Sophia, ending all possibility for further private conversation.

On the way home, Sophia searched for a compelling argument that might encourage Aidan to relinquish the guardianship. During tea she had observed Ariel carefully. Lighthearted and laughing, Tom's youngest sister showed no indication that her abduction had any lasting effects. Yet had Aidan been less attentive to her absence or less dogged in his pursuit, Ariel's life would have been much different.

It was another story to add to Sophia's collection. In Italy she'd gathered information about Aidan like a starving woman hoarding crumbs of bread. But the picture the scraps created only revealed an enigma. He had acquitted himself admirably in the wars, but where exactly he'd served or what he had done, she had never known. He had a reputation as a gambler, but never sustained irreparable or even substantive losses. He had engaged in one or two duels, but why or over whom, she didn't know. And she could never ask; she couldn't risk revealing to Tom how much Aidan remained in her thoughts.

She'd never been able to reconcile the stories. In some he was ruthless and remote; in others he was engaging and seductive. But none described the young man she'd loved. The Aidan she had known was confident and ambitious and witty and kind. His touch had made her feel safe long before it had made her burn.

She still remembered the day they had parted. Aidan's father—an armchair patriot—had bought his younger sons commissions as they came of age, promising a piece of land and an annuity when they defeated Bonaparte. For Sophia and Aidan, the settlement was their hope of a life together. Soon, he and his brother Colin were set to join their older brother Benjamin, an adjutant to Wellington, on the Peninsula.

She'd waited in her uncle's summerhouse to say good-bye. She had determined to be brave, to let him go without crying. But when he came to her—calling her "my only love, my heart"—his own eyes were already wet. She'd touched his face, wiping his tears away. He'd pulled her into his embrace, and they'd made love, savoring each tender caress as if it were their last; then they'd dressed each other tenderly, carefully, memorizing each touch.

"Will you wait for me, Sophie?" His eyes had searched hers earnestly.

"Do you promise to come home to me?" she'd teased.

He refused to tease back. Instead, he'd pulled her into his arms and held her against his heart. "If you are waiting, there's not a bullet in Boney's army that will keep me from you."

She pulled back just enough to look in his eyes. "There's nothing in the world that would keep me from waiting. No man alive compares to you." She put both hands on his cheeks to emphasize her words. "You are my love, my only love."

He'd lifted her, laughing, and swung her around in a circle. "How can I be so lucky that the cleverest, most beautiful girl in the whole world loves me? A girl who can ride and draw and conjugate Latin and Greek. You know I'm not worth you." He'd kissed her forehead. "But I'll try, sweeting; I'll devote my whole life to being worthy of your love."

She'd felt without a home for so long that his words had

fed her lonely soul. She'd closed her eyes, savoring his love, the feel of his hands, warm in hers. The moment had been perfect. Then his hands were gone, leaving her bereft. She'd opened her eyes to find him kneeling before her.

"Sophia Elliot, when I return, will you marry me, be my wife, live with me, have children, laugh, cry, grow old with me? Will you be my fiancée from this day forward?"

She'd laughed at his alteration of the marriage rite. "From this day forward, yes, my love, yes."

He looked sheepish. "I haven't a ring or anything, nothing for you to remember me by."

She'd kissed him, longingly, sweetly. "I don't need anything. But I do have something for you, a token of my love, to remember your . . . fiancée . . . by." She'd held out a folded piece of oilcloth, no bigger than his thumb.

He'd unwrapped the gift, a small hardboard wafer on which Sophia had sketched a self-portrait. "I drew it mostly with ink to get the lines sharp enough."

"It's beautiful. I can see your spirit, here in the shape of your eyes, in the curve of your lips."

"I know you can't take it with you. But I wanted you to have it."

"I can take it. Look here." He'd pulled off one of his boots to reveal halfway down a slit in the lining that formed a shallow pocket. "It's just deep enough." He put the wafer in, then pulled his boot back on. "I must go my love, but until I return, I'll carry you with me in my heart"—he smiled mischievously—"and in my boot."

He kissed her once more, a perfect kiss filled with longing and tenderness and passion. Then he'd stepped away, still holding her hand. Their fingertips had been the last thing to part.

* * *

After a decade of rumors and stories, Sophia wondered if she had known Aidan Somerville at all. Or if, like her, he had simply changed. If she could transform from a trusting girl who'd leapt freely into love into a more sober woman with an estate to administer and a child to rear, who might Aidan have become? More than anything else, remembering the authoritarian tone of his missive, she wondered which man she would meet tomorrow.

Chapter Five

"No, no, no, I need no introduction." Ophelia's voice carried as she approached Sophia's room.

Sophia stepped back from the balcony, pushing the French doors nearly closed, and depositing her cat on the ottoman.

In the hall, Ophelia waged a small battle with Dodsley. Sophia could only hear Ophelia's part, but she could well imagine Dodsley's objections from Ophelia's responses.

"Of course her ladyship will see me—whatever are you thinking, Dodsley?" . . . "Well, I can't imagine why it would matter if her ladyship is dressed or not." . . . "We are family, after all."

Sophia reached the door to her dressing room just as Ophelia flung it open. Her sister-in-law strode victoriously into the room, resembling far more closely Boadicea the warrior queen than the weepy Shakespearean heroine her parents had named her after. Sophia nodded her acceptance of her sister-in-law's invasion, and Dodsley, looking woeful, retreated.

"Oh, darling, I can only stay for a few minutes." Ophelia kissed Sophia on both cheeks. "But I brought you a gift for your meeting with Aidan this afternoon." From behind

Ophelia, a footman entered carrying a dress box followed by Sally and a wan young girl Sophia didn't recognize.

"Over there, Phillip. Put it on the ottoman, then meet me downstairs." Ophelia waved her directions, then turned her attention back to Sophia. "I've just picked it up from the modiste, but I'm sure it will fit. Your Sally has been so good about giving us your measurements, and I brought the modiste's girl along in case. We have plenty of time before two, and I will be back to help after I deliver Sidney."

"Oh, Phee, I've already chosen . . ."

"No, not one of those dreadful black things you have worn till the fabric is thin. If you wish to have any influence over Aidan in this guardianship, then you must be *Lady Wilmot*, a woman of his class, a woman he cannot command. If you are available to meet with him, it must be because you *condescend* to do so."

The modiste's girl opened the dress box and began to remove layers of paper until the dress was visible. Then she raised the dress from the box. French in design, the day dress was formal, suitable for visits in the late afternoon or family dinners. The muslin was a cerulean blue decorated with small, black raised dots. Narrow black lace repeated at the neck, the waist, and the wrists, then in five flounces alternating with black, brocaded-satin ribands at the base of the dress below the knees.

"Oh, it's lovely." Sophia lifted the muslin in both hands, feeling its weight and texture between her fingers. Then taking the dress from the seamstress, she held it in front of her before the pier glass. "But for half-mourning, the color . . ."

". . . is beautiful," Ophelia interrupted, "and it will be beautiful on you. Tom was very specific that the dress should be ready by the anniversary of his death. He must have intended you to wear it when you met with Aidan."

"Tom?" Sophia's eyes misted, but only for a moment. "But how?"

"You are not the only one who received a letter." Ophelia motioned Sally and the seamstress into action. "Mine came some weeks ago and included a fashion plate and that exquisite material. Tom gave me permission to reject the design if it were out of style, but it was lovely. Now put it on. I'll be back within the hour."

"So that's how it is then?" Barlow assessed the clothes Aidan had chosen for his meeting. After more than a decade of service, Barlow measured Aidan's mood better than any other man.

"Yes, that's how it is. To dress too much *à la mode* would suggest I can be swayed by society or by the vagaries of public opinion."

"Or by an old lover, barely out of mourning," Barlow muttered.

"I never claimed we were lovers."

"No need to; I had my own eyes in the camps for that." Barlow held out the forest-green superfine waistcoat with matching velvet collar. "Beware vengeance, your grace. It clouds the judgment."

Aidan adjusted the puffed edge of the neckline, then lifted his chin for Barlow to twist the starched linen into a complicated cravat knot. "Much between us remains unresolved, that's all."

Barlow snorted and went to the wardrobe to retrieve Aidan's boots.

Barlow was wrong, Aidan assured himself. His revenge was already a decade in the making; he would not misstep. During the long years of the Wilmots' absence, he'd mastered the double-edged reply. "I was there when they met" suggested that he'd known of Tom's tendre for Sophia from the first. Instead Aidan meant that he had never forgotten the day he and Tom had gone to a country fair and seen Sophia, in a blue muslin gown with flowers embroidered above her feet, sunlight falling on her rich dark hair. Her serious gray eyes had met Aidan's gaze and not turned away, and he had found himself desperate for an introduction. No, if anyone asked Aidan's opinion of the Wilmot marriage, he would offer a knowing wink and a conspiratorial "clever Sophia," appearing to compliment Lady Wilmot's success in catching a husband when he actually meant that Sophia had deceived him thoroughly.

Aidan already knew what he wanted from the end of their affair, for an affair it would be. He would gain Sophia's trust, then betray it, watching the expression in her large gray eyes change as she realized his deception. Confusion, disbelief, awareness, hurt, betrayal, and then perhaps even despair. Best yet if he could leave her wondering not *if* but *when* he would reveal her frailty. Yes, he would leave her no peace as she had left him none.

But he did not yet know how to accomplish that revenge. First he would have to meet his opponent and take her measure. Would Sophia be the lover of his youth, the cold fortune hunter who married Tom, the distant and inscrutable statue of Aldine's experience—or the ghost in the garden filling him with desire? Aidan would adapt his campaign and his demeanor to whichever Sophia came to their meeting.

Straightening his cuffs, Aidan examined himself in the mirror. His clothes were well-tailored, boasting enough color to suggest wealth and class and enough restraint to convey power and control. Exactly the image he wished to convey—he wanted to leave no room for Lady Wilmot to remember the callow boy she had so easily deceived. "This will do."

Barlow snorted, brushing the shoulders of Aidan's coat. "It's one thing, your grace, to destroy a person for the nation's sake; it's another to do it for your own ends. In the end, you'll wound yourself as much as her ladyship."

"My enemies would say that sympathy is no longer part of my nature and that I have no heart to wound."

"A man who judges his own character by the opinions of his enemies is a fool," Barlow countered.

Aidan pretended not to hear. If he lacked sympathy, it was Sophia's doing. And if she suffered for his hardness of heart, then she deserved no better. He could hear his father's admonition as if it were yesterday: "Never trust a woman, lad. Their affections are only as deep as your pockets."

Chapter Six

Aidan arrived at the Wilmot house promptly at two. A solid Georgian, with three floors above the ground level, and one below, the house faced north into the last block of Queen Anne Street, abutting the lower estates of Portland Place. At the corner there, Chandos Street led south to Cavendish Square, to the park—and to his house. After receiving Tom's letter, Aidan had waited until night, then he had traced his path from the now spent flowers in the Cavendish Square garden, out the iron gate, up the block, and around the corner, until he'd found the Wilmot home, several houses in. The ghostly Sophia in the garden had been no ghost.

Lady Wilmot—as he reminded himself to call her—had instructed her staff to expect him. Her butler opened the door at the first knock, then disappeared to deliver Aidan's card. A lithe Italian wearing secondhand gentleman's clothes took Aidan's cloak and gloves. Likely Tom's clothes, Aidan realized with a pang.

Waiting, Aidan felt unexpectedly unsettled. To calm himself, he assumed the posture of an officer at ease. Hands folded behind his back, he turned his attention to a mental inventory of the house. Pocket doors on either side of the entry led to public drawing rooms, but the butler had disappeared instead through a third doorway, leading to the back of the house. A large open stairway curved on his right, up to a second-floor landing, where a large Palladian window filled the whole space with light. On a sunny day, the window could light the front of the house, an efficient floor plan, given King George's regressive tax on windows.

Aidan paid little attention to the hall furniture; it had most likely come with the property. The paintings on the walls offered precise architectural scenes of Italian cities. Tom's choices, Aidan assessed. Rational, intellectual.

No hint of Sophia, her taste, or her preferences. Oddly, he relaxed. In the larger scheme of his life's experiences, this was not so significant a meeting. His own life, the lives of thousands of British soldiers, did not depend on the outcome of his and Sophia's discussions, and he doubted Lady Wilmot would kill him with her penknife if he made a misstep. No, he thought, and breathed deeply, this was simply another diplomatic mission. He would set her at ease, so that he could discover what she held valuable and what she deemed expendable. And when he knew what she hoped to gain and what she was willing to lose, he would know how to proceed. Until then, he would give nothing away.

When Dodsley returned, Aidan followed the silver-haired butler to the back of the house.

Competent, serious, responsible. Sophia repeated the words, as she waited for Dodsley to escort Aidan to the library. A woman who could be trusted with the care of her own child. A woman who can command, she heard Phee's voice correct her.

Even in cerulean blue, the dress Tom had sent her was subtle and reserved. She would not greet Aidan in frothy silks and remind him of those silly, ill-educated society beauties he knew best. "Hothouse flowers," Mary Wollstonecraft had called them, arguing that such women should be educated, if nothing else, to become fine mothers. *I am, if nothing else, a fine mother.* In Sophia's hair, black brocaded velvet twisted through the bun above the nape of her neck, complementing the black ribbons in the dress. Seeing herself in a color other than black, she could almost hear Tom's voice whisper, "Courage."

Her dress and her house—both chosen for her by Tom—bolstered her confidence. When she had returned from Italy, she had immediately claimed the library for her own. A harmonious room, long and narrow, the library boasted a fireplace in the middle of the interior wall, flanked with bookcases and cabinets on each side. She'd hung Tom's portrait over the mantel, and sometimes she felt as if his spirit comforted her. On the exterior wall, bookcases alternated with tall windows, and beyond the windows, a wide expanse of lawn bordered with flower beds made up the garden.

When she felt anxious and unsettled, the library's order offered a peaceful calm. Order suggested control, a control over her life and circumstances that she had never felt she had.

Treasures from her married life filled the room. Near the garden door stood her easel. In the bookcases behind it, topped by busts of the Greek poet Sappho and the botanist Carl Linnaeus, were her botanical books and her collection of bound woodcuts and engravings. The cabinets below the bookcases held her pots of paint, her cakes of watercolor, brushes, and paper. She rarely painted anymore, but she often used the easel to sketch her botanical illustrations, laying out the image in pencil or pastel, then moving to the desk to trace the lines with pen and ink if the sketch was destined to be engraved. Her portfolio of sketches rested in a wooden frame like those in print dealers' shops, but made of finer wood and more richly finished, a gift from Tom at Ian's birth.

In the middle of the room—across from the windows and in front of the fireplace—stood a low couch with tall curving sides. Ever considerate, Dodsley had moved three chairs from the wall to flank the couch, giving her several choices for seating depending on how the meeting was proceeding.

At the far end of the room stood the enameled partner desk she had shared with Tom. On her side of the desk, looking toward the fireplace and Tom's portrait, were her writing materials: a pot of ink, several tempered quills of different sizes, a penknife, blotting paper to absorb extra ink, and in the drawer, several sizes of writing paper.

Behind Tom's side of the pedestal desk, Sophia had arranged their scientific library. The bookcase to the right, under the bust of the Greek philosopher Hippocrates, held her husband's books and translations: on the top shelf were her husband's books as printed by his publishers—all neat quartos similarly bound in dark green morocco with gilt titles on their spines. As accompaniments to the printed books, the remaining shelves held bound copies of Tom's manuscripts. Each time Tom had sent the fair copy of his book's manuscript to the printer, she had gathered up the original manuscript pages and taken them to a bookbinder.

In opposition to the crisply uniform printed books, the manuscript books varied in size and height, ranging from tall folios to squat octavos, depending on the paper that had been available when her husband had been writing. Each volume evoked a different place and time in their marriage. The folded foolscap paper reminded her of alpine plants and snow; the grape watermarked paper on which Tom had written in a messy brown ink reminded her of oak galls in Italy and of laughing over a scrofulous French novel in a monastery library.

She ran her fingers across the raised bands on the spines. By touching Tom's works, she imagined somehow she could still draw on his strength. The messy pages reminded her of the best part of their marriage: the hours of cooperation, discussing the best angle from which to draw the plant, the right way to describe its habitat. The manuscript books comforted her, suggesting that her life had not disappeared, but remained preserved in the leaves she had saved.

At the end of one row, an open space waited for Tom's last manuscript, now at the binder, and she placed her hand in the gap. If Tom had been like his printed books, even-tempered, clearly ruled, and unambiguous, then Sophia found in the bound manuscripts an image of her life: pages of disparate sizes all bound together with scribbles in the margins, marked out passages, and added leaves.

The transformation from manuscript to printed books offered Sophia the hope that somehow meaning could still come from the disorder of her life. Perhaps she could yet become what she was meant to be. Perhaps some good could come from this co-guardianship.

Sophia moved to stand in front of the long window nearest her easel. From there she could look into the garden, taking strength from the marigolds and forget-me-nots in Ian's bed. She wished to be standing when Aidan arrived, to meet as equals: he was not a suitor to be greeted with an upward glance and a smile upon rising. Nor would she welcome him as a friend with a polite embrace or the offer of her cheek. No, she would nod gravely at his entrance, offer her hand, and gesture him to a seat.

The door opened to admit him. As in the park, something in the air changed with his presence. She turned to face him.

When she had last been this close to him, he had still been a gangly youth, all legs and arms, tall for his age, and thin. Now his height had become lean muscle, and his shoulders were broad in the form-fitting green jacket. She could understand why women speculated about who his next mistress might be. Once more she felt like the sixteen-year-old girl who had first looked into those deep blue eyes and felt her world shift.

His movements reminded her of the panther at the Royal Menagerie, all pent energy. And like the panther, he seemed predatory, coolly assessing her vulnerabilities. She remembered suddenly and vividly the press of her body against his, the passion of his kisses. She could not allow herself the memories: if she remembered, if she trusted him again and told him their secrets, how would she survive when he left again? She breathed slowly and drew herself inward, forcing a pose of indifference.

When Aidan entered the room, Sophia was standing in the light of the window, and it took some time before he could make out her features. For a moment she was the ghostly Sophia who had met him in the park, and he felt the same elation and panic. Then she moved away from the light of the window and walked toward him, holding out her hand. The illusion of the ghostly Sophia was replaced, more disturbingly, by the actual woman. But emotion still clutched at the bottom of his stomach—not the pressing lust he had felt with other women, but the unfamiliar ache of desire.

He'd forgotten the look of her, and he found himself—propriety be damned—indulging in a long, assessing gaze. Her nut-brown hair carried the same weight and luster as when he had last seen her. Her gray eyes, always large, seemed more pronounced now, and the line of her cheekbones more defined with age. She was, if anything, more striking. But her eyes looked as if laughter had not reached them in many years.

He had not given much credence to Aldine's description; Sophia had always hidden her passion behind a veil of reserve. But this was no veil. It was something else, an absence of engagement, as if she were not in the room beside him, but rather watching from a great distance. Had it not been for the blue vein pulsing beneath the alabaster skin of her neck or the warmth of her hand as he took it up in greeting, he could easily have imagined this woman as a statue of Carrara marble.

"Lady Wilmot." He brought her hand to his lips, offering the expected formal kiss, his lips barely brushing the back of her hand. But to test the limits of her reserve, he held her hand a moment longer than appropriate. She offered no response to the greater intimacy of his gesture, not even pulling her hand away in dismay or shock. She only looked at him, her eyes remote, before responding gravely, "Your grace."

"My condolences on the loss of your husband. He was a fine man." Her reserve angered him, but he kept his voice placid.

"Thank you. I have known few finer." Her gaze shifted past him to the portrait of Tom over the fireplace. In it, Tom was seated beside a table filled with books and papers, his right hand resting on the table next to an inkwell and pen, his left hand holding a sheaf of papers in his lap. He was looking up at the viewer, as if he had been interrupted in the act of reading. But Tom's smile and the hint of mischief about his eyes suggested the interruption was welcome. Aidan remembered with poignancy many times in their youth when Tom had used that same smile to smooth their paths. The artist had captured Tom's spirit, but he had made no attempt to hide the thinness of Tom's body or the unhealthy red on his cheek.

"When was this painted?"

"About six months before Tom's death, when Frederick Buchanan visited us. I assume you know Buchanan from Harrow as well."

Aidan listened to her speak. Her voice carried no inflection, as if talking about her dead husband offered her no more pause than she might feel ordering afternoon tea. Further evidence she had not loved Tom at all. But of course Aidan could see that proof in her dress as well. Certainly, the details were black, but the blue was too vivid. At best, the dress only nodded at half-mourning. He tamped down his rising anger. Many widows had not loved their husbands, but Tom had deserved mourning. Sophia should have mourned.

"Yes, I knew Buchanan; he was talented even then." Aidan tucked the name away: a portrait painter who had spent hours observing minute details would be useful in learning more of Tom's death. "Why did you let Tom be pictured so?" Aidan asked, without turning from the portrait.

"So?" For a moment she sounded perplexed. "Oh, you mean dying? I don't see the portrait in that way. That's simply how Tom looked for much of our marriage and all of Ian's childhood. You might prefer the portrait of Tom in the drawing room, painted before we left England. In it he is younger, healthier, more as you remember him."

Aidan turned from the portrait to assess the room and its contents. He made his body, his tone, mirror her distance. "May I sit?" He took over the social pleasantries. He would not allow her to assert her place as hostess or as the boy's mother.

"Certainly." Unruffled, she held her hand out to the seating facing the fireplace, and Aidan chose the sofa, leaving her one of the three chairs remaining. She chose for herself the middle chair, neither too close nor too far away. It was, Aidan noticed, the diplomatic choice, saying neither "I wish to be confidants" nor "I prefer to remain aloof."

"Would you like some tea?"

"After our discussion. I don't think we'll find this conversation too onerous?" His smile said "have confidence in me." To emphasize his comfort, he leaned on the arm of the couch and stretched his legs out to the side. Such a pose, drawing attention to the leanness of his frame and his long, muscular legs, displayed his form to its best advantage. "I was surprised to receive Tom's letter after so many years."

"No one would think ill of you if you wished to decline or to be guardian in name only." She folded her hands primly in her lap. "I'm sure this must be an unwelcome, and unexpected, obligation."

Aidan willed his expression to remain pleasantly inscrutable. "I was surprised. But, as you know, Tom and I grew up together. I've decided—in his memory—to fulfill his wishes toward his son. I'm not in town often, though I keep a house here. I will be traveling to my estate in a few weeks. I'd like to take the boy with me. I could return him to you before Michaelmas?"

Aidan saw the almost imperceptible stop in her breath. But she didn't refuse. Perhaps Aldine had misread Sophia's attachment to her child.

"Ian." She spoke slowly. "His name is Ian."

"Ian," Aidan repeated. "I would like to meet him."

"He's in the nursery with his tutor."

Aidan offered her a smile, one he used at balls, pleasant without suggesting intimacy. "Should we call for him? Or surprise him in the nursery?"

"We should call for him." She stood to pull the bell hanging from the side of the fireplace. "Before you decide to take Ian to your estate for the summer, it might be best to see if you two suit."

He had gained little information thus far, except that Sophia's reserve was so engrained that many might believe it her natural manner. Seducing this remote Sophia would offer him little satisfaction. This Sophia wouldn't care if she lost her reputation. She was too far removed from society to feel its stings. But he was not deceived. He remembered the mischievous young woman who had once hidden a family of mice in a suit of armor to convince her cousins that the gallery was haunted. No, he would draw her out of her solitude, earn her trust, bring her back into society, make her care once more about living, then snatch it all away. He would make her regret Tom's death.

Dodsley arrived with such speed that the man was either curious or protective. As Sophia and Dodsley spoke at the door, Aidan wondered how much Sophia confided in her butler.

Turning back to Aidan, Sophia offered a polite smile. "Ian should be down presently. I mentioned he might meet a friend of his father's today, but I haven't explained the guardianship. I saw no reason to broach the subject if you preferred to withdraw."

As she spoke, Aidan rose and stood before the portrait, positioning himself to watch her, unobserved, in the mirror. Was she only so controlled when she knew she was being watched? "I understand. . . . How old is Ian? Tom's letter didn't say."

She looked at her hands. "Nine."

"He's lived abroad his whole life," Aidan prompted. "His transition to English society may be difficult."

Her eyes narrowed slightly, with irritation, or something else. "Naples was home to a large community of expatriates and British military. Our house was often full of English children as well as Italian. Tom insisted that Ian feel at home among strangers."

"How is his Latin?" Aidan changed the topic, wishing to observe her responses to different topics.

"Quite advanced, and his Greek studies have already begun." Her pride was clear in the lift of her jaw.

"That would place him in the fourth form."

"I know, but he will be younger than the other boys in fourth form." She paused. "And Harrow is not known for its tenderness."

"Yet Harrow friendships will serve him a lifetime. He will lean on those relationships as he grows to manhood, chooses a wife, begins his own family. Had he been reared in England, I wouldn't think this so vital. Michaelmas term begins in September, so we have almost six weeks to introduce him to other boys already there."

Her gray eyes widened.

"He already knows—I assume—Ophelia's Nathaniel and Malcolm's wife's boys. I can take care of the introductions to the other boys, if you will host an afternoon party." Aidan turned to face her, expecting her agreement.

"Since our return, Malcolm's stepsons have not been much in London. And Nate is so boisterous that Ian often finds him overwhelming. Ian's like Tom in that way."

"Then Toby and Jack will be more suited to his personality. They are both thoughtful boys, though mischievous."

"Some boys remain with a tutor until Cambridge or Oxford, so I'd hoped to delay Harrow a little longer, to give Ian more time to adjust," she objected mildly. Aidan was pleased to see distress in her eyes.

"You returned to England a year ago, am I right?"

"Yes. After Tom's funeral."

Aidan raised an eyebrow.

"Tom was concerned that the Italian nationalists would make our situation dangerous," she explained.

"Ah, a wise man. But if you returned last summer, then Ian has already had ample time to adjust." Aidan paused, wanting to see if she would lie to keep the boy with her. "If the problem is inadequate funds to cover his expenses, I will be happy to pay. As I am his guardian, that would only be reasonable."

"No, it's not that." She spoke deliberately. "Aldine can confirm that we have adequate funds. I have the accounts here if you wish to inspect them." She gestured to a cabinet behind the desk. "Ian has already lost so much this year—his father, his home—that I hoped to avoid separating him from his remaining parent."

"Boys are resilient. And summers and holidays are more than adequate time for a boy to be with family."

She grew quiet and stared into the distance, her body completely still except for the movement of her chest as she breathed. It was easy to see why Aldine thought her a kind of living statue. But Aldine was wrong; there were signs of the woman behind the mask, just subtle ones. The tightening of a muscle in her hand or her jaw, the darkening of her eyes. Perhaps one had to have known her in her youth to notice the signs. Had this been some other woman Aidan had met on a diplomatic mission, he would have wondered what created such control. But he found that he lacked curiosity about what sorrows she had suffered since they had parted. No, the passionate Sophia he had loved would have stood against him with every fiber of her being. Was this a ploy? Did she believe she could circumvent him by appearing to accept his will?

At that moment, the door opened. A boy, tall for his age but thin, walked into the library. Aidan was struck by how much Ian looked like Tom: the same dark hair, the same serious eyes, the same pensive look.

Immediately, Sophia's demeanor became expressive, and Aidan saw for himself the transformation Aldine had described. Her dark eyes, before so restrained, smiled. Rising, she held her hands out to the boy and drew him against her in a quick hug. "I mentioned that the Duke of Forster would be visiting us today."

The pair turned to him, Ian at Sophia's side, her arm resting across his shoulders.

Before Sophia could offer formal introductions, Aidan stepped into the space between them and offered Ian his hand. "I'm pleased to meet you, Ian. Your father and I grew up together. I counted him as my closest friend." Aidan wanted to see if his assessment was accurate, or if the boy would shrink from the introduction.

But Ian stepped from Sophia's side without hesitation. Taking Aidan's hand, Ian met his gaze. "I'm happy to meet you, your grace; my father often told me stories about you."

Aidan was right: Ian was self-possessed, even able to speak of his father with affection but not visible grief.

"My father asked me"—Ian reached into his pocket and withdrew a small, carved wooden soldier—"to give you this when we met."

The soldier was the banner-bearer from a set of soldiers Aidan's father had given him. Aidan took the soldier carefully from the child's hand.

"My father said that he won it from you, but that I should return it." Ian watched Aidan turn the small figure over in his hand. "He said you would understand."

"Yes, Ian, I do understand." Aidan was once more in the tower of his childhood home, a room that he, his brothers, and Tom had claimed for their games. From the height of the tower, they had imagined themselves knights of the realm, protecting the land from invaders. Many afternoons they had enacted battles from history, using the set of soldiers from which the banner-bearer came. Benjamin on his university holidays had spent hours with his five younger brothers, reading from Malory or other medieval romances.

Aidan found Tom reaching across the years to him. The banner-bearer had always been Tom's favorite. Tom insisted he was the greatest hero because he entered the battle first and encouraged the others to remember their cause. Tom had been an idealist even then, believing that causes mattered. In contrast, Aidan had always known—perhaps because Aaron had been stronger and more cruel than his younger brothers—that the battle often went not to the strongest or the most faithful but to the most strategic.

"The paint was chipping off, but Father and I repainted it there." Ian pointed to the bottom of the banner. "And here." Ian pointed to the bearer's cloak.

Aidan turned the figure over once more. "You did a fine job with the repairs; they are barely visible." He handed the figure back to Ian. "The banner-bearer would like to remain with his troops."

Ian smiled, gratefully. "Thank you, sir; I have another, but this one is my favorite. Would you like to see my other soldiers? None are as good as he is, but I have them set up to fight the Battle of Hastings. He leads the Saxons. I'll show you how to tell which are Saxons and which are Normans."

"Ian, I'm not sure that the Duke has time." Sophia tried to intervene.

"No, Sophia." Aidan used her name without thinking, her name on his lips feeling like a caress. "I have time." Aidan turned to Ian. "I'd be pleased to review the troops with you, Commander."

Chapter Seven

Sophia watched helplessly as Ian led Aidan from the room, neither looking back. Spent, she sat on the couch, leaning into its curved side.

When Aidan had first entered the library, he'd seemed so real that the colors in the room faded around him. Tom, all kindness and bland manners, had never walked with such vitality, not even when well. The chill that had settled in her bones years ago had lessened as Aidan drew near to her, and the kiss he'd breathed onto the back of her hand had made a place below her stomach tighten with expectation. She should have expected to react to the physical contact strongly, she reassured herself; no one but Ian and Tom's sisters had touched her since her return. But even so, for an instant she had wished Aidan would fold her in his arms and reassure her that Tom's plan hadn't been misguided.

However, when Aidan had released her hand, she saw nothing in his face to encourage such confidences. If anything, the line of his jaw had become more severe over the years, reminding her of his older brother Aaron. She braced herself for harsh recrimination or even cold hatred. But he offered neither. His every sentence conveyed distance and a disinterested practicality.

Just as Ophelia had predicted, Aidan treated her with a civil solicitude, an appropriate manner for discussing business with the widow of an old friend or, apparently, for meeting with a former lover. It was as if they had never kissed, never held one another in their arms, never made promises . . . never loved. It was as if she meant nothing to him.

Unbidden, she remembered her first glimpse of him, young and laughing with his friends. She had suppressed the memory for years. But now, having seen no trace of their passion and no hint of the laughing, charming boy he'd been, she let herself remember.

It had been sunny, the first pleasantly warm day. She'd walked with some of her Elliot cousins to the local village fair. With a small allowance from her uncle, she had already bought rosemary soap from the Misses Bornfield, spinsters who lived near the pond at the edge of town, and some ribbon for her hair. At the end of the booths, a crowd cheered the morris dancers.

She'd noticed Tom first. Tall and thin, he watched the dancers over the heads of those in front of him. Someone hidden by the crowd had called his name, and he'd responded with a call and a waved arm. His wavy dark hair fell over his eyes, only to be pushed away by elegant hands. She'd noticed him because he was a stranger and handsome.

Then, Aidan came into view, eclipsing Tom. She had been struck by Aidan's beauty, broad shoulders tapering to narrow hips, thick black hair, and deep eyes. The two were clearly relations, perhaps even brothers, but something in the vitality of the one overshadowed the other. Tom, enamored with the rural dances, hadn't noticed her watching, but Aidan saw her immediately.

He'd winked, and followed that wink with a slow, confident assessment of her dress and person. Sophia had lived too many years with her cousins to allow any attempt to embarrass her, so she had waited for his eyes to return to hers, then she'd mimicked his assessing gaze until he laughed aloud.

When the crowd shifted, she'd soon wished she had been less daring. Tom and Aidan's third companion, Charles Culvert, was the son of a neighboring landowner. Seeing her, Charles waved, then made his way to her side, his companions in tow, to make introductions. Aidan had pretended they had already been introduced—another dare she couldn't ignore, and she'd gone along with the charade. In the company of her cousins, they had spent the rest of the afternoon together, and the next afternoon, and the next, until the beginning of Michaelmas term, when the whole group left for school. But Tom and Aidan had returned again at the next holiday, and the next, and soon, she'd come to expect seeing them at the end of every term.

Sophia and Aidan's hadn't been a proper courtship. He hadn't met her in her uncle's drawing room or conversed with her aunt while Sophia embroidered demurely. No, with her cousins as chaperones, she had met him in the fields for long walks or in the orchard with the fruit trees in bloom. She'd fallen in love with him while throwing rocks in her uncle's pond and watching the fish dart among the rushes. He had listened to her ideas and argued with her as if she were one of his friends from Harrow or Cambridge. He had made her feel valued and confident.

But today, his nonchalance had made clear that she had been no more than a youthful indulgence, long ago set aside. He had moved on, to war and whatever missions he had done there, to a role in parliament, to managing his estates . . . to a life not influenced by love for her. Certainly he had broken off all communication with Tom, never answering any letters until even Tom ceased to write. But was that the result of anger—or simply of time and distance?

In Italy, she had known men—and women—who could cover a well of hatred with a polite façade. She didn't know if Aidan had grown into a man capable of such dissimulation. But would the cost of believing Aidan sincere and finding him deceptive be greater or less than the cost of mistrusting him at every step? No, she had spent a decade fearing how he might respond when they met again and had been wrong in all her predictions. She would not spend the rest of Ian's youth suspecting Aidan—until Aidan gave her cause.

Sophia weighed the decision carefully. If Ian were not involved, she might force the discussion. But Ian's well-being was her only concern. Yes, she would follow Aidan's lead. If he chose to ignore their failed love, then she would ignore it as well. She already had years of practice pretending disinterest in news of Aidan; now she could simply pretend disinterest in Aidan himself.

As Aidan accompanied Ian to the nursery, the boy offered a short tour of the house and its inhabitants. Ian pointed out a study, a morning room, and a door under the stairwell that concealed the servants' stairway, leading down to the kitchen, the household offices, and Dodsley's and Cook's rooms.

As they ascended the stairs to the first-floor landing, Ian indicated the general arrangements of the rooms: a music room, the gallery, the drawing rooms. The second floor was devoted solely to bedrooms, family to the left and guests to the right. Most conveniently, Ian indicated Sophia's bedroom. "Mama's room is there at the end." Ian waved his hand toward it. On the third floor were the nursery and the staff rooms.

Ian had Tom's talent for knowing all the household secrets: Dodsley loved opera and would sometimes play the piano and sing robustly in the music room ("with Mama's permission, of course"). Cook was disappointed at not finding pistachios in London for any reasonable price because without them she was no longer able to make her famous

lemon cake. His tutor Mr. Grange (who "smells of pickles"—
Ian wrinkled his nose) pined after a squire's daughter, but
hadn't the money to offer for her. Their lame cat Artemisia
("Papa named her for a plant") liked to lie in the sun on the
balcony outside his mother's bedroom and pretend to catch
birds, so Sophia left the door unlatched and open. Ian's stories were useful and charming, though Aidan was certain
Sophia would not have approved of her son's easy confidences.

Ian was so delighted to escort him to the nursery that
Aidan felt a twinge of conscience. He had accepted Ian's offer
for reasons other than a desire to get to know his ward better.
Certainly the boy's resemblance to Tom was too great for
Aidan to refuse the boy's request. But he also needed some
time, having met Sophia, to plan his next move. Ian's invitation gave him that time. It also allowed him to escape from
the gaze of the ever-vigilant Dodsley and wander the house
unimpeded. Aidan imagined that he would play soldier for a
quarter hour or so, then begin his investigations. If he happened to run into a suspicious servant, he would simply claim
to be lost.

The nursery was painted, not the typical drab whitewash,
but a pleasing terracotta that spoke of Ian's Italian childhood.
The walls were hung with botanical drawings. Aidan knew
the most common—pansies, violets, roses, columbines—but
others were more exotic.

"Mama painted them," Ian offered proudly. "I get them
when she's finished. I like that one best." Ian pointed to an
image labeled *"Rosa chinensis."*

Aidan knew it from his mother's garden, the *Mutabilis*
rose, with buds and flowers from yellow to salmon to red. He
noticed the clarity of the line, the purity of the colors, the
delicacy of the touch. From her early promise, Sophia had
developed into an artist of sensitivity and skill.

"Finished?" Aidan prompted.

"Mama drew the illustrations for Papa's botany books.

After the engravers return the illustrations, I can have the ones I want. Papa gave me this one special before he died."

"They are quite lovely." Aidan had attributed the easel in the library to an interest suitable to women of her class. Clearly it was far more important. Perhaps an interest in Sophia's art would offer a way past her reserve? He stepped closer to examine the images.

"She and Papa would sit in the loggia. In the morning he would translate and write, and she would draw the plants he was writing about."

"Really?" Aidan focused on Sophia's drawings. He didn't wish to hear about the companionability of the Wilmot marriage.

"Then in the afternoon they would argue."

"Argue?" Aidan found himself more interested. "About what?"

"Well, not an angry argue," Ian clarified. "Papa always called it an intellectual disagreement. Mama would compare what he had written to the Latin and tell him how to make it better. Papa would quote something in Latin, and Mama would quote something back, until they found a new sentence they could agree on. Papa said Mama had the best mind of any man he knew."

Aidan knew Tom was right. Sophia's agile intelligence had fascinated Aidan from the moment he'd found her translating Greek in her uncle's garden. Her aunt's opposition to her education had forced her to wrap her Greek dictionary in oilcloth and tuck it inside a lidded urn. But he shook off the memory. "Why do you like this one best?"

"I like the hummingbird. Mama put it in the picture because I liked to feed them in the garden. Papa liked this one too. He always said it wasn't fair that Mama could fix his work, but he could never fix hers. Her illustrations were always perfect. This is the only picture that Papa declared wasn't perfect. So it was special."

Aidan looked back at the image, the strong lines, the delicate coloring. "Why isn't it perfect?"

"Hummingbirds don't feed on roses." Ian's tone hinted that he expected an adult to have a better knowledge of the feeding habits of hummingbirds. "Mama had to make a second one for Papa's book, but that one wasn't nearly so good."

"Because it didn't have a hummingbird?" Aidan speculated.

"Yes."

Aidan found the conversation strange—and strangely compelling. He'd learned more about Sophia and Tom's relationship in a few minutes than he had in all his years of questioning tourists. He now knew to seek out and follow her advice. He was going to become indispensable to her, as necessary as light and water to her precious plants, then he would withdraw and leave her bereft. Missing his companionship as much as his touch. Abandoned, as he had been.

Aidan turned from looking at the pictures in time to catch the boy wiping a tear on his sleeve, and he was moved to compassion. Whatever Aidan's business with the mother, the boy deserved kindness. "Thank you for showing the pictures to me, Ian. Now, where are those soldiers?"

Ian's face brightened. He pointed to the far corner of the large room. There on a low table, toy soldiers stood on a thick green cloth. Tufts of fabric bunched up under the green created hills and valleys, and blue cloth cutouts set on top signified rivers and oceans.

In the shape of his face, Ian looked far more like Sophia, but he resembled Tom in his mannerisms, the way that he tucked his head to the side when thinking or his way of looking into the distance when planning. Even his sighs were colored with Tom's inflections, so that Aidan could easily forget the years and imagine himself with Tom once more, playing soldiers before either of them knew what losses soldiers face.

But Ian's ability to think strategically far surpassed Tom's at the same age. Tom had hated to lose even a single soldier. He would work so hard to save each one that he would often find himself surrounded or otherwise lose the game. Ian knew he would sustain losses, but worked to minimize them.

Aidan quickly realized that he wouldn't be able to offer the game only half of his mind, lest he lose the battle and change the course of English history. Soon he was embroiled in a game of strategy with a sharp-minded boy. When Sophia came to the nursery to see if Aidan needed to be rescued, he was surprised to realize over an hour had passed.

"Oh, Mama, please, not yet." Ian's disappointment surprisingly mirrored Aidan's own.

"If you would like, Ian, I could come by tomorrow, and we can enact another battle." Aidan spoke without thinking.

Joyful, Ian turned his face up to his mother. "Would that be acceptable, Mama?"

Aidan nodded his willingness, and Sophia, seeing his acknowledgment, smiled broadly at Ian. "Of course it's acceptable. His grace will send us a note letting us know when to expect him."

Aidan stood and offered Ian his hand. "Excellent battle, Commander; we meet on the battlefield tomorrow."

On the way back to the main floor, Aidan stopped on the landing in front of the large Palladian windows to look out over the garden. "I believe we still have much to discuss."

Sophia felt her knees weaken, but her hand on the stair railing steadied her. So, he had not forgotten their past, but only delayed broaching the subject. She felt the pressure of her heart heavy in her chest. The silence extended between them for several moments, but she ignored the growing quiet, waiting until she could speak deliberately.

"Certainly, your grace. Would you like to return to the library?"

"Not *your grace* . . . Aidan." He gave a distant smile. "We were all so young, even children together. Surely—if nothing else does—that gives you the right of my name." He turned down the final set of stairs.

"Then . . . Aidan . . . what remains for us to discuss?" She braced herself for his answer, keeping her eyes on the stairs as they descended.

"The past and the future," he offered enigmatically.

She swallowed, waiting for the next sentence.

"And by that of course, I mean Tom and Ian. . . ."

She felt relief and disappointment in the same moment. So, they were to be cordial, ignoring the passion that had once connected them. But she had little time to consider the implications of that position; Aidan had continued speaking.

"Should we conclude our discussion of the guardianship now? Or would some other time be more convenient?"

Sophia thought of her preparations, her clothes, her hair, the air of distance she'd worked to maintain. Waiting would gain her nothing but more anxiety. "Perhaps we should make some preliminary decisions."

Aidan held open the library door, and she entered, walking once more to the middle chair on the assumption he would again pick the couch. This time, Aidan chose the chair next to hers. She tensed.

"I can see why you wish to keep Ian here rather than send him to Harrow. He is sociable, but there is something . . ." Aidan's tone remained pleasantly cordial.

"Like Tom." Sophia hoped spending time in the nursery had changed Aidan's perspective on Ian.

"Yes, like Tom. In his manner."

"Tom would have hated Harrow, had you not been there." She allowed herself to relax slightly. "Ian is not ready to have to work so hard to make friends or to be isolated from family."

"I can see that. We will keep him with a tutor this year. But I still wish to introduce him to boys already at Harrow, so that he has friends once he is there."

Sophia felt such relief that her body seemed to have lost all its sinews. "I'm pleased you agree that's the wiser course."

"I'm even willing to leave him with you for the rest of the summer. I have a house not far from here; I could easily see him when I'm in town. At some point he might benefit from spending time on the ducal estate, but there's no hurry." His voice was low, confidential, his body leaning toward her just slightly. "Whatever Tom might have imagined, it is for the two of us to decide."

Sophia was surprised; he offered her everything she had wished for. All she had to do was agree.

Then she remembered the look of joy on Ian's face and the weight of Tom's letter in her hand. "Delaying Harrow for a year is best. As for the other, I had hoped to convince you to let him stay with me, but, seeing him with you . . . knowing that Tom talked about you to him, that Tom chose you to stand in his stead as father. Much as I will miss him, Ian should go with you. He needs more than a mother now."

"I don't leave for some weeks. Why don't I spend time with Ian to see if having him accompany me would be a good decision? With your permission of course?"

"Of course." She couldn't help but agree; Aidan seemed to have become more accommodating during his visit with Ian.

"Then I will see you tomorrow." He rose to the sound of Dodsley's sharp double rap on the door.

"Excuse me, my lady. A messenger has arrived with a package from Mr. Murray."

"Thank you, Dodsley. You may place it on the desk." The butler followed her instruction, then returned to the hall, pulling the door closed behind him.

"It must be an important package for your butler to interrupt," Aidan offered.

"It's from Tom's publisher. I've been expecting it," Sophia acknowledged.

"Why don't you open it? It may require a response by return of the messenger."

Sophia wondered why Aidan was being solicitous, but his face revealed only a bland politeness. "If you don't mind . . ." She pulled on the twine, but the knot was tight.

"May I?" Aidan held out a knife. She wondered where he had kept it.

He cut the twine with one swift pull. Inside the heavy paper wrapper were several books in publisher's boards, each one with the title handwritten on the front cover, ready to be bound in the style of her personal library. Sophia looked quickly at each title, disappointed. The package had not contained the materials she'd expected.

Aidan, however, showed real interest in her choices, picking up each of the titles in turn. "Poetry, novels, science. It's an eclectic selection Murray has sent you."

"Mr. Murray has been very gracious, and I read widely."

"I can understand *Don Juan*. I've heard copies sell as fast as Murray can print them, though Murray's wise not to put his name on the title page. The slightest hint of sedition can put a publisher in prison. But Fanny Burney's *The Wanderer*? The reviewers dismissed it as quite inferior to her other books."

"The reviews claimed it was quite *unlike* her other books, because Burney's heroine must make her way without the advantages of wealth or family connections. That piqued my curiosity."

"Then, you must let me know if it proves worth reading." He raised an eyebrow at the next volume. "Priscilla Wakefield's *An Introduction to Botany*? I would have thought Ian had no need of Wakefield."

"It's for me," she admitted.

"For you?"

"I'm interested in how children are taught botany," she explained.

"Well, other than the Wakefield, we share some similar tastes. I have a substantive library in town, and you are welcome to draw on its contents at any time. Perhaps sometime you will tell me whether you find Burney's heroines better with or without wealth or family. But for now, I will leave you to that rake, Byron, knowing you will be well entertained. I will send round a note arranging a time to visit Ian, tomorrow."

Sophia felt more than watched Aidan leave. Just as with his arrival, one moment the room was filled with his presence and the next it was empty. It was foolish, she told herself, to feel bereft. Somehow seeing him had resurrected both her grief for Tom and for the Aidan she had lost as a girl. But he had drawn the limits of their relationship to their roles as Ian's guardians—nothing more. Whether such a silence was wise or not didn't matter, not now, and not with the things she still had left to do.

Chapter Eight

Once Aidan was out of the house, Sophia turned back to the stack of books sent to her by Murray.

Several months past, she'd contracted with John Murray of Albemarle Street to publish her husband's last book—a work on European plants suitable for English gardens. Murray was known for publishing some of the finest books in England, and Tom's book would appear in two volumes, quarto. The proofs had arrived the day before. They lay on her desk, waiting for her approval.

But Mr. Murray had also been interested in a project of hers, and her book was slated to appear simultaneously with Tom's. It occurred to her suddenly that Aidan might not approve of her aspirations to authorship. If he had become a hard man like his father or his brother Aaron, it would be best to conclude her business with Murray quickly, before Aidan could object.

She looked at the clock next to the fireplace. Ophelia planned to visit before dinner while Sidney attended a committee meeting at Westminster. If Sophia hurried, she could still meet with Murray.

Dodsley tapped at the door to the library.

"Dodsley, please tell Sally to meet me in my dressing room. I'll be going out, and I wish to change into a walking dress."

"I'm sorry, madam, but your brother is waiting in the green drawing room."

She groaned. The only thing worse than meeting with Aidan to discuss Ian's guardianship was meeting with Phineas at all.

"I forgot he was to visit. Is the purse-lipped Chloe with him?"

"No, madam, but your brother appears agitated."

"Oh, dear." She smoothed her skirts and walked to the library door. "Send a tea service and ask Cook if she has any of yesterday's tea cakes. I would rather not meet the savage beast without refreshments."

Sophia regretted dressing with such care for her meeting with Aidan. If she had remembered Phineas was to visit, she could have changed into something dowdy. But she couldn't change now; keeping Phineas waiting was never a good decision. At least, she consoled herself, Chloe had stayed home, saving Sophia from having to explain yet again why she and Tom had spent so many years surrounded by "papists and idolaters."

As she entered the room, Phineas was pacing away from her. She chose the most comfortable chair. No reason to be miserable during the inquisition.

"How kind of you to visit, Phineas. Dodsley is bringing us tea. Please take a chair." She always encouraged Phineas to sit when he visited. Pacing accentuated the angularity of his build and the narrowness of his limbs. His awkward gait always reminded her of a crow pecking for seeds.

He stopped before her, looking much like a dyspeptic Nero, his thinning hair brushed forward against his face.

"Was that Forster"—he grimaced on the name—"leaving just now?"

"Yes."

"Rather late for him to pay his respects to the family of the dead," Phineas spat, then strode away from her.

Phineas expected no response, so she said nothing. Instead, she wondered how Phineas knew Aidan had not visited before.

"He isn't known for being scrupulous of propriety." Phineas waved his thin arms. "They say he's seduced half the widows in the *bon ton*."

Suddenly, Phineas stopped pacing and stood still. He examined her dress, her hair. "My God, did you invite him here? Surely you can't be thinking of returning to your Italian ways and taking a *cavalier servente*?"

Phineas always thought the worst of her. Irritated, she considered telling him that she'd never taken up Italian ways—whatever those were—or had a *cavalier servente*. But she let the accusations pass. Narrow-minded as Phineas was, he was still her brother, and his children were Ian's cousins. Since Tom's annuity offered her protection from Phineas's pettiness, she could endure his sermons and accusations.

Phineas continued unrestrained. "If you take up with Forster, people will soon remember the circumstances of your marriage to Wilmot." Phineas was well agitated now, pacing with greater energy. She looked at her hands to avoid seeing the crow-like flap of his coattails. "That's likely why Forster is visiting now: as Wilmot's friend, he cannot have forgotten how easily you were compromised. He must think you a wanton, and it's not as if he would be seducing an innocent."

She felt her back stiffen, but she told herself "quiet, quiet." Appropriate women for Phineas were silent. Talking back, she had long ago learned, only lengthened his lectures.

"Wilmot might have married you to save your reputation,

but you shouldn't expect Forster to do the same. If your liaison became public, I would feel obligated—for the sake of my family and my status—to turn you from our door." Phineas paced back to the other end of the room.

Yes, Phineas would throw the first rock to stone her, though he would enjoy it more if he could make a speech on her weak morals first.

Dodsley tapped at the door with the tea service, and she nodded him in. "Tea has arrived, Phineas; can I serve you? Cook has prepared those cinnamon cakes you like so well. You wrote that you had a request for me?"

If Phineas liked anything as much as being the judge of social mores, it was Cook's cinnamon cakes. He sat immediately to tea. Sophia watched his hands as he buttered his cake. He'd married well—the widowed wife of an industrialist for whom he'd worked as a clerk. His wife's fortune had been sufficient for Phineas to buy a country estate and embark on a life of leisure. Even as a clerk, he'd kept his hands soft and clean—no inked fingers, no callouses. Neither one would do for a man rising in the world.

"You haven't told me why he was here." Phineas sugared his tea with one, two, three teaspoonfuls.

"We met to discuss a request in Tom's will."

"What request?" Phineas glared at her across his narrow, beaked nose.

"Forster is Ian's co-guardian." It was always a delicate balance, offering little more than what Phineas could hear at his club or from a parish gossip.

"No, no, no. . . ." Phineas's howl sounded like the cry of the little owls in Naples. "This will not do. Of course *you're* not suitable to serve as the child's guardian. But we can have no connection with that man, not now." Phineas set his cup down sharply, and she watched the liquid roll against the side of the cup.

"We must think. We could challenge the guardianship in

Chancery—I investigated how one does that last year. But that will cause gossip."

He'd already investigated how to challenge a guardianship in Chancery? She let the implications of Phineas's words flow past her, as he gulped down his tea in two large swallows. Whether it was true or just one of Phineas's tests of her reactions, she didn't know. She wondered how he would respond if she threw the teapot at his head. But even that act would require more energy than she had. Better to be still and let him imagine her grown compliant with age.

"Are you certain the guardianship papers are in order? Could you convince him not to take up the guardianship?"

She tried to sound meek. "You have always told me it is not a woman's place to oppose a husband's wishes. Tom's will is quite clear on this." She held out the plate with the cakes.

Mollified either by her answer or the cakes, Phineas took up a second cake and motioned for her to pour him another cup of tea. "Certainly, you should submit to your husband's wishes. I always worried that you would follow in our mother's footsteps, so I've been relieved that since your return you appear to have avoided her foolish notions."

Sophia bit her lip. It was one of Phineas's favorite complaints: how their mother's behavior had embarrassed her family and how Sophia—as her daughter—was fated to embarrass them as well. Exactly what her mother had done to deserve such condemnation, Sophia had learned in her girlhood not to ask. Doing so had only prompted a lecture on woman's frailty and need for obedience.

Crumbs fell on Phineas's trousers. He brushed them to the floor. "Well, if nothing's to be done about the guardianship, perhaps we can make use of the opportunity."

He wrapped two cinnamon cakes in a piece of table linen. "Lord Craven has offered me a seat in parliament. He is the only voter in the borough, so the seat is assured. He comes to town in two weeks. As I have no established house here, I wish for you to host a dinner party." He reached into his coat pocket. "Here's the guest list. You've been reclusive, so many will come simply to see you."

"I've been in mourning. No one should be surprised not to have seen me."

"I've been pleased that you showed an appropriate respect to your husband's memory. But you could have been visiting in the afternoons and going to private dinners for the last six months. No one will find it inappropriate for you to host a small party. To build alliances in parliament, I'll need to draw on Wilmot's connections."

He paused, looking her over once more. "I was going to ask for Chloe to oversee your choice of gown for the evening, but that dress will do. You'll need to wear a black shawl to tone down the blue, but it's modest enough and shows your rank."

She focused on reading the guest list. She knew all the names, and several—like Craven—had visited their villa in Italy.

"Two weeks should be ample time to make arrangements. Chloe will be with me and young Bartholomew and Chloe's Melissa." He never referred to his stepdaughter as his own. Phineas pulled another package from his pocket. "Chloe has written the invitations. Your footman should deliver them today."

Sophia nodded. He picked up the last cake on the plate. "Oh, and send an invitation to Forster. As Ian's guardian, he's likely to be seen with you. We must let it be known why. It wouldn't do for the *bon ton* to assume you his latest conquest. I'll spread the word at my club."

"I would like to invite the Masons, and our cousin Malcolm Hucknall and his wife."

"Wrong political opinions." He handed her his empty cup. "But Ophelia could help you avoid any mishaps as hostess. And since she's Wilmot's sister, no one will think her presence remarkable."

He stood, stuffed the cakes in his overcoat, and repositioned his hat. "I'll let myself out; I'll send Cook a menu. You'll need to hire additional servants for the evening. I don't have any in town." He walked to the door. "Perhaps I will bring Chloe with me when next I visit."

And with that, he was gone.

On the scale of meetings with Phineas, that one had gone, she thought, quite well—she was only the worse five tea cakes, some table linen, and a dinner party. She didn't know whether she should feel pleased or annoyed—both at Phineas and at herself. By refusing to defend herself, she had avoided a row. Now she appeared close enough to his ideal of womanhood that he would allow Chloe to visit. A disheartening thought. Chloe exhibited the vivacity and charm of a garden slug.

But her meeting earlier that afternoon with Aidan—the passionate love of her youth—made Sophia wonder at her own acquiescence to Phineas's demands. Had she really changed so much? When had she decided that giving in was just easier? Was there no passion left, no cause she would wish to champion? And worst of all, by keeping silent and calmly serving tea while Phineas impugned her character, had she finally become the sort of woman he and her aunt would praise?

Chapter Nine

Aidan was rereading Tom's letter when Ophelia swept into his study, clearly frustrated.

"It's lovely seeing you, Ophelia." Aidan suddenly remembered Tom joking, *"There are two rules for managing my sisters when they are upset: notice their clothes, and compliment their taste."* Tom had developed his rules when his sisters were barely out of the schoolroom, but Aidan thought they might still work. "Is that a new dress? It looks lovely on you; the green offers a perfect accompaniment to the rich auburn of your hair."

"Don't compliment me, Aidan Somerville. Not while I'm ashamed of you," Ophelia objected, but the tense set of her shoulders softened slightly.

Aidan stood and stretched his hand out, directing her toward the couch. Her use of his childhood name signaled ill. "I'm not sure what you mean. I've seduced no innocents. I haven't taken a new mistress, though my old one left me months ago. I've no new lovers among the widows of the *ton*. And I pay my creditors when their bills come due. What is there to be ashamed of?"

Ophelia looked at his hand, then at the couch. She moved

toward it, but did not sit. "I can't stay; Sidney expects me to gather him up from Whitehall. But I had to stop in. I've just come from Sophia. For a man reputed to know how to please women, I really expected you to . . . to . . ." Ophelia sputtered.

"Expected me to what, Phee? Seduce her in the drawing room?" Aidan found himself almost amused. From the moment his father had agreed to help rear Aidan's orphaned Gardiner cousins, Aidan had considered Tom's three sisters as his own. He preferred their easy laughter to the watchful aloofness of his elder and only sister, Judith. But he hadn't anticipated Phee's casting herself as Sophia's avenging angel. No, that was more the role he would expect from Judith; he would have to mollify Phee.

"No, certainly not." She began removing her gloves, pulling on each finger with short brisk movements. "You couldn't know, but I've been worried about Sophia. I was pleased Tom named you co-guardian. I thought it would protect Ian against that worm Phineas. But I never expected you to take Ian from London."

"If you must know . . ." He sat on the couch and patted the space beside him.

Ophelia refused the seat again. "I must."

"I offered to make just the occasional visit. *Sophia* insisted I play a greater role in her son's life."

"She believes she's fulfilling Tom's wishes." Ophelia shrugged. "She's spent too much of her life doing as Tom wished, though I never understood why. Had my brother been a saint, he wouldn't have been your friend, Aidan Somerville." Ophelia wasn't yet appeased.

"I assure you, Ophelia: she believes Ian would be best served by spending the summer at Greenwood Hall."

"But *you* can't possibly believe it. Even with a child as agreeable as Ian, I don't give you three days before you want to send him back to his mother."

"That may be true."

"Of course it's true. I've known you your whole life. Besides, it's not a good idea to take Ian away. Sophia's fragile, worn out . . . by grief perhaps, but something more as well. You must have seen it. She's more likely to defer to another person's opinion, less likely to express her own."

"To tell the truth, Phee, Sophia appeared perfectly in control, a bit reserved perhaps, but otherwise self-sufficient and calm."

"Then you don't deserve half the credit for observation I've given you. Ian will be fine, but Sophia shouldn't be left alone."

"Then perhaps Sophia should accompany us." A splendid idea. He wondered why he hadn't thought of it before. A summer in his country home, the two of them—and Ian of course. Little possibility of interference. One hundred possibilities for seduction.

Phee finally sat on the couch beside him. "Actually, Aidan, that's not a bad idea. It might even be brilliant. I've often suggested Sophia take a week at Tom's country place. But she refuses. Leaving London might offer the recuperation she needs. Of course you would have to host a house party. She couldn't come alone with only Ian."

"It's a big house. She's a widow. He's my ward." Aidan patted Ophelia's hand as if to console her.

"That won't matter if someone in the *ton* objects." Ophelia pulled her hand away in refusal. "*Her* reputation may be spotless, but *yours* isn't."

"I could have the dower house prepared for her and Ian," he suggested.

Ophelia considered his words. "Actually, that might work. Of course Kate and Ariel and I could make a trip to the country as well."

"You are always welcome at Greenwood Hall." Aidan offered the expected invitation.

"Oh, I feel so much better." Phee leaned over and kissed Aidan's cheek. "Now we must convince Sophia. She's wary of you. Apparently tourist gossip in Italy did not stand you in good stead."

"I'm yours to advise, Phee. What would you have me do?" Aidan knew that by appearing to follow Ophelia's guidance, he gained the chance to allay any later suspicions she might have.

"I want you to be charming and solicitous, but more subtle. None of those hungry looks that make women run after you. *And* I want you to escort her to my house for a family dinner tomorrow night. I won't tolerate excuses. It's been far too long since you dined with us."

"Then I will offer none. If Sophia agrees, I will play coachman. A charming, solicitous, *subtle* coachman."

Ophelia smiled broadly. "Then it's settled. Of course, you must promise that once you are ensconced in the country, you won't grow bored and seduce her for entertainment."

"Phee, I'm crushed. You think I would seduce the wife of my childhood friend and the mother of my ward?" Aidan pretended to be wounded.

"Well, to be perfectly honest, neither of you is married. If you were discreet . . . well, I would offer no recriminations. She's not the sort of woman you typically prefer, but perhaps you could find her attractive. It might even bring some life back into her. . . ."

Aidan sat back in his chair, laughing, and stretched out his long limbs. "Phee, I've never known you to encourage me in an affair, so I'm unsure what to say. I will promise you this however: if I were to seduce Sophia, it wouldn't be from boredom."

* * *

Ian was lively and animated at dinner, hardly able to contain himself.

"He knew the battle as well as Papa." He pulled his leg up to sit on it in his chair.

Sophia pretended not to notice. Ian rarely forgot his table manners, and she didn't wish to interrupt his excitement. "It was kind of Forster to stay so long."

"He said he would come back tomorrow. I've planned another battle, a harder one this time. I wonder if he'll know it." Ian bounced back and forth on his bent leg.

"Which battle, darling?"

"Bosworth Field, though I have to put little pieces of paper on the men to show which side they fight on. When Papa lost—he always played Richard—he used to run around the room, and call out, 'a horse, a horse, my kingdom for a horse.' Then he'd let me stab him. Papa said I made a fine Henry Tudor. Do you think Forster knows about Richard III?—he was a hunchback and murdered his nephews. Or will I need to tell him?"

"The Duke was very well-read when your father knew him. But if he doesn't know, I'm sure he wouldn't mind your telling him. He always liked to learn new things." It was dangerous to think of Aidan as he had been as a young man, but his kindness to Ian had made Sophia remember his unusual patience with his own younger brothers, patience she'd always believed he'd cultivated to make up for Aaron's many cruelties.

"I'd like him to know. It would be fun for him to say the line—Papa said it was from Shakespeare. Do you think Forster would read me the part? I'd like to hear it from the play. Papa never read me the play because I was too young. But I'm not too young now, am I?"

"No, darling, you're not too young."

There was almost no need to answer. Ian's pleasure ran

faster than his words. Forster was well on his way to becoming her son's hero.

Sophia listened as Ian detailed each step of the battle to come, how Henry Tudor's troops would be outnumbered, how Richard would divide his army into three groups, how Richard's noble allies would fail him.

She asked questions about which generals led which troops and how they positioned themselves on the battlefield. Ian had not been so excited since before his father died. Perhaps she and Aidan could share a mutual affection for her son, and if there was nothing else between them, that mutual affection could stand for friendship.

Sophia kissed Ian good night, entrusting him to Sally's care. She watched as the pair, laughing, ascended the stairs to the nursery, before she turned to her own room.

At the door's opening, Artemisia ran from the open balcony doors, not to greet her, but to escape into the hall and down to the kitchen, where she would spend the night hunting mice and being disappointed. Even mice were afraid to intrude on Cook's domain. "At least," Sophia said, more to herself than the cat, "you have the good grace to rub against my ankles before you abandon me."

Her voice stilled on the word *abandon*. She knew—and had known long before she realized that Tom would die— that she held so tightly to Ian because she had suffered so many losses of her own. Before she'd turned fifteen, she'd lost all the people she'd loved: her parents, her beloved aunt Clara, then her adored governess Mrs. Lesley. Perhaps that was why Sophia had acquiesced when Aidan had told her he was going to the wars. Everyone else she'd ever loved had left; why not Aidan as well?

Sophia blinked her tears away. To distract herself from sad thoughts, she curled up on the chaise longue to read, long,

round pillows behind her back, and an oil lamp at her side for
when the evening light waned.

Perhaps a book would quiet her restless mind.

She first opened Burney's novel, but the plight of the
heroine—nameless, alone, reliant on the kindness of
strangers—only made her more sad. So, she turned to *Don
Juan*, an anonymous satire on literature and society that
everyone attributed to the exiled Lord Byron. The poem recounted the love affair between a hapless Don JOO-un (as
the rhyme told her to pronounce it) and the older, beautiful,
and married Donna Julia. Throughout, Byron offered clever
digressions on the work of other English poets. Sophia found
much of the first canto amusing. But at Donna Julia's defense of women trapped in unfulfilling arranged marriages,
Sophia grew pensive. Donna Julia's farewell to her lover
reminded Sophia of herself and Aidan.

Closing the book on her finger, she leaned her head back
against the arm of the chaise. Tears welled in her eyes, but
did not fall.

She had believed their passion would connect them across
the years, that they could not meet without emotion, even if
it were hate. She had been wrong. And like Donna Julia,
she was left with a heart still his, remembering every caress
as if it were burned into her skin.

Yet, she consoled herself, the meeting she had dreaded for
a decade had come and passed. And she had survived.

Tomorrow she would set her love for him behind, knowing that no spark was left. But for what was left of tonight,
she would mourn.

She opened the book to the place marked by her finger.
She read again Julia's parting lines to Juan, this time adapting them as a farewell to her passion for Aidan:

> *"You will proceed in pleasure, and in pride,*
> *Beloved and loving many; . . . but I cannot cast aside*

> *The passion which still rages as before,*
> *And so farewell—forgive me, love me—No,*
> *That word is idle now—but let it go."*

That night Sophia dreamt of Tom. He was handing her the papers. "Are you sure you want the responsibility of these? I could send them to Aldine with instructions to keep them sealed. When it was time, you could instruct him how to proceed."

She'd refused. "The risk is too great. They could go astray. Someone could read them. They will be safer with me."

He'd covered her hands with his hands and pressed a kiss to her forehead. "You are remarkable, Sophia. Few women would agree to this."

It had been the last time they had touched.

For a decade, Aidan's dream had begun the same. Sophia slipped into his room, smiling, her long dark hair loose around her shoulders, a white shift sheer against her limbs. Locking the door behind her, she would run soundlessly into his arms, kiss his neck, his face, his lips. Her hands would caress his chest and back. She would thread his hair through her fingers, as she held him tightly, passionately. She would lead him to the edge of the bed, holding her finger to her lips for silence. He would watch, silent, as her clothes dropped to the floor around her feet. In bed, he would be entranced by the sight of her, naked above him, beneath him, caught in the embrace of her long, slender arms. He would revel in her caresses, then sate his desire in the softness of her body, as she called his name in ecstasy.

If Aidan could have awoken at the moment of their shared climax, he might have found the dream a pleasant residual of youthful passion—a strange quirk of memory that allowed him to enjoy her body over and over. But the dream never ended there. It always shifted to any of a series of endings, all betrayals. Sometimes she would simply disappear from his arms to the sound of mocking laughter. Sometimes he would search for her, calling her name in the darkened halls of his family home, but finding only the echo of his own voice. Other times she would run away from him, and no matter how hard he ran he could never catch her. Frequently he would find her in a lighted ballroom, dancing, being swept away by partner after partner, always out of reach. Often, she ran into the arms of another man, a man he trusted and called friend, and that man would lead her into a waiting carriage. Aidan would stand on the porch steps, helpless to stop the carriage, watching it disappear into the night, her name unvoiced on his lips.

He always awoke shaking with frustration and anger, his heart racing and his body covered with sweat. The dream had visited him less frequently over the years, the benefit of brandy or an intoxicating woman. But its intensity never lessened. For days after, he would revisit the dream while waking, playing the scenes over in his mind. He allowed himself the torment. He never wanted to forget the dream's message: that he was a fool. And each time, he renewed his pledge that no woman would make him a fool again. And for nine years, no woman had, his heart protected by Sophia's betrayal.

But a year ago, the dream had changed. Sophia came to him in joy as always, and they made love passionately, but when she disappeared from his bed, he found himself in the churchyard of an English village, following her through the gravestones. Suddenly she was gone, and Aidan stood at an open grave, watching a wooden casket be lowered into the ground.

At the side of the grave stood Tom, dressed in black mourning clothes, thinner, older, with a red flush on his cheeks and leaning on a cane. Tom held out his hand, saying, "I have never had greater need of a friend or brother." Aidan, moved by the sorrow in Tom's eyes, took a step toward him, but he disappeared before Aidan reached the other side of the open grave.

This night, Aidan awoke to his name being called by a male voice he would have known despite the separation of many years: Tom's voice. He threw himself from the bed, listening as the voice came from the garden below his open window. As he pulled open the long glass doors onto the balcony, Aidan was struck suddenly by memories of childhood, of climbing down the balcony at his father's house to meet Tom for nighttime adventures, of patrolling the woods at the edge of the estate, playing Arthur's knights or Norse marauders, and of circling their rowboats in the pond to fight as Nelson's armada. Aidan felt the loss of his friendship with Tom slip past his defenses and settle as an ache in his memory.

The garden was lit by a full moon, with mists passing below on the grounds, shrouding the familiar shapes of the hedges and walkways into new unfamiliar ones. The ridges of the old flower beds, now unkempt, appeared like so many graves. A dark figure stood beside one of the beds, and, as in Aidan's dream, held out his hand to Aidan, then disappeared.

Aidan caught himself as he was about to climb down the balcony. Moved with sudden and surprising emotion, he stretched his hand out to the garden where he was certain Tom had stood, but where now there was only fog and darkness.

Chapter Ten

Charters pushed hard against the garden door, pressing his shoulder against the crack of rotten wood. The door fell open, broken against the latch.

The house had few servants. An old butler too deaf to hear the groan of the wood as it collapsed. The cook, his wife, too arthritic to move quickly, if at all. Charters left the broken door as a payment for the sweet lemonade and savory cakes the cook had always saved for his visits when he was young. Perhaps it would be enough to save the staff from suspicion. The house was characteristic of the aged: careful locks at the front, rotting doors on the back, as if a burglar always entered through the main door rather than hopping the wall at the mews.

The late Lord Montcrief's study opened directly off the back, still carrying the faint smell of death. The glass-fronted cabinet of curiosities sat prominently before the desk, the key in the lock. Charters shook his head: Montcrief would not have been pleased to see his treasures so unattended.

Charters pulled the key from the lock and dropped it on the floor, to suggest haste. The piece he wanted was wrapped in soft flannel, pushed to the back of the drawer beneath the cabinet. Montcrief had always thought it a copy, but Charters knew different. He unwrapped the antique Damascus blade reverently, felt the knife's heft and balance, then slipped it into the empty scabbard at his waist. From the cabinet itself, he gathered half a dozen of Montcrief's smaller objet d'art and put them in a bag. He slipped back out of the house into the night.

At the wall closest to the mews, Charters poured the items from the bag on the ground. A burglary gone awry; the pieces recovered. That's how the newspapers would tell it. Then, he let himself out the garden gate, locking it behind him, his hand caressing the hilt of the knife.

As he walked away from the wall, Charters wondered wryly if he should thank Aldine for all his help. Most of the documents Aldine gave him to deliver appeared mundane: a death notice, a house being let, an investments report. But others contained information some would pay to keep confidential, and still others would pay to learn. Without Aldine's deliveries, Charters wouldn't have known that Montcrief's treasures still remained in his old home. Nor would he have known that Lady Wilmot still employed Luca Bruni, one of Tom's confederates in the spy game. A member of the Carbonari in the household of a British peer. Charters could make much of that.

He rubbed his thumb on the smooth hilt as he walked. Had both Forster and Lady Wilmot signed the same set of papers? If so, what business connected the two? Charters would have to find the papers later on his own. But where? He'd already searched all of Aldine's files related to Lady Wilmot and found nothing. And Aldine never carried papers home. It was a complication.

Forster was a complication as well. At Harrow, they had been in the same form, well-matched rivals, both in their studies and at chess. Both third sons, they had no guaranteed sinecure. Instead, each was forced to be reliant on his wits and skills to advance. During the wars, Charters had listened for Forster's name, learning the young officer had been with Wellington at Badajoz and Salamanca. After that, Forster had been nowhere for several years, though rumor had placed him in clandestine circles.

Charters had been imagining a pretty game of cat and mouse with the lovely Lady Wilmot, ending—as they so often did—with her apparent suicide or accidental death. But Forster was one of the few men in London who could fit the pieces together. Was Forster involved somehow with Lady Wilmot? If so, Charters had less time than he'd imagined. But complications often made the game a more worthy challenge.

Chapter Eleven

Working all morning in the garden with Perkins, Sophia didn't realize until well past noon that Forster had never sent round a note about visiting Ian. She should have been angry, but she was only surprised and disappointed. She had almost convinced herself that Aidan would care about Ian's feelings, but this was exactly the sort of behavior she had predicted to Tom. Perhaps it was for the best. If Forster couldn't play with a child for an hour or so when he had himself suggested it, then she had little to fear from him as an interfering guardian. But she was unexpectedly sorry to have been right.

Ian, however, would be hurt and out of sorts. Though his father's illness and death had made Ian mature, he was still young. She would need to soothe his disappointment. Perhaps a visit with Nate or a trip to the Royal Menagerie as a treat. Surely Dodsley would know where a boy might like to go in London.

She dusted her hands on her gardening apron, cursed under her breath, and went to comfort her son.

As she approached the nursery, she heard Ian's laugh, boisterous and excited. Thank God, she thought, for Luca. But in the nursery she found Forster, sitting on the floor, surrounded by soldiers, and Ian, animated with delight.

Ian saw her immediately. "Mama, Mama, I won. I beat him. And look . . ." He grabbed up some soldiers and ran to her, putting them in her hands. "Forster brought me the set he and Papa used to play with. See . . ." He ran back to the pile of soldiers and picked out the banner-bearer. "See how he matches some of the men. This set has four armies, so that I can have bigger battles." Ian threw his arms around her waist. "Isn't it tremendous? Forster says I may keep them. May I? May I?"

Sophia could not refuse such pure joy. "If Forster is certain that he wishes to give the set to you." She looked at Aidan, who had unfolded himself from the floor and was brushing off his trousers.

"I'm certain."

Ian cheered and hugged Sophia again.

"Tell his grace thank you for his gift," she reminded gently.

"I already have, Mama," Ian said. "He told me I had to have your permission to keep them. May I show Luca my new soldiers?"

"Certainly. You may play until we dress for dinner, but remember we dine at your aunt's tonight." Sophia was barely able to finish her sentence before Ian, yelling for Luca, ran from the room, leaving her alone with Aidan.

She turned to him, still smiling at Ian's happiness. "I'm sure Ian will value the soldiers. When he is older, if you wish for him to return them for your own sons to treasure, I'm sure he will."

"They have been in a box for many years. I'd rather Ian enjoy them." Aidan did not acknowledge her comment about sons.

"That is very kind. I can't think of anything that Ian would value more. He and Tom used to play at soldier for hours. . . ." She let the sentence fall off into silence. Aidan was standing close by, not so close that she felt ill at ease, but enough for her to be aware of his height, the breadth of his shoulders.

She shook herself inwardly. Her awareness of him was nothing unusual. She had always been aware of him. "How long have you been here?"

Aidan laughed. "Long enough to realize that the last time I sat on the floor playing soldiers, my bones were much younger." He leaned forward slightly, narrowing the distance between them, "Lavender. That's it. You smell like lavender."

For a moment, Sophia thought Aidan had intended to embrace her, and her heart leapt. But it was only the lavender.

"I've been in the garden . . . planting. I thought you had forgotten him—you didn't send a note—I was coming to console him. I was so relieved to hear him laughing."

"Can you forgive my lapse in etiquette?" He smiled apologetically. "I had intended simply to deliver the box with the soldiers, but Ian saw me at the door, and . . . well, after that we were deep in the throes of battle." He leaned into her once more and breathed deeply. "I've always loved the scent of lavender. Perhaps you could show me where lavender would grow best in my garden."

"If you would like. I seem to have used up all London had remaining this far into summer. I've written the estate for more. Perkins can bring some to your garden when he returns with the new plants."

It had been easy to reject Phee's recommendation to seduce Aidan out of the guardianship before she'd seen him again. But now with him so close, she felt torn between her heart and her head. Her heart wanted to step into his embrace and taste his kisses once more. But her head told her not to break their civil distance lest the resulting conversation turn acrimonious and destroy their ability to care for Ian together.

"With Ian as my ward, I will come to town more frequently. It would be embarrassing to let the garden remain in disrepair," he offered confidentially. "I don't live far. You can even see the barest corner of my rooftop from the nursery windows." Sophia searched his face, but found no hint that he'd recognized her in the park.

"I'd be happy to offer whatever advice you find useful." Anything to encourage him to come into town rather than take Ian to his estate. She led him to the stairs.

"The plants should arrive next week?"

"Yes. Perkins has family on the estate, and I told him there was no reason to return quickly."

"Then I look forward to next week." They descended in companionable silence.

Dodsley met them at the foot of the stairs, then disappeared to retrieve Aidan's coat, hat, and gloves.

"As for tonight, what time would be best to collect you and Ian?"

"Tonight?" She struggled to remember what she might have agreed to. "We have promised to go to Ophelia's for a family dinner."

"Yes, and Ophelia has asked me to play escort. She insists the ducal carriage will be more comfortable than, as she said, 'that claptrap carriage of Tom's.'"

"Oh, dear. I knew it rattled." She could not refuse, not with him living so near. Dodsley, returning, helped Aidan into his coat, and Sophia noticed how the broad line of his shoulders fit exactly. "Would an hour before be sufficient to arrive on time?"

"We'll have time to spare." Aidan put on his hat and gloves, then, offering a gracious half-bow, took his leave.

Aidan considered his morning well-spent. He'd set his footman to watch Sophia's house and report when Ian went to the park with his nurse. Then, he had timed his arrival to coincide with Ian's returning home. He wanted to give the soldiers to Ian without Sophia present.

He had moved the soldiers to London for his nephews, but

he had never been able to part with the box—or even open it. He'd justified it to himself by saying the little devils could not treat things with care. But in truth, the soldiers, horses, wagons, and cannons were not simply toys to be set on a felt battleground, but reminders of a youth spent with Tom. As Ian—so nearly resembling his father—lifted each figure from the box, Aidan allowed himself to remember. Their tricks and games. Their scrapes and secrets.

Sharp-witted and funny, Ian knew stories from Aidan's shared youth with Tom. But Ian also asked questions that suggested someone had been sending Tom reports on Aidan's activities for years. The information went beyond typical tourist fare.

But who?

"Ian"—Aidan had laughed, after a pointed question about his expenditures at his club—"did your mother tell you stories about me, too?"

Ian looked into the distance. "No, Mama never talks about her childhood, and Papa told me that I shouldn't tell Mama the stories he told me about you."

"Why?"

"Papa said it would make her sad, so we made you a secret."

The stories Tom had told Ian seemed clearly designed to make the boy accept Aidan's guardianship. But why keep them a secret from Sophia? True, Sophia wouldn't have wanted her child to romanticize the scrapes of a youth run wild. But was there more to it?

At the thought of Sophia, Aidan smiled despite himself. Sophia transformed by Ian's joy, though still reserved and cautious, was more filled with life than the Sophia he had met yesterday. Yesterday's Sophia was bolstered by her library and the protection of Tom's portrait. But today's Sophia, caught off guard at finding Aidan in the nursery, had none of those supports. Even her clothes made her more human, a light muslin gardening frock, stained from grass and mud. He wanted more time to watch her reactions, to learn how to shape his demeanor to gain her trust.

At least that's what he told himself.

Aidan stopped on the sidewalk, letting the street vendors move around him. Only one person could have sent Tom such detailed intelligence. Recalling the address, he caught a hackney for the offices of Leverill and Cort.

He arrived in the City some thirty minutes later. He knew what he wanted—no, needed—to know. But how to encourage the stocky solicitor to comply? Where Sophia was concerned, Aidan rarely told the truth. At first, he'd lied to conceal his growing affection from a father who believed all women avaricious: "Beware of women, my boy: if you steal a kiss, they will snatch your purse." Then after Sophia's marriage to Tom, he'd lied to preserve the possibility of revenge. But Aldine was not the sort of man one could easily manipulate, and Aidan was left with telling the truth . . . or at least a portion of it.

A brown-haired clerk with small dark glasses and a limp met him at the entrance and escorted him to Aldine's office. The odd-looking fellow had accompanied Aldine to deliver the guardianship papers. Something niggled at the back of Aidan's memory—an unsettling mix of familiarity and distrust, as if he had recognized something hiding in a shadow. Likely, the sensation was just an echo of the world of suspicion and subterfuge in which he had worked during the war. But before he could trace the feeling, the clerk knocked on Aldine's office door and announced him.

Aldine sat at a desk piled high with paper, surrounded by shelves and cabinets, filing drawers and cubbyholes. Papers rolled tightly rested in the range of cubbyholes to his right. But what would have been chaos under other men had the appearance of a studied order under Aldine. Aidan knew without question that Aldine could place his hands in an instant on any papers he wanted.

Aldine began to rise, but Aidan waved him back into his seat, then placed his overcoat on the back of a chair and sat. "I have some questions."

"About the guardianship." Aldine anticipated.

"In a way. To what extent did your correspondence with the late Lord Wilmot include information about my life?"

Aldine smiled enigmatically. "The late Lord Wilmot wished to remain apprised of your . . . activities. I provided news from various sources."

"You had me watched." Aidan interpreted.

"My predecessors did so. I preferred different methods."

Aidan raised an eyebrow.

"A traveler at an inn near your estate gathers more than adequate information about the status of your rents, your crops. A young blade in need of funds listens well at your club. The firm has ears in most of the clubs, gambling hells, and brothels, even at Almack's. But be assured: none of my listeners would have found it striking for your name to appear on my list."

Observing was easy when the subject didn't know he was being watched. And Aidan hadn't thought of himself as an object of investigation since the war.

"I did no less for Wilmot than I would do for your grace. I assume you wish to know what information I sent Lord Wilmot." Aldine took a roll of papers from one of the cubbyholes, then spread the roll out on his blotter and placed weights on each corner to hold the papers flat.

Aidan leaned forward to read the documents, but Aldine motioned him back.

"You will refuse to let me read your correspondence?"

"No. Lord Wilmot gave his permission to make the correspondence available to you, at your request. But it is to remain a secret from her ladyship, until such time as you give your consent. I sent the information about you separately from our regular correspondence, including it in the embassy packet. A young clerk collected it from the ambassador's staff."

"Did you find Wilmot's wish to conceal his correspondence from Lady Wilmot suspicious?"

"You may form your own judgment." Aldine took his hat off the rack. "Will you accompany me? Or would you prefer I bring the papers to your home?"

"I'll accompany you." Aidan pulled on his coat.

"I assume you are not averse to subterfuge?"

Aidan nodded his agreement.

Aldine continued, "Then, I'm accepting your offer for coffee at your club. As we leave, we should discuss the horses you intend to purchase at Tattersalls."

"I see you still listen," Aidan said.

"I remain his young lordship's agent." Aldine opened his bag and left it at the side of the desk, and lifted his overcoat off the rack. The two men walked out of the office discussing the merits of the ponies to be auctioned on Monday.

Outside the offices, Aldine hailed a hackney and followed Aidan into it, settling into the back-facing seat. "Solicitor's offices are not always secure."

"The papers you laid out on the desk?"

"A diversion."

"Your open valise by the desk is also a diversion."

"I wish it to appear we had nothing to discuss but ponies and coffee."

"You suspect one of your clerks?"

"I'm uncertain." Aldine looked out the carriage window, and Aidan followed his gaze. They were close to his club.

"I assumed we were traveling somewhere other than my club."

"Can I trust you to keep our destination a secret? Or must we travel with the windows shuttered?"

"You have my word."

Aldine tapped on the roof, and the hackney slowed. He handed up a slip of paper, and the carriage changed direction. "After his lordship's death, you spent weeks in London, making inquiries," Aldine explained, almost offhandedly.

"I thought I'd been subtle." Aidan hid his chagrin. Malcolm had also noticed his interest. Had others found it remarkable as well?

As if anticipating the line of Aidan's thought, Aldine offered, "I doubt if anyone else noticed. I simply saw a pattern in the reports I received. You suspected Lord Wilmot's death was not natural."

"He was not yet thirty." Aidan shrugged.

"No, not yet thirty. But we lost many not yet thirty and not yet twenty, in the wars. One grows inured to the reports."

A companionable silence grew between them, both men understanding how much had been lost in defeating Bonaparte.

Aidan watched the buildings change, the neighborhood grow less mercantile and more rural. They were heading north and east, out of the City, toward St. Pancras and Camden Town. Aidan calculated how much time he would need to return home in time to change for dinner. Eventually the hackney stopped in an unassuming neighborhood, little more than a crossroads with brick row houses on either side. The carriage pulled into the mews behind one row. Aldine directed Aidan through an apparently unused kitchen, to the front of the house, and into a cozy drawing room. The decorations suggested a spinster with an affection for lace.

Aldine pointed Aidan to an upholstered armless chair, then slipped from the room.

The maple furniture was decades old, in the style of Queen Anne. A hoop with embroidery half-finished lay to the side of the sofa, and a book open on the writing desk gave the impression of a resident returning soon. But the air in the room was stale and the table not recently dusted. The room was staged to appear as if someone lived in the house. If Aidan were a betting man, he would have said that Aldine lived somewhere else.

Aldine returned with several pasteboard hat boxes stacked high enough to hide his lower face.

"Tom would have liked this." Aidan motioned at the room, the hat boxes. "As a boy, he was always squirreling things away, creating hiding places in books or under drawers, tapping the wall of every room to find the secret passageways. At Harrow, he even had a suitcase with a false bottom where he would hide his treasures."

Aldine opened the lid of the top hat box to reveal it was filled with letters. "I'm pleased to know my circumspection would have pleased his lordship. I moved most of my correspondence with Lord Wilmot here when I realized you had suspicions about his death."

"Most?"

"I left enough to avoid questions if a clerk noticed we had no documents, but nothing of note. These boxes concern you; you will find copies of every communication we sent his lordship interleaved with his responses. His lordship indicated you may read in my presence."

Aldine picked up a newspaper and moved to the couch. Aidan opened the first box.

The reading was sobering, a detailed record of his sins. The reports began with his return from the Continent after Aaron's death. The names of all his mistresses, their whereabouts, how much he had spent on them, their settlements on parting, which gambling hells he preferred, even the nights he'd appeared at Almack's. It was better and worse than a diary. At least Aldine had been scrupulous in recording the good with the bad.

In the end Aidan felt weighed in the balance, and he found himself wanting. The only information Aldine hadn't recorded was Aidan's work for the Home Office. It would have explained some of Aidan's behavior. But whether that would have counted him a sinner or a saint, there was no way to tell. He'd be a fool if he ever gave Sophia permission to read the documents.

He was grateful Tom had withheld the information from Sophia. If she knew even a tenth of the information hidden in the hat boxes, his campaign would be doomed. When Ophelia had confided that the comments of tourists had made Sophia wary of him as Ian's guardian, Aidan had passed it off as nothing more than the idle chatter of bored expatriates. Sophia had made no attempt to dredge up their past, not even when he had given her the opening on the stairs. But now he better understood in how damning a light the stories placed him and how reticent Sophia would have been to broach the rumors she'd heard, given his role as Ian's guardian. But Ophelia was right: to allay Sophia's reservations, he would have to be charming, solicitous, and subtle—though not for the reasons Ophelia would assume.

Chapter Twelve

In the middle of the library floor, Ian had laid out one of his favorite games, The Magic Ring. Printed on heavy paper then glued to sturdy linen, the game showed a knight reclining at the middle of four concentric circles, each circle connecting to the next to form a spiral. The spiral itself was divided into 50 steps, each one illustrated with a hand-colored symbol that told the player what to do when his marker landed there.

Ian rolled the six-sided die. "Two!" He leaned forward to move his marker. "That takes me from step 26, the Basket of Flowers, to step 28! I'm more than halfway to the center!"

The symbol for step 28 was an open chest filled with riches.

"Do you get a reward or punishment for landing there?" Sophia asked.

"A reward: ten counters from the bank."

Sophia counted out ten dried peas from the bag Cook had provided somewhat reluctantly.

Grinning, Ian added them to his already large pile. "If we go by peas, I'm winning."

"You still have to beat me to step 50." Sophia leaned over

the game board to read the instructions printed in the margins. "Last turn I landed on 38, the Dove of Peace, so this turn I get to double whatever I roll."

She sat back, looking for the die on the floor between them, but couldn't find it. She felt the floor and looked in the folds of her dress. "Ian, do you see . . ."

"Look up, Mama."

She did, only to hear "Catch!" as Ian tossed the die a bit too far to her right.

Sophia stretched as far as her dress would allow and caught the die inches before it hit the floor, even though it set her off balance. Pulling herself back upright, she raised one eyebrow. "You forget that my cousins were more devious than you. I know that trick."

Ian shrugged and grinned. "But you caught it."

"Incorrigible." Sophia shook her head. "That's what you are." She looked at the clock. She didn't want to be lounging on the floor when Aidan arrived. They had plenty of time to finish the game. "Let's see." She cast the die. "Oh, dear."

Ian laughed. "One. Double that is two. Now you're on 40—oh no, the Lobster!" He held his hands out to her, opening and closing them like a pair of claws.

"Is that bad?" Though Sophia had played the game in her childhood, she pretended to have forgotten it entirely to give Ian the pleasure of teaching her.

Ian leaned over the rules and read them aloud. "It says here: 'Who falls into his claws is pinched back as many pictures as his next goes will spin.'"

Sophia grimaced and moved her marker. "Well, if I have to go backward, let's hope I throw another one. Your turn."

Ian shook the die next to his ear, then blew on it.

Sophia laughed. "Where did you learn that?"

"From Nate. He says Uncle Sidney always does it when he plays. It's for luck." Ian blew on the die once more.

"That's only a superstition."

"We'll see." Ian cast the die. "Five." Ian counted the steps as he moved his marker, the banner-bearer from his army set. "Number 33, the Magic Circle!"

Sophia reached for the die, but Ian snatched it from the board before she could reach it.

She held out her hand. "Isn't it my turn?"

"Mama," Ian offered in mock exasperation, "if you would read the rules, you would know." He pointed at the rules. "The Magic Circle 'immediately entitles the spinner to two new goes.'"

Ian threw the die. "One." He moved the banner-bearer forward one step to step 34, Fortune.

"See, you shouldn't have teased me," Sophia gloated.

"No, see what it says here. At Fortune, I gain eight counters from the bank, move my marker to step 44, then throw again."

Sophia added eight peas to Ian's pile. "What's at 44?"

Ian counted. "It's the Heart. Here are three peas for the bank."

"Why?" She took the peas from his hand.

"He has to pay 'a token of his expected constancy.'" Aidan's voice came from the doorway behind her. "Of course I always found constancy of a much greater value than three dried peas . . . and much harder to come by."

Sophia stiffened and bit back a retort. With her back to Aidan, she closed her eyes for a moment to collect herself. *Of course, he'd arrived early, and in time to offer a disquisition on constancy. But be gracious—gracious for Ian's sake. You cannot afford to offend him.*

Sitting on the floor, she twisted to acknowledge Aidan. "Dodsley did not announce you had arrived. If you would be so kind as to wait in the entry, we will join you momentarily." To rise without damaging her skirts, she would have to perform a series of ungainly acrobatics, and she wished not to perform them in Aidan's view. Any proper gentleman would retreat—but would Aidan?

Sophia turned back to Ian. "Count up your peas. We'll note where we left off and finish tomorrow."

Fine leather Wellington boots walked from behind her to the space between her and Ian.

"If you wish to finish, we have time." Aidan crossed his ankles and lowered himself gracefully to the floor.

All on the floor together, there was no reason not to finish the game. She nodded assent, and Ian blew on the die once more.

"Ian, you don't believe that works, do you?" Sophia prodded gently.

"It worked before, and I need a six to get to the center. All the steps between here and 50 make you lose turns." He blew on the die and shook it beside his ear, then threw. "Six!"

Sophia watched Ian move his marker to step 50, symbolized by an illustration of a Knight at his ease. "You've won!"

"Not yet. Now I have to throw a one, two, or three twice before I win. Otherwise, I have to go back steps. It's your turn."

"This is too complicated." Sophia pretended petulance, placing her hand to her forehead.

"Not if you read the rules," Aidan echoed Ian genially.

Sophia glared at Aidan, then cast the die. "Two. Ah, back to the Dove of Peace. Does landing on the Dove of Peace require me to throw again?"

"Yes, and double it," Ian reminded. "But blow on the die, just in case."

"I'll brave the consequences of not blowing on the dice." She threw. "Five." She picked up her marker. "Doubled, that is 10."

"I told you to blow on it." Ian began counting the peas in his large pile.

Sophia counted ten steps, her marker landing on a symbol of a grave. "Oh. Is this bad?"

"That's the Grave." Ian returned his peas to the bag. "The rules say 'who plunges himself in this dreary mansion is deemed dead and has entirely lost the game.'"

"I seem to have arrived in time, then, to save your mother from an early grave." Aidan looked at Sophia's tiny pile of peas. "I don't think there's any reason to count, do you?"

Sophia shook her head, and Ian began putting her peas into the bag. Sophia picked up the game and unsuccessfully tested several ways to fold it to return it to its box.

To Sophia's surprise, Aidan reached out and took the game gently from her hands, then folded it on the first try. She didn't know whether she should be grateful or offended.

"Mama pretends to like games she knows I like," Ian said. Then he added more quietly, "Papa and I used to play."

"I always enjoy being with you." Sophia tousled her son's hair and tickled him out of his fleeting sadness.

"See." Ian grinned at Aidan. "Because she doesn't like them, she loses, even when all she has to do is throw dice."

"Well, perhaps I can play them with you," Aidan suggested. "But I rarely lose."

Ian picked up the banner-bearer and put it gently in his pocket. "I would like that, your grace."

"If your mother doesn't like games, what does she prefer?" Aidan focused his gaze on Ian, not Sophia.

"Ahem, I can hear you talking about me." She waved her hand, as if they had not noticed her.

"Other than me, she likes plants and painting." Ian looked at his mother, then at Aidan. "I'm not sure she likes you yet."

"Ian!" Sophia chastened. "Remember your manners." She

tossed her son the bag of peas. "Return these to Cook." She held the game up to him. "And the game to the nursery."

Ian tucked the game under one arm and left, tossing the bag of peas up and down like a ball, clearly enjoying the sound of the peas falling against one another.

"We had to promise to return the peas before we left. Cook needs to set them to soak." Sophia started to arrange her skirts, trying to imagine how to stand without looking like a cow struggling to escape a bog.

Aidan stood as gracefully as he had sat. "May I help you up, my lady?" He held out his hands. "Perhaps it will give you cause to like me . . . if only a little."

She didn't look into his eyes, only at his hands. "Your kindness to my son gives me ample cause already." She adjusted her dress to keep it from getting caught underfoot and took his hands. They were strong and warm. Aidan pulled her up gently and set her on her feet. She ignored the warmth that spread up her arms and into her belly.

"Then perhaps I can find other kindnesses to perform." But before she could respond, he bent down to pick up her marker, a green crystalline stone, flat on the bottom, but with one vertical crystal emerging from a pool of other smaller crystals. "I don't recognize the stone."

"It's vesuvianite," Sophia offered, hoping to distract him from Ian's revelation.

"From the volcano?" Aidan held the crystal in the light.

"Thereabouts. We had gone on an excursion to the side of the crater, and Ian traded for it because I liked it." She watched Aidan examine the stone, turning it to catch the light in its facets.

"Traded?" Aidan held out the vesuvianite crystal to her.

"Ian treated our gardens as his personal bank, and cuttings from it were his currency." Without her fingers touching his, she lifted the crystal from his palm and returned it to the mantel below Tom's portrait.

"I didn't realize Ian inherited your love of plants." Aidan folded his hands behind his back, watching.

"Oh, he doesn't love them; he loves what he can do with them." She walked toward the partner desk to retrieve a long black cloak. "He'll manage his estate well, but if he weren't a lord, he'd be perfectly happy in trade."

"He has a ready mind and quick wits, traits valuable in any pursuit . . . which must lead us to the question: how do we convince him he is wrong?"

She pulled the cloak over her shoulders, then turned to her reflection in the garden window glass. "Wrong?" She used the excuse of arranging the shawl over her décolletage to avoid facing him.

"Do you harbor an aversion to me?"

"I harbored an aversion to sharing the guardianship. Ian noticed my reticence and presumed it was tied to you. Nothing more." She set her face in a grave reserve and turned back to face him.

"Yet if Ian believes it is dislike, it will make my role as guardian difficult. Unless you help me convince him he is wrong." Aidan had moved to stand near her. He was closer than she'd expected, or wanted. For just an instant, she once more imagined Aidan as a large predatory cat hunting her. But his voice was conciliatory, even deferent.

She wanted to object, but it was her fault for letting Ian, her ever-perceptive son, see her discomfort. "I have no idea how to be other than I am. What do you propose?"

"When Ian is present, you pretend to feel comfortable in my presence. If it helps, pretend I am someone else. Seth, perhaps, or Clive. Pick someone of your circle with whom you feel most at home, and behave to me as you would to them."

"Malcolm, though I haven't seen him for some time."

"Then pretend I'm Malcolm."

"You and Malcolm are nothing alike," she interjected before she could catch her words.

"I always thought we were much alike." Aidan looked bemused.

"Oh, no. Malcolm wears his childhood in Kentucky like a badge of honor, and when it suits him, he even puts on a hint of Daniel Boone."

"And me? What am I like?" Aidan quizzed.

Ian came to the door of the library. "Mr. Fletcher says to tell his grace that only God can stop time."

"Mr. Fletcher?" Sophia asked, grateful to avoid more explanation.

"My coachman. He's been with the estate since before I was born, which gives him the right—or so he tells me—to order me about. Shall we go?" Aidan offered her his arm, and, aware of Ian's careful gaze, she took it.

"Eighteen carriages for a family dinner?" Sophia groaned as Fletcher drew up to the Masons' large Kensington home.

"Nineteen if you count ours, Mama." Ian leaned out the window, waiting for the carriage to stop and allow his escape.

"Ophelia defines small somewhat differently than most. But take heart: she's limited by the word *family*." Aidan unlatched the door and allowed Ian, already perched at the threshold, to jump down. Ian ran to the front door and let himself in.

"I assure you that I did rear my son to have manners." Sophia shook her head.

"Ophelia is his aunt; Nate is his friend. Besides, he's saved us the trouble of being announced." Aidan stepped down from the carriage, then held out his hand. Sophia took it, steeling herself against the thrill of his touch. "I am certain you will manage the hordes admirably, but if you require assistance, I am at your service."

The front door flung open, and Ophelia greeted them.

"A small family dinner?" Sophia pointed at the line of carriages.

"I didn't invite anyone you don't like." Ophelia embraced Sophia, then Aidan. "Of course some, like Malcolm's wife, you haven't met yet."

"Malcolm is here?" Sophia peered into the open hallway for her cousin.

"Yes. I knew you would be pleased." Ophelia took Sophia's arm in hers and walked toward the door, Aidan following. "So you must forgive me the others."

"You said there was no one I didn't like." Sophia pulled away to look Ophelia in the face.

"There isn't." Ophelia waved Sophia's objection away. "Just a few that you might not prefer. Come along. Aidan, show her into the saloon. Now that you are here, I'll call for dinner."

"Are we late?" Sophia whispered to Aidan, lapsing without meaning to into old patterns of familiarity.

"No, the others came early." Ophelia had overheard. "I thought it would be easier, if they were already here when you arrived. It's your first excursion in company since your mourning ended, and you are the guest of honor, you know." She moved away to call the servants and to announce Aidan and Sophia's arrival to the company.

"I thought you said she was limited by the word *family*," Sophia accused in a whisper.

"Well, everyone here is someone's family . . . just perhaps not yours or mine or Ophelia's." Aidan brushed his wavy hair back from his face.

Sophia stopped in panic. "But what if I don't remember

them? It's been ten years—some of them were children when I left. What if I don't recognize members of my own family?"

"Then, if you allow me, I will remember them for you. Leave it to me: no one will suspect if you don't remember them." Aidan extended his arm. "Ready?"

She took a deep breath before tucking her fingers into the bend of his elbow. "Yes." They entered the dining saloon.

"Sophie!" a slender blond man wearing an embroidered green waistcoat exclaimed. He began to make his way toward them.

"Your youngest Elliot cousin. Ralph. One of the twins," Aidan offered sotto voce.

"Ralph, is that you? Why you were barely out of Uncle Lawrence's nursery when I left!" Sophia extended her arms and offered an embrace.

"We were eight." He waved toward another man at the pianoforte. "John is here too."

John, wearing a pink waistcoat instead of a green one, came to embrace her. "We're thrilled with our gift. Thank you." He kissed her on both cheeks.

The two men, nearly perfectly identical, stood side by side, grinning. Colored waistcoats aside, Sophia knew a way to tell the twins apart, if the difference had not disappeared as their faces aged. She watched for the telltale double-dimple in Ralph's right cheek, his twin having only one.

"Yes, the cage is perfect," John continued. "We've wanted a larger iron one for some time, but haven't had the funds."

"We certainly couldn't get the money from Father." Ralph jostled John's arm.

"Not given how much our evil stepmother Annabella hates Fire and Brimstone," John jostled back.

The twins laughed. The twins spoke so quickly, one almost on top of the other, that Sophia had no time to ask "what gift?" before they moved on. She looked to Aidan for help, and reassuringly he patted the hand she had placed on his elbow.

"I hadn't realized Fire and Brimstone were still alive. How old are they now?" Aidan asked.

"At least twenty. Macaws can live for more than fifty years in captivity. With the larger cage—it's as long as the side of our study—they seem much happier."

"Yes, they must have known it was a gift from Sophie, because they have been singing her lullabies since we put them in it," John offered sweetly.

Sophia remembered. After her marriage, she'd wept at leaving the twins, whom she had sung to sleep since their own mother had died when they were four. To appease her, Tom had brought his birds from his estate and convinced her they could learn her songs. But in the weeks she'd sung to them, all they had ever offered were imitations of various street singers' calls. "They learned the lullabies?"

"Yes, all of them. When we closed our eyes, we could imagine you were in the nursery with us, they imitated your voice so well." Ralph's cheeks reddened at the revelation.

"Of course, over the years, they've parsed the songs together in their own way," John added. "But we still find them . . ."

The twins looked shy for a moment, then continued in one voice, "comforting."

"Didn't they have different names when Tom had them?" Sophia questioned.

"Oh, yes, but at eight, we found Heraclitus and Parmenides a little daunting." For the next several moments, the twins shared the conversation, finishing each other's ideas, often in mid-sentence.

"So, we converted them from Greek philosophers into religious enthusiasts."

"In honor of Annabella's puritan leanings."

"We thought she might like them better if they were named after something she liked hearing about."

"And the birds took to their new names with appropriate enthusiasm."

"Yes, within days, they were calling each other Fire and Brimstone."

"Especially whenever she came to the nursery."

"Which wasn't often once we got the birds."

"We were very grateful to you and Tom for that."

As quickly as they'd begun talking, the pair fell silent.

Overwhelmed, she held out her arms and enfolded both young men together. Both whispered at once, "We missed you, Sophie. The birds couldn't replace you."

"Perhaps some day I could hear the birds sing?" she asked when the embrace ended.

The twins suddenly looked sheepish. "That wouldn't be a good idea. They lived with us at Harrow. Now they stay with us at Oxford and at our club between terms." Their voices trailed off, and they turned to Aidan for help.

Sophia refused them his aid. "So, in other words, your birds are not only named after hell, but they sound like they are personally acquainted with the region?"

"Well, yes!" Ralph agreed, then fell into silence when John elbowed him in the ribs.

Sophia patted each one's arm. "Tom would completely understand."

Sophia soon learned that Ophelia's idea of a family dinner extended beyond Sophia's handful of blood relations to include Tom's family, Aidan's brothers, the local clergyman, several spinsters, the magistrate, and a handful of families whose daughters, though still too young for the London season, needed experience navigating social situations with strangers. Ophelia, eschewing precedence, had created a playful and original seating arrangement, based, she claimed, on drawing names from an envelope. But Sophia could see that it intermingled rank and gentry artfully, instead of sequestering her with Aidan, his brothers, and her cousins at one end of the table.

Sophia was seated at dinner between the parson and the magistrate, but happily both men were congenial companions, adapting their conversation to her interests and experiences. The parson had read Tom's *Systematical Botany* and applied Tom's observations to his own botanical pursuits. The magistrate was interested in Sophia's perceptions of the state of Italian politics.

Aidan was seated far to her right, surrounded on all sides by the daughters of her ever-affable cousin Hal Elliot, the twins' eldest brother and her senior by almost a dozen years. Across from her Hal conversed to his left with a dignified, gray-haired woman in her sixties whom Sophia remembered to be Tom's aunt Millicent and to his right was Malcolm's wife Audrey. Sophia could hear only snatches of a conversation that centered on the relative merits of various writers for the stage, but she kept finding her attention drawn to Audrey, whom Malcolm had introduced as his fair-haired gypsy.

The food was generous, the conversation jovial. By the end, Sophia realized that Ophelia had not lied: the people she had invited *were* Ophelia's family if not by blood, then by proximity and affection.

After dinner, Kate and Ariel played a duet on violin and cello, joined by the twins who were surprisingly accomplished baritones. The mill-owner's two daughters, singing in tightly harmonized voices, led the whole company in several popular songs.

Sophia's dance card, for Ophelia insisted on the convention even for a family dinner, filled quickly. Country dances with the twins were followed by a reel with the magistrate, whose round cheeks grew red with the exertion.

Malcolm had reserved the first dance after the break. "I believe this dance is mine," he said, holding out his arm to Sophia.

The local brewer offered a regretful good-bye as Malcolm led her to the dance floor. "You seem to have won his heart."

"I only asked some questions about the variety of his hops." Sophia leaned into Malcolm's arm.

"He's sending you a hogshead of his finest porter," Malcolm rebutted. They stopped at the edge of the dancing floor, waiting for the musicians to retake their instruments.

"I asked very good questions." Sophia stepped back to regard Malcolm intently. "But let me look at you."

Malcolm submitted to her inspection, straightening his crimson waistcoat and deep gray jacket, then standing straight.

"Marriage suits you. Your eyes are still that devastating green that drove the local girls mad, but the loneliness is gone."

"Of all the cousins, only you ever knew I was lonely." Malcolm placed his hand behind her back as the musicians finished tuning, and they stepped into the space reserved for the dances. "But you are right: marriage does suit me, though getting Audrey to the parson all in one piece almost eluded me."

"Tom and I were concerned when you wrote of her injuries, but she seems to have recovered fully."

He looked adoringly across the room at his wife, dazzling in a rich salmon satin. "Yes, thank heavens. I would never have forgiven myself otherwise." At the first strains of the waltz, he began to lead Sophia in circles around the floor. "Audrey has convinced me it would be bad form to reject your gift, that I would not have refused had it been a bequest in Tom's will."

"That's the perfect way to think of it: as a belated gift from Tom." Once more Sophia found herself in the uncomfortable position of having no idea what gift she had given, and this time Aidan was not present to offer her help. Remembering the twins' birdcage, she offered, "And it's not so great a gift that you couldn't have purchased it yourself."

He shook his head, but never missed a step of the waltz. "No, I could never have raised the funds to buy it." He pressed his hand against her back to lead her into a spin outward, then lifted his arm to bring her back. "But you, sweet cousin, never forgot all our hours planning what we would do if we owned it. We're partners now, Sophie, whether you expected to be or not."

She squeezed his hand. She knew what his gift had been. "Your father sold that land to make his fortune in Kentucky; now it's yours again, to build your fortune here. It's a gift that cost me nothing; it was part of an inheritance Tom received before he died. From what I've seen of Audrey tonight, you don't need any other partner."

She watched Malcolm's eyes focus behind her and light up with love. On the turn she saw Audrey, talking with Aidan's brothers, her blond ringlets tied up with a wide green brocaded ribbon to highlight the green accents in her salmon gown.

"When we were young, I always wanted to marry someone like you: clever and funny and brave." He paused. "But I'd given up finding someone like that, until I found Audrey."

"I'm not sure I remember how to be brave, Malcolm . . . if I ever was." She heard the music drawing to a close.

"You'll remember, Sophie." He spun her out for one more turn. "I know you will."

At the last turn, they stopped in front of Aidan. It was to be his dance, a rousing Scottish reel, but taking his leave of

Malcolm, Aidan took Sophia's hand and drew her away from the dance floor.

"I have some intelligence you will find helpful. Shall we take some air on the terrace?" He led her to the curtained glass doors of the terrace.

Outside the night was cool, the light of the evening fading gently on the horizon.

"I'm hoping you plan to tell me what other gifts I've given . . . and to whom."

He considered the other couples on the terrace, but none were close enough to overhear. "It took some coaxing, but eventually Ophelia confessed." He held out a list in Tom's hand, with more than two dozen names, each one accompanied by instructions for a gift.

Sophia read it over. "This includes everyone in our circle before we left England: my cousins, your brothers and Judith, Tom's sisters. But how?"

"Tom was wealthy. Most of the gifts are not extravagant. In each case, Tom picked something the person desperately wanted, but for some reason could not or would not buy for themselves. Ariel's cello, Kate's violin, Hal's new hounds, Clive's set of Malone's edition of Shakespeare, Colin's landscape of Dedham Vale by John Constable. The only gift I think he got wrong is Judith's; I can't imagine her wanting anything so impractical."

Sophia read down the list again to Judith's gift: a robust collection of novels from the Minerva Press. "That makes perfectly good sense to me," she said, laughing.

The last name on the list caught her attention. "Benjamin Somerville to receive William Stansby's 1634 printing of Malory's *Morte D'Arthur*." She grew sober. "Even a gift for Benjamin."

Aidan nodded, but said nothing.

"Tom never believed Benjamin was dead. He couldn't have left him out."

Aidan took the list from her hands, then folded it, and slid it inside the top of his boot. "Now you can enjoy the rest of the evening without the fear of exposure."

"But how? And why?" Sophia frowned into the growing dark.

"According to Ophelia, the gifts were originally intended as bequests. In many cases, Tom had chosen the gift, but for the others, he enlisted Ophelia's aid. Ophelia contacted your agent Aldine, and together they determined what each person would receive, suited to the person's temperament and desires. In most cases, Tom approved the choices, but he died before the bequests were written into his will," Aidan explained gently.

"That answers how, but not why. Why did Ophelia pretend the gifts were from me?"

"During mourning you withdrew, even from those who would have eagerly offered you comfort. By making the gifts into a game, Ophelia hoped to remind you of your deep connections with your cousins and my family."

"Like brother, like sister." Sophia grimaced. "The temptation to manage is irresistible."

Aidan heard the bitter undertone in Sophia's voice. As the diplomat he had been, he took a moment to consider the situation. Ophelia had felt keenly her sister-in-law's isolation, and though she had not intended to be cruel with her game, she had caught Sophia off guard. Similarly, Tom had not considered that Aidan might be cruel as a co-guardian; instead he had foolishly entrusted his wife and his child to Aidan's better nature. In each case, Sophia's actual well-being had been ignored in pursuit of what Tom or Ophelia might deem a higher good. Aidan finally broke the growing silence. "I suppose it doesn't help to say that they only manage those they love."

Sophia sighed. "I know. Tom believed any problem could be solved by the application either of reason or affection. Ophelia is like him in that. . . ."

She paused, and he saw the faintest hint of tears in her eyes. Unexpectedly he felt his heart move in sympathy, but before he could console her, she straightened her shoulders and prepared to return to the saloon.

"May I see that list again? I have other gifts to give."

Chapter Thirteen

The proofs for Tom's final book—a catalogue of European plants suitable for English gardens—had arrived the day Aldine had informed her of the guardianship. But with Aidan a new presence in their lives, Sophia had been unable to address them. This morning Aidan had taken Ian to St. John's Wood to watch a cricket match with some boys already in residence at Harrow. In the quiet of the house, she turned to her task. Laying the manuscript next to the printed proof pages, she began to compare them, line by line.

The proofs to the first volume had been so accurate that she'd been tempted to send the rest of the pages back without reading to the end. But her sense of obligation made her read every page. By noon, she'd realized that her task would not be as easy as she first imagined. In the second volume she found small but unexplainable errors on almost every page. Random bits of Latin interrupted sentences that made perfectly good sense without them. An easy solution would have been to remove all the Latin, except for the fact that Tom sometimes quoted Latin as part of the sentences.

It made no sense. She groaned in frustration and rubbed her forehead with her fingers. Then, breathing deeply, she returned to her task.

When Dodsley arrived with a pot of tea, she realized with chagrin that it was almost two. The warmth of the tea felt good against her hands.

However frustrating, the proofs were useful in focusing her mind on something other than Aidan. Since they had met to discuss the guardianship, Aidan seemed always to be interrupting her—every day, he'd found a way to engage her in conversation, about Ian mostly, and what plans he had made with her son for the following day. She couldn't complain; he never took Ian even as close as the park without making sure she knew and approved. His attention to her opinion was flattering, but it only made her thirst for more: for more engagement with his quick mind, for more chances to be near him. And her desire made her feel foolish.

Forcing herself to turn back to the proofs, she saw an error far worse than all the others. According to the text, plate 48 was supposed to be an engraving of a rose, *Rosa chinensis Mutabilis*—simple enough. Her illustration of the rose had been one of her favorites, single flowers opening a rich red, ripening to a salmon pink, then fading to yellow.

But here was an engraved illustration of a far different plant. She knew the plant—the agave. She even knew the original engraving, a large foldout that had fascinated her as a child. Sophia pushed back from the desk and walked to the bookcases behind her easel. She kept her father's copy of Philip Miller's 1763 *Gardener's Dictionary* near her prints and paints. Her father had avidly admired Miller, the gardener at the Apothecaries' Physic Garden at Chelsea, and its pages still smelled like her father's study, reminding her of the hours she'd spent as a child tracing the book's full-page botanical illustrations. She found the illustration in an instant and laid the proof beside it. It was the same. Not just the same plant, but the same illustration.

Unfortunately, finding where the image had come from

did nothing to make the proofs correct. This last mistake had surely come from Tom's hand. He had even signed the illustration according to the common practice: he'd used Latin for the verb *made*, or in this case *drawn*: *Fecit T. G. W.* Why hadn't he asked her to draw it for him?

If the incorrect image was from Tom's hand, what of all the bits of misplaced Latin. Had Tom "made" those errors too?

She couldn't imagine that the Latin phrases had been added accidentally by the press. No, setting Latin phrases added another step into the process of composing the type. The compositor would have to work from one type drawer for the English and another for the italicized Latin. And no compositor would just "add in" Latin arbitrarily, unless the publisher had an angry or malicious compositor intent on making Tom's book a financial failure—and that was unlikely. Could Tom have added nonsense letters to the fair copy he had written out neatly for the publisher?

In the case of a malicious employee, she could alert Mr. Murray.

But if Tom's fair copy was the problem, continuing to read the proofs was useless. She would have to wait for Mr. Murray to retrieve Tom's fair copy from his printer to finish her task.

But the agave print she could track down on her own. She removed the image from the proofs and folded it small enough to fit in her reticule. Though Tom had drawn the image, he hadn't engraved it. If she could find the engraver, perhaps she could discover what Tom had been thinking.

Aidan was in his study, catching up on correspondence, when his younger brother Edmund opened the door.

"Hey-o! Haven't seen you at Brooks's for days." Edmund chose the most comfortable chair, then turned it backwards.

"Ian and I spent the day at St. John's Wood, watching cricket with some boys already at Harrow." Aidan blotted the remaining ink from his pen and set it on the rest. "Drink?"

Edmund nodded at the whiskey. "How do you find your new ward?"

Aidan poured two shots of whiskey and handed one to his brother. "Reserved, but not shy. Like Tom, he is a thoughtful observer of people." At the cricket match, Aidan had watched with a certain amount of pride as Ian drew his social circle wide, including those who were good-hearted and congenially holding at a distance the ill-natured boys. Signs that—like his father—Ian had the makings of a statesman. "We're going to Smithfield tomorrow. You're welcome to join us, though I'm sure you and Clive already intended to be there."

"I might. I'd like to see Ian. I haven't seen him or Sophia since the last time I came to town with Seth." Edmund brushed a wave of dark hair from his face. Of all the brothers, he and Aidan shared that feature, but there the resemblance ended. Edmund's disposition was as sunny as June. "In fact, I called on Sophie this afternoon to apologize for missing Phee's dinner, though I suppose three Somerville brothers is enough for any party. But she'd already gone out."

"Women often call on one another in the afternoons." Aidan turned back to his papers, annoyed. He'd known that Seth, as the Wilmot estate manager, visited Sophia, but he hadn't realized his other brothers visited as well. And he wasn't sure what rankled more: the visits or his not knowing.

"On foot? Without a maid? I arrived after she left the house, but I could see her walking at the end of the street." Edmund inhaled the aroma of the whiskey, then drank. "I found it somewhat odd."

Aidan folded the paper and met his brother's eyes. "Did you offer to accompany her?"

Edmund turned serious. "No. There was something about her carriage. I don't know. I thought that as Ian's guardian you might prefer if I discovered where she was going."

Aidan raised one eyebrow and waited.

"She went to the British Institution."

"She's an artist. Perhaps she went to see the old masters on display?" Aidan turned back to his papers.

"She didn't go to the public galleries."

Aidan sat silently, waiting, saying nothing that would reveal interest.

"She was downstairs in the Institution office. A man was examining a document for her with a magnifying glass. At some point Sophia wrote what he told her on a slip of paper. The man folded the document she'd brought and started to place it in his overcoat, but she objected and he returned it. She put both in her reticule."

"Could you see what the document was?" Aidan was suddenly interested.

"No. Do you want me to find out?"

"Can you do so without garnering attention?"

Edmund smiled broadly. "What do you think?"

Chapter Fourteen

Aidan was considering his next move. His men were positioned along the top of a tree-covered ridge. From that vantage point, they could see most of the valley below. Ian's troops were gathering on the ridge on the opposite side of the valley, hiding behind rocks. They had been playing this engagement for the last several afternoons, and the next few minutes would determine the course of the battle. Aidan was running scenarios in his head. To move his troops there would put him at risk of . . .

"You made Cook very happy with the pistachios. You should ask her to save you a piece when she makes her lemon cake," Ian announced without looking up from the green felt landscape.

"I'm pleased they made Cook happy." Aidan placed his next figure. "They weren't that hard to find."

Ian considered his next move, then shifted a squadron of men to the side. An inconsequential move, Aidan thought with surprise.

"I'd like to find something that would make Mama happy." The boy spoke quietly, as if to himself. "She doesn't laugh much anymore."

Aidan paused, giving his brain a moment to shift from one strategy to the next. "I've seen her laugh with you." Aidan moved some of his men into the brush on the downward slope of the ridge.

"I know. She says I make her happy. But it's not the same. She used to laugh all the time. And not just with me."

"Do you know when she stopped laughing? Could she just be sad because your father died?"

"No, she stopped laughing before he died. I don't know when. She was in the hall one day, watching the men take away the trunks to come here. I realized I hadn't heard her laughing for a while." Ian chewed on the end of his finger as he stared at the playing field. He moved his soldiers.

"She sent trunks back before your father died?" Aidan moved some of his soldiers farther down the slope to the point where there was no more brush before them, only open ground to the bank of the river running through the middle of the valley.

"For a couple of weeks. Papa made us promise to return to London as soon as he died."

Aidan knew this. Sophia had told him as much when they had met to discuss Ian's guardianship. "So, she was packing because she thought your father was about to die? Couldn't that be a reason to stop laughing?" Aidan, paying close attention to the tone of Ian's voice, absently moved more soldiers down the slope.

"No." Ian sounded frustrated. "We didn't expect him to die yet. She thought we had at least another year. I think she quit laughing because she didn't want to come back here."

"Do you know why?"

"No." Ian moved some soldiers farther to the right. "She is happier when she's in the garden or with me. But she can't be with me or in the garden all the time."

"No, I suppose she can't." Aidan further solidified his

position on the face of the slope. "Is there something you would like me to do?"

"I'd like for you to make her laugh . . . though I think it will take more than a bag of pistachios." Ian sat back on his heels. He motioned toward the felt, smiling. "I'd also like for you to surrender, Commander."

Aidan looked at the position of his men, focused for a forward attack, and at Ian's men who had somehow flanked him and were now taking the ridge behind. Disbelief, then recognition, then a touch of admiration. "I see, Commander, that I have been outmaneuvered."

Aidan stood, stretching. From the nursery window, he could see down into the garden, to Sophia sitting near the newest of the beds, a raucous mix of every-colored flowers that somehow reminded him of Tom. "Perhaps I'll have more luck with laughing. Do you think your mother would like a game of croquet?"

"That should make her happy." Ian carefully reordered the soldiers in ranks and battalions.

"Why?"

Ian stopped for a moment, a red-coated soldier in his hand. "Because, your grace, she'll beat you."

Then he turned back to the green felt landscape and began setting up another battle.

Sophia sat on the garden bench, surveying how her plans were developing. Perkins had found an old sundial under the debris of one garden bed. They'd laughed that the trees had grown up so much that time stopped every day at seven. She would need to find a space to place it.

Her plants were growing well. Next year the perennials would have matured enough to fill their allotted spaces, but this year, while they were settling in, she'd need to supplement with some annual plantings. It was too late to grow from seed, so Perkins was investigating what was available from the nursery gardens in Lower Thames Street.

She let her bonnet fall back, lifted her face up to the sun, and closed her eyes. Without the distraction of her plants, her thoughts turned to Aidan. For the last week, she'd seen him every day, but always unexpectedly. He never sent a note to indicate when he intended to visit. It kept her unsettled, but for Ian's sake, she allowed Aidan's intrusions.

Today he had been reading the newspaper in her morning room when she had come down for breakfast. And no one had warned her. Somehow Aidan had seduced—there was no other word for it—her servants. She'd started to feel like her house wasn't quite hers, but it was only for another fortnight. After that Ian would be gone, and she would have the whole empty house to herself.

At the same time, Aidan's kindnesses to Ian seemed limitless. For the past week, he had been taking Ian with him to events in town, introducing Ian to his circle, particularly those with young boys near Ian's age. Ian had told Aidan of playing bocce in Italy, and with her permission, the pair had set a croquet game up below her garden beds. For the last several days, he and Ian had alternated between playing croquet or soldiers.

On Monday, Aidan had taken Ian to Tattersalls to "help" choose a new horse for his stables and returned with a pony for Ian to ride at Greenwood Hall. The pony was to have been housed in Aidan's London stable, but Ian had grown so attached to the animal—terrorizing his tutor by asking to see it every hour—that Aidan had sent over his own carpenter, groom, and stableboy to repair and ready another stable in Sophia's mews. This morning the pony had arrived at its temporary home. Aidan had even loaned one of his grooms to Ian, so the boy could ride whenever he wished. There had been no way to object without disappointing Ian.

It was a consolation, though, that the ward and the guardian were getting on so well. At least, she wouldn't worry when Ian left with Aidan. There would be ample time to grieve when Ian was gone. For now she tried to enjoy Ian's daily presence, his laugh, his enthusiasm.

At the same time, she could never see Aidan without the clench of longing at the pit of her stomach. It never lessened, but she was growing used to ignoring it. Would she have to grow used to ignoring him all over again when the summer was over?

Something hit her foot, and she looked down. A croquet ball. She reached down and picked it up, feeling its weight in her hand. A game of hide and seek? She waited, not turning around, expecting Ian to steal up behind her as a surprise.

"Ian suggested I challenge you to a game of croquet."

She started, feeling his voice echo in her bones.

"I'm sorry. I thought you would have heard me approach." His tone was all solicitude.

She turned to face him, but he stood between her and the sun. "I should have heard. But I was imagining how this bed would grow over time. . . . What did you ask?"

"Croquet. Ian seems to think I need a break from being beaten at soldiers. He suggested you and I might play a round. He's in the nursery setting up tomorrow's battle."

"Did he tell you I'd beat you?"

"He did mention that. But I find it difficult to believe him. I'm quite good."

She stood up and shifted so that the sun stood between them and she could see his face. "You haven't played in a country where bocce is a blood sport and the women in your salon pride themselves on ruthlessness. It makes croquet look like . . . afternoon tea."

"Then I look forward to the challenge."

"As do I, but the ground is too wet. That's why I was only sitting here."

"Watching your garden grow."

"Imagining it grow."

"Then you must compensate me for the loss of a game by escorting me to my garden and giving me some advice on how to reclaim it. Your man Perkins delivered some lavender, but I haven't a clue where to place the plants."

She'd thought he'd forgotten her offer, and her heart leapt.

"I'll need just a few minutes to put on a walking dress. Would you like to wait on the terrace?" She rose and ran her hands down the side of her skirt, straightening and smoothing.

"It's not necessary to change; we could cross behind the garden, around the mews and stable yard, and into the passageway behind my house. Of course, if you would prefer the more conventional route, I'm happy to wait."

His slight inflection on the word "conventional" taunted her. But she saw nothing in his face save the exceptional politeness that greeted her each time they met. He was right: for convention's sake, she should change clothes and walk properly down the public street, not slip down an alley in a work dress with a known rake. Phineas would be horrified.

"It doesn't make sense to change to go from garden to garden. So, yes, let's slip through the mews. My sketchbook is on the terrace."

As Sophia walked to the terrace to retrieve her pencil and papers, Aidan watched her walk, enjoying the gentle sway of her hips, the elegance of her carriage. When he'd first come upon her, she had looked so peaceful with her face open to the sun, her bonnet away from her face. Then a look of such sorrow had crossed her face that he felt a surprising sympathy. He wondered what she had been thinking of at that moment. . . . It was not, he was sure, how her plants would grow.

The path was not a direct one. Out the gate, around the mews through a short alleyway between the houses directly behind her, then through a paddock, and another alley into a passage behind his house.

"I had no idea one could make that into a path, and I'm a bit disturbed to find that my gate doesn't appear to lock. Is that how you simply appear without announcement?"

"Guilty as charged. But your gate does lock—it's just that the lockmaker for your gate and mine appears to have been a shiftless sort; my key opens your gate, and yours, I assume, opens mine."

"So it isn't that my servants have lost all sense of loyalty. . . ."

"I never give them the chance to intercept me."

"That explains a great deal."

Aidan paused at a wall heavily covered with vines and pulled back a section to reveal a door. "After you." Sophia passed through ahead of him. The path into the garden had almost disappeared on the inside of the garden wall as well; unmaintained, it was thickly covered with leaves and dead branches. She paused to look around her.

Directly in front of them, about ten feet from the garden gate, stood a hedge thick with years. A gap in the hedge at their right opened to a path she assumed led to the house. To the left in the corner of the grounds was a gardener's shed and a small greenhouse, also neglected and unused. Sophia assessed the view. "You can't see the house from here. This hedgerow nicely hides both the gate we came in and that shed there, so we wouldn't want to interfere with it."

She turned to follow the path, but her heel caught on a downed branch. Aidan reached out just as she stumbled and pulled her against him to keep her from falling. She stood still catching her balance, then looked up. He was examining her face so intently that she could imagine his lips against hers. Then his face shuttered, and he set her back on her own feet as if setting a vase on a mantel, precise and without emotion.

"That was clumsy of me." Her waist burned where his hands had caught her.

"No, the apologies are all on my part. I should have had the twigs and branches cleared away. May I offer you my arm?"

Sophia was both tempted and wary. Tempted to feel his body closer to hers, and wary that she might reveal the desire that had flared with his touch. Yet there was no way to refuse without appearing impolite. She took his arm cautiously, maintaining a separation between his body and hers.

The garden showed vestiges of an earlier design. At the bottom had been a small wilderness, with five box shrubs grouped to suggest they had once been topiary, but no hint of their former shapes remained. She could see the upper stories of the house, Palladian in its lines, above another hedge that grew about ten feet in front of them. If she guessed correctly, on the other side of the hedge would be the remains of knot gardens, leading to whatever terrace backed the house.

"Has the property been in your family for some time?"

"No, I acquired it when I returned from Europe—or rather, I won it at cards," Aidan answered. "It had been empty for some time, and I never saw any reason to hire a full staff. But after I became duke, this house became a sort of refuge."

"So no one would object to my reshaping the garden to more contemporary tastes?"

"No, when they are in town, all my siblings lodge either at the ducal residence, or—like my brothers Clive and Edmund— at their clubs. As for me, I live here irregularly, so the only expectations you would have to meet would be your own."

"Other than lavender, are there plants that you particularly like? Colors? Textures?"

"I would enjoy it most if you did as you thought best. My garden is your palette, my lady. My only requirement is that you must share with me what you are planning."

She was surprised and intrigued that he would let go of his authority in his own garden. At her villa in Italy, though the shape of the garden was to her taste, it had not been her design. Tom and Ian had collaborated on the design, placing the beds and creating the effect. Sophia's part had been to make the design come alive each year. Even in the London house, she hadn't begun from nothing, but worked within the constraints already present.

Here, however, in this overgrown mess, she could make something beautiful—something of her own creation.

"Well, then, you see how those trees there and the hedge have grown together . . ." As she spoke, Sophia grew more animated and assured, and soon, without thinking, she had curved her body conspiratorially into his.

Despite himself, Aidan found it fascinating to hear Sophia assess his garden. He had thought Tom had been the botanist, and Sophia his assistant. But he quickly realized that Tom had been the scholar and Sophia his muse. She was the artist, thinking about color and shape, texture and time. Planning not only what plants would look well and bloom together, she also considered thoughtfully the succession of colors across the seasons. When he watched her sketch the bare outlines of his garden, noting the placement of the trees and shrubs, he saw a new garden emerge in the swift movements of her pencil.

He asked questions, encouraging her to explain her recommendations. As she spoke, he saw glimpses of his old Sophia. The one whose mind he thought had matched his. The thoughtful passion he had seen in their youth was tempered into a different key, one muted, but more richly inflected. He realized that in other circumstances, he would have been pleased to call this woman friend.

But he wasn't ready yet to give up his revenge, and after that, there would be no space left for friendship. Strangely, the thought did not give him the same satisfaction as it had even a week ago.

Chapter Fifteen

Aidan returned home to find Harrison Walgrave lounging in the study, a glass of Aidan's finest claret in his hand, reading the *London Times*.

Walgrave lowered the shipping news. "Ah, Forster, you've returned. I hear you've become guardian to Wilmot's heir?"

"I have." Aidan examined Walgrave carefully. They'd been comrades during the war, but Walgrave was the man least likely to cool his heels waiting for an old friend, not even with a fine claret and a newspaper to keep him company. "What of it?"

Walgrave elided Aidan's question. "You've been spending time with her ladyship?"

"With the boy, mostly. I'm taking him to the country, and I wanted to know him a bit better before we leave." Aidan omitted that he'd spent the afternoon in Sophia's company and that he'd decided Sophia would be joining them at his estate.

Walgrave folded the paper and leaned forward. "How well do you know her?"

"Who's asking? You or the Home Office?" Aidan chose not to sit. If this was to be an interrogation, he had no wish to make it appear otherwise.

"It depends on your answers," Walgrave countered.

"I was with Wilmot when they met."

"And . . . ?"

"Tom inherited an estate near her uncle's. From Harrow, we knew Malcolm Hucknall and some of her Elliot cousins, so we rusticated at Tom's estate holidays and summers." Aidan leaned against the side of the desk. "My father bought me a commission. Wilmot proposed after I left. Until last week, I had had no communication with Wilmot or her ladyship in a decade."

"Tell me about her." Walgrave watched Aidan intently.

Aidan knew this was a test of his objectivity. Walgrave would compare Aidan's answers—and level of detail—against what he already knew from other sources.

"Then or now?"

"Then and now."

Aidan offered the information as if it were a field report. "Her parents died years before we met. Her uncle had educated her without regard to her sex according to her parents' wishes, but neither her brother nor her uncle's second wife approved. At some point she was distressed that her governess had left unexpectedly. As I remember, the governess was her only friend. After that, she had a great deal of freedom, with her cousins acting as rather poor chaperones."

"Most of that we already knew. What else can you tell us?"

"Sophia was witty, good-natured, and mischievous."

Walgrave raised an eyebrow at the use of Sophia's first name. "What about now?"

"Lady Wilmot appears much changed from her girlhood. Her solicitor describes her as a statue. Her sister-in-law says she is exhausted by grief."

"What do you think?"

Walgrave wanted Aidan to identify with Sophia, to anticipate her perceptions, inclinations, and her dispositions. But

Aidan had no desire to predict the turn of her mind. "I haven't formed an opinion."

"What about their years in Italy?"

"I know almost nothing. Wilmot always wanted to take the Grand Tour. I suppose living abroad was his way of doing it, even with a wife in tow. In Wilmot's defense, he chose Naples. After Marengo, Naples was never central to any conflicts, and by the time the Wilmots reached Italy, Bonaparte was already in Russia. It was a fairly safe choice."

Walgrave listened, looking at the liquid he twirled in his glass. Stopping, he looked directly into Aidan's eyes. "Could she be a spy?"

"For us or for someone else?"

"Either."

If Aidan wanted a public revenge, this was his opportunity. A single word to Walgrave. But with the Home Office involved, the stakes were too high. Sophia's life and Ian's future. No, unless Aidan had proof, irrefutable proof, he wouldn't sacrifice Ian.

Aidan held Walgrave's gaze as he answered. "As a girl, her education made her thoughtful, but not radical. She was as suspicious of Bonaparte as any of us. As for her present opinions, I haven't had occasion to observe. What exactly do you want to know?"

Walgrave set the paper to the side and leaned forward.

"The Home Office would like you to spend more time with her. Some information important to our interests has made its way into England from Italy, carried, we believe, by one of the realm's peers or his family in the last year. Only three families have returned from Italy in that time. The other two have been thoroughly investigated, but your lady has proved difficult. She has kept the strictest mourning, her only visitors family. She rarely goes out, but when she does, she visits a bookseller or a print shop where she could pass information easily. Her staff is surprisingly small, so we haven't been able to place a servant in her household."

"What am I looking for?"

"You have the official story." Walgrave poured himself another glass of claret.

"What's the unofficial one?"

"I did tell them you would ask. But I won't tell you if you are simply going to stand there glowering at me." Walgrave gestured at a chair, and Aidan sat. "In Italy Lady Wilmot hosted a salon, making the Wilmot household a gathering place for members of the Bourbon government in Naples *and* for Carbonari revolutionaries. Wilmot collected information for us from both. To protect the information—and obscure his part in collecting it—he would encode it, then send duplicate copies. One by our courier, if we could get one to him, and another by whatever means he thought might be successful. Over the years, he used the mails, other travelers returning home, the embassy packet. The key to the code he never sent the same way twice. Once he wrote a letter to the editor of the *Gentleman's Magazine* praising a rather obscure passage in Horace and commenting on a specific word in a specific translation. That word was the code key. His last communication indicated he was sending us a list of names. We believe it includes English peers who sold information to our enemies during the wars. But we have not heard from our courier since before Wilmot's death. Even if we had received one of Wilmot's copies, we wouldn't be able to decode his message without the code key."

"So, one dead—and one missing . . . presumed dead?"

Walgrave nodded.

Perhaps this was the information Aidan had waited for. "If you suspect Lady Wilmot might be a traitor, do you also suspect her in her husband's death?"

Walgrave looked thoughtful. "Wilmot was dying. No one gave him more than another year, so if Lady Wilmot wanted her husband dead, all she had to do was wait. As for the list itself, we don't know if it didn't arrive because it no longer exists, because she doesn't know what she has, because her own name is on that list, or because she's conspiring with those whose names are."

"Blackmail?"

Walgrave shrugged, pouring the last bit of claret into his glass. "I can say this, Forster. If your *Sophia* has the list or the code key, and she doesn't know what she has, she could be in grave danger."

Walgrave reentered the private suite at the Home Office where the more clandestine projects were planned.

Behind the desk sat Walgrave's commander, his body broken in the wars, a long disfiguring scar down the middle of his face. His eyelid on one side was puckered badly, and his lips, where the sword had sliced through the corner of his mouth, didn't meet properly. When the commander stood, he could walk only with the aid of a cane, his leg having been crushed under a horse's terror. He'd lost everything in the wars, even his name.

Joseph Pasten, his adjutant from the wars, sat reading reports at a table nearby. It was said that Joe had saved his commander, carrying his body to safety, hiding him, and nursing him back to health until he could be left alone long enough for Joe to find help. It was also said that no doctor would have attempted where Joe had succeeded.

"Have you chosen a new name yet, sir?" Walgrave posed the question as he did each day. "When we received the news that you were both our new head and officially dead, the men began steeling themselves never to use your old name, sir, but as time goes on, it's making conversations a bit difficult."

"Whatever my name will be, it won't be 'sir.'"

Walgrave chose his favorite chair and pulled it next to where Joe was working. "Have you convinced him to choose something?"

Joe shook his head. "He can be quite stubborn. He has no wish to return to his old life, but he's unwilling to let it go entirely."

"There is nothing wrong with my hearing, gentlemen. To the point, Walgrave, did Forster agree?"

"Yes, but I had to tell him a bit more than we hoped."

"Well, that's not unexpected. Has he realized that Edmund is watching Sophia for us?"

"Edmund doesn't think so. In fact, Edmund managed it so that Forster asked *him* for help."

"Good. Then let's see how this plays out."

Chapter Sixteen

Aidan had bought the Exmoor pony for the look of sheer joy on Ian's face, but it was proving valuable for getting Sophia and Ian out of the house. This morning Sophia and Ian were riding in Hyde Park . . . and Aidan was searching the volumes in the bookcases behind her desk.

He opened each of the printed books, thumbed through the pages, read the marginalia, and examined their bindings and the pastedown pages on the inside of each board. He found nothing.

Most intriguing to him were the manuscript versions of Tom's books, offering a record of Wilmot family life. The manuscript volumes contained the fair copies sent to the printer and the messy early versions, pages with corrections and comments in the hasty hand he knew as Sophia's, responses and additional comments in Tom's. Ian had not exaggerated his parents' cooperation.

Equally clear was Ian's place as a treasured child. The books recorded not just the parents working together, but Ian's developing intellect and ability. In one volume, Aidan found the rude pencilings of an unformed hand. In the next, Ian's name practiced in the unused areas of the pages, and most recently, Ian's answers to questions posed to him in the ample margins reserved for his parents' own commentary. Aidan had never longed for a child, but these evidences of Ian's growing intellect held an unexpected charm. A space on the shelf indicated that one book was missing.

Below the shelves of the bookcase was a locking cabinet, but he found the key quickly in a desk drawer. Inside were the estate and household account books. He pulled them out.

He caught himself automatically reviewing the figures— wages for household and gardening staff, costs of transporting crops to market, improvements to fencing and drainage, repairs to the manor-house roof. Under Sophia's guidance (he knew it wasn't all Seth's capable supervision), her husband's already ample estate had grown more robust. Indeed, the estate was flourishing.

Closing the estate ledgers, Aidan moved to the household accounts. The figures were recorded first in a secretary's neat copperplate hand, then confirmed by Sophia's own scrawled notations in the margins. He wondered who served as her secretary. By now, he thought he'd met all her servants.

The accounts revealed that Tom had established a handsome annuity for Sophia as part of her wedding settlement, and she had just the month prior received her semiannual payment. All her bills had been paid for the quarter; she had set in a store of coal for winter, buying in summer for the advantage of lower prices; and the household staff had already been paid their wages. In each category, she was well within her allotted budget.

Though he learned a great deal about Sophia's household and estate management, Aidan found nothing to answer whether Sophia had the coded documents or the code key. And certainly, if she were engaged in blackmail, she would be unlikely to record the amounts in ledgers available to her secretary and her estate manager.

He worked efficiently. The only books remaining were those nearest Sophia's easel. But those would have to wait.

He could hear Ian's voice, chattering happily, as he and his mother entered the garden from the mews.

By the time Sophia entered the library, Aidan was lounging on the couch, legs stretched out, and a newspaper sufficiently rumpled to suggest a man at his leisure. He watched her as she entered the room, irritated to see her again in black. It was odd: The manuscript books had fascinated him as the easy concourse of two minds. But while they had signaled companionship, they contained no scribbled endearments, no loving asides. The pages only made him more convinced that Sophia had not loved Tom with any degree of passion. Yet Sophia's mourning dress made that greater claim, embodying a devotion he was certain she did not feel and continuing to place the reminder of Tom between them—Tom, who had always been the block to any revenge Aidan might wish to take, and whose child now stood equally in the way.

"When do you intend to set aside your mourning clothes?" he asked off-handedly.

Sophia had made no acknowledgment of seeing him in the library when she entered, and she remained silent as she stood behind her desk, facing the bookcases. She removed her hat and placed it on the low shelf that extended out over the locking cabinets. She turned back to the desk, toward him, then offered a slight shrug.

"This is all I have to wear. We dyed my clothes for mourning, and I haven't ordered new ones yet. I'd thought about bleaching them, but . . ."

"Are you out of funds?"

"No, it's not that. I . . . I just . . . After Tom's death, so much *had* to be done—returning to London, moving everything into a new house, getting Ian settled, all of it. Some things were just too much to face. Now, I have nothing suitable to wear that isn't"—she held out her skirts—"black."

"We'll have to remedy that for you to enter society again."

The look she gave suggested both resentment and suspicion.

"For Ian," he offered.

"Oh, of course," she relented. "You just sounded like Tom."

"What do you mean?"

"Before he died, Tom made me promise to 'regain my place in society.'" She shifted her voice to mock Tom's words. "I'll tell *you* as I told *him*, I never had a place in society to regain. I was a poor relation to country gentry before I married Tom. I'd never even been to London."

She said it as if Aidan hadn't known her then, as if they hadn't talked for hours about where he would take her on her first trip to London. He remembered their conversations vividly. Clearly she did not. He buried the sudden and unexpected anger.

"*Was* country gentry. Even if you were not *Lady* Wilmot, your son is *my* ward. Society will welcome you to further an association with me." He looked over her dress more closely, noting each curve and line of her body. "But not in those clothes." He sat up straight and rose, picking up his hat, but leaving the newspaper as a reminder of his occupation during her absence. "This afternoon. I'll be by at two to escort you to a modiste."

"What do you know of modi . . . ?"

Aidan turned to her with a stare that stopped the words in her mouth. "Madam, I have clothed many a mistress in your absence, and no one has ever questioned my taste—in clothes or in women. Be ready at two."

He turned on his heel and was gone.

Chapter Seventeen

Aidan left Sophia's library to pay a call to Madame Elise, the most fashionable and most exclusive of London modistes. Other peers might wait for months for an appointment, but Aidan was never kept waiting. Only Aidan knew Elise as Lizzie, the daughter of one of his father's cottagers, seduced by his eldest brother Aaron into being his mistress, then beaten half to death in one of Aaron's drunken rages. Only Aidan had known where she had gone when she ran away, for he'd given her the money to start a sewing business in a fashionable area of town. They'd chosen a French accent to hide her, but it—along with her exceptional craftsmanship— became the foundation of her success. Despite the war with France, French fashions—and refugee French modistes— were all the rage.

When Elise had heard his very specific instructions for Sophia's new wardrobe, she'd raised an eyebrow. Her unspoken question: was Sophia Aidan's new mistress? Just as with Walgrave, he could have easily allowed Elise to believe what she wished and to let her circles of gossip begin to link his name with Lady Wilmot's. But once more, he considered his obligation to protect Ian.

Any revenge would have to be private, known just to himself and Sophia. So, he'd told the truth, or most of it: that Sophia was the mother of his ward, recently out of mourning. Then he'd surprised himself by asking Elise for her discretion. But the conversation gave him other ideas, and he spent the rest of his time planning how to breach the defenses around Sophia's heart.

Aidan arrived promptly at two, his plans for charming Sophia progressing nicely. He found her in the hall, gloves in hand, waiting for him alone.

"Do you wish to wait for your maid?"

"I'm a widow. I can ride in a carriage with my son's guardian without a maid," she offered stiffly, then softened. "Ian spent the morning reading Greek with his tutor, then he and Sally escaped to the park. I hadn't the heart to call them in."

"Then we shall go as you wish." He held his hand under her elbow as she descended the steps, then left his hand there until they reached the carriage. He opened the carriage door and started to offer his hand to help her up. But instead, he stepped behind her and, without warning, lifted her up and into the carriage. He couldn't see her face to gauge her reaction. She moved to sit on the far side of the carriage, giving him space to step in behind her and close the door. He took the backwards-facing seat, across from her.

"But," he teased, "what will Phineas say?" It was an old game, established long ago to take the sting out of Phineas's petty cruelties. He wondered if she would play.

Caught off guard, she laughed. "I didn't expect that."

"Which part? My gallant help or the reminder that your brother is a self-important prig?" Aidan welcomed the opportunity to be alone with her in close quarters. He stretched his legs across the space between them, resting them against the side of her right leg.

"I suppose both. I've been gone so long; I'd forgotten you know Phineas." She shifted her body to create a space between their legs.

"Ah, to know him . . ." He let pass her off-handed suggestion that she had forgotten their shared past. He would remind her of it here in the carriage. He leaned forward, shifting his leg again to touch hers. "Was he a devoted correspondent when you were in Naples?"

"I heard from him precisely three times a year, on my birthday in a long letter in which he detailed the various costs of maintaining a household in a civilized country, and on his birthday in a longer letter in which he detailed . . ."

"The various costs of maintaining a household in a civilized country."

"Yes, and in each one, a brief sermon on moral obligations, which always ended with my needing to donate my pin money to this or that endeavor Phineas wished to support."

"Of course. And the third time . . ."

"His request to visit Tom's estate to collect a Christmas ham. Poor pigs."

"I would have expected more."

"In actuality, there *were* more." Her voice shifted from amused to pensive. "I found them in a packet after Tom's death, Phineas's fat letters and copies of Tom's slender replies, all in a cover marked, 'only read these if you must.'"

"Did you read them?" Aidan regretted the change in her voice, but—for Walgrave at least—he needed to know the extent of Phineas's correspondence, if not with Sophia, then with Tom.

"No. I trusted Tom's judgment. So, I determined that Phineas didn't wish for me to read them either." She shifted again, once more creating distance between them.

"How did you determine that?" He kept his voice light, conspiratorial.

"Phineas never fails to remind me that a wife must obey her husband in all things."

Aidan laughed aloud, pleased at each glimpse of the old mischievous Sophia. "I doubt Phineas would approve that particular application of Scripture."

"I doubt it as well. But should I answer?"

"Answer?"

"What would Phineas say?"

"Yes, do." He was pleased she had agreed to play.

"It is no *more* inappropriate to ride unchaperoned in a carriage than it is to accompany a man to his modiste to choose a new wardrobe." She mimicked Phineas's intonation so well that Aidan—who had not seen her brother in years— could once more hear his voice.

"Ah, that's it exactly. Why do you put up with him?"

"Before my father died, he told us to take care of each other, and I suppose I feel that obligation. But I must say, it was easier when we were half a continent away and Tom was alive to bear the worst of it."

"Have you ever done anything Phineas approved of?"

"Actually I have." She shook her head, smiling. "I hired Cook. He visits, I believe, solely to eat her tea cakes."

"Ah, Cook. I brought her pistachios some time ago, hoping for a taste of her famous lemon cake."

"One must stake a claim early for a piece of Cook's cake. Between Ian and Dodsley, I barely get a crumb."

"Ah, unfair, my lady." Aidan pretended to be hurt.

Sophia laughed, relaxing against the seat. The conversation about servants gave him an opportunity to discover some of the information Walgrave needed.

"Counting Cook, how many servants do you employ?"

"Enough for the needs of our household," Sophia answered obliquely.

"Let me try: there's Sally, a maid-of-all-work who serves as Ian's nurse and helps you dress; Cook, Dodsley, Perkins, and a footman. . . . Have I missed anyone?" Aidan leaned back, as if counting her servants, but, in fact, using his motion to bring his legs once more against her calf. This time, when his leg brushed against hers, she had no room left to move away. She had to allow the subtle pressure or ask him to move. He was certain she wouldn't openly acknowledge his touch, not when he pretended to be unaware of it.

"Ian's tutor, a Mr. Benedict Grange."

"No secretary?"

"Not anymore."

"I'll send you some servants in the morning."

"I don't need more servants."

"You will."

He'd hoped that the constant pressure of his legs against hers would remind her of what they had been, of the passion they had shared in their youth. But by the time they arrived at Madame Elise's, he had only succeeded in reminding himself. The scent of her hair, newly washed, with hints of lemon and rosemary, the rise and fall of her chest with each breath, the soft pressure of her calf through the layers of her walking dress against his leg, each one captured his senses.

At Madame Elise's, Sophia's dreary clothes and her wary reserve gave proof to Aidan's words that she was not his new mistress—as did her insistence that the bill come to her. At first it had gratified her that Madame Elise had not assumed she was another of Forster's mistresses, then she realized that Madame Elise knew all of Aidan's mistresses and had identified Sophia as not one of them. At some level it disappointed her, creating a dull ache at the back of her chest, but she told herself, it was for the best.

Even so, Aidan had resisted her choices of colors, insisting that, after a year, she did not have to limit herself to lavender and gray. When she would not be moved from half-mourning, Madame Elise had smiled and patted Aidan's arm. "You will be *très contente* with my designs, your grace. I can do much with the *materiel seul*. She will still be *sensationelle, non?*"

After choosing patterns for a small wardrobe—two morning dresses, two evening dresses, a riding habit, and three walking dresses—Sophia and Aidan took their leave of Madame Elise. Aidan opened the door to Madame Elise's shop and let Sophia pass before him into the street. It was just short of half past three. The streets were still lively with the sounds of vendors and children chasing one another up and down the sidewalks.

She heard a commotion to her right, and a rough voice crying "thief."

A child of perhaps six ran past. Agile and small, the child ducked around her, and down the alley on the other side of Elise's shop. A large broad man burst through the crowd. Sophia had no time to think, no room to move out of his way.

Suddenly Aidan pulled her out of the way of the pursuit and against his chest. She could feel his breath against her neck. His arms held her tight, and she turned her face into his chest, listening to his heart beat fast. She knew she had to move, but now that she was in his embrace, she wanted only to remain in his arms.

"I'm not hurt." She tapped his arm. "You can let me go."

His arms released slowly. Stepping back, she followed his gaze. He was watching the crowd for the man who had almost run her down.

"Yes, but you could have been. There's no excuse. . . . It

was obvious he couldn't get through without knocking others down."

"That's the second time you've kept me from being hurt. I must thank you."

"No thanks necessary. I would have a hard time explaining to Ian how I allowed his mother to be mauled in the street." Though Aidan appeared placid and at ease once more, his eyes continued to search the crowd as he escorted her into his carriage. Sophia wondered how much Aidan hid behind that bland composure.

Aidan settled himself into the carriage, feeling uneasy. Were the child and his pursuer just that, or was someone trying to harm Sophia? Had he seen a knife flash in the instant before he pulled her back off the sidewalk? He could not be sure. But if she were in danger, he was obligated to Ian and the Home Office to protect her. Now, though, having pulled her body tight against his and held her in his arms for the first time in a decade, he wanted to touch her again, to draw her into the dark of the carriage and kiss her senseless. Acutely aware of her nearness, he fixed his legs far from her own.

The silence gave Sophia time to think. She'd been foolish not to bring a maid. She would have liked to believe that his legs brushing up against hers in the carriage had been an attempt to seduce her, but each time she looked at him, he was looking out of the window. Surely, if he had seduction in mind, he would at least look into her eyes. Or make a joke. But apparently he thought so little of her, he wasn't even aware of how his legs felt against hers.

And in the street, when he had swept her out of the way, he had not taken the opportunity to embrace her. No, his were only the natural reactions of a man brought up in polite society. He would behave in the same manner, she was sure, to any other woman of his class, and likely even to Madame Elise, with whom he seemed to have a long history. But Sophia found herself disappointed. She longed to feel his touch once more, and she wondered how he would respond if she were to move across the seat, and lift her lips to his. She waited some time before she spoke. "Madame Elise said one of the plainer dresses might be ready in time for the dinner party."

"Dinner party?"

"I assumed you had seen the invitation. Wasn't that the reason you insisted on a modiste?"

Aidan laughed. "My lady, all invitations go into a pile for my secretary to refuse. I don't even read them."

"I haven't received a refusal."

"*Yet.* He sends them out seven days before the event. So what is this dinner party for?"

"Phineas is sitting for parliament in a rotten borough, and he wishes to begin forming political alliances."

"And I'm invited?" Aidan sounded genuinely surprised. "Is he mad?"

"Phineas wishes for people to know Tom made you Ian's guardian, so that if they see us together, they won't think . . ." She trailed off, wishing she had not begun that sentence.

Aidan heard her hesitation. He needed little help to imagine what Phineas had said, but he couldn't resist forcing her to finish the sentence. "Think what?"

She looked down into her hands. "Phineas fears for my reputation. . . . Well, to be honest, he fears I will do something that will thwart his ambitions."

"Ah. So that's how everyone at my club knows Ian is my ward." There was nothing Sophia could say, nothing that wouldn't tread on dangerous ground. She turned her attention to the streets passing outside the carriage window, and the silence lengthened.

They had been driving long enough that they should be

nearing her home, but none of the streets looked familiar. Instead, they drove through parts of London she had never seen: buildings farther and farther apart, interspersed with fields and crops. She shifted against the seat, beginning to feel ill at ease.

"There's somewhere I thought you might like to visit before returning home."

"Do you intend to tell me where?"

"I'd prefer to surprise you, if you are willing. Dodsley knows we will be late returning."

Sophia nodded her assent and watched out the window, trying to imagine where Aidan might be taking her and even more why he would wish to surprise her. They were traveling south toward the river. She could smell the water in the air.

Only a few minutes later, the carriage turned down an alley, faced on one side by a long brick wall. The coachman opened the door. Aidan jumped down and held out his hand for her to join him. An inset door in the brick wall opened to a garden beyond. "If my memory serves me, you once said you wished to visit the Apothecaries' Physic Garden in Chelsea. I hope that is still the case."

She was stunned. She didn't ask how he had remembered; in some ways she didn't dare. If he felt her marriage was a betrayal, then she didn't dare open those old wounds. But if he *had* felt betrayed, why would he reveal that he remembered their conversations about what they would do together in London? It was a puzzle. At first she had been relieved not to have to address the question of their past, but in the last few weeks, she'd wished she could broach the subject. If it were true that he held no animosity for her decisions all those years ago, perhaps they could start anew—even if only as friends. Her heart lifted in a way she had thought no longer possible. Before she could answer, before she could thank him, he continued.

"Ian told me you have met few other gardeners since your return to London. In about an hour, William Anderson, the curator here, will meet us for a tour. Until then, I thought you might like to wander. To our north are the greenhouses, the hothouses, and the library; to the south, from here to the Thames, open beds with specimen plants."

"I don't know how to thank you. . . . Of all the places in London . . ."

"Then don't thank me. Whither will you go first, my lady?"

She looked down one of the garden paths faced by perennial herbs of varying colors and textures. "I want to see everything. Let's go that way."

The garden, though only four acres, was lush with plants. The first section—thirteen long beds ranged horizontally to one another—held the perennial plants and herbs, and after that lay a large section of twenty vertical rows of tender and annual plants. Each section was bordered by box and other edging plants. Between the annuals and perennials were glass cases that provided artificial heat to succulents and other tender exotics.

As they walked down the rows, Sophia pointed out interesting plants or read to him the label of an unfamiliar one, interpreting the technical information into layman's terms with ease. She frequently pointed to a plant she was considering for his garden and asked if he liked some aspect of it, its color, or leaves, or texture, or height.

Surprising himself, Aidan grew increasingly interested in how she thought about the plants, what characteristics appealed to her. At the same time, his attention was repeatedly drawn to her, to the way she moved gracefully down the rows, to the scent of her hair, to the tapered length of her fingers as she pointed to one plant, then another. But it wasn't just the physicality of her body. It was also the clarity of her expression as she talked about the plants, the extent of her knowledge. And he found he wanted to know more of her, of how she had changed since their youth, of who she had become as a woman. "Tell me what you see in the plants as we pass them."

"Do you really wish to know?" Sophia searched his face for an answer.

"I would not have asked if I didn't. . . . And how can I resist learning from such an authority?"

Her soft smile pulled at his heart and his loins.

"Designing a garden is both an art and a science. First you must think about how the color and texture of one plant's leaves complement those of another. Then, you have to imagine the influence of time on the plants, how the plants will grow across the season and how one season of color will give way to another. This bed is arranged by family, showing the apprentices the various habits of the plant. See how these leaves are small with rounded edges. In my garden I'd want more contrast, so I'd put that next to a plant with a different leaf shape and texture, and if possible, a different color. And to give interest, I think about theme and variation, so I might put the same plant at each end of a bed, or at key points across the garden, to unify the garden, without being monotonous."

Halfway through the upper part of the garden, they sat to enjoy the prospect down to and out over the Thames. The seat was just large enough for two.

"How are you liking the physic garden?" Aidan asked.

"It's lovely. I haven't enjoyed myself this much since . . ." She paused, pensive. "For a very long time."

"Since when?"

"Tom wasn't sick yet. He and I were collecting plants in the mountains, some beautiful native flowers I'd never seen in bloom. I had my chalk and watercolors, and I was trying to match the hues. This sort of luminescent white with a touch of pink at the center, very delicate. Ian was little, perhaps two; he'd just learned to walk. He was forever slipping away from his nurse to hide in my skirts. I kept having to stop and give him back to his nurse, until Tom came and caught Ian up in his arms, and turned him in circles over and over. Ian laughed and laughed. And I was able to match the colors. Then, Tom and Ian sat and watched me paint. Tom sitting cross-legged on the ground, with Ian standing in his lap, pulling on his face, as children do. The sky . . . the sky was a cornflower blue with almost no clouds."

"What happened?"

Her face shuttered. "Tom fell ill, we made no more excursions, and Ian grew up."

"I hadn't intended to bring up sad memories," he offered, surprised to find he meant it.

"It's not your fault; it's the day. That sky is almost the same color, and we're sitting beside marigolds, such gaudy plants, but Tom's favorites. Their acrid smell never fails to remind me of him. It wasn't possible for me to come here and not think of Tom. But it's still lovely. And I've always wanted to visit."

"I'm glad I remembered correctly then."

They had only examined the top half of the garden when a servant arrived to escort them to their meeting with Anderson and their tour of the greenhouses and library. Flanked on either end by greenhouses, the main building offered a symmetrical arrangement popular fifty years before. It rose three stories, and the ground floor was divided visually by three sets of three arched colonnades, with a triangular pediment over the middle three arches. "I've told him you are the illustrator of Lord Wilmot's works and a botanist in your own right," Aidan whispered as they approached the entrance where Anderson, a tall, burly Scotsman, stood waiting to meet them.

Anderson's generous heart compensated for his rough manners, and before five minutes had elapsed he and Sophia were chatting like old friends about gardens in London. "Do ye know ol' Lord Whitney's house, empty now? It's within a block o' two of ye. The caretaker could let ye see it. Give him my name. Before ye go today, I'll show ye the plans of his great iron conservatory, built to entertain his guests. His wife Alisoun hated the guests to see the servants stoking the stoves during her parties, so the old lord put the stoves and wood-sheds on the sides with their own servants' entrances. Last thing he did afore he grew too frail to come to town was to in-stall a giant statue of Flora atop all that plate glass and iron."

By the time the three took their tea by the sea gate, Sophia and Anderson had determined what plants they could trade, when she would visit again, and who in the community of plantsmen she would most enjoy meeting. Aidan's servants had laid out a small feast—apples, oranges, and nectarines, lemon sponge cake, jam tarts, cheese, and bread—in the shade of one of the two Cedars of Lebanon, both over two-hundred years old. This Sophia was more like the girl Aidan had known, confident, assured, lively. Gone was her wary reserve, melted away by the rows of plants she had greeted as old friends and by the love of botany she shared with the gruff Scot. When the time came to return home, Sophia and Anderson parted with clear regret.

Aidan handed Sophia into the carriage, then went to speak with his driver. She closed her eyes and rested her head against the wall of the carriage. Something subtle had changed between them. Or perhaps she had simply decided to let their relationship play out as it would. Thinking of Tom in the garden, she had realized he had been right to appoint a second guardian. If anything happened to her, Ian would be safe from Phineas, safe with Aidan. She was finding it harder and harder not to trust Aidan. Or, to be honest, it had always been too easy to trust him. When he was kind, he reminded her of his youthful self, and she found herself less and less able to maintain a cool reserve. Despite her reservations at the guardianship, things might still be well—if only she could forget her memories of his touch.

At some point she would broach their past, apologize, if nothing else. But every day she seemed to find a reason to postpone the possible conflict. And this day, this companionable day, was one she wanted to remember untouched by recrimination.

When Aidan stepped into the carriage, Sophia was sitting with her eyes closed, breathing deeply. He watched her chest rise and fall, let his eye follow the line of her décolletage down across her chest, stomach, and legs. He wanted her. He'd felt it all day in his stomach and his loins, felt it when he'd seen her that morning wearing black, felt it in Elise's shop when he'd imagined her in new dresses (and out of them). But their conversation in the garden had evoked the hottest part of his desire. Over the years he'd forced himself to forget her quick wit and the easy banter of their two agile minds. He'd forgotten the allure of her intellect. He would have to forget it again after their affair ended, but now he knew it would be difficult.

He seated himself across from her once more, again taking the backwards seat, and settled in for a quiet drive, folding his arms across his chest and leaning against the side of the carriage. But as soon as the carriage started moving, she leaned forward and reached out her hand to touch his. "This has been a marvelous day. Thank you."

"I'm glad finally to have been able to fulfill the promise I made you."

"I never expected you to remember. It was so long ago, and so insignificant."

"None of the promises we made were ever insignificant."

And there it was . . . the past laid present between them. She couldn't avoid it.

"No. They weren't insignificant. And I have no excuse. Only that I could not have remained in my uncle's house any longer. So much changed after you left, and Tom offered me an . . . escape. Can you forgive me?"

His pause was long, as he sat, his arms still folded across his chest, regarding her intently. In the silence that stretched between them, she could almost hear Tom's voice whispering, *"Patience."*

"Yes." His voice was firm, deliberate.

"Yes?" she repeated in surprise. "I didn't expect that."

"We were young, too young perhaps to know our minds."

She wanted to object: She had known her own mind. She simply hadn't been allowed to follow it. But his was an easy answer, one that didn't require other explanations. So she let it stand.

"Thank you." She touched his hand once more, covering it with her hand. "I must apologize for resenting that Tom made you guardian. Ian adores you, and you have been exceptionally kind, not just to him, to both of us."

"Tom was a good man. If nothing else, his request made me realize the time for holding grudges had long past."

"Then perhaps we can be friends," Sophia offered cautiously.

"Perhaps we can be." Aidan offered her a wide smile and was repaid by hers in turn. "It occurs to me, if you would consider it, that when I return to my estate with Ian, you might wish to go with us. The house is large, or if you are concerned about the proprieties, I could send word to open the dower house. I even have another garden in disrepair that you could take in hand."

"I would like that very much." She knew she spoke too quickly, agreed without even a moment's pause. But it was a lifeline, a way to hold on to Ian just a little longer.

By the time they returned to her house, they had sketched out the details. They would leave shortly after Phineas's dinner party and spend the rest of the summer and fall at Aidan's distant ducal estate in Monmouthshire.

Chapter Eighteen

When Sophia awoke, streaks of color were not yet brightening the dark sky. But her dreams, influenced by the Apothecaries' Garden, had been filled with color: purples by yellows, oranges and reds, blues and whites all in one. It was cacophonous, and jarring . . . and beautiful. It was her vision for Aidan's garden, but not what she'd originally planned.

The lines had all been there in her drawings, but not these particular details. It wasn't a design she would normally create. The long stalwart lines of the Italian cypresses rooted in raucous beds of color. But having seen it in her imagination, she wanted it.

She picked up the sketchbook and colored in the plants with a bag of pastel crayons she kept near her dressing table. Tom had joked that she couldn't be long without paper to sketch on, and he'd kept her supplied with blank-page account books. This was the last one he'd given her, and she'd resisted filling the last dozen pages, but she began to draw today without thinking. She sketched quickly, preserving the outlines of the beds and colors from her dream.

When she was done, she moved to her wardrobe. She needed to see if the garden she imagined could actually take shape in Aidan's yard, or if it were one of those ideas possible only in a dream world.

Since she knew the mostly private path to Aidan's yard, she saw no reason not to use it.

She wouldn't run the risk of meeting Aidan—he'd said he intended to spend the evening at his club—but she still should not be noticed. Sally had laid out a morning dress, but she ignored it. Instead, she drew from the closet a dress she had often worn in Italy when she walked the hills searching for botanical specimens. Now dyed black, it was more of a shift than a dress, with two drawstrings to pull the heavy cotton in above and below her bodice. The top drawstring pulled the puffed sleeves of the dress in to cover her shoulders. It was a plain dress more suitable for a servant than a woman of rank, but she would only be slipping from one garden to the next. With a black lace fichu, she covered the exposed skin between her shoulders and the nape of her neck.

She slept with her hair braided, and now she simply pinned the braids against her head and placed on top an oversized poke bonnet that hid her face. Over it all, she draped a long cloak with a hood, and she pulled the hood over her head. She stood in front of the mirror to test her appearance: no one could recognize her.

Tucking her sketchbook and pencils under her arm, she ran down the stairs and into the dark.

Within five minutes, she had slipped inside the door at the bottom of Aidan's garden. She'd seen no one. It was too early yet. The darkness had lifted only enough for her to find her way.

It felt exhilarating, like those years long past when she had slipped out of her uncle's house to watch the stars on the lawn, or to hunt for night-blooming plants in the forest, or—much later—to meet with Aidan.

She wished she hadn't remembered that last. It brought

him too close to the front of her mind. But she pushed his image away, focusing on the lines of the dream garden she could still see in her memory. She began to walk the garden, testing her plans, oblivious to the sounds of the houses coming alive and the horses in the mews stirring in the lifting darkness.

Aidan had been standing at the window for at least an hour. He had come home half-drunk from his club, stripped down to his underclothes, and put himself to bed.

The dream began as always, with pleasure, then Sophia had disappeared, and he'd dreamt of Tom. This time Tom stood near a pond, hand outstretched, pointing at the body of a dark-haired child floating facedown. Aidan plunged into the water, searching, but the child had disappeared. In the clear water, he saw bodies floating beneath the surface. Men from his regiment, their horses, Ian, Sophia, his brother Benjamin. He tried to pull them to shore, but they turned to skeletons in his arms.

He'd awoken in a sweat, gasping with grief, his heart drumming fast. He tried to distract himself from the dream, by imagining Sophia in his bed, his hands running down her body. But the grief and fear remained and the sense of impending danger.

The light of the sunrise was only beginning to streak the sky, tinging the tops of the houses as it approached him from the east. In the garden below him darkness began to lighten gradually, revealing glimpses of movement in the trees. A figure in a long cloak walked in and out of the shadows. For a moment, uncertain in the half-light, he wondered if he were awake or sleeping. He threw the last of the whiskey to the back of his throat, and the burn called him to himself. Someone was in his garden. He picked up the folding knife he kept on his dressing table, wishing he hadn't left his pistols in his study.

His balcony was supported by broad columns and a trellis, an easy route to the garden, quicker than running through the darkened house.

He had no slippers, but the grass was soft. He walked stealthily, staying in the shadows, keeping his attention on the dark figure near the trees. He was close; he could call out, demanding the figure identify itself, but then he might risk being shot if his intruder had an accomplice. The figure turned toward the back of the yard and the gate.

He moved swiftly. Taking hold of the back of the cloak, he flung the intruder to the ground and himself after. He heard a sharp breath as the weight of his body knocked the wind from the intruder's lungs. Only when holding the intruder down on the grass, did he smell it: lavender. Sophia. And not a dream.

He pulled back the cloak, only to be frustrated by her bonnet twisted half-round. He pulled the string under her chin and pushed its sides away from her face. She looked at him, half in fear, half in expectation.

There was no resisting his passion, the call of the dreams too strong. Her body was beneath him, its curves soft against his legs and chest. He could feel himself grow taut, primed by dreams and danger. He kissed her—not the tentative kiss he'd imagined as a start to his seduction, a sweet kiss that would disarm her. No, this was a kiss that spoke of years of longing. Of seeing her again in the half-light of his dreams.

But the urgency in his kiss surprised them both, and for a moment she didn't react. Then, as if giving in to some inner debate, her body answered his, returning the pressure on his lips, her legs moving against the confines of the cloak to arch slightly against him.

He kissed her again, less hard but no less desperately.

Tasting her lips, the inside of her mouth, he waited for her to push him away, but she didn't. Instead, she matched his fervor. He didn't stop kissing her, didn't dare risk giving her a moment to reconsider. He slipped his hand between them, under the thick material of the cloak. Untying it at the neck, he felt below it the thinner material of her dress. He kept his kisses deep and rocked gently against her lower body. When he pulled his mouth away from hers to kiss her neck, she traced her own line of kisses across his forehead and into his hair.

His hand found her breast, gently caressing the side. Then moving to the center, he felt the lace of a drawstring and pulled it. She wore no other undergarments. His hand rubbed soft flesh between his fingers. She gasped and struggled, but not against him; her arms were tangled, he realized, in the cloak between them. He pulled at the material with her, releasing her arms, and she pulled him closer, rubbing her hands up and down his back, pulling his hips against hers.

His one hand still cradling her breast, he kissed down her neck, smelling the lavender water on the skin below her ear, then moving farther still, down the center of her chest, kissing the line of her décolletage, then taking the center of her other breast in his mouth. She arched against him again, as he teased her with his teeth and then with the thumb and forefinger of his hand. She was breathing soft, thick pants as he pulled the second drawstring and slid his hand down her belly. The material gave way enough for him to caress the intimate folds beyond her soft tufts of hair, and beyond that to slip his fingers into her core.

He wanted to undress her there. Bury himself in her body. Claim her once more for his. But he also knew that this moment of unthinking passion was too fragile. The sun already lit the garden, leaving only their patch below the trees in half-light. The birds had already begun calling to one another; the horses in the mews had begun to whinny for their breakfast. Sophia with her eyes closed had not realized the change, but the moment she opened her eyes, she would withdraw from their passion.

Had her legs not been entangled in the cloak, he might have had a chance. But to undress her farther he would have to move off of her, and that would break the physical contact that held her out of time and thought. Though everything within him said "try," he gave up the thought of taking her in the garden.

But he could at least leave her satisfied. He kissed back up her neck to nuzzle her ear, whispering, "Let me give you pleasure, Sophia," as he pressed his palm against her mound. She arched her hips into his hand, and he covered her mouth once more with his lips. Caressing with tongue and fingers, he waited until she shattered in his arms.

She kept her eyes closed for some minutes, as the heat of her body calmed. He watched her, forcing himself to breathe deeply, wanting to appear in control when she came back to herself. And in truth, he had found satisfaction in proving she was not impervious to him and that he could use her passion to his ends.

"You've been drinking. I could taste it on your lips."

"That's not why I kissed you."

She put her hand to her lips, feeling them, the heat still lingering, her flesh swollen with passion. "That was more than a kiss."

"It's still not the reason."

"Why then?"

"Because you came to me, and I remember . . . how it felt. Be my lover again. Here, in my garden or in my bed." Though he knew she would refuse, he added, "We could go there now. With your cloak, no one would recognize you. This was just a taste of the pleasure I can give you. Come with me."

Sophia looked to the house, her silence revealing her temptation. "But Ian?"

"Isn't here. He doesn't even know you are gone. In fact, given that garb, I would bet no one knows where you are. Not clever, my Sophia." He pressed his lips hard against hers once more, whispering against her cheek. "I could make this house a seraglio with you its only concubine, and no one would ever suspect." He pressed another kiss to her lips, until she matched him kiss for kiss. "Besides, why did you come here in the dark if not to become my lover?"

"The garden . . . I dreamt about it. I wanted to see . . ."

"You came to see my garden," he repeated, disbelieving, but he knew it was the truth. Nothing else explained her movements in the dark.

"Yes. The garden."

"You understand how I could have misunderstood." He nuzzled the skin of her neck.

"I thought you would be at your club."

"It doesn't matter; we can't ignore this." He brushed her hair back under her bonnet and tucked her curls behind her ear. "Perhaps before, but not now. Will you consider it?"

"Consider what?"

"Becoming my lover." Her breast was still exposed, and he cupped his hand around its fullness and leaned over to kiss it, pulling hard against the nipple until she gasped with renewed passion. "If you are worried about disclosure, we could wait until we arrive at my estate. I've already sent word to open the dower house. Malcolm and Audrey have a house close by. It would be easy for Ian to spend a day . . . or a night with their boys."

The moment he took his lips from her breast, she began to redress. He watched as she put on reserve and civility with each layer of her clothing. When she was finished replacing her dress, fichu, and cloak, she held out her arms for Aidan to help her up. He rose, then pulled her up after him, setting her off-balance at the same time, drawing her into his arms. He kissed her once more, a gentle persuasive kiss.

He set her back from him with regret, his body still taut with desire. He had been carried away by the passion that rose so swiftly between them and by his own heated responses to her body under his. But on the chessboard of his seduction, he could not have planned a better move. She had come to him—her reason was irrelevant. And now, he could begin a more active pursuit. Until they left for his estate, he would distract her with stolen kisses and torment her with gentle touches. And then, once they were far from interruption, he would remind her of exactly how enjoyable an affair with him could be.

Sophia looked down at the ground where they had both lain, the imprint of their bodies still visible in the bent grass, then she turned away toward his garden door, walking quickly. Aidan was right: the passion had been there. She simply hadn't realized it was smoldering on his side as well as hers. She was grateful her clothes were black, no green stains to reveal their tryst. And it had to be only a tryst. He was too dangerous to her peace and calm.

Once at his garden door, she thought to object to his proposal, but as if reading her thoughts, he interrupted. "What do you plan for the garden?"

"That seems so insignificant now, after . . ." She looked back at the garden.

"I told you yesterday: nothing between us has ever been insignificant." Aidan pulled her bonnet up around her face, then lifted the hood of her cloak to conceal her face entirely. He followed her out into the alley and walked behind her toward her house.

"I don't think I can describe in words what I've imagined. Will you promise to let me work until the design is fully executed? Not critique or complain before the thing comes together?"

"I'll leave the garden to you, but in return you must promise not to make a decision before we get to my estate."

Against her better instincts, she nodded agreement. They walked the rest of the way silently, and at the door to her garden, she bid him good-bye and slipped inside. Leaning back against the closed garden door, she shut her eyes, recalling every moment from the time he'd knocked her to the ground.

She shook her head, willing the tears of recrimination from her eyes. How could she? What had she been thinking? She'd been exhilarated by her dream, not considering Aidan might be home, might find her, might misunderstand her intentions. But what else could he think? Finding her in his garden in the half-light, how could he not think her a light-skirt?

He'd offered to make her his lover.

She should be insulted. And yet, the worst part was that she wanted to say yes. Even if it only lasted for a few months, to have him once more, to hold him and breathe in the musk of his skin. Phineas was right: Aidan wouldn't marry her, and if they were discovered, she'd be ruined. But she was a widow. . . . If they were discreet? When it ended, she would simply withdraw to the country, leaving London to him and his next mistress and eventually to his bride. All paths led to sorrow: If she rejected his offer, she would regret it for the rest of her life, and Aidan was not a man to give her another chance. If she accepted . . .

Troubled, she entered the library. She could hear the house coming awake. She set her cloak and bonnet aside and walked to the pier glass between two bays of windows to examine her reflection. Would the flush on her cheeks tell of her indiscretion?

In the window's reflection, she could see a package on her desk and walked to examine it. From Mr. Murray. She flexed the edge of the package. Paper, not books. Tom's fair copy returned from the printer—something to take her mind off the persistent problem of Aidan and her passion.

But first she had to focus on putting her plans for Aidan's garden into effect. She drew up instructions for Perkins, complete with plant lists and diagrams of the plantings as she had dreamed them. In the light of day, the design was still exhilarating. Even if it hadn't been, she couldn't retreat now.

As she wrote the plans, however, she found herself constantly distracted by the smell of grass on her skirt, the hint of Aidan's scent on her neck, the remembered taste of his kiss on her lips. No, she would never be able to concentrate with such reminders, and she withdrew to her room to change into a more suitable morning dress.

Returning to the library some time later, she turned to Tom's fair copy. Placing the pages next to the proofs, she began to compare.

Soon it became clear that Mr. Murray did not have a malicious printer: the proofs were set exactly as Tom's fair copy had indicated they should be, errors and all. She could not imagine why Tom would have made such mistakes. But perhaps as she made the corrections, Tom's intentions would become clear.

That left only one task: to recreate the book she and Tom had worked on in Italy, using the messy manuscript pages she'd recently had bound. It would take hours, but it had to be done.

* * *

She was only one-hundred pages from the end when Ian's tutor, Mr. Grange, tapped on the library door. A slight man in fashionable clothes, Mr. Grange was a contradiction, self-important in his speech but self-effacing in his carriage.

"Her ladyship summoned me to an audience." Grange stood in the doorway, looking at his shoes.

"Please come in and sit. I have a favor to propose." She motioned to the chairs before the fireplace. The tutor flipped the tails of his coat over the sides of the chair, and sat between them as precisely as if he had studied his movements in a mirror.

Sophia chose the chair opposite him. "My brother has asked me to host a dinner for his political associates next Thursday. My sister-in-law in Kensington has invited Ian to visit her son Nate for the evening of and the day after the party. I was hoping you might be free to take Ian to his aunt's house and remain at her home supervising Ian and his cousin. In all, two days."

"I typically teach other boys when I'm not with his lordship. My days are quite full." Grange crossed his legs, one ankle to the other knee, his back perfectly erect. His eyes focused on a point somewhere around the tips of his toes.

"I understand that you might not be able to alter your other obligations."

"It will be difficult; my services are highly valued by my patrons across Mayfair. I would not wish to give preference to one child over the others." Never looking up, Grange rubbed a smudge on his shoe with his thumb until it disappeared.

Sophia noticed a hole in the shoe's sole. She looked away.

"Of course, Mr. Grange, I understand that might be awkward. But if you were able to open your schedule, my sister-in-law and I would recompense you for the loss of the other income, and I would provide a bonus for the additional time spent accompanying Ian to and from her home."

"Precisely what services would her ladyship expect? I am not adequate to the task of playing nursemaid." Grange took a small notebook and stub pencil from his upper coat pocket and began to make small unreadable notations in a crabbed hand.

"Ian will have Sally for his nurse. He would need his lessons, but perhaps an excursion in the countryside, looking for botanical or mineral specimens, would offer a diversion from his more traditional studies. His cousin might choose to accompany you . . . for an additional fee, of course. My sister-in-law's son is also somewhat boisterous."

"I could provide them with adequate exercise to check their exuberant spirits." Grange looked up from his notebook only for a moment, blinked, then returned to writing.

"If you deem it appropriate or necessary."

"Excellent. And what arrangements will be made for lodgings?" He paused in his notes, and without looking up, waited until she began speaking, then returned to his scribbles.

"You will be the guest of my sister-in-law and her husband, the Masons, taking your meals with the family."

"I will not be lodging in the nursery." Grange looked up; his large eyes, owl-like, stared for a minute, blinked twice, and stared again.

"No, you will be provided with one of the guest rooms."

"Excellent." He returned to his notebook. "I assume we will be traveling in your carriage rather than in a hired hackney."

"That can be arranged."

"Excellent." He licked the tip of his pencil and began writing again. "I will need an advance of funds, should any unexpected expenses arise in delivering his lordship's studies."

"Of course. Will you require anything else?"

"No, that will be sufficient." Grange snapped the notebook shut. "I will inform you on Monday if I am able to arrange my schedule to suit your request." He placed both the pencil and the notebook back in his pocket. "With your permission, my lady, I take my leave."

"Of course."

Grange stood up as precisely as he had sat and walked swiftly to the door.

She watched Grange go, always surprised at their interactions. But if she knew the tutor at all, she knew he would agree on Monday. As much as he loved teaching, he loved money more.

She looked up at the clock. She'd already been working longer than she'd hoped, and she was still not finished.

Hours later, Sophia finally finished marking all the corrections to the proofs. She rose from the desk and walked around the library, stretching her arms in front of her and stretching her neck to one side then the next.

Aidan walked into the library. Unannounced. Again.

"I looked for you in the greenhouse."

"I wasn't there." She could hear the irritation in her tone, and it galled her. This morning in his garden had shown her how little control she had in his presence. Her ability to remain calm, a trait that had served her so well in the last year, had deserted her. At the same time, she had been more than generous with Aidan's lack of propriety, arriving and interrupting as he wished. Perhaps it was time to be less generous.

"Dodsley said that you've been working all day, and it's after four. Your man has made quite a bit of progress in my neglected garden. We thought you might like to inspect it. But"—his eyes followed her gaze to the papers on the desk— "if you are engaged . . ." He walked behind the desk and picked up a sheath of the pages. Then he leaned back against the edge of the bookcases, turning the pages slowly. Sophia tried to focus on his face and his words, not to look at his body, not to look at his hands, turning the pages slowly . . . not to remember the feel of those hands against her skin.

"I was working, but I'm just finished, and I'm about to go out." Her voice was determined and stern. Reaching past him, she set about returning the stack of paper to its former order.

"Out?" Something in his tone made clear that he expected an answer, and it rankled her.

"Yes. Out." Impatient and annoyed, she took the pages from his hands, confirming that he had only the printed proofs from volume one, not any from volume two. "I will be unable to inspect Perkins's progress today." She began to rewrap the proofs in their brown paper covering. However, when she reached for the twine to tie it up, Aidan's hand covered hers, stopped her from wrapping the package.

She turned, fully intending to ask him what he thought he was doing.

But she hadn't realized how close he was. She turned without meaning to along the curve of his arm, into the space before his chest. She could smell the scent of the afternoon rain still on his clothes, feel the warmth of his body so close to hers, and she suddenly longed to lean into him, let his heat once more dispel the chill in her bones.

He leaned to kiss her, and she realized that after the garden, she would be lost if she allowed it. Instead, she bit her lip hard, recalling herself to sense. He leaned closer. She twisted to face the desk, putting her back to him and pulling her hand from beneath his.

"No, Aidan. This is not the time."

Undaunted, he breathed against her neck, then brushed the hair on the side of her face with his face, and whispered in her ear, "Wait here. I will return." He was gone as abruptly as he had arrived.

Sophia stared at the library door, stunned. She felt a complicated mix of emotions: anger, relief, and frustration. Angry that he assumed she would do as he said and wait. Relieved that he had left before she'd given in to her desire and responded to his kiss. And frustrated . . . with the errors in the proofs, with the time (and money) it would take to repair them, and most of all with Aidan, for entering and leaving her life as he always had . . . on his own terms. She pulled the twine tight, breaking off the ends with her hands. Then, picking up her cloak, she turned to escape through the long glass door behind her desk.

"Don't go." Aidan's voice was soft.

She turned to object, hot words ready to spill out. But she caught them just in time.

Looking cautious, Aidan stood in the doorway, holding a tray on which he'd assembled a feast: Cook's sweet Scottish scones, butter and cream, Sophia's favorite orange marmalade, some slices of apple, and a triangle of cheddar.

"I thought it was music that soothed the savage beast," she offered in half-conciliation. How could he, after all these years and her marriage to Tom, be so thoughtful of her needs?

"In your case, food has always worked best. But since Cook appears to be off for the afternoon, I had to make the tray myself," he offered with a shrug. "I hope it's acceptable. Dodsley will bring a pot of tea when it's hot. But of course, if you must go, I can return all this to the kitchen."

It was his acknowledgment that he couldn't stop her if she chose to leave that made all the difference. That, and the grumble in her stomach. "No, I can stay—at least for some tea." She made a space on the desk for the tray.

Setting the tray beside the proofs, he pulled a chair to the side of her desk and stretched his legs into the space beside her chair. "Now, tell me what's so important about these papers that you haven't time to see your plans for my garden come alive. Perhaps I can help."

"I can't imagine that you are interested in this."

"There's no way to know until you tell me, and you are clearly frustrated. Ian says you and Tom often worked alongside one another. I cannot replace Tom, but perhaps I can serve as a poor substitute."

The thought of Aidan's helping her was more appealing than she wished to admit, even in her most private moments.

"These are the printed proofs for volume two of Tom's last book." She pointed at the printed pages partially wrapped in the brown paper. "I was about to return them to the publisher with my corrections." She held her hand over a second stack of paper. "These are the pages of Tom's manuscript that he prepared for the printer and I delivered to his publisher. And this"—she placed her hand on the third set of pages—"is the bound *original* manuscript of Tom's book, the one we finished while in Italy and he copied out fair. Or at least I thought he'd copied it."

She explained it all to him, the perfect clarity of volume one, the odd errors in Latin in volume two. . . .

"And this." She reached for her reticule and removed the misidentified engraving. She unfolded it. "This isn't one of my illustrations."

"Looks deadly. What is it?"

"It's an agave, an American plant. Tom must have drawn it for the engraver, but he wasn't particularly careful, and this is an odd illustration."

"Why?"

"Well, it's just wrong for the book. Tom was writing on Mediterranean plants that would do well in an English garden, and so it's not even from the right part of the world. Even if it was, it's wrong as a botanical illustration."

Aidan raised an eyebrow in question.

"Let me explain. It ought to show the plant in its various states at once: seeds, fruit, flower. This is just the plant in flower. And the reference in the text to this plate is to a rose."

"Would Tom have made such a mistake?"

She shook her head in disbelief. "Only if his illness affected his memory more than I imagined. But then he died shortly after, so . . ." She shrugged. "I can't be sure. But the errors I've found in the proofs are all in his fair copy."

"You didn't make the fair copy?"

"No, Tom always copied the manuscript out himself. He joked that I could draw a fine line and sign my name with aplomb. But more than that, and my script turned into a messy scrawl worth neither the ink nor the paper."

"Did you use Tom's regular printer? Perhaps Tom's printer would have known what to do with these errors you are finding."

"Tom always used a subscription printer, a bear of a man named Holst. I always thought that Tom's books had a big enough market that he didn't need to publish them by subscription. And Holst was the only bookseller from whom one could order the books. I always insisted that the books needed a wider circulation than Holst could give. So when I returned to England, I contacted Murray, and he agreed with me. This time, at least twenty shops will sell Tom's book."

"Could it be that Holst would have known how to deal with these 'errors'?"

"What are you saying? That Tom added gibberish to his fair copy and added plates that make no sense, just so that the publisher had to take them out before printing it?"

"That's exactly what I'm saying. You say that Tom wasn't affected mentally by the illness."

"No, not even at the end."

"Then there's something else going on here. May I escort you to Mr. Holst's?" He held out his arm.

Despite knowing she might regret it later, she took his arm. But Holst wasn't in. In fact, his shop was closed up entirely. A sign in the window indicated he was on a provincial tour distributing books. He would return in a fortnight. Or a week after they left for Aidan's estate. But there was something here; Aidan could feel it. He might have just found the very information Walgrave needed.

Chapter Nineteen

It was the night of Phineas's dinner party; his guests would be arriving in only an hour.

Sophia and Aidan waited in the library for the Hucknalls and the Masons to arrive. She'd invited them to come earlier than the other guests. In part because their presence would give her courage for her first dinner party without Tom, but it also ensured that Phineas's guests would find ready conversation when they began to arrive. Ian was on his way to Kensington to visit Nate—he didn't like Phineas either.

Sophia's dress was the blue one Tom had made for her and Phineas had approved. Madame Elise had been unable to finish any of her dresses in time. Sally had taken special care with Sophia's hair. A halo of soft curls surrounded her face, and more curls were tied up with dark string around the beads she wore in her hair.

Aidan amused himself browsing through her books, picking up one, flipping through its pages, then turning to another. It was odd, really, for a man with a rich collection of his own to spend so much time examining her books. But, he was doing no harm, and due to his coming and going through the garden entrance, no one knew how much time he spent in her house.

Almost no one had refused her invitation. She wondered if that had more to do with the fact that the Duke of Forster had let it be known he would be in attendance or if Phineas really had so many friends. Either way it was the largest party she'd held in a very long time. For years in Italy, she'd hosted a salon, bringing together local Italians of good birth, representatives of the Austrian government, the occasional English travelers living in Naples, and every itinerant artist whose work she'd found intriguing. Tom had named their villa *il museo*, the home of muses. But with Tom's illness, the salon had proved too taxing, and she'd let it go. To find herself back in the role of hostess after so much time was daunting.

A tap at the door signaled Dodsley's presence. "My lady, the Masons and the Hucknalls have arrived." Ophelia and Audrey entered with arms intertwined, already laughing over some joke. Both women embraced Sophia, greeting her with kisses on both cheeks. Their husbands followed, debating a parliamentary vote to be held on the Bank of England's monetary practices. After kisses and handshakes, Sophia noticed that Dodsley remained.

"The modiste has sent round your dress for this evening, my lady. I've placed it in your dressing room. The seamstress is waiting in the kitchen if you need her."

"Thank you, Dodsley. As for the seamstress, let her go. I'm already dressed, and Phineas will prefer this gown."

Aidan intervened. "Sophia, why not look at the dress?"

Suddenly suspicious, she nodded assent to Dodsley.

Sophia didn't bother to close the door to her dressing room. She didn't intend to wear the dress, only to look at it.

It was lovely. The smoke-gray silk made half-mourning beautiful. The bodice was scooped from her shoulders to her décolletage with a narrow black-trim border, a design repeated in the black sash at her waist, and in the black border at the bottom of the skirt. Dark red vertical stripes, so narrow as to be imperceptible at more than a small distance, gave the fabric depth and richness.

But it wasn't one of the dresses she had ordered. Only Aidan could have convinced Madame Elise to ignore her requests and make this . . . this beautiful dress. Sophia let the fabric run through her fingers. So soft.

She held the dress up before the full-length mirror.

"You must wear it." Aidan spoke from the doorway.

"Why?" She hadn't realized he'd followed her.

"Because it's beautiful. Because it suits you."

"No, I meant why did you . . ."

"It seemed the right thing. Phineas forced you into having this party. No woman should have to reenter society in a gown her guests have already seen."

"There isn't time. I've sent the seamstress away, and Sally has left for Kensington with Ian and Mr. Grange."

"Knowing Elise, the dress will fit perfectly. But the seamstress is still here. I've called for her."

Shaking her head, Sophia looked at the dress once more. "Phineas will not approve. . . ."

"Phineas never approves. Accept it . . . as a gift to the mother of my ward. No one will ever know. Or if you prefer, Elise can send you the bill. But wear it."

She was torn. She hadn't had a dress so beautiful in years—not even Tom's cerulean blue one—but to accept such a dress as a gift . . . After the tryst in his garden, she should be wary of taking gifts, of suggesting he might think of her as a mistress. She was saved from deciding by the sound of Ophelia's and Audrey's voices.

"Forster, what are you doing at my sister's bedroom door?" Ophelia demanded with mock seriousness.

"It's her *dressing*-room door, sweet ladies. And you would both approve. Help me convince her to wear the dress her modiste has delivered." Aidan stepped aside to let Ophelia and Audrey see the dress.

"Oh, it's lovely. Of course you must wear it," Audrey exclaimed.

"Yes, there's no choice," Phee agreed.

"Come now. It won't take long. We'll help you into it." Audrey took the dress from Sophia's hands and laid it out gently over the ottoman.

"And you"—Ophelia turned back to Aidan as she shut the door in his face—"you go down to entertain any guests who arrive early."

The fire was low, but still burning when Sophia returned to her dressing room hours later. The house, which only an hour ago had rung with the sound of voices, was now quiet. Exhilarated by the conversation and the success of the party, even if it were not one she would have chosen to give, she had thought she would be too awake to sleep. But the moment the last guest had taken his leave, she found herself spent. Ophelia and Sidney had chosen to return to Kensington rather than spend the night, so she was alone.

The design of her dress made it simple to remove on her own: the black sash under the bodice covered a drawstring that tightened the dress to fit, and covered buttons secured the bodice in the back. She undid the buttons, then loosened the sash, and stepped from the dress. She laid it over the ottoman, smoothing out the fabric.

She couldn't remember the last time she'd worn a dress so lovely. Of course she would pay Elise for the gown. It was time to set a limit to Aidan's liberties.

As she changed into her nightdress, she thought of Aidan. All evening, aware of Phineas's watchful eye, she'd taken care not to look in Aidan's direction. But she could not be unaware of him, her ear always listening for his voice. A number of the guests had spoken highly of Tom, several claiming his friendship from Harrow. Phineas had increased the guest list, inviting a number of men whose names she did not know. One, a slender man with a thick raised scar across one hand, had told her a tender anecdote of Tom's school days that had brought tears to both their eyes. It had gratified her to hear Tom spoken of so well. She'd felt almost guilty to have Aidan present.

She covered the nightdress with her favorite Italian robe and picked up the book Mr. Murray had sent her that afternoon: George Crabbe's *Tales of the Hall,* out only a month.

Artemisia came howling, pushing open the door between the bedroom and the dressing room. The cat headed for the ottoman. "No, no, no, you don't. No walking on the beautiful dress." Sophia caught the old tortoise shell in her arms and turned her belly up to scratch her chest. "What has sent you from your balcony before breakfast? Is it raining again?" She looked to the window, but saw no rain. Odd. "Well, you and I are going to read before bed." Holding book and cat together, she entered the bedroom, kicking the door to the dressing room shut with her foot.

Inside her bedroom, she caught the fading notes of a cologne, not hers. She stiffened. The smell was too strong to have lingered from Ophelia or Audrey.

To be alone in the family suite now felt less like a luxury. She looked to the bell pull at the fireside. No, that's foolish, and what would she say? *Dodsley, would you mind checking under the bed for a monster?* Even if she pulled the bell, Dodsley wouldn't know to hurry.

The low fire illuminated the seating area in front of it. Two tall Queen Anne chairs fronted the fire, facing each other, both empty. She raised the wick of the oil lamps on the wall until they illuminated all the corners of the room.

The curtains on her bed were tied close to the posters; no one there. Nothing. Silly.

Murmuring to the cat, she carried Artemisia to the balcony. The door was open, as usual, but as she drew near, the hint of cologne strengthened. She drew away from the balcony, just as curtains moved.

Two hands caught her, one at the waist and the other over her mouth. She was pulled in against the intruder's body, dropping the cat, which ran under the bed.

She barely heard the rough whisper, "don't scream." She bit the man's hand and stomped with her ankle flexed back hard on the man's foot. He released her. She fell forward, running to the fireplace and grabbing the iron poker.

The intruder followed her. She turned, poker held high, ready to strike.

"Sophia, it's me." Aidan stepped back, hands extended in submission. "I didn't mean to startle you. I was waiting by the fire, but I heard your voice in the dressing room and thought your maid might be with you. So I hid."

Still holding the poker, she walked toward him, fear now turned to anger. Her hands shaking, and her breath ragged. She slapped him across the face, hard.

"I take it you didn't get my note?" Aidan rubbed his face where she'd hit him. "Could you put down the poker?"

"Note?" Glaring, she replaced the poker.

"On your dressing table. I told you I was waiting." He sounded sincerely apologetic.

Sophia was unmoved. "You left a note on my dressing table where any of the servants, or nosy guests for that matter, could find it, saying you were waiting in my bedroom? Are you mad?"

"I didn't say I was waiting in your bedroom." Aidan leaned on the edge of her bed, rubbing his foot with the hand she hadn't bitten. For a moment she thought he looked pleased.

"Then what did you do?" Sophia glared. "Write it in code?"

"In a way. I wrote 'what light through yonder window breaks.' I assumed you would fill in the rest. Or at least remember."

"I don't want to remember." But she did, without wanting to. Aidan's using bales of hay to convert the barn loft into a makeshift balcony, then reciting lines from her least favorite Shakespeare play, before he climbed the ladder to kiss her. "I always hated that play; star-crossed lovers, my foot. Just foolish children playing at being in love."

Aidan's eyes flashed. He crossed the room in only a few steps. Taking her shoulders in his hands, he pulled her against him and kissed her hard on the lips. She could taste his anger. "I was never playing, Sophia." He set her back away from him.

She retreated to the other side of one of the chairs in front of the fireplace, increasing the distance between them. She began to say something, but stopped. She touched her lips and breathed deeply, one long breath.

Aidan breathed the next breath with her. "I must apologize. I returned to tell you how beautiful you looked tonight, luminous. And to congratulate you on a deft handling of the conversation, particularly when Lord Craven joined Malcolm and Sidney's debate on the economic practices of the Bank of England, and the whole started to turn heated. But I arrived before the last of your guests left."

"So you hid in my bedroom." She was not mollified.

"Not intentionally . . . Well, yes, intentionally. I didn't wish for your guests to wonder why I'd returned." His voice had returned to the level calm she had grown to expect. "I thought this would be the room where I was least likely to be discovered. So, I wrote you the note, and I fell asleep before the fire. I only woke when I heard your voice. Will you forgive me?"

"How did you get here?"

He looked at the balcony.

"You didn't."

"It's a useful skill, you know."

"Tomorrow, I'm having that trellis taken down." She held her arm out and pointed to the window. "But you can use it tonight—to leave."

He took her hand, though she resisted, and placed it over his heart. "First let me accomplish the task I came for. You looked beautiful. Your handling of the guests was skillful. The meal exceptional. If Phineas doesn't thank you profusely, he's more of an ass than I would expect, even from him." He kissed her gently on the cheek and walked to the balcony. "Until the morrow, my lady." And he slipped over the edge.

She followed him out, listened as he climbed silently down, and watched him walk away in the darkness of the garden. After he had disappeared into the shadows, she returned to her dressing room.

She found the note—written on her own notepaper—exactly where he had said it would be.

Chapter Twenty

The following afternoon, Aidan walked through the garden to see that Sophia had more than kept her word. Perkins had trimmed the climbing rose, removed the trellis, and begun to dig a small pond at the base of her balcony.

He entered the library to find it filled with flowers. He groaned. He should have realized it would happen. A number of the male guests were bachelors or widowers, and Sophia was a young widow of means. Even had she not been beautiful in the dress, its gray and black calling into relief her dark hair and eyes, she would have had suitors. Her cool distance had warmed over the last weeks into a soft reserve. Any of the men of rank would have seen her as a fine match.

As for Aidan, he'd spent the evening making sure not to look at her, not to respond each time he heard her voice. Phineas was openly suspicious, and it didn't suit Aidan's purposes for Phineas to meddle. Aidan had left early to avert speculation, but he'd slipped back through the mews, hoping to capitalize on her success—and on Ian's absence—to begin their affair earlier than he'd promised.

Somehow he'd let the night, the nearness of her, the smell of her skin, all carry him away. But he was not a young man to be carried away by his passions. He could wait. For, in her room, angry and wielding a poker, Sophia had resembled the spirited woman of his youth, and he'd known that retreat would be his best strategy. But this new Sophia—certain of herself and her limits—was a woman worth seducing.

He picked up the stack of calling cards and began to sort through them, making two piles. No and maybe.

"Separating the sheep from the goats." Sophia looked over his shoulder as she walked past him, a vase of flowers in her hand. "That's thoughtful of you, but unnecessary."

"Unnecessary? Your remarriage would affect Ian. Therefore it's my obligation to offer my advice." Aidan felt unexpectedly provoked. He wanted her to have nothing to do with any of them, but could do nothing to stop her if she so wished. He held up the cards one after another, assessing their senders. "Blakey, inveterate gambler; Debenham, old enough to be your grandfather and opposed Wilberforce and the abolitionists; Ratchett . . ."

"Why don't you just focus on the ones who are acceptable? It's the smaller pile." Sophia seemed to be enjoying baiting him. She had placed the vase on a table near her easel and taken out some pieces of charcoal.

"By my count, six." He drew close to watch her pick out a piece of large paper, turn it to the unused side, and attach it to the easel.

"So many. Surprising. Tell me their names, nothing more." Her manner had changed in the last several days, more vibrant, less weary. It wasn't the success of her party last night, though that was part of it. At last she appeared at ease with him.

"Montmorency, Bentinck, Courcy, Desmond, Montalbert, and Sinclair."

"Excellent. Now if you could throw all the cards in the bin, I would be grateful. I intended to be away from home if any of them called, but I'll be especially careful to avoid those six." She began to sketch, long lines and short curves, looking to the vase and back to her paper.

"Whatever for? All have either substantial fortunes, or peerages, or talent, connections, ambition, education." He stepped to stand directly behind her. He resisted the urge to put his hands on her shoulders. The memory of last night's kiss was still too present in his mind.

"I have no intention of remarrying. Besides we'll be gone in less than a week; it would be silly to encourage any of them, only to have to correspond with them for months." The first of the flowers came clear in the lines of her drawing, then the next.

"Well, you'll have to remember that tonight when they crowd my box at the opera wanting to talk with you."

"Tonight?" She set down her pencil and looked over her shoulder at him. She looked longingly back at the still life, barely begun. "Ian is staying in Kensington until tomorrow with his cousins, and I thought to spend the evening here, painting."

"It's Kate's birthday; Ophelia and I discussed the outing last night, but you were busy with your guests. I picked up the remainder of your wardrobe this morning at Elise's, so you have no excuses. Your maid is putting the clothes away as we speak."

He watched her face transform with suspicion.

"Don't worry. These are the dresses *you* ordered. And Elise is sending you the bill. I just served as delivery man."

"Not a single party dress was ready yesterday, but today the whole wardrobe is done?"

"Odd, isn't it?" He ran his hand through his wavy dark hair and feigned innocence.

"More than odd." She held his eyes to emphasize her point. "But if it's likely to happen again, I will need to find a modiste more interested in my trade."

"I'm certain this was a special circumstance." It was neither an admission nor a promise, but it was a retreat of sorts.

Nodding knowingly, she turned back to her painting. "I didn't realize Kate liked the opera."

"If you must know, Ophelia suggested the new water drama at Sadler's Wells. I hastily proposed the opera instead." Aidan met her eyes and smiled, disarmingly. "You once confided that you wished to see the opera."

"Oh, but when we first got to Italy, we went many times," Sophia objected.

"But *I* have never taken you, and you have never been to the opera in London." His voice held a hint of sternness, then he lightened it. "Besides, you have grown too used to seclusion these past months, and after last night's success, you should celebrate with an evening out."

"Even so, what would Kate prefer for her birthday?" Sophia looked at the unfinished image with clear regret.

"Kate will enjoy being wherever her suitors can easily find her," Aidan reassured. "And as for your painting, I promise that when we arrive at my country house, I will set up a studio where you can paint all day if you wish." He watched her expression turn from disappointment to pleasure. He wanted to tempt her, to make her look on their trip with eager anticipation.

"Well, then, I suppose I cannot refuse."

"I'll pick you up in my carriage then. Three hours from now will allow us to slip into my box just late enough to avoid interference from your new beaux." He threw all the calling cards in the dustbin as he left.

Aidan's box had one of the better views of the stage. The first row was taken by Ophelia, Kate, and Ariel, who chattered excitedly and waved at their friends in other boxes until the music began. Sophia and Aidan were seated in the second row.

Their bodies concealed behind the three women, no one could see Aidan's subtle liberties. A leg that leaned against Sophia's gently, a hand lingering on hers as he handed her the program or the opera glasses. Had there not been the kiss in the garden, that exquisite moment of passion, even she might have believed him unmoved by her nearness, and she suddenly saw their last trip in a carriage in a new light. Had the passion been present all along—and not just on her side? Before she had steeled herself to ignore his touches, but now each glancing touch reminded her of his lips against hers; the touches kept her off-balance.

Before her marriage, she had imagined just such a night at the opera, the swell of the music surrounding them, feeling its rhythms echoed in her chest. But she'd never imagined she and Aidan would be sitting in a box together; no, she'd imagined being crowded into his side in the crush of the upper galleries. She closed her eyes, listened to the intricate harmonies of the singers. She felt the nearness of him, imagined she was once more a young girl in the first flush of love and he was the charming boy who had stolen her heart. Then, she let the present moment replace the past longed-for one. It might have been ten years too late, but in every other way, it was almost perfect.

At the intermission, all gracious good manners, he offered to retrieve lemonades for them all. Sophia accepted with a grateful smile, but Kate and Ariel had already identified another box they wished to visit. "We'll be back before the next act." And they—with Ophelia in tow—slipped out of the box, laughing and whispering behind their fans.

Aidan stood. Sophia watched her dream of him merge into the real man standing before her. "I'll be back shortly. But let me give you some privacy while I'm gone—or rather conceal you from all those suitors you insist you don't want." He smiled and drew the curtain partway.

As Sophia waited, she wondered what her life might have been like if she'd married Aidan instead of Tom. In the past weeks, Aidan had been considerate, kind, and often even charming, and in his garden . . . Even the memory made her flush.

But she often caught glimpses of another, harder man under his charming façade. Was the change in him the result of his experiences during the wars, or just the natural consequence of aging? If they had married, would he have retained more of his youthful good humor? Or would the strain of living on little money (for neither of them had fortunes) have evoked the same sternness she puzzled over now? Or would none of it have mattered? Was their character as adults somehow predetermined and not fully a creation of the events that had transpired to separate them?

She heard a footfall behind her and began to turn. But a gloved hand covered her mouth from behind, and an unknown person pulled her chair back into the darkest part of the box. She grabbed the arms of her chair to keep from falling, but before she could react, fight, or scream, she was stunned into silence by the glitter of the knife blade as it moved to her neck. With one hand on her mouth and the knife in the other, the man whispered.

"Lady Wilmot." The man's voice was cultured, English, and vaguely familiar. "If you scream or attempt to attract any notice, I will not hesitate to use this blade. Your friends will find you, blood ruining your precious dress, a gaping wound at your neck. Then your son will have no parents to care for him. If you agree to be still, place your hands in your lap."

Sophia slid her hands from the sides of the chair and clasped them together in her lap.

"Good. I'm going to move the knife to your back, so that no one grows suspicious if it glints in the light."

She watched the knife move out of the corner of her eye. The knife was old, a curved blade with swirls in the metal. She tried to remember its pattern in case she needed to recognize it later. The knife slipped from her view. She felt its point behind her heart.

"I'm going to release your mouth—I have some questions for you. But be assured: I'm an efficient killer. If you attempt to gain anyone's attention, you'll be dead before they understand you are in trouble." To emphasize his intention, he pushed the side of the blade into the skin across her backbone. He moved his hand from her mouth to her shoulder, his fingers holding her so tightly that they bit into the skin at the base of her neck.

"I had business with your husband. He died before that business was concluded. As a result, I have business with you. Your husband had some papers of mine. He was to send them to England for me, but those papers never arrived, and I was unable to find them in your villa in Naples."

Sophia stifled a gasp.

"Therefore, you must have brought them to England. You will return those papers to me, or . . ."

"I've gone through all my late husband's papers," she whispered. "There was nothing that belonged to anyone outside the family."

The knife pressed harder against her back.

"Let me explain it more clearly, Lady Wilmot. In the last week of his life, your husband entertained a man who brought him these papers."

"No one visited my husband the week before he died. He was too ill for guests," Sophia tried to explain.

"Your husband, my dear, had visitors even on the night of his death."

Sophia gasped again.

"Your husband was a spy, Lady Wilmot. He took sensitive materials and converted them into code, so that they would be secure to send by mail to England. But the code hasn't arrived, nor have I been able to find the papers themselves. I give you one week to find my papers and deliver them to me, or . . ."

"Or what?" she whispered.

"Let's just say that I find suitable punishments for those who anger me. Something that you'll regret losing till the day you die. Or I might kill you—though, I assure you, it would not be a simple death."

Sophia heard laughter in the hall, the sound of Aidan's voice. She tried not to react. But the man heard it as well.

"I must be going. Don't turn around until your friends return." He released her neck, but kept the blade of the knife at her back. "I'll send you a messenger at the end of the week with instructions for handing over the documents. And Lady Wilmot: tell no one."

Then the blade was gone. And the box was empty.

Sophia pressed her hand to her neck and felt the heavy thud of her pulse. She'd heard him leave, but she was afraid to move. Aidan would be here in a moment, then she would know her assailant was gone.

"Lemonade, my lady."

She breathed in deeply, then out. She was safe.

But Ian? She had to go home. Then she remembered: Ian was in Kensington with Nate. Not in London. Safe.

But she still had to leave.

She didn't answer when he offered the lemonade. He knew something had changed. He'd watched her face as she listened to the music, open, joyful, so like the young Sophia he had loved. He'd left her smiling, relaxed, finally comfortable with him.

Then, in the time he'd been gone, that woman had disappeared, replaced by a Sophia who was visibly disturbed and wary.

She stood to gather her reticule and shawl. "I need to go home."

"Did someone trouble you while I was gone?"

She looked startled. He'd hit on the truth.

"Which of your suitors was it? Sewell's a bounder and a rake; I saw him in the corridor earlier." Aidan kept his tone level, but his was a cold anger.

"None of them. It wasn't anyone I . . ." She remembered the whispered warning, how little time had passed between her assailant's leaving and Aidan's arrival. Her assailant might still be close, listening. "I . . . I'm not feeling well. Would you mind escorting me home?"

He knew that look, remembered another time when her voice had trembled in the same way, when she had turned up her chin just as bravely. Once again, he had to help, whether he wanted to or not.

"I'll call for my carriage." He turned to go.

"No! Let me go with you." She grabbed his arm. "I don't want to . . . explain to Phee or the girls why I'm leaving. They'd feel obligated to cut their evening short. I don't wish to ruin Kate's birthday."

"You don't want to take your leave of them?"

She shook her head no.

"All right then." He pulled her shawl over her head, veiling her face. "We've been seen together in my box, but with Phee and her sisters as chaperones. If people see me spiriting you away through the back of the theater, we'll start rumors. So we must be quick." He looked out of the box into the hall. Intermission had not yet ended. Most of the boxholders remained in the gallery taking refreshments. For another moment or two, the hall would be empty.

"Stay here." His box had easy access to the actor's quarters and the prop storage room. A long-ago mistress who'd sung in the chorus had given him a key, and he still kept it hidden in his box. He walked to the end of the hall, slipped the key into the lock, and felt the bolt turn. He returned.

"There's a door down the hall to your right. It's painted the same color as the wall. Walk in front of me, but quickly." Shielding her body from view, he hurried her to the end of the hall. He could hear voices approaching. The end of intermission had been called.

He opened the door, and they were through. The storage room was barely lit, only a lantern at the opposite end of the room and, below it, an outside door. He pulled the door tight behind them and relocked the latch. He stepped in front of her. "Let me lead. I know my way."

She said nothing. Nothing, when he took her hand and led her through the darkness, through the narrow space between the rows of costumes. Nothing, when, hearing a door open to their right, he pulled her tight against him out of the sight of the actor who picked up a prop, then left as he had come. Nothing, when finally at the outside door, he opened it and looked outside. Nothing, *until* he tried to leave her safe in the storage rooms to call for his carriage.

"My coachman always parks on a side street near the theater to avoid the crowds. I will get him. Wait here, but keep your face covered."

"No. I'll go with you."

"It's bad enough that I'm sneaking you out of the theater without telling Phee we're leaving. Or that I've taken you out of the public space into the isolation of a prop room. Now you want to walk through the dark into an alley to get in my carriage."

He stood facing her. In the dark he could hardly see her

face. She leaned her head against his chest. "Please." He smelled her hair, the hint of lavender. He wrapped her in his arms. She lifted her face. He touched her hair, her neck. She responded with ardor. Perhaps he had misinterpreted her distress in the box; perhaps she had simply decided on a night of passion.

But this wasn't the place for the seduction he had planned. Soon they would be at her house. He brushed his lips against her forehead. "Home first." He shielded her from view as he opened the doorway, then pulled her out behind him.

"Quickly."

The door opened into an alleyway near the back of the theater and into near complete darkness. Unless someone came upon them face-to-face, there was little chance of being recognized. The greater danger was of course his empty box and people's noticing that she had left with him. But the coach, his coachman, and a postboy were not far . . . just ahead.

At the coach, he handed her in, the only observers those of his household. With a word to the postboy and a coin to deliver a message to Ophelia, he returned to Sophia.

In the dim light of the coachman's lantern, he could see she was sitting as if she were looking out the window, into the darkness, but the curtain was drawn, and her hands twisted in the fringe of her shawl. He sat next to her and pulled her toward him, resting her back against his chest. He tapped the roof, and the carriage began to move.

Her hair was up, tied again with beads, but the curls felt soft against his cheek. No reason not to follow up the spontaneous kiss with a more measured pressing of his advantage. He brushed his lips against the side of her neck. She stiffened, but did not pull away. He blew softly against the back of her ear, breathed in the faint scent of lavender water from her hair. He kissed slowly a line from her ear to her shoulder, ran his hand from her shoulder to her hand, and let it rest there, her hand under his.

He kissed again, this time from her shoulder back to her ear, into her hair, savoring each step. As in the garden, it was as if his dream had merged in the darkness with the real Sophia. He felt the ache of desire as he had each time he'd dreamed of her for the past ten years.

When she tilted her head to let him reach her neck more easily, he moved his hand, not back up her arm, but across the center of her body, pulling her tighter against him, but stopping right below the line of her breasts. She did not resist. He whispered her name in her ear, and she leaned back farther into him. Only then did he move his hand, upward for a moment, then back down across her body, back to her hand.

Ian was in Kensington. There would be no reason not to stay. Given her passion in the garden and at the theater, her willing acceptance of his touch in the carriage, he found it difficult to believe she would say no.

Aidan opened the door to the library, then helped Sophia remove her cloak. He walked past her to the sherry on a table at the far end of the room. He poured two glasses, filling hers to slightly more than she normally drank. Once more pushing her limits . . . but he would have to be subtle. Even now he could see her stiffening in the light, the pliant Sophia transforming once more into a statue. He'd promised to give her time to decide, so he had to give her a reason to choose him, tonight.

He walked toward her, the hand with her drink outstretched. She took it from him, but didn't drink. She fingered the outside of the glass.

"Thank you for bringing me home. But I'm fine now, and you can go. I was just a bit overset." She walked away from him, holding the glass.

"I can't let this fine sherry go to waste." He stood, waiting for her to offer him a seat. But when she didn't, he sat on the edge of the desk near her. "Besides, something happened, and I will not leave until I know what. Who disturbed you in the box? I promise I won't call him out."

"I don't know." Still turned from him, she crossed her arms under her bust, as if comforting herself.

"You don't know?" Aidan willed himself to appear at ease. But he still felt in his body the tension from touching her in the carriage.

"I didn't know him, though his voice sounded familiar." She put her hand to her neck and rubbed behind her ear absently.

"Then what did he say to upset you?" Aidan took a long drink from his sherry and refilled the glass.

"I can't tell you." She turned to him, her eyes imploring, then looked away.

"Can't or won't?" He let the question hang, waiting on her answer.

She pressed her fingers against her temples. "He told me not to tell anyone what he said."

"Who do you trust more? A man who comes to your box and threatens you, or me?"

"When you frame it like that, I suppose I must choose to trust you." She smiled wanly. "The man said Tom had some papers that belonged to him, and he wanted them returned."

Aidan hadn't been prepared for that. He'd thought Sewell had imposed on her, upset her with licentious comments or an inappropriate kiss. And Aidan had been honest when he'd said he wouldn't call out whoever had upset her. Not when it had sent her into his arms. But this, this might lead to what Walgrave wanted. "Describe him."

"He came up behind me. I didn't see his face, only his gloves and the knife."

"Knife?" Aidan felt his temper spike. "He had a knife."

"Yes." She looked up, remembering. "It was long, curved, with a pattern in the metal."

Not a penknife, though those could still do sufficient damage, but a Damascus blade. Someone who was serious about his knives. A collector or an assassin. It was simply unbelievable. But to what purpose would she make up such a tale? No, her distress in the box had been real. Whatever Aidan's reservations, appearing to believe her was the better tack.

"Why didn't you tell me earlier? I might have been able to catch him." But even as Aidan said it, he knew it was unlikely, not in the press of the theater, and particularly not at intermission. But it would have been a way to test her story.

"I didn't think. I wanted to come home. And he didn't hurt me, just threatened to do so if I don't find what he wants. So go, please. I have imposed upon you enough, but I won't be able to sleep until I find whatever it is he wanted."

Sophia turned away from Aidan, dropping her fichu on the couch. Her dress scooped from shoulder to shoulder. At the base of her neck, Aidan saw the bruising imprint of fingers, and he saw a thin line of blood, now dried, across her backbone.

His heart went cold. "Sophia. Tell me the story from the beginning, trying not to leave out any details. That way, I'll know what we are looking for."

The library, the nursery, the study, and her bedroom. Sophia insisted those were the only places where Tom's things might be.

She'd answered Aidan's questions directly, and for the most part he believed her. She had been startled by the intruder into his box and afraid more for Ian than for herself. He even believed that she didn't know what exactly the intruder wanted her to find. But she'd hesitated when he'd asked if Tom had any secrets he should know. Now his job was to find them out . . . if not for her, then for the boy and the Home Office.

He'd gone along with her insistence to start in the library, though he'd searched most of it already. At the end of each shelf, he refilled her glass of sherry. At one point he had excused himself, claiming to visit the water closet, but instead he had slipped to the kitchen to retrieve Cook's jar of laudanum. The sherry had hidden the taste.

Then he waited for her to succumb to the aftermath of fear, liberal doses of alcohol, and a drop or two of laudanum. There was much to be done—and better done without her. He felt a twinge of guilt at drugging her unaware, something he rarely felt when working for the Home Office. But he forced himself to see it as a sort of kindness, allowing her to sleep heavily through a search that only would have distressed her further. He promised himself that he would make amends to her later in some way, even if she never realized what he had done.

While he waited, he searched the part of the library he hadn't yet examined. He missed nothing, feeling the binding of each book for irregularities, watching that the end papers were firmly glued down. He watched for odd marks that might indicate a key for a code. But without the coded documents themselves, what good was a key? Tom's marginalia revealed only an active mind arguing with an author.

Completing the last rank of shelves, he turned to find Sophia, still wearing her silk opera gown, folded asleep over a ledger.

He walked to her side and touched her hair. He let his fingers trace gently its sensuous curls, thinking of how one day soon, he would trail his fingers down each one of her limbs. Tucking one hand under her arm, he lifted her to her feet, cradling her head and shoulders against his side. He felt her resist. "Bed. You are overtired."

She shook her head, but didn't move out of his arms. "Not yet. Need to search."

"Whatever it is, you won't recognize it without rest. Come along. We'll begin again in the morning."

He led her through the lamplit hallway and up the stairs. The remains of a fire placed her bedroom in a seductive half-light.

The dress was elegant in its simplicity. And he'd spent much of his time at the theater imagining the most efficient way to take her out of it. This particular design relied on two long ribbons, each one beginning atop a shoulder, then crossing between her breasts below her bodice, and wrapping flat across her chest to her back, making a bow in the front and another in the back. Once the ribbons were undone, the whole fell to the floor, leaving her in only a shift. She wore no stays. He lifted her out of the puddle of silk and half-carried her to the bed. He was too aware of her body, thinly clad, pressed to his.

Her hair was, once more, sewed up in ringlets by beads on dark-colored threads. By the flickering light of the bedside lamp, he cut the threads with his penknife. Her hair fell over her face, and he brushed it back with his hand, allowing the soft ringlets to run through his fingers. His desire for her ran hot as it had all evening, but he tamped it down.

He pulled the covers over her, thankful for the dark that made it impossible to do more than imagine the press of the transparent chemise against her limbs. But his imagination was more than sufficient. He could imagine himself stretched naked above her, his chest covering hers, his thighs between her legs. He turned away.

In the morning he might have to face her anger or embarrassment when she realized who had undressed her and put her to bed, but until then, he had the run of her room and of the house.

He began with her dressing table. The only note was his,

quoting *Romeo and Juliet*. He was strangely satisfied to find no notes from lovers, but she also had no cards from friends either. Convenient, but sad.

She had no face paints, only a sweet-smelling soap in a dish next to the basin and a jar of lavender water. Her jewelry box held a few trinkets, none of any value. He wondered where she kept her jewels, then wondered if she had any jewels at all. He'd thought she had not worn jewels as a nod to Tom's death. Now he wondered if Tom had ever bothered to give her such gifts. He felt a mixture of jealousy and disdain. He had never left a mistress so unadorned.

At the bottom of the jewelry box was a long ribbon and a key at its end. What did the key open? He'd find the lock, then retrieve the key.

She had a small shelf of books in her bedroom. None likely Tom's, but he searched and found nothing. No love letters. No remembrances of Tom; all of those were in the library in the manuscript books. No treasured notes in Tom's hand, not even, Aidan realized, the letter that she had received from Tom invoking the guardianship. Proof she had a hiding place, and he'd already found the key.

He next made short work of the study. Everything was neatly arranged: old bills, all marked paid, in one pile, new bills waiting on the beginning of the quarter in another. The ledgers he'd already examined in the library.

Though he'd already spent time in the nursery, he searched there as well. The only papers were the illustrations from Tom's books Sophia had given to Ian for decorations. Aidan looked once more at the rose and the hummingbird, recalling Ian's glee when Aidan hadn't known why the image was wrong. Something niggled at the back of his memory, but wouldn't come clear, so he set it aside and continued searching.

Many of the books had inscriptions from Tom to Ian, "his dearest son," and snippets of advice for him as he grew. What sorrow it must have caused Tom to know his son would grow up without him, having only flyleaves of books and letters and portraits to keep Tom's memory alive to a boy not even ten? Aidan paused over one particularly loving passage. Whatever happened, he would not abandon Tom's son or let Tom's memory fade.

Aidan returned to Sophia's bedroom, picked up her dress—hopelessly wrinkled—and laid it over an ottoman. He returned the key on the ribbon, pressed it into his finger to remember its length and shape. It was a simple key; he might not even need it if he could find the lock.

From the balcony, he retrieved the cat and brought her into the house, then pulled the door to the balcony closed and locked it. From now on, Aidan would be spending his nights guarding the house. A man who would accost Sophia in an opera box with Aidan only footsteps away would think nothing of entering a darkened house with few servants. He took a quilt from the foot of Sophia's bed and carried it back to the library.

It was still dark outside; he had several hours to sleep before the house awoke. He made himself as comfortable as he could be on the chaise longue.

Tomorrow—he had already begun to think ahead—he would speak with Dodsley and Cook; he would send for men to guard Sophia's house; he would meet with Malcolm and Walgrave. He would find the lock that fit the key.

They would still leave town. Only the timing had changed.

Aidan awoke to the sound of the library door opening. Dodsley was placing mail on Sophia's side of the partner desk. Aidan realized he had never seen Sophia sit on what had been Tom's side. He would consider that later. For now he needed Dodsley as an ally in protecting Sophia. He sat up.

"Sir, I had not realized you were here." Dodsley's voice was impassive.

"I was hoping to speak with you privately. I need your help." Aidan rose.

"My loyalties, your grace, are with her ladyship." Dodsley assessed Aidan closely, noting his clothes, his tailcoat on the back of the chair, his boots in front of the couch near the fireplace.

"I was hoping that was the case." Aidan stepped to the hearth to retrieve his boots. "When did you begin service with the Wilmots?"

"I came in a sense with the house. Mr. Aldine purchased the property for her ladyship while she was still living in Italy."

"For her ladyship?" Aidan returned to the chaise and sat, boots in hand.

"Yes, your grace. As Mr. Aldine can tell you, the house is not part of his lordship's estates. It belongs to her ladyship outright. Her late husband and I corresponded to determine if our ideas of service would be complementary, and I chose to remain when my former employers removed to the country."

"You did not know her ladyship's late husband?" Aidan pulled on the right boot, then the left.

"No, his late lordship died abroad shortly after purchasing the house. I have always been in her ladyship's employ."

"Then, I'll be frank: her ladyship was threatened last night at the opera. We'll remove to my estate at the end of the week, but I'd like to keep a close eye on her until then."

"She will not like that. Her ladyship may appear compliant, but she follows her own mind."

Aidan wondered how many people knew Sophia as well as her butler. "That's why I need your help. I need to stay in the house without anyone—particularly her ladyship—finding out."

"Her ladyship sleeps too near the guest rooms for you to use one of them. But Luca's room was in the family quarters, close enough to hear if she calls out. It abuts the rear stairs, so it would be easy to come and go unobserved. I can have it prepared for you."

"Luca?"

"His lordship's secretary. He accompanied the Wilmots from Naples and remained here some months before returning to Italy."

Ah, the other handwriting in the accounts and on the guardianship papers.

"It's essential that the staff not reveal I'm staying here."

"The staff is fond of her ladyship and his lordship. No one will tell tales if they are in danger."

"I'd like to have more men about the house. They will be in my employ. Are there places to be filled?"

"Certainly, your grace. I can place one in the garden with Perkins; that would cover the yard. Another footman would serve for the front of the house. You have a groom already in the mews, but Cook would welcome an errand boy. That would cover the servants' entrance. Of course I will be watchful, as will Perkins and Cook."

"I'll send three to fit those jobs. They will arrive this afternoon."

"But her ladyship, sir, will she not notice the extra servants?"

"She will, but she won't object."

Chapter Twenty-One

Aidan spent the next several nights watching over Sophia and Ian, slipping into her house after dark, slipping out before dawn, changing clothes, and returning as if he had spent the night in his own bed. Sophia had accepted the additional servants on the argument that they were present to protect Ian. But, in the pit of Aidan's stomach, he knew she and Ian weren't safe.

At the same time, remembering their kisses in his garden and their caresses in the carriage, he wondered if she was safer with him *in* or *out* of the house. Those newer encounters merged with other memories, older ones, of limbs entwined, of hands and faces touching, of kisses down the line of her spine as she lay spent on the pallet he'd made for them in a forest clearing.

He imagined the ways her body would be different, after a child and a decade. He imagined the swell of her breasts, the flare of her hips, the planes of her stomach. It wouldn't matter: his body would still fit into hers. Having seen her again, he realized he'd been waiting, wanting at least one more chance to wrap his body around hers.

Over the years, he'd reduced his desire for her to sheer sensation, devoid of emotion. He'd wanted to possess her body once more, to reassert his youthful claim to her passion. He'd wished to feel her move beneath him, given over completely to him and to the pleasure he would bring her.

But at least until this danger was past, he reminded himself, he was obliged to guard her, to think only of her welfare. Protecting her from the threat of an unknown enemy seemed to only heighten his desire. He wanted her to be safe, even from himself.

A tray on Sophia's nightstand held a pile of letters. Resting against the bolster, she sorted through them quickly. Aidan had been right. Since the dinner party, she was on everyone's invitation list. Or at least everyone in Phineas's party, but she held little sympathy for their political views.

She wondered about Aidan's political views, but she couldn't discuss politics with him, not with the question of Tom's patriotism unanswered. Since the threats at the opera, she'd been reconsidering their years in Italy. Tom's visitors at odd hours, his insistence that the country was on the brink of revolution. At the time, she'd discounted it as a well-connected exile's interest in the political winds of his adopted country. She wished she'd known more. Had Tom really traded in secrets? And for whom? Tom wouldn't betray England. . . . She knew he wouldn't.

At the bottom of the pile was a small envelope, the address in Luca Bruni's hand. Luca had been inseparable from Tom, had accompanied him everywhere.

She broke the seal, unfolded the paper, and read. Luca had arrived two weeks after the funeral of his sister Francesca. Though his niece Liliana had expressed a stoic acceptance of her mother's death, Luca was unwilling to leave the six-year-old in a convent school, not with the political climate so unstable. He wished to return to London and bring his Liliana with him, to be educated there *sotto la sua tutela*.

Sophia read his commentary on the political situation in Naples differently than she would have done even a day ago. No, if Tom's actions had compromised Luca's position in Naples, she could not refuse his request to return. With Francesca dead, it was only right to give Liliana a home; Sophia would not consign the child to another's care.

Sotto la sua tutela . . . under your tutelage. Rearing a girl posed different problems than rearing a boy. With Ian, she had never had to make the choices her own parents—Oliver, an Oxford-trained clergyman, and Constance, daughter of an Oxford tutor—had faced in educating her. In their parishes her parents had seen the virtual enslavement of married women, unable to own property, without rights to their own income or even their children. The Elliots determined not to sacrifice their daughter on the altar of accomplishments. No, their Sophia—her name meaning wisdom—would be educated as if she were a boy.

In the village school where Sophia grew up, area boys and girls learned to do sums, to read, to write in a neat hand, and to understand geography, but only boys learned more. By the time she was nine, Sophia knew Latin and Greek grammar, geography and arithmetic, some algebra and geometry, and classical and English history. Proficient in botany, she could identify the plants in their village by their genus and species, and she could draw a plant in its habitat, matching its colors with remarkable skill. But it was a path that had isolated her, even from children of her own station.

If she were to rear Liliana, she would have to decide whose values she would pass along.

There would be difficulties. The Brunis' presence would be hard to explain to Phineas, perhaps even harder to Aidan. But if there were controversy or danger, she would face it. She was a widow of means; Tom had made sure of that.

Certainly, Tom had kept things from her—he would have claimed out of love. But she had let him. From the moment she had discovered she was increasing, she had deferred to Tom's judgment and allowed him to manage their lives. She had done so because she had believed she knew him, his character, his values, his ideals. And even when she disagreed with him—as with the guardianship—that faith in his good sense and affection had eased her mind. She had believed she knew all his secrets, but in the end, she hadn't. And now those secrets endangered them all.

No, she would not let another person determine what information she needed to know again. She would not trust her causes to another's good will. She would choose what battles she would fight and which she would set aside. She could make her own choices and live with their consequences.

She took out her notepaper and wrote two words: "come home." Enclosing a bank draft with more than adequate funds for passage for two, she folded the letter. But she hesitated before sealing it. Given Tom's activities, corresponding directly with Luca might not be wise.

She placed Luca's original communication and her unsealed response in another cover. Addressing it to Aldine, she asked him to review the correspondence, then send her response by the fastest, most secure route to Naples.

Chapter Twenty-Two

"Is he alone?" Aidan walked past Walgrave's butler.

"I can announce you, your grace."

Aidan watched a maid carry a silver tray from the servants' stairwell toward the back of the house. "No need; I can announce myself."

The butler made no attempt to stop him. He knew when to interfere and when to step aside.

As foul as Aidan's own mood was, he could tell that Walgrave's was fouler.

Walgrave sat at the table in his morning room, a coffee service beside him. A pile of government reports covered the table.

Walgrave growled when Aidan entered. "Did you know that half of the bank notes in the North are forged? That last year *alone* there were no less than 140 capital convictions for forgery? That last year more women were hung for forging and passing forged bank notes than were hung for murder?"

"You're on the secret committee, I take it." Aidan turned a chair backwards to face Walgrave.

"I wish someone would take it; it's a nightmare. More than a decade ago the Bank of England stopped paying its obligations in cash. Now every bank in the land issues

its own notes. The number of forgeries has risen . . . let me
see . . . 281 convictions since the suspension of cash payments. Before the suspension, only 3. This report here"—
Walgrave lifted a manuscript in front of him—"tallies the
number of individuals imprisoned simply for having forged
notes in their possession. Holding the notes, even if you
never spend them, is as much of a crime as forging them,
and the penalty just as deadly. And this one"—he pointed
to another manuscript—"recounts the newest fraud: a pair
of swindlers pretending to be bank examiners who steal true
notes by pretending they are forgeries. They duped our man-
agers at half a dozen banks before we realized their game.
The committee has to alleviate this evil, without, *without* I
say, simply reinstating cash payments."

"Then my news won't improve your morning." Aidan
leaned forward. "Apparently the Home Office is not alone in
believing Lady Wilmot possesses the missing documents."

Walgrave raised an eyebrow in question.

"A man threatened her at the opera."

"When?" Walgrave leaned back in his chair.

"Three nights ago."

"And you are just telling me?"

"I've been ensuring that she and her son are safe," Aidan
countered.

"Did you see the man?"

"Had I seen him, I would not be asking for your help."

"Of course. How has the search for the documents gone?"

"I've searched the house, including the servants' quarters.
Sophia mentioned she sent some trunks to Wilmot's estate,
so I'm thinking of traveling there on the way to my own
estate. I haven't found any list of names or any other sort of
document that might be state secrets, except . . ."

"Except?" Walgrave lifted his pencil to write a note.

"Someone should examine the fair copy to Wilmot's last
book. It's filled with odd nonsense phrases in Latin. They

may be nothing but the product of Wilmot's decline. But Lady Wilmot says his mind wasn't affected. There's also an engraved plate of some sort of cactus plant. If Wilmot converted the document he received into code, then the plant might be the cipher key, and the Latin phrases . . ."

"The code itself. Brilliant. Do you have a suggestion for how we should acquire the documents?"

"I have a print from the engraved plate here." He withdrew the picture of the agave from his pocket. "You might want to also retrieve Lady Wilmot's corrected proofs from John Murray's. In that copy she's marked all the phrases that aren't supposed to be in the book, making it easy to see which bits might be code."

"We'll have that done by morning."

"I think it best—given the threats—to take the Wilmots with me when I leave the city. I can protect them more easily at Greenwood Hall."

"Ah yes. You have gathered a small militia there."

"Just old soldiers with no other place to go."

"And completely loyal to you."

"As I am to them."

"It sounds like a reasonable plan. One we will support with whatever resources you need."

"I need a diversion, something to allow her to travel from Wilmot's country seat on to my estate, but leave everyone thinking she's still at her country home."

"We can do that—let us know when and where. Easier than stopping the flow of forged notes, at least." Walgrave turned back to his papers.

Aidan didn't mention the key on the ribbon or the fact that he hadn't had a chance to look for the hiding place it opened. Walgrave didn't need to know that, not yet at least.

* * *

Malcolm Hucknall watched from a comfortable chair as Aidan worked his way across the saloon in their club. A handshake here, a shared laugh there. Had he not been a duke, one would have thought Forster was canvasing for election to parliament. But Malcolm knew better: Aidan was on the hunt for information. Aidan took almost an hour to make his way to the shadows where Malcolm was most often to be found. Old habits die hard, and Bonaparte back in exile still had not ended the threats to England.

"Looking for something?" Malcolm held up his hand to order a drink for Aidan.

"You." Aidan pulled out the chair and seated himself.

"You could have found me over an hour ago." Malcolm nodded to the barmaid. "Or sent a note and met me at home."

"I needed to see who was in town."

"And?"

"Everyone I expected, and some I didn't."

Malcolm nodded. "Who is most interesting?"

"The ones who have returned from the Continent in the last year and remain in town: Ratchett, Debenham, Desmond, and Brice. All four were at Phineas's dinner at Lady Wilmot's. Three have attempted to call on her recently as old friends of her husband."

"Jealous?"

"That's not my motivation, old friend."

"Oh, dear. Whenever you call me 'old friend' I know something is dire, and I'm about to be conscripted. What have you done now, another duel for me to second? What brother, father, uncle, or husband have you offended? I thought you were out of harm's way spending so much time with Lady Wilmot." Malcolm grew silent. "Oh, God, you haven't, have you? Not Sophia? I noticed she appears less grave, but it's not because you've . . ."

Aidan cut him off. "There's no duel. And I'll have you

know I have never found myself in any woman's bed who didn't happily invite me to it."

"Are you saying that Sophia . . . that Sophia and you . . . You haven't taken advantage of her grief to get into her bed? That would be low even for you, Aidan."

"For the sake of our long friendship, I'll ignore that last, and no, Malcolm, I am not bedding your cousin. For God's sake, she's the mother of my ward."

"The fact that she's my cousin didn't stop you before." Malcolm concentrated on the liquid in his glass.

"You knew?" Aidan was stunned.

"I suspected, but I've never had the opportunity to broach the subject." Malcolm raised his glass in salute. "Nor have you ever given me the opportunity. You must be in deep, *old friend*, to have fallen for such a ploy."

"Damn, Malcolm. It was a youthful indiscretion, and she chose Tom." Somehow the conversation had gone awry.

"I've always wondered about that. If she were going to throw you over for someone else, why Tom? She wasn't in love with him." Malcolm swirled the bourbon in his glass. "No, something happened. Have you no curiosity?"

"What do you mean?" Aidan wasn't sure he wanted to hear Malcolm's observations, but he needed to know.

"You'd been gone less than a month, and Tom had gone on some business to the coast, leaving us cousins and your brothers in the country to run wild. Sophia was withdrawn and pale. I thought she was pining for you."

"What changed your mind? The wedding?" Aidan couldn't hold the resentment from his voice. Malcolm ignored it.

"I found her weeping in the chapel over a letter from Tom. I decided I must have been wrong about the two of you. Had I been five years older, I would have wondered what that letter said."

"You didn't ask?"

"I was young and uncomfortable with women's tears. Lately, however, I find my old questions returning."

"Well, set them aside—whatever they are. Lady Wilmot is in danger—as is my ward. I need your help. I haven't time to worry over misunderstandings a decade old."

"Unless those misunderstandings have some bearing on her troubles now. You owe it to yourself and the boy to ferret out what happened that summer. But what do you need?"

"Audrey mentioned that you are taking a tour of the Lakes."

"We leave in a week. We've leased a lodge near Keswick for a fortnight."

"Take Ian with you, and leave day after tomorrow. I'll pay any additional expenses, and I'll send several of my men from Greenwood Hall to stay near you." Aidan outlined the events of the previous week, the threat at the opera, and the continuing search for whatever the unknown assailant believed was hidden in the Wilmot household.

"That isn't the whole story."

"It's close to the whole story."

"Will anything I don't know endanger Audrey or the boys?"

"If I believed so, I wouldn't ask. I have a plan, but I need to know that Ian's safe to play it out. And there's one problem."

"No plan is ever easy with you."

"I need the trip to look like it's your idea. And I need you to exclude Sophia from the invitation."

"First you want me to protect the boy—which I will do, for Sophia's and Ian's sakes. But I have to mastermind the plan as well. If that's the case, I have to tell Audrey."

"Do you trust her to keep this a secret?"

"More than I trust you."

Aidan knew that Malcolm was only half joking.

Chapter Twenty-Three

Sophia had awoken with a desire to paint figures as she hadn't done in years. She'd begun a portrait of the bust of Boccaccio, but she'd grown dissatisfied. No, she wanted to sketch faces she knew: Ian, Dodsley, Cook, Sally, Luca, Mr. Grange . . . and Aidan. After making a rough sketch, she wanted to develop Aidan's portrait. Perhaps by doing so, she could reconcile the youth she had loved with the man he had become. Soon she would have to decide whether to accept Aidan's offer or refuse it. But if she found the courage to leap, could she survive when he left her again?

She uncovered her paints. On the prepared canvas, she blocked in the light and dark of his features in umber. She imagined his face: the lines on his forehead when he concentrated on a game with Ian; the way his left cheek dimpled when he smiled; the way a memory—perhaps of the wars—would pass over his face, leaving no soft lines. She mixed a range of flesh tones on her palette, each in its own puddle of color. She was about to add the first half-tone to his cheek and forehead when Aidan entered the library without introduction, his eyes dark, his manner controlled.

His voice was low, but tense. "I've received some disturbing news by rider."

News from outside London. News about Luca and Liliana would have come from the docks. Behind the easel, her hands unclenched.

"Someone broke into your country house and attacked Seth." His voice never wavered. "That's all I know."

Relief turned to concern. "But how do you know? I haven't received any news from the estate." She met him in the middle of the room.

"Colin was visiting Seth and sent a special messenger. How long will it take you and Ian to be ready to leave town? You will be gone some weeks."

"Within the hour."

"I will be back in an hour. I'll arrange for changes of horses along the way. We should be at your estate by tomorrow evening." He turned to leave, but she placed her hand on his arm.

"If you wish to go ahead, Ian and I can follow. On horseback, you could be there hours earlier."

Aidan's control slipped. "You do not understand, madam. You are not safe. You have been threatened. Your country home has been robbed; your estate manager attacked. Whatever your enemy is seeking, he has not found it. I cannot protect you and Ian here, but I can on my estate. Be ready."

He strode from the room.

Malcolm waited at the crossroads for the carriage carrying his family. As planned, Audrey's older son, Jack, rode slightly ahead. When he saw Malcolm, Jack signaled the coachman to stop.

It took only minutes for Malcolm to dismount and trade places with Toby in the carriage. Audrey's youngest—*his* youngest—was thrilled to be trusted with his stepfather's powerful bay. Malcolm settled into the coach, alone—even if only briefly—with his wife.

"It's kind of you to let Toby ride with Jack." Audrey curled into his side, his arm resting around her shoulders.

Malcolm pulled her even closer and nuzzled her hair. "It wasn't kindness, but the tantalizing memory of other carriage rides with my wife." He breathed her hair, the scent of spice, of exotic lands.

She laughed and kissed him deeply. "Yes, but on those rides we could pull the curtains. . . . Today"—Toby rode slightly ahead of the carriage windows—"we'd be questioned. And besides," she said, her tone turning matter-of-fact, "that's not why you chose to ride in the carriage instead of out."

"Ah, my wife." He still found the phrase delightful. "So perceptive."

"I don't need to be perceptive to know something is amiss."

"Do tell." He rested his legs on the opposite seat of the carriage, relaxing the muscles.

"Well, let's see." She brushed his blond hair with her hand. "Day before yesterday, we were to leave London in a week. Yesterday afternoon, we were to leave tomorrow, but with three boys, not just two. This morning, you send a note saying to be ready by noon. Then promptly at twelve, one of Aidan's luxurious carriages arrives to carry us away, driven by two coachmen who look as if they served in the Peninsular campaigns."

"It's Aidan's idea. We may as well travel in style." Malcolm nibbled her ear.

"What is Aidan's idea?"

"We're to take Ian far away and keep him safe, with the help of those coachmen who used to serve in His Majesty's infantry. Beyond that, I'm not sure. There might have been a plan before the attack on Seth, but now it's all an improvisation."

"What about Sophia?" Audrey offered, her green eyes filled with concern.

"Aidan will look after her."

"Getting Ian away isn't simply a ploy to get her alone?" She stared into his eyes, looking for the truth.

"He wants the boy safe. Besides, Aidan's not as scandalous as they say."

"You, darling, are not the one to judge who is scandalous." She smiled. "Besides, it's not his reputation. It's something about the way each one looks when the other is in the room."

"Not the way they look at each other?" Malcolm's expression turned pensive.

"No, they look anywhere *but* at one another. One could almost believe they despise each other . . . but the tone is wrong." Audrey closed her eyes as she rested her head on his shoulder.

"I'll have to watch more closely." Malcolm grew silent. Whatever obstacles he and Audrey had faced, they had overcome them. Would Aidan and Sophia find each other or pass each other by?

"How long will Ian be with us?" Audrey snuggled in closer to Malcolm's side.

"Until it's safe . . . or we tire of traveling." Malcolm kissed the top of her head.

"So, more than a fortnight."

"Perhaps. But we have carte blanche to enjoy ourselves; Aidan is paying the bills."

Sophia watched Aidan from the carriage window. His anger, fueled—she knew—by helplessness, made the confines of the carriage unbearable. Sophia had been grateful when they'd stopped to let Ian ride post with Fletcher, and Aidan had announced that he would ride. To keep watch, he'd said.

He'd always been an accomplished, even elegant, horseman. As a girl, she'd loved watching him. She'd admired his instinctive handling of a headstrong horse, his unconscious adjustments to its movements. But now, his skill had transformed to an enticing sensuality. She felt the pull even in her bones, reminding her of the strength of his embrace, the passion of his kisses.

But without knowing if Seth would be well, she could not spend the carriage ride considering Aidan's proposition. Instead, her memories turned to the first time she'd traveled this road: when as a ten-year-old orphan she'd gone to live with her uncle Lawrence and his wife Clara. For the first several years, when Clara was alive, their home had been a comforting refuge. In Clara's straightforward view, being educated *as* a boy was no different than being educated *with* boys. So, Sophia had learned everything Clara's boys did, from instruction in letters and science, to archery, fencing, and dancing. Clara had also taught Sophia practical things: how to plan a meal or remove a stain, how to make a poultice to cool a wound or fever. Recognizing Sophia's interest in botany, Clara had expanded it by introducing her to Annie, the local herbalist. "Now don't be afeared; I've known Annie since I was a girl, and she'd never harm a soul. And she knows what healing can come from plants like no one else."

Sophia still remembered the day Phineas, in whom none of their parents' radical ideas had taken root, had discovered Sophia's irregular education. She'd been reading Mrs. Inchbald's plays when she was summoned to her uncle's study.

When she had entered the study, book in hand, Phineas had looked smug and superior. "See, see there, reading without supervision. As a female, she hasn't the strength of character to resist identifying with wicked characters. Immoral reading leads to immoral actions." Phineas had turned to her. "Give the book to your uncle, Sophia."

She had quietly handed the book to her uncle. "Your

brother believes that by not supervising your reading materials, we are neglecting your moral character." The argument was a favorite of moralists like Dr. Gregory, whose best-selling book advising women to be silent in company had drawn the ire of Mrs. Wollstonecraft. Sophia, not knowing what words would be safe, had looked at her feet.

"Your brother wishes to approve the books you read." Her uncle read to her from Phineas's list. "Books on deportment by Mrs. Trimmer, devotional materials, novels by Maria Edgeworth, and plays by Hannah More. What do you think of this arrangement?"

Phineas smirked, knowing the trap he'd set. If she objected, she did not know how a proper woman behaved. If she didn't object, she could read only what he wished—if she read anything else, she would prove that she lacked moral character. She'd stood quietly, trying to imagine a way out, when Clara had placed her hand on her husband's arm. "Let the child be, Lawrence. It's right that Phineas be concerned for his sister's welfare, but we must abide by *your* brother's wishes in educating his daughter." Lawrence had nodded his agreement. Phineas's expression had changed from confident satisfaction to malice.

But when kindhearted Clara died of influenza and her uncle remarried, Sophia's new aunt, Annabella, disapproved of all but the most narrow education. Her governess Mrs. Lesley began to include in Sophia's lessons more feminine accomplishments: "We can't, my dear, give your brother anything to criticize." Mrs. Lesley had also retrieved from the library Phineas's various books on deportment and placed them prominently in the nursery bookshelves. Sophia learned French and how to embroider. But most of all she drew. She took what she'd learned about shape and color from her studies of plant forms with her father and added lessons on perspective from the Italian masters, identifying horizons and distance. In the manor gallery, she and Mrs. Lesley drew the portraits of her distant relatives. She began to paint, and in painting found solace. She and Mrs. Lesley would sketch or watercolor in the fields, capturing specific moments of light and color, then Sophia would return to the nursery and transform her sketches with texture and color until the scene was both nature's and hers.

Early in the marriage, her new aunt, pious like Phineas, had visited the nursery. "My husband has told me I'm not to interfere with my niece's education, but I do not approve of . . . of this." She waved her hand at the maps on the walls, the books of science on the shelves. "What was the girl reading when I came in? It wasn't French."

"No, madam; it was Greek. Her father wished her to know the language sufficiently to read the Holy Scriptures."

Annabella had demanded that Sophia read aloud again, this time translating into English. Sophia had looked at her book—Sophocles's *Antigone*—then recited a short passage from the Book of John on brotherly love. Mrs. Lesley had nodded at her performance. Her aunt had been mollified. But she demanded Sophia spend more time in the drawing room, reading books on deportment, acting as amanuensis for her aunt's letters, and embroidering.

In Annabella's view all artists were "degenerates and wastrels," and the only appropriate artistic expression for a girl was imitation. Sophia could watercolor engravings of pastoral landscape scenes or the scenes from Shakespeare Annabella had purchased at a printshop and had bound to illustrate her expurgated edition of the Bard. Some time later, Sophia had found a paper envelope addressed to her by her uncle and, inside it, the key to a tower folly built by her grandfather, far beyond Annabella's willingness to walk. There, she and Mrs. Lesley had hidden Sophia's paintings, paint pots, brushes, and paper. Within the year, Mrs. Lesley was gone, her aunt claiming the governess had found another position. But Sophia knew Mrs. Lesley would have at least said good-bye.

Sophia wiped away the wetness of tears from her cheeks.

No, given such sad memories of growing up near Tom's estate, only Seth's injury could have convinced Sophia to travel this road once more.

At Tom's manor house, they were met by the housekeeper and Audrey's two boys. Jack and Toby were not much older than Ian, close enough in age not to mind his presence, yet old enough that Ian idolized them. The boys were anxious to explore, but their mother had allowed them only the gardens. With Ian, they could search the crannies of the rambling house.

Sophia watched the boys disappear up the stairs, whispering conspiratorially. Aidan was right: Ian needed his own English community. Once she and Ian were safe, she would help Ian form those friendships as Tom had asked.

Seth's rooms were in the family wing. There he rested on a chaise wearing a long dressing gown over an untucked shirt and breeches, his head and arm bandaged, his eyes closed. Malcolm and Audrey were seated across from him in two upholstered armchairs, sipping glasses of Mountain. Malcolm rose to greet them.

Sophia hastened to Seth's side. "Why aren't you in bed, old friend?" Kneeling on the floor, she placed her hand on his forehead to check for fever.

Seth opened his eyes, his pupils large and unfocused. "The doctor said rest, not bed."

"He meant bed," she chastised.

"I'm near the bed." Seth shrugged and grimaced at the movement.

"Next time, let the thief steal whatever he pleases," Sophia chided. "You matter more than any object a thief could cart away."

Sophia's affection for her estate manager surprised and irritated Aidan. Seth had never indicated this depth of friendship in any of his conversations over the last decade. The sudden surge of jealousy took Aidan off guard.

"I intended to surprise the intruder, not be surprised," Seth offered.

"And that's supposed to mollify me?" Sophia brushed the blond hair from his eyes.

Seth smiled wanly. "It's the best I can do for now. I see you've brought my oaf of a brother."

Standing up, Sophia stepped out of the way.

Aidan dropped to one knee at Seth's side, his manner all tender solicitude. "Can you tell us what you remember?"

Malcolm interrupted. "I've already quizzed him mercilessly; he remembers little after leaving the lodge. Most of our details come from Colin."

"Ah, yes." Aidan looked around. "Where is my brother?"

"After we arrived, he rode out to escort Judith the rest of the way here," Malcolm explained. "She arrives day after next to cart Seth away."

Audrey caressed Malcolm's arm absently. "We've decided to accompany Judith home. Her manor is on our way to the Lakes."

"I begged them to come." Seth groaned. "I need protection from Judith's tender mercies."

"Judith isn't as forbidding as you boys make her out to be," Sophia objected.

"Ah, but you aren't her sibling," Aidan countered. "Like her Biblical namesake, Judith has always been judge, jury, and executioner when it comes to us boys."

Audrey hid a yawn. "It always surprises me that such powerful men can be cowed by a woman as tiny as Judith."

"You didn't grow up with her. Judith makes Wellington quake. I've seen it." Seth groaned.

"Judith is exactly what you boys made her be," Audrey observed.

"Actually"—Malcolm smiled—"Judith likely kept the whole lot of Somervilles—as well as me and Tom—from growing up milquetoasts or dandies."

Sophia pulled a chair to the chaise behind Seth's head and sat with her hand on his shoulder. "Tom thought Judith felt obligated to counter Aaron's influence."

Aidan was spared acknowledging Tom's perhaps too apt observation by Audrey's half-whisper. "He's asleep again. Should we move him to the bed?"

"No, let's leave him be. I'll stay with him until morning," Aidan said. "It's been a long day. I'm sure you wish to retire."

Malcolm nodded. "I'll remain here a while as well."

The two women rose to retire. Audrey took Sophia's arm. "I thought we would visit the nursery to see that the boys are in their rooms. Then I can show you the rooms the house-keeper prepared for you." Sophia agreed, and the two women took their leave together.

At the nursery, Sophia and Audrey found the bed from Ian's room dismantled and moved into his step-cousins' room. Audrey's boys had been describing the route of their trip, from investigating Roman ruins near Windermere, to fishing and sailing on Derwentwater, and climbing Helvellyn, as well as a dozen other plans. At some point, they had determined it would be more fun if Ian could come along. Sophia and Audrey had barely crossed the threshold when they were greeted by three boys begging for Ian to accompany them.

"Please, Mama, may I go?" Ian's face was radiant. "I've never been to the Lakes."

Sophia knew that she would not be able to refuse him, not if she meant to help him forge friendships. But so soon?

Her only hope was that Audrey would not wish to manage another child.

"Boys, boys." Audrey calmed her sons. "Lady Wilmot and I must discuss this privately. We will let you know our decision in the morning." But as soon as she and Sophia stepped into the hall and shut the door, Audrey smiled broadly. "I intended to offer just such a plan. Our boys get along famously, and, having a third boy along will ensure that my two quarrel less. Besides"—she drew close, dropping her voice to a whisper—"it might be safer for Ian if he were far away right now. Malcolm mentioned the threats at the opera. We would have my boys, Malcolm and me, and Aidan's sturdy coachman, all keeping watch."

Sophia thought of the house, silent and empty without Ian, then of the knife glinting in the opera box, and she agreed.

Aidan watched Sophia leave, arm in arm with Audrey. Now that he'd seen that Seth's color was good and that he could speak in clear sentences, Aidan could relax somewhat. Judith would take over Seth's care; no one dared die when Judith was in charge. Ian would travel to the Lakes with Malcolm's family, and there, far from the danger that threatened in London, Malcolm's and Aidan's men would keep him safe. Having fulfilled his obligation to his ward, Aidan would focus on Sophia, protecting her, but also exploring the passion that flared between them.

"I'm still of the mind that you have a chance to set things right," Malcolm said.

It took Aidan a moment to realize Malcolm was talking. "Why do you think things need setting right?" Aidan quizzed, trying to determine what he had missed.

"I don't know what happened between you. I don't know why she married Tom," Malcolm mused. "But your rooms adjoin. Don't waste this chance."

"At my club, you were appalled that I might have seduced your cousin. Today, you invite me to her bed." Aidan thought the best solution was to admit nothing. "I find myself confused."

"I've been thinking of my own life . . . how Audrey and I almost let each other go. Both of us so hardheaded we thought we were being rational and even noble to ignore our hearts. In the wars, Aidan, we learned to ignore our feelings, to focus on what we could control. That might be the way to survive battles, but it's not the way to live." Malcolm drank more wine. "You loved each other once—I'm certain of it—so, if you can find even a moment's happiness with Sophia, you should pluck that moment as if it were a piece of fruit, and squeeze out every drop of juice, taste every piece of pulp, leaving nothing behind."

"When did my rational old friend become so dreadfully sentimental?" Aidan grumbled.

"When I saw Audrey, blood staining her ball gown, collapse on the parquet floor of Lady Sheppard's ballroom."

Aidan's stomach twisted at the thought of Sophia wounded. "Sophia will be guarded every moment, of that you can be certain. I will let no harm come to her."

"I had a dozen men in that ballroom, and I couldn't protect Audrey," Malcolm chided. "Don't let this chance slip away; it might be your last opportunity to make things right."

Aidan nodded as if in agreement, and Malcolm fell silent. Soon, both men were asleep in their chairs.

Chapter Twenty-Four

The problem with sending Ian to the Lakes was one of logistics, and Malcolm and Aidan worked out the details over breakfast. If Sophia and Ian were being watched, then they had to obscure when Ian had left, with whom, and for what destination. Eventually it would become clear that Ian was no longer with Sophia, but if their plan were successful, it would be difficult—and thus counterproductive—to pursue the boy. Keeping Sophia primary in the blackmailer's attention was dangerous, but essential.

The plan wasn't foolproof. But Sophia had trusted Malcolm from her girlhood, so when he'd taken her hands and promised that he would keep Ian safe, she could not say no. In their youth, Malcolm had been her ally against Phineas, the steady one among her run-wild cousins. She'd been his first friend in England when his mother, the youngest Elliot sibling, had sent him home from Lexington, Kentucky, to be educated with his cousins at Harrow. Sophia had been pleased when he found Audrey, a woman of spirit and conviction but a tender heart.

Until Judith arrived and the company scattered, what mattered was keeping everyone within view. The boys were allowed free run of the house, but outside, they had to be accompanied by one of Forster's men. Both of Audrey's boys—Jack and Toby—were responsible and observant. Ian would be well watched.

The others spent their time entertaining Seth with gossip from balls and gambling rooms, descriptions of the latest routs, and tidbits from their club and Tattersalls. Sophia was surprised once more at how small the *ton* was and how far (and how quickly) news carried. If she were to become Aidan's lover, she could only do so in the country.

Late in the evening, when the boys were safely tucked into the nursery, terrifying themselves with ghost stories, the adults played faro, then whist, at a table near Seth's bed. Audrey beat them all, to Aidan's and Seth's open dismay, and Malcolm's and Sophia's amusement.

The next morning, Judith arrived promptly at ten. Seth was bundled into the carriage by eleven with Colin and Judith at his side. By half-past eleven, Judith's carriage was on its way home.

Half an hour later, Ian took a sad farewell of his cousins on the front porch of the house, while the Hucknalls waited for their carriage to be pulled round. Anyone watching would have seen the boy appear to argue with his mother, then run angrily into the house. A few moments later, the carriage pulled up, and Malcolm, Audrey, and their two boys left, heading as if back to London.

Stopping in the village for ribbon, Audrey left the carriage door open wide. Anyone walking past could see that no one traveled with the Hucknalls but their own two sons. Ian, thinking it was a fabulous game in which he would surprise his cousins after an hour on the road, remained hidden in a false seat compartment until the Wilmot estate and its village were far behind.

Then the carriage turned north to Judith's estate and the Lakes beyond.

* * *

Sophia had watched the carriages until they disappeared into the distance. Her uncle had sent a note inviting her to dinner, and, without the excuse of Seth's injury, she'd been obligated to accept for her and Aidan. It would delay her decision by another evening: would she act on the passion that increasingly flared hot between them?

The housekeeper had prepared a tour of the house, kitchens, and pantries, and though Sophia would have preferred to retreat to her rooms, she knew it would disappoint the staff not to observe the expected rituals.

Her obligations were fulfilled late in the afternoon, leaving hours before she would have to dress for dinner. Aidan had offered to walk with her in the gardens. But she had asked the housekeeper to offer her regrets, claiming she needed to lie down. Instead, she went to the attics above the nursery.

From Italy, Sophia had sent their books and papers to London, finding those items more of a comfort than a sad remembrance. But she'd sent five trunks—what was left of Tom's things—directly to the estate, to preserve them for Ian who would someday want reminders of his father. She had never intended to unpack those trunks herself, and she certainly didn't want Aidan watching when she did.

The housekeeper had indicated the trunks were in the central attic space. She began with the one trunk of Tom's clothes she had kept for Ian. As she lifted its lid, Tom's scent—sandalwood—rose from the tweed jacket lying on top. She held it up and pressed it to her face. Soon it grew wet with her tears.

When Sophia pleaded a headache, Aidan wondered what she intended to do without him. Over the past weeks he'd come to believe two things: that she didn't know anything about the papers they were seeking, and that she was hiding something else, perhaps equally dangerous. Whatever it was, he wanted to know all her secrets. He'd reported the first to Walgrave and the Home Office, and he'd taken steps to address the second. He rarely left her alone, and when he did, one of his footmen reported on her actions. Within minutes, he learned that her ladyship had asked her maid, the housekeeper's daughter, to help her change into clothes suitable for the attic.

He arrived at the top of the stairs as she opened one of the trunks. She lifted a jacket—clearly Tom's—from the trunk and placed it in her lap. From his vantage point, he could see her hand caress it softly, her finger trace the line of the patterned material. Then she'd pressed it to her chest like a well-loved child and buried her face in it.

Suddenly Aidan realized that he and Malcolm had been wrong. She *had* loved Tom. The knowledge felt like a blow to his gut. It had been easier to believe her a fortune hunter who had cared little for her husband. Over the years Aidan had decided that their passion had been only a physical pleasure, not a joining of two hearts—something Sophia easily set aside for wealth and a title. Sophia's choices, he had convinced himself, were made out of heartless self-interest.

But this, *this* was evidence of love. For all these weeks, she had been so self-possessed, so contained and elegant, but when she'd held Tom's jacket, Aidan glimpsed what he hadn't wanted to see. Under her self-possession was a woman uncertain, clearly still affected by the loss of her husband. He'd seen the same stance in others, women whose husbands had served in his regiment and whom he'd notified of their deaths. He should have seen the similarity sooner; Sophia would not be one who heard of her loss with public sobs and hysterics. No, she would be the one whose façade never faltered, whose eyes might glisten momentarily with tears, who would see the bearer of the bad news politely to the door, then lean up against it and weep.

He coughed, pretending to clear his throat.

"How long have you been there?" Sophia stood, wiping her hands on her apron.

"Only just arrived." He looked around as if counting the trunks. "Do you have all these to go through? May I help or would you prefer to face them alone?"

She shrugged. How was it that when he was away she wished him to stay away, and when he was with her, she wished him never to leave? "Five isn't so many. For the most part, I packed like items together: books with books, papers with papers. These trunks held things we wouldn't need. Those two"—she pointed to the back of the room—"were shipped at least a month before Tom's death, so it depends on when he got the papers. We could leave those till last."

She pointed to a smaller wooden trunk. "That one should have nothing in it but mementos . . . reminders of Ian's childhood. Things I couldn't bear to discard."

She pointed to the two larger wooden trunks beside her. "These two hold Tom's things. This blue one I made for Ian, things to remind him of his father. That red one—well, truthfully, I don't know what's in it. After Tom died, Luca put everything remaining of Tom's there."

Aidan recognized the red trunk: the one Tom had brought with him to Harrow and later to Cambridge; it had a false bottom. "I'll take the red, while you finish the blue?" Aidan found a stool and sat before the trunk. "To make sure we don't miss anything, let's take everything out, examine the trunk itself, then put everything back."

Sophia began emptying her trunk. The first layer yielded clothes, Tom's court dress, gloves, a pair of glasses. For a minute Aidan was mesmerized by the movement of her long slender fingers as she checked each pocket, felt every lining.

He turned to his own trunk and angled it so as to watch

her movements and conceal his own. He lifted the lid. On top was a delicately knitted blanket—likely a child's—and Aidan wondered why it wasn't with Ian's things. He set it aside and caught a hint of bergamot. Underneath were the sorts of things Tom would have traveled with: a portable writing desk, a case filled (still) with toiletries, a razor, tooth powder, various unguents mostly dried, several notebooks with soft leather covers tied shut with leather straps—Coptic bindings, Tom had always called them. All dated to the early years of Tom and Sophia's marriage. Aidan set them aside to review later.

"Tell me, who is Luca?" To open the hidden space, he needed to distract her.

"Tom's secretary in Naples and mine here for a time." She uncovered toy animals Tom had carved from scraps of wood.

"Tom's secretary?" Aidan felt along the edges for the latch. "Was he with you long?"

"Almost from the day we arrived. When he was eight, he climbed a tree next to our garden wall to watch Tom work with his plants. Tom never ran him off. He said Luca reminded him of you as a boy, always watching from some vantage point."

"I was likely stealing apples. Tell me more."

Telling stories made the work easier. The next layer contained penknives, a wooden flute, and botany notebooks all in Tom's hand. Sophia flipped through the pages of each one, holding them upside down to let anything placed between the pages fall free. "Tom and the child struck up a friendship. Luca was fascinated with plants, and Tom found him a kindred spirit. He was of gentle birth, but impoverished, and Tom hired him as his assistant."

"Assistant?"

"Tom claimed that any young boy who would watch him so intently for days on end had ability. Tom paid him exorbitantly. But his wages helped his remaining family, a sister, survive."

"Where is Luca now?"

"He returned to Italy some weeks ago. His sister, who had remained at our villa, died, and her daughter, Liliana, was left with the remaining staff."

"Left at your villa? The child had no other relatives?"

"Other than Luca? Yes, but . . . He and Liliana would live with us, if he wishes to return. Perhaps he will stay there, maintain the property, oversee the gardens. He's very capable."

Aidan felt the indentation where he knew the board would release. In their youth, he had opened it in seconds. He coughed again to cover the click of the spring.

Sophia looked up with concern.

"It's nothing; just a bit of dust."

"I'm almost to the bottom. . . . Just a minute and I'll come help you."

Aidan felt in the space . . . paper . . . He pulled it out. A small packet of letters all in Italian, several in Tom's hand. From the dates, all were too old to be the papers they sought. He slid the packet into a pocket inside his waistcoat, hiding his motion by picking up the child's blanket. He pushed the board back in place as he coughed again. She was already standing to come help him.

"Perhaps this should go in the box of Ian's things?" He held out the blanket.

Her reaction was unexpected, a look of pain that disappeared in an instant. "No, it's not a child's blanket. It was Tom's—to keep out the chill of the evening. Luca's sister Francesca made it for him." She turned her face away.

Without thinking, Aidan rose, took her in his arms, pressed her to his chest, caressed her hair. He meant only to comfort her, but his feelings had grown too complicated, even confusing. She might have loved Tom, but Aidan could still evoke her passion. He'd proved that already. Today he wanted more; he wanted all of her. He wanted to remind her that though Tom had been her husband, her first kisses had been with him. No, whether it was jealousy or renewed affection, he wanted her to remember everything they had been to one another.

He lifted her chin and kissed her lips lightly. He looked for some reaction, but she had closed her eyes. So he pressed his lips against hers more firmly, more insistently, the need for her that he had been suppressing swelling between them. He felt her body arch into his, as she stood on her toes, her breasts pressing against his chest.

He pushed back the scarf in her hair, nuzzled her ear, then kissed her neck.

Sophia had not expected him to embrace her. From the look of sympathy on his face, she had thought he intended only comfort. But she found herself remembering his kiss at the opera, his touches in the carriage. These present moments merged more and more with their past passion. Renewed grief made her reckless.

She turned her head to let him kiss her neck more easily. She wound her arms around him, one caressed the back of his neck, the other pulled him closer at the waist. He took advantage of her willingness, pressing his lips more insistently against hers, touching her lightly with his tongue, tasting the honey of her lips, and feeling the softness of her skin, until she opened her mouth to him. He kissed her lightly, then, teasing her mouth with the tip of his tongue, he explored that space that had been denied to him for too long. He longed to evoke the same open passion that he had found when he'd kissed her as a young woman, but still she held back. He increased his fervor.

Suddenly she gave in to her passion, let her tongue follow his, allowing him to touch the depths of her mouth. He felt her hands move against his back. He let his hand move to the side of her chest to caress its edge. When she gave no objection, he moved his hand more centrally, exciting her passion so that she would not refuse him.

He wanted to draw her body more closely against his, to feel her pressed fully against the length of his frame.

"Sophia." He whispered her name as a caress. "Let me love you. Pretend we never parted, that there is nothing in the world but the two of us."

Sophia's eyes, dark with passion, searched his face, looking for some help in deciding. He pulled her tighter against his body, pressed his arousal against the plain of her belly. He moved his hand to cover her breast. He whispered into her neck below her ear. "I want you"—he punctuated his words with kisses—"want you as I have wanted no other woman." He sucked her earlobe as he caressed her breast. He felt her body begin to rock against him, but he held himself in check. He laved a line of slow kisses from her ear to her shoulder and back. "I want to give you pleasure, pleasure as I gave you in my garden." He moved to kiss her mouth, and she responded with ardor, mouth open, welcoming him.

Sitting on one of the closed trunks, he pulled her into his lap, never stopping the pressure and pull on her breast, the kisses on her neck and mouth. He leaned her against his chest, leaning her into the curve of his arm and freeing the other to slide up her leg slowly, past her ankle, her knee, squeezing the swell of her thigh. He felt for the slit in her drawers and slid his fingers between the fabric to press against her flesh. She gasped and tightened her embrace, hungry for his touch.

"Tell me you'll be my lover." He stopped caressing. She moaned in objection, but he refused to continue. "Tell me. We will not have misunderstandings between us . . . at least not about this."

She opened her eyes and met his.

"I will be your lover." Then realizing where they sat, she pulled out of his arms and stood. "But not here. Not surrounded by . . ."

He rose and kissed her thoroughly, not allowing her to remember any more. He took her hand and led her down the stairs, stopping at the foot of the stairs to press her against the wall and kiss her deeply, to press his body against the cleft of hers. He wanted to keep her desire hot.

He kissed a line from her neck to her décolletage then to her breast, kissing her through the fabric of her gown. "I will meet you at your room."

He set her back from him. She nodded her agreement; taking his hand, she pressed his palm to her lips. Then she turned away, still holding his hand. Their fingertips parted last.

In her room, she stood at the foot of her bed, uncertain how to proceed. Should she wait for him naked in the bed or allow him to undress her? She couldn't imagine how to go about taking any man to her bed, much less Aidan. Her body still ached for him, but she had begun to feel foolish. She wanted him. But was wanting him wise?

She heard a tap at the door, and she was surprised that he didn't simply enter. It would attract less attention. But no matter.

She considered lowering her blouse to reveal her décolletage, but she reconsidered. She had never been a wanton, and she wasn't sure she could play the role successfully now. She opened the door wide.

The housekeeper's daughter waited with a tea tray. "My mother thought you might like a bit of tea." Seeing the door opened wide as an invitation, she walked past to set the tray on the table. "Do you wish to have your bath drawn soon?"

Sophia looked to the clock on the mantel, surprised at the time. "Yes, please. Will you bring a tub to the room?"

The maid left. Sophia shut the door in time to see Aidan entering the room from the adjoining bedroom. She had assumed the adjoining room was empty, but had neglected to ask the housekeeper the arrangement of the guests. He had heard the conversation.

"I suppose it's good that I didn't arrive in my dressing gown."

"I didn't realize how long we had been in the attic." She lifted her palms apologetically.

He walked to her and placed a kiss on her forehead. "Neither did I. But there is time. Now that we have agreed to become lovers, there is time."

Chapter Twenty-Five

Sophia had originally chosen a sober dress for dinner, one that would garner no attention and no criticism from her aunt. But after her breathless encounter with Aidan in the attic, she wished to be beautiful, or at least to wear a beautiful dress. At Elise's shop she'd been entranced by a moss-green silk—an earthy hue, almost colorless, except when caught by the light. The silk was patterned in narrow vertical columns: delicate grape vines, with stylized leaves and dots of fruit, alternated with pale, almost ivory, columns whose texture resembled basket weave. The pattern had reminded her of Italian vineyards, the Neapolitan air tinged with spice, her gardens alive with color. But she'd seen no dress in Elise's pattern books that suited the material. She'd almost set the bolt aside when Elise had joined her. "I could only find just enough, *ma cherie,* for a single dress. Most women do not see how lovely it is, so subtle, so I do not sell it. But you, you can see, no?" Sophia had nodded. Elise had promised it would be Sophia's favorite dress.

The dress's only ornamentation was a repeating pattern of triangular points, in two rows at the base of the skirt, the first beginning slightly below her knees. A third row of points ran across her back, mirroring the deep curve of the neckline in front, all edged in a deep burgundy-velvet rickrack. It reminded Sophia of the points on a harlequin's costume, an unexpected and delightful detail, quiet in its execution.

For Sophia's hair, Elise had provided wide ribbon in the same deep burgundy. The maid tied it in bands, one near Sophia's forehead behind the curls around her face, and the second farther back, allowing her hair to trail in long curls down her back.

But, disappointingly, Aidan was not yet in the entry when she arrived, and the footman had already helped her into her cloak by the time he appeared. In the carriage they had sat apart, saying little, only their hands touching. But their promise lay between them.

The party was small, just herself and Aidan, her uncle and his wife and their children, Elizabeth and Frederick. Her aunt had offered a family dinner, and Sophia quickly realized why. Annabella hadn't wanted any competition in making a match between her daughter and "the Duke." To think that Sophia had been worried that Annabella might be suspicious of her relationship with Aidan.

To seat Elizabeth across from Aidan, where he could appreciate "her clear skin and perfect manners," Annabella had been obliged to leave Sophia at his side.

"Your grace, isn't the pale yellow of Elizabeth's dress becoming against the green of her eyes?" Annabella paused behind her daughter's chair, placing her hands on the girl's shoulders. Sophia saw her step-cousin blush at her mother's narration.

When Aidan smiled blandly, Annabella moved to her own seat. "She will be offering us some entertainment after dinner: she can play the harp and sing so to make your heart break." Annabella nodded to the servants to begin the meal.

"Elizabeth will be taking her season next year, but of

course if we could find her a suitable match before that we would be quite happy. . . ." Annabella looked with anticipation for an acknowledgment from Aidan, but received none. "I would hope you would promise to dance with her in London." She lowered her voice to a stage whisper. "She's a good girl, knows everything that's important for a woman to know."

Aidan nodded.

"Of course, that wasn't the case with my niece here." Annabella leaned back to allow the footman to fill her wine. "No, it always surprised me how well Sophia married. But I take some credit there."

Sophia almost choked on her fish.

"She wasn't much interested in marriage, you know." Annabella motioned to the servants to wait on the table, all without slowing in her conversation. "And her mother had given her such immoral ideas." Annabella emphasized her words with a roll of her eyes and a snort of disapproval.

If Sophia had thought that her aunt would have grown more circumspect with age, she was wrong. She knew there was no deterring her aunt from any story she wished to tell. Sophia turned her attention to the design on her plate, green Chinese tigers on a translucent white background, with gilt edges all around. Very expensive. She wondered how often the china was used or if it had been brought out solely to impress the eligible Duke of Forster.

"Immoral?" Aidan was suddenly engaged in the conversation.

"Well, you can't expect to educate a girl like a boy and not have it come out badly. Her parents taught her all sorts of things no girl needs to know, then neglected all the things that she *must* know to make a good match." Annabella leaned forward, her face a mask of dismay. "Why, when I married Mr. Elliot, Sophia didn't know how to sit or stand elegantly, she couldn't play any instrument or sing, she knew only country dances, and she couldn't arrange flowers."

Aidan remembered that girl, so refreshing in her honesty, open in her passions, willing to run across a field in pursuit of a butterfly, willing to laugh. He'd fallen in love with her from almost the first moment of seeing her. Recently, he had begun to see that girl once more. Suddenly Aidan realized that, like Ian, he longed to hear Sophia laugh.

"Half the time she'd be in the fields, botanizing, coming home with scraps of plants and dirty fingers; the other half she'd be in the library reading," Annabella offered confidentially as if she spoke to a kindred soul.

"That doesn't sound immoral." Aidan knew any defense of Sophia would only draw attention. "It's only a different sort of education."

"But she had no sense of how to catch a man. So, of course, I had to help her." Annabella paused to emphasize the generosity of her act. "I was thrilled when Lawrence and I met your brother Aaron at a dinner, and he seemed perfectly in need of a wife. But, when he came to ask for permission to hunt on our lands, Lawrence was in the lower meadows. I could have sent your brother the short way through the fields, but Sophia had gone into the forest. He was dressed so fine that I sent him along the forest road instead."

Sophia hadn't forgotten that day, the man on horseback who had cut her off then begun herding her with his horse off the path into the dark of the woods. When she had tried to run, he had jumped from the horse and pressed her against the side of a tree. In a flash of memory, she was back in the forest, his wet mouth pressing her lips into her teeth in hard, unwanted kisses, his leg pressed between hers holding her in place. One hand had pulled her skirt up to her hips. She felt again the paralyzing fear, her helplessness against his physical strength.

She dropped her fish fork, and it clattered against her plate. As if he knew the course of her thoughts, Aidan placed his hand on her leg. Its firm pressure brought her back to the present moment.

Her aunt glared, then shrugged. Evidence that Sophia was still somehow unsuitable as a wife. "Your brother must not have seen her. I'd thrown young man after young man into her path. But she never seemed to be interested in catching their attention. When I realized that she didn't know how to attract a man, I let her go off with her cousins, hoping she might be able to meet young men more freely. And we could make a match that way."

Sophia wondered how she had never realized her aunt's plan. She had seen those days of freedom as an odd lapse on her aunt's part and cherished them. She'd never imagined that her aunt had wanted her to be caught in a compromising position that would lead to marriage.

"Were they good chaperones, her cousins?" Despite his hand tight on hers, Aidan's tone revealed only a pleasant, polite interest.

"Oh, la, I don't know, your grace." Annabella shrugged dramatically. "You would know better than I. For a while, I had some hopes you would fall for our Sophia, but then you left for"—Annabella waived her hand dismissively—"wherever it was."

"Forster served His Majesty on the Continent," Sophia offered softly.

"Well, no matter." Annabella offered another dismissive wave. "I found her a wealthy industrialist, a bit older, willing to marry her even though she lacked accomplishments. But in the end it was Lord Wilmot we found courting our Sophia. Surprising, but a good match."

Sophia felt her aunt's "our" like a painful refrain. She had never been "our"; she had only been an unwanted ward to marry off. She felt deeply sorry for her young cousin—to have a mother who would go to such lengths to entrap a man.

"Found courting?" Aidan's tone encouraged greater revelations.

"Oh, don't you know that story? Most romantic." Annabella pressed a piece of linen to her lips. Her hands were weighted with two large, jeweled rings.

"Forster isn't interested in such an old story," Sophia intervened, increasingly uncomfortable with her aunt's conversation.

"Nonsense, Lady Wilmot," Aidan broke in. "I'm fascinated."

Her aunt raised her chin triumphantly and leaned forward as if she told the story in confidence. But it was clear that she had rehearsed the story many times over the years. "Sophia felt unwell and missed the last ball of the season. At the ball, I told Lord Wilmot the disappointing news that she had remained home. Apparently, he wished to check on our Sophia, because when we came home . . ."

"Earlier than expected, I presume?" he asked, smiling, but Sophia noticed the smile didn't reach his eyes.

"Well, I recall that I had a sudden headache. . . . But when we came home, Sophia and Lord Wilmot were in the drawing room, and Lord Wilmot announced their engagement. I hadn't noticed he had a tendre for her, but after that he courted our girl most assiduously, got a special license, made it clear to the whole county that it was a true love match."

"It's a shame then that Lord Wilmot died so young. . . . True love matches are so rare," Aidan offered, and Sophia wondered if others heard the hard edge to his voice. "Don't you think, Miss Elliot?" Aidan turned the conversation deftly to engage Sophia's young cousin and removed his hand from Sophia's leg.

Without the comforting presence of his hand, Sophia felt like the lonely girl she had been in her aunt's home. Though it couldn't matter now, she hadn't wanted Aidan to believe that she had set out to seduce him into marriage.

How relieved he must be to realize how barely he had escaped the trap. The fledgling trust between them would evaporate. But she would not reveal how deeply she felt their loss of contact. She was no longer the awkward girl who would rather read a book than go to a ball. No. Tom and Italy had taught her much about how to manage a conversation, and she'd rallied in more difficult situations than this.

Having decided to be the woman she had become in Italy, Sophia found the conversation moved more smoothly, ranging from crops and yields, to the latest novels, Elizabeth's interest in music and Frederick's in shipbuilding. Even her aunt became less a scheming shrew and more appealing as a woman concerned with her children's prospects and futures. Sophia hardly had to work at all, the conversation glided almost of its own accord, everyone contributing. Even if the table wasn't filled with the riotous laughter she remembered from her childhood with her cousins jockeying for space in the conversation, still it wasn't the icy repast she'd anticipated.

Aidan had managed to control the rest of the dinner conversation, engaging Sophia's uncle in a discussion of methods to increase yields in fields and the merits of enclosing wasteland and her cousin in a discussion of the various ships in his Majesty's Navy. By the end of the hour's entertainment, when Elizabeth revealed a real talent for the harp and a lovely singing voice, he felt less interested in killing Sophia's aunt.

But under his calm exterior, Aidan felt himself on the edge of something. Listening to her aunt's glib testimony, he felt unreasonably angry . . . angry that Sophia had been left in the charge of such a woman, angry that he had never seen Sophia's days of freedom as a plan to force her into a marriage, any marriage. And by placing Sophia in his brother's way . . . Aidan felt his heart grow cold at the memory. Foolish woman, not understanding that for all his brother's easy manner, he had a quick temper, a fondness for the feel of flesh against his fists, and a penchant for unprotected women.

It had been hours before Aidan and Sophia had been able to escape into his carriage.

"Well, your aunt is quite a woman."

Sophia remained quiet.

"I thought I had seen the most inventive of matchmaking mamas, but your aunt seems quite ruthless. You never told her about your encounter with my brother in the forest?"

"We agreed no good could come of it. Remember?" Her voice was lifeless again, as distant as the day they'd met about the guardianship. The advance of the afternoon disappeared in the dark between them.

He drew her to his side and placed an arm around her shoulders. "I remember. We had only just met at the fair, and I had been unpardonably forward. In the forest, I was afraid you wouldn't trust me, and I wouldn't be able to get you away from him unmolested."

"I thought you were kind, up until the moment you told your brother that I was 'a pitiful country virgin who would make any reasonable man miserable for the whole of his life.'"

"I said that?"

"You did, but I understood that you needed him to find me unappealing. It's important that you know: I never knew our time together had been part of some plan. After you left, it was clear she intended to marry me off, but I never knew before. I only knew she'd manipulated the night with Tom."

"Tell me what happened that evening, Sophia. How did my fiancée"—Aidan bit the word—"and my best friend come to be in a compromising position. It's only fair to tell me."

"Yes, it is only fair." Her voice sounded far away, her face turned to the carriage window, looking out in the dark.

"Before you left, we agreed it wasn't necessary to announce our engagement, that I could wait for you because my uncle wouldn't force me to marry against my will. My aunt was furious that you had left without a declaration and even more adamant I should marry soon. Phineas brought a factory owner from Manchester—a Mr. Mortimer—to visit. He was fifty or older, with wooden teeth, and the smell of liquor on his breath. I thought if I avoided him, he would turn his attentions to some more amenable girl, but my aunt encouraged him over my objections. He tried more than once to force a kiss or an embrace. So when I found he would be at the festival ball, I determined to remain home, even though the servants all had permission to attend. My aunt was eager to leave me behind."

Sophia paused, lost in her memory, and Aidan waited until she picked up the thread of her story once more.

"Tom had planned to leave the next day. When he found I'd stayed at home, he sought out my aunt to send me his farewell. Instead, he overheard my aunt giving Mortimer instructions on how to gain me as a bride that very night. Annabella had left the conservatory doors open and given him directions to my room. She even gave him a key in case I'd locked my door, saying I had been playing coy to win his affections. It would be best, she said, if we were 'discovered' in my bedroom. She told Mortimer to use whatever encouragement he thought necessary, and Mortimer called for his horse."

"Tom would have been horrified."

"He was. He had no time to find my uncle, but his horse had already been called, and he knew the shortcut through the fields. Even so, he had only minutes before Mortimer would arrive. Tom slipped through the open conservatory door and followed my aunt's directions to my room. Tom had already realized that, without servants in the house, he might be able to thwart my aunt's plan only by offering to marry me himself. But he didn't tell me that part. Instead, he told me to run to the mews and take his horse to Annie's; I grabbed a cloak and ran to the front hall. But it was too late; we could hear Mortimer in the conservatory. We had just enough time to slip into the drawing room before he entered the main hall and took the stairs to my room. Unlocking the front hall door was too risky, so we thought to escape through the open conservatory door. But Mortimer had left his footman standing guard on the path. We could hear Mortimer return to the main floor, opening door after door looking for me. And Tom told me I had to marry him, that there was no way I wouldn't be ruined, and I couldn't risk that Mortimer would still want to marry me. Tom promised to find you before the wedding and to help us run away, you and I. He said he wouldn't mind my jilting him for you. We could hear Mortimer drawing closer and closer. I thought of his clammy hands and his putrid breath, then I looked at Tom's kind face, and I agreed."

"Then your aunt and uncle arrived home."

"Not quite. Tom saw the door to the conservatory opening and pulled me into an embrace that must have looked convincing. Mortimer pulled us apart, flung his gloves in Tom's face, and challenged him to a duel. *That's* when my aunt and uncle returned home, to Mortimer decrying Tom as a rake and a ruiner of young women."

"How did Mortimer explain his presence?"

"He had followed Tom, seen him let himself into the house. My aunt, not wishing to be discovered, railed that I was a light-skirt ruined by lust. My uncle looked distressed. But Tom declared that he was the happiest of men because I had agreed to be his bride. Since I was wearing my cloak, we appeared to be eloping."

"What did your uncle do?"

"He asked me if Tom was telling the truth, and I said yes. Then he embraced us, gave us his blessing. He thanked

Mortimer for his concern, told him there was no cause for a duel since Tom was to be his ward's husband, and escorted Mortimer to the door. My uncle told Tom to meet him in the morning to discuss terms and to let himself out the way he had come in. Then he took my aunt's arm and escorted her from the room."

"What happened then?" Aidan kept his voice softly encouraging, just enough to prompt the story to continue. He'd seen men like this in the war, telling of the loss of a battle or a friend, drifting to a place where they relived the memories as they told them. For years, he'd wanted her confession, and this might be the only time he would hear it.

"Tom and I went to the drawing room to plan. We wrote letters to your father, hoping to find you. The next morning Tom and my uncle agreed on terms; my settlement was more than generous. Tom stayed until the end of the week, convincing people that ours was a love match: he met me after church with flowers; he bought me ribbons in the village; he announced to all that he was the luckiest man alive. It was a fairy tale: the orphan ward beloved by the rich lord of a local estate."

"Why did Tom leave at the end of the week? Not on business, I assume."

"No, he went to London for a special license and to search for you. But he could find no news." Her words if anything sounded more rote. "I realized that though we had loved each other, it wasn't meant to be."

Aidan felt a pang of conscience. Tom hadn't found him because he hadn't wanted to be found. But he would make it up to her. "It was meant to be. Your aunt interfered where she shouldn't have."

"Had I realized her intentions, I wouldn't have stayed home that night. . . . But I didn't know, and then it was too late." She began to cry, and he pulled her head to his shoulder and held her . . . as he had when they had hidden from his brother.

Chapter Twenty-Six

Back at Tom's manor house, Aidan escorted an emotionally exhausted Sophia to her room, then, with a gentle embrace, took his leave. He had much to consider after Annabella's revelations at the dinner table and Sophia's subsequent confessions. He carried a glass of claret to a chair near a lamp in his room. When he'd returned from the attic, hot with passion and anticipating the beginning of their affair, he'd hidden the packet of Tom's papers. Retrieving them, he laid them on the table next to a folded packet made of well-worn oilcloth.

At first he'd wished to be present when Sophia experienced emotional moments, like going through her husband's things, in order to spark a liaison. He'd intended to use her unspent passion for him and any unresolved feelings for her husband to his advantage. He had cared little how distasteful his plan might be, for he had not planned to build a relationship built on real attachment.

But somehow over the last weeks, his revenge had lost focus. Over the years, having no interaction with Sophia, he had found it easy to write the story of their past as he wished. In it, just as his father had predicted, Sophia was a fortune-hunting orphan, who used her beauty and wit to steal his heart, then abandoned him when another richer lord expressed his interest. Aidan had ignored anything that contradicted the story he'd created.

But now he began to see the holes in his narrative. If she had been a fortune hunter, surely she would have wished to keep her engagement to a poor soldier a secret, leaving her possibilities open for another better match. But he had been the one who wished to keep quiet, postponing the conflict with his father until after he'd received his annuity.

Even more striking, somehow in his anger, Aidan had forgotten the depth of her intelligence and the tenderness of her heart. He'd never imagined love might have played a part in her marriage. Then, to see her still so affected by Tom's loss. To watch her draw herself together and muster the strength to look him in the eye and pretend she was unmoved . . . It had forced Aidan to reconsider their youthful liaison. Perhaps what he had seen as mutual passion had been no more than an indiscretion for her. She had been an innocent, of that he was certain, and he suddenly had to consider she might not have been fully aware of the route their passion would take. But then they had both been innocents.

All these years he had thought himself foolish to have trusted her, to have believed she could be faithful despite his absence. He unfolded the oilcloth. Inside lay the wooden wafer on which Sophia had sketched herself in pen and ink. Her face was little damaged by time, though the wafer's edges had smoothed to a fine finish. He'd carried her portrait with him through the wars, unable to leave it at home, unable to let it go. In the hidden pocket in the lining of his boots, she'd gone everywhere with him. He'd unwrapped her portrait hundreds of times over the years, to remind himself of her faithlessness. But now, he looked at the portrait anew. He saw once more the generosity of her smile, the warmth of her eyes.

Perhaps he had been foolish not to have trusted her more,

the woman he believed understood his sense of duty. Even if he hadn't trusted Sophia, why hadn't he trusted Tom, a man he'd known would never betray him?

He knew the answer: Aaron. The eldest son, the bully. Even without being duke, Aaron had almost run the estate into the ground. When Aaron died, as far as Aidan knew, only their father had grieved. Judith and Benjamin had each protected their younger brothers in their own way, but Aidan had been the one who openly stood up to Aaron and the one most frequently punished for it. Aaron had taught Aidan that trust was foolish and that attachment only led to pain. A favorite fishing pole, a bird's nest filled with eggs, an affectionate barn cat, nothing was safe if Aaron wanted it or wanted to destroy it.

Their father had been a negligent accomplice in Aaron's terrors. Married twice, he had cared little for the women who bore his children, and more for the wealth or power they brought to the union. In that way he was a man of his generation and class, and the women he married had no expectations he would be otherwise. And perhaps Aidan's upbringing had made it easier to believe that any man of greater fortune or position would just as easily suit Sophia's fancy, that she would jilt him the first chance she got if the money and the title were better.

And yet, save for marrying Tom, Sophia had never deceived him. If he had read her letter, rather than torn it unopened into small bits and watched them sink into the bay, perhaps he would have saved himself the torment of the last decade.

He turned to the packet, ten letters in Italian. Would these prove or disprove Sophia's story or would they be about something else entirely? All he knew was that Tom had hidden them where only he or Aidan could find them.

The letters were in chronological order, the earliest dating back some eleven years. He looked over them as a group first. Only two were in Tom's hand, and both of those late in the correspondence. The others were in the same ornate Italian script. Of those only the first—a brief but effusive thanks for a basket of food, medicines, and money—was addressed to "your lordship." The next three letters offered no salutation, but they indicated an intimacy between the Italian letter writer—who signed only with the initials *FB*—and the letter's recipient. Aidan skimmed them quickly: sorrow at their separation; despair at the idea of marriage to another; some warm passages in which the writer anticipated a joyful and happy reunion; requests to remember his obligations to her; thanks for various presents, jewels, dresses; her delight at his gift of a small house at the edge of the city with a view of the sea. Aidan stopped reading, stunned. Tom had had a mistress almost from the moment they arrived in Naples. It was no different from the behavior of other men of his class, but Aidan had thought Tom better than other men.

He felt angry on Sophia's behalf. Tom had bought his mistress jewels, but Sophia had none. Tom had bought his mistress dresses, dozens every year, but Aidan had seen Sophia's wardrobe, and unless she had left the majority of her finery in Italy, she owned few gowns suitable to her rank.

Had Tom neglected his wife so obviously—and had Sophia known? He thought of her tearful moment holding Tom's jacket. No, she couldn't have known. Or had she loved her husband only to find he cared little for her? He thought again of Tom's letter instituting the guardianship; his old friend offered more concern for his son than for his widow. Had Tom regretted marrying Sophia? Did he find his unselfish act had come at too great a cost?

Once more Aidan could see Tom's hand reaching out to him from beyond the grave. Yet he still had no idea how to appease his old friend's spirit.

Chapter Twenty-Seven

In the morning, a box arrived by footman from her uncle. Sophia opened it to find a series of almanacs, one for each year from 1774 to 1798, and all filled with her mother's fine, precise hand, along with a small set of books tied in twine. On top was a note, sealed with her uncle's signet. She opened it carefully, not tearing the paper under the wax seal:

> *My dearest child,*
>   *These are your mother's journals, kept until her death. Your father wanted you to have them on your twelfth birthday, the age your mother was when she began writing them. But in my grief for my dear Clara, I forgot his wishes, and by the time I remembered I had remarried, and Annabella declared them inappropriate for a young girl. Not realizing my wife's hatred of bluestockings or how she tormented you for being your mother's child, I acquiesced. I realized those things too late, after you were engaged to marry a fine man, though I fear not the man you would have chosen.*
>   *I regret few things, but one most deeply: that I married a woman who could not love you.*

*I had forgotten these books until last night, when
you walked into the room with your mother's beauty,
intelligence, and grace. My brother had no greater
wish than that you would grow up like her: a woman
of conviction and passion who feared little and loved
deeply.*

*If you ever wish to talk about your parents
privately, I will arrange it.*

> *Your ever most affectionate uncle,*
> *Lawrence*

It was too much, she thought. All the things that had come
to light in the last day: that her uncle hadn't sanctioned
Annabella's behavior; that he had valued her mother. Perhaps
if Sophia had known, she could have confided in him.

Aidan was completing some tasks Seth had left him,
giving her several hours to herself. She took the box and retreated to the depths of a hedged maze where a giant copper
merman, green from oxidation, rose in the middle of a
sunken pond.

She began at the beginning. The first volumes were more
exercise books than diaries, and Constance recorded her
responses to and observations of her schoolwork in the margins. Sophia began to trace the development of her mother's
mind and ideas. It was strange in some ways to be reading
her mother's words from when Constance was not much
older than Ian, and Sophia was often moved to offer advice
or sympathy. She wished she had received the books as her
father had intended, when she was herself the age of her
mother.

Quickly however, the content shifted, and Constance
came alive. Clever and witty, she was used to being the center
of an intellectual if aloof father's attention. Her comments on
the local society and on her first visit to London had been
incisive, but touchingly naïve. She'd had a brief attraction at

sixteen to a soldier bound for the American wars. She was never presented at court, never danced at Almack's; but she stole away to the dark alleys of Vauxhall with a young man and had her first kiss. She deemed it a great disappointment.

Through her father's connections, she became a teacher at a boarding school in Hampstead. Her charges were moneyed: daughters of wealthy merchants, the unacknowledged— but cared for—daughters of various nobles, and American heiresses sent to England for culture. Most of her students were well aware of their precarious positions in society—all knowing they needed good matches to stabilize their fortunes and knowing equally well that their good looks and other charms, more than their education, would ensure their future happiness.

Constance, unmarried, had grown discontented. She looked at the idea of marriage anew, wondering if that were the path her heart would take, with its responsibilities for house and home. She saw no other choice she could make as a woman, or as a woman of her class.

Then something happened, something that troubled Constance and transformed her. She'd gone to a market to buy ribbon and paper. There a girl, not older than fifteen, was drawn by a halter into the square, as if she were cattle. The man who led her was in his sixties, apparently her husband. A man from the docks, a sailor, stood to the side. The girl looked at the sailor imploringly, and an old woman spat "adulteress" on the ground. The bidding began, the men in the crowd jostling and calling out slurs. Once the men took her lover's measure, they found it amusing to raise the price. Eventually the sailor stopped bidding, unable to buy her, and turned away, leaving her in the square. One of the drunken men won the day, gaining a "housekeeper for life," he said, for six shillings.

The story was so real in the journals, Constance's outrage so palpable, that Sophia understood better what experiences had made her mother the woman she was. As a teacher, Constance made little more in a month than the sailor, but she'd pressed seven shillings into the drunk's hand and bought the girl herself. Constance told the girl she was owned by no man. The sailor had been the girl's childhood sweetheart, gone to wars, and returned to find her in a forced marriage. The girl, weeping, begged for help in finding him, so Constance accompanied her to his boarding house and watched as the two embraced.

Sophia followed her mother through the years. Constance's father had been a scientist, and Constance had had the best midwife in the county. But even then the fear of not surviving childbirth or the weeks after was never far from hand. Her joy in her infant daughter Sophia was tempered only by her fears of leaving her without a guide in the emerging new world, a world of potential equalities and great tyrannies.

Constance hadn't at first been a republican. She distrusted the mob, having seen it for herself in the angry faces of her peers when she raised the question of the morality of the slave trade. But she'd become a republican through seeing the daily injustices created by the wealth of the aristocracy and the poverty of the people.

Sophia's mother's voice swept over her, reminding her of all she had forgotten, the way her mother cared for the poor and the sick, the late night knocks on the door, watching her mother dress quickly, kiss her on the cheek and leave . . . sometimes for days at a time, caring for those who needed both her and her knowledge of healing plants. Sophia remembered asking each time if she could go, and her mother had promised every time, "when you are older, Sophie, we will go together."

At the end, Sophia found a letter from her father.

*I've read your mother's journals, dearie, and I
hear her voice so strongly, it is as if we have sat
down before the evening fire to talk. There is nothing
in these journals that you cannot read without
benefit. Some (like your brother) would read
unsympathetically, caring more for the voice of
society than that of conscience. It takes a woman
of great strength to forgo luxuries to which she had
grown accustomed. How it humiliated your brother
when she no longer purchased sugar, and a certain
class of visitor stopped visiting.*

*Our Constance was a woman of convictions,
convictions that eventually took her away from us,
but her journals record those things she found
valuable. She followed the dictates of her conscience,
but she never forgot that conscience was heart
guided by reason and a careful examination of moral
and intellectual obligations.*

I loved her, as I love you.

Papa

Sophia realized her memories of her mother had been
colored by Phineas's embarrassment, then recast by her
step-aunt Annabella's disapproval. The Constance she discovered in the journals was not a virago or a shrew as
Phineas and Annabella would have her remembered, but a
deeply moral young woman who would not be silent when
faced with injustice. Constance's values as expressed in the
journal were far closer to Sophia's own than she had ever
imagined. Somehow, growing up, Sophia had come to regard
her mother as scandalous, but the journals gave Sophia
back the passionate clergyman's wife and teacher, who ded-
icated her own life to caring for others. Perhaps had Sophia
been able to read the journals as her father had intended, she
would have felt less obligated to try to mollify Phineas or

Annabella. Perhaps with the words of her mother embedded
in her heart, Sophia would have trusted her own conscience,
even when it had set her at odds with those in power over her.

She was so absorbed with her reading that she never heard
the footsteps approaching from behind her on the path.

Aidan finished Seth's responsibilities and went to find
Sophia. In the morning room, he found the estate papers she
had been reviewing that morning, but the cup of tea beside
them was cold. Nor was she in the library. He took the stairs
to the family rooms and rapped sharply on her bedroom door
before he turned the knob. But the room held only the faintest
hint of lavender. His stomach twisted. He opened and closed
doors to all the bedrooms down the hall, shutting each one a
bit more loudly than the last.

At the servants' staircase to the nursery and attic, he
stopped. He could hear soft footsteps descending the stairs.
Of course, she had been in the nursery or the attic, going
through Tom's trunks. The tightness in his stomach eased.
Smiling, he positioned himself to the side. When the door
opened, she would walk into his arms, and he would surprise
her with a kiss. A penalty, he would tease her, for hiding
herself away.

The door opened. A mob-hatted maid backed into the hallway, holding a basket of linens. Dropping his arms, Aidan
fell back, almost tripping over his own feet.

"Your mistress. Have you seen her?" Even to his ears, his
voice sounded abrupt.

Startled, the maid turned to face him, then dropped to a
curtsy. "No, your grace. Not in the nursery or the boys' rooms."

He pushed past her, past the upper floor to the attic, taking
the stairs two at a time. The attic. He would find her there, as
he had the day before. He flung the door open. But the air
was still, and the trunks unopened.

Not in the morning room, the library, her bedroom, or the attic. His list gave him no comfort. She had agreed not to leave the house without being accompanied by him or one of his men. Did she forget—or had she been taken? Malcolm's words about not being able to protect Audrey rang in Aidan's memory.

The muscles tightened in his jaw and neck. He'd been in the ballroom the night Audrey had been stabbed, seen Malcolm holding her to his chest, blood down the front of his waistcoat, calling for help, and begging her not to die. What if Sophia were hurt, bleeding, dying, and Aidan didn't find her in time? He pushed the thought away.

Beyond the trunks, the attic windows looked out over the front lawn. He shoved the trunks aside and surveyed the area. Four of his men had arrived that morning. Two stood talking, positioned to see both the house and the entrance from the road. Their stances were alert, but not anxious. So, she hadn't gone out the front of the house.

He took the narrow attic stairs too fast, almost falling midway down. Catching himself against the walls, he chastened himself to be calm. No old army officer who had lived through the barrage of a hundred cannon should be reacting to a misplaced woman with such haste. Deliberate and thorough—that was the way to find her. Yet his heart still pulsed hard in his chest. He hurried down the remaining stairs, opening doors to the rooms he had not checked before, and calling her name. Nothing.

By the time he reached the main floor, the housekeeper stood waiting at the base of the stairs, hands folded before her body. "Her ladyship was last seen in her garden, your grace."

He began to turn to the back of the house, but stopped. "When? And by whom?"

"Several hours ago, your grace. Cook and I saw her pass by the kitchen window."

"Alone?" He cursed himself for not having fully informed her staff of the danger. He'd thought his men would be sufficient.

The housekeeper's face grew concerned. "We did not notice, your grace. Should we . . ."

But he didn't hear the end of her sentence; he was already moving to the back of the house. From the raised terrace along the house's back, he watched for any hint of movement or flash of color, for birds taking flight in surprise, for noise turning to silence. For anything that might reveal her location.

He bit off a curse. This was not the time for panic. She was likely in the garden, unaware that no one knew where she was. He had to be deliberate. He looked at the face of his pocket watch; if he didn't find her in ten minutes' time, he would call for his men, inform the house, and make a broader search. But he could already feel his body tensed as if for battle.

He crisscrossed the garden, but he did not call for her. If there were an intruder, he did not wish to offer an alert. But she was nowhere. Not in the kitchen garden, not in the knot garden farther from the house, not in the wilderness at the bottom of the lawn.

Panic tightened at the back of his throat. How would he explain to Ian that he had failed to protect his mother? How would Ian ever forgive him? How could he forgive himself? He pushed the thoughts away and turned back to the house, prepared to call a search.

Then he remembered. There was a maze built of stone and hedges, past the wilderness, created by Tom's grandfather for his bride. Tom had taught Aidan its secret rhythm of turns, and he had long ago taught them to Sophia. He stood for a moment, torn. His weight balanced on the balls of his feet, and his arms taut, he considered his choice.

If she had been taken, then the time spent searching the

maze would be time lost. He should return to the house, call his men, begin a widening search. But with hours since she had been seen, it would be almost impossible to find her. Once more, he saw the line of blood across her back when she removed her shawl. No, she was simply . . . misplaced.

He ran.

Down the path that led through tall trees to the maze. At its entrance, he realized, he would have to be cautious. It would do no good if he lost his way in the maze. In the decade since he had last visited Tom, the hedges had grown tall enough that once inside, he would have no way to gain his bearings. He would be able to see nothing but hedge and sky.

He paused, wanting to rush in, but knowing he had to remember the pattern first. Even so, his first few turnings led him to a dead end. He was forced to double back, his hands fisted at his side. Starting over, he forced himself to move slowly. Left, left, right. Left? Or was it right again? He made his way farther and farther in.

At the middle, though, he found nothing. No Sophia. Only an empty bench where he had prayed she would be. Fear tasted bitter on his tongue. He turned in his tracks, then back again, trying to get his bearings. He would have to retrace his steps, or lose even more time.

As he began to leave the middle, he heard a soft motion down a path to his right. He waited, hoping to hear it again. But a bird hopped from the bushes, regarded him, then flew away. Not Sophia. But down the path he saw the edge of a fountain in a partially hidden alcove. If she were not there, then she was likely taken, and he had failed to protect her from her enemy, failed her, failed Ian, failed the Home Office. He wanted to run to find her, to take her in his arms, but he was afraid it would be only one more place that Sophia wasn't. Instead, he walked slowly, silently, down the lawn path.

And there, in an alcove, he found Sophia, a box of books

at her feet, lost in reading. Safe. Suddenly he could breathe again.

His first impulse was to embrace her, then rail at her, but he knew she would not understand. He barely understood himself; he had not realized how important just the sight of her had become to him over the last weeks. He stood watching her, letting his emotions pass over him: fear, then anger, then relief, and finally desire. Then he waited still, allowing his pulse to slow, keeping track of how long it took before she realized she was no longer alone.

She lifted a hand, tucked her hair back behind her ear, all the while absorbed in her reading. It wouldn't do to tell her she could have been in danger; she would just tell him that she wasn't. His logical Sophia.

His. The word surprised him. All along he had been telling himself that he wanted her to trust him again so that he could gain his revenge. But in the course of protecting her, something had changed. The truth was that he wanted her to trust him—not for revenge, not because he was obligated to Tom or Ian or even the Home Office, but because he wanted her again to be . . . his.

He shifted his weight, and the gravel crunched under his feet.

She looked up, her face troubled. "I've been reading my mother's journals—my uncle sent them to me this morning. Phineas was always embarrassed by her because she would never let an injustice pass by. After her death, I thought I should be embarrassed too. But I see it differently now. She was Judith's age when she died; I was Ian's. She was always brave, choosing her own conscience." Sophia looked down again. "I haven't been brave for a long time."

He sat next to her on the garden bench, but facing her, one leg on either side. He pulled her into the circle of his arms, and she leaned her head against his chest. "You sat in an opera box with a knife to your neck, and you thought to remember the shape and design of the blade. Bravery comes in many forms." He kissed her hair.

She let his comment go by. "I would have liked to remember her as brave before this."

"You weren't allowed to. Phineas, your aunt—they couldn't let you."

"I suppose not. But I want to be more like her. I spent too many years letting Tom make the decisions and, apparently, take the risks."

"Tom was always one for a secret. He likely thought he was protecting you and Ian." Aidan pulled her in more tightly against his chest. Somehow the mention of her life with Tom no longer troubled him.

"Perhaps." She was silent. "In with the journals was a key. My uncle sent it. I know what it opens, and it's not far. Will you come with me?"

"Yes." Whatever her secrets were, he wanted to know them, wanted her to share them all, to trust him fully as she had once long ago.

"Thank you." She leaned down and slid the box under the stone bench to protect her mother's notebooks from the elements. She looked into his eyes. "I should apologize. I know I shouldn't have come to the garden alone. I wasn't thinking until I was already here. So, I made sure to sit where no one could see me." Her soft smile made his heart warm. "Anyone from outside the estate would have made too much noise trying to find me. But I should have thought first."

"I have considered putting a leash around your ankle as if you were a falcon, and tying you to my wrist, so you couldn't wander."

She smiled and kissed him, a tender, sweet kiss that reminded him of their first. She started to stand, and he pulled her back, kissing her once more, a kiss of fervor and passion, igniting the fire in her eyes.

She put her hand on his chest and looked into his eyes. "Tonight. I promise. But come with me first."

He stood up and pulled her to her feet. "Lead on, my lady."

Tom's estate extended past the gardens through an orchard and, across a deep stream, a hay meadow. At the farthest corners, the forest that led to Annie's house edged the property. The forest lay primarily on her uncle's land, but Tom's land and her uncle's abutted briefly there. Sophia and Aidan did not enter the forest, but walked around its edge, onto her uncle's land, and then up a hill to a ruin built sometime in the middle of the last century, when ruins were all the rage. In the meadow, the folly offered an elaborate but small fortress: a central hall, decorated in the family colors, and above that, four corner turrets.

The door to the main hall was unlocked, the air of the dining hall grown stale. Sophia walked to a wall tapestry covering most of the back wall and pulled one edge back to reveal a door.

"Can you hold this out for me? I'd rather not have to brush spiders from my hair."

Aidan held the tapestry, and she took her uncle's key, turned the lock, and pulled the door back. It resisted only briefly.

"Do we need a candle?"

"No, there will be plenty of light. We just have to manage the first two turns of the stairs in the dark."

"Cobwebs?"

"Cobwebs. But . . . Yes, here it is. A broom." Her voice caught. "It's almost as if no one has been here, but that doesn't make sense."

"It doesn't?"

She didn't answer. She brushed away the cobwebs before

her as she ascended the stairs. He followed, wondering why she had never brought him here before.

After two turns in darkness, the stairwell grew lighter as they ascended. The staircase ended in a single room with two windows, the smaller one facing the countryside, the other one, larger, facing in to the center of the folly. On the inside corner stood a small fireplace, long unused. Next to it, a door led out onto the roof of the main hall. In the middle of the room, an easel held a canvas shrouded by a heavy cloth. Along one wall about twenty finished canvases leaned against one another.

There was little else: a padded chair next to a small table, a larger table covered with paper and drawing pencils, a set of shelves holding books. All covered with a thick layer of dust. Sophia surveyed the room. She walked to the outer window, silent.

Aidan recognized some quality about her that refused any questions, so he turned to the paintings along the walls. The first canvas was unpainted, but he tilted it forward to reveal the next. Several still lifes with fruit, a landscape of the countryside from the view of the small window; all good but unremarkable, indicative of a developing but not mature talent. The next stack were portraits, of Sophia's cousins in their teens; one of her uncle and of a woman in middle age who Aidan assumed to be her aunt Clara; one of Clara alone; one of another woman in plain dress, perhaps a governess. Each showed increasing promise; Sophia's gift was for capturing expression. Her cousins, never still, were positioned at angles from one another, almost as if they were in motion; her aunt held in her lap a lattice-topped pie, her mouth offering a bare hint of a smile, while her eyes glinted with secret humor. Why, he wondered, did Sophia move to watercolors and to scientific illustration? Why had she two portraits of Tom, but neither by her own hand?

Sophia had moved to the table, shifting one layer of paper to reveal the next, all sketches.

He wondered about the portrait on the easel, and he moved to it. Taking up the corner of the cloth, he pulled it away just as Sophia cried out "no."

Of all the pieces in the attic, it was her best work: the face was still young, not yet fully formed, but the detail was remarkable. The lines around the mouth suggested generosity, the eyes good humor, the chin firm and a bit stubborn. The texture of the hair was rich, each strand containing a range of blacks and blues to give a sense of life and energy. The expression was thoughtful with a hint of mischief. This was no lifeless rendition; it was one that revealed the emerging character of the young man being painted. Even Aidan could see that it was a portrait of the man she loved. If he had any questions before of how she had felt about him, this would have dispelled them.

"I didn't know you painted me." He reached out his hand and took hers. "You must have done it from memory. I don't remember sitting for you." He pulled her into his side and held her against him.

"You sat a thousand times. Every day we were together, I memorized your features. The angle of your head when you were amused, or angry, or puzzled. I knew the bones in your cheek, the line of your jaw, the way your hair curved in front of your ear. It made it hard to forget you; I knew your face so well. It haunted my waking and my sleeping, until I realized if I didn't dull the memory, I'd go mad."

"I didn't forget you either." He reached into his boot and teased out a folded piece of oilcloth. "I have the same pocket sewn into the lining of every pair." He held out the oilcloth, and she unfolded it to see the portrait she'd given him when he left.

Tears welled in her eyes, but they did not fall. "I didn't think you would have kept it. Not after . . ."

"I tried to get rid of it, but I couldn't. I kept thinking somehow it wasn't true, that you hadn't really left me. I went a little bit mad, thinking you hadn't loved me. Perhaps I've never recovered." His eyes never left the portrait.

"I did love you, Aidan, with all my heart. I never stopped loving you."

Aidan pulled her more tightly to his chest and kissed the top of her head, then stroked her hair as she leaned her face into his chest. They stood silently for some time, their hearts too raw for them to speak or move.

Sophia broke the silence first. "But we are together. After all that has happened to separate us, we are together now, and whatever happens . . ." She pulled out of the circle of his arms to look into his face, her eyes searching for some confirmation.

"We will be together," Aidan assented.

Smiling, she took the oilcloth from his hand and covered the portrait. "If we leave soon, we should arrive in time for supper."

"Did you find what you wanted to learn here?"

"Yes. I was never the unwanted responsibility. My uncle gave me this room when he married again. I thought it was just temporary, an apology for his wife's narrow-mindedness. I assumed he would give it to his own children when I was gone. But nothing has been moved, not even my pencils on the table. The cobwebs . . . He left them to let me know that. I just wished I'd known then."

"Would it have changed anything?"

"I don't know."

"Does it change anything now?"

"Yes. And no."

They talked about mundane things on the way back to Tom's park: the beauty of the forest; the state of the orchards and the crops. They retrieved Sophia's mother's journals from beneath the stone bench. Aidan insisted on carrying the box; Sophia insisted on taking some books from the box to share the load.

She'd called for a bath to be prepared before dinner, and the maid had just finished filling it when she returned to her room to change. She instructed the maid to prepare Forster a bath as well.

They both arrived at dinner in evening dress, or at least evening dress for the country, to eat a hearty country meal of roasted duck, rice pudding, stewed apples, and greens.

They ate largely in silence, separated by a long table and by memories no longer held at bay. He'd seen in the portrait the truth of her heart.

Chapter Twenty-Eight

When Sophia returned to her room after supper, she unlocked the adjoining door and left it ajar.

But she had no idea how to prepare to begin an affair. She thought to change out of the gown she'd worn to dinner, but into what? She had only serviceable shifts for night wear, and none of them in silk, none of them remotely beautiful. When they were young, it hadn't mattered what she'd worn. She hadn't worn anything for long. But she wasn't young anymore.

What if her body, older by a decade, reshaped by a child, was a disappointment? What if he found her uninteresting? She was a woman of little experience, welcoming a man—Ophelia's words rang in her memory—known for his skill in the bedroom.

Her marriage had been companionable, but Tom had never looked at Sophia with desire, and—still in love with Aidan—she had been relieved. Over time, her friend the Countess d'Abrennes, pitying her, had offered suggestions on how to attract a man's attention. "Why deny yourself, *ma cherie?*" the countess would coo as she threw the bocce ball. "Grasp happiness wherever you find it. If you find it with a lusty young Adonis, *où est la mal?* I could introduce you, no?" The countess had sent her a book of engravings that Sophia found more intriguing than shocking. She had begun to sketch copies of some of the engravings, but stopped. She could never see them without imagining herself and Aidan in each pose. But she'd seen enough to know how little she knew.

Certainly the passion had run hot between them since his garden, and his long looks at dinner had just begun the night's seduction. But no matter how much she wanted him, no matter how much she still loved him, she had no expectations that once the night was over, he would want her again.

Now she simply waited. She'd loved him her whole life, and she couldn't allow herself to care if it was a good idea or not. She only wondered what his response to her would be.

Aidan stood before the mirror in his room, imagining all the paths to Sophia's seduction. The room was darkened, and in the mirror, the shifting shapes of the oil lamp reflected, making cold bodies of flame. It reminded him of their passion, hot then cold, but never absent, always reflected back in memory. He could see her again as in his dreams, their limbs entangled. His dreams merged with their kisses in the garden and his carriage. In the half-light he wondered if he was sleeping or awake.

Was he really going to her room or was this simply another version of the dream come to torment him? It felt real. It felt like all the dreams of holding her close were about to become real in the next room. But this time he would not lose her. He put his hand out and placed it on the doorknob, but paused. Once he opened the door, it would begin. They would possess each other once more, touching that place within each other's souls that had once joined them more than any words. And nothing would pull them apart again.

He stopped to examine himself, looking objectively at his

body, a decade older. He considered how it would be best to approach her. He was still dressed in his evening clothes. Should he draw out the tension by meeting her clothed? He'd already imagined how he would undress her, but should he expect her to play valet? Some women liked to undress their men, but would Sophia? Would it excite her or make her shy? No, he wished to leave no possibility she would change her mind. He would dress more simply, leaving no need for her to interpret his desire.

The women of his past disappeared as he thought of Sophia, and the memory of those liaisons faded in his renewed desire. His dreams of Sophia had, if nothing else, kept their lovemaking fresh in his memory. For a decade, he had compared all other women to her, and now, he was to have her again. He hoped, forever.

Aidan came to her in undress, a silk banyan buttoned loosely at his waist. A rich yellow, the long dressing gown was embroidered with an elegant, curving vine pattern. She wondered if he greeted all his mistresses thus. From the adjoining door to their rooms, he walked to the hall door, turned the key in the lock, then placed the key on her dressing table. They would not be disturbed or interrupted.

A triangle of smooth flesh visible where his banyan crossed over his chest revealed that he wore no clothes beneath the gown. Her desire increased. She waited for him to approach her, not because she was playing coy, but because she could think of nothing else to do.

Without touching any other part of her body, he leaned his mouth to hers, first kissing just with his lips; then, when she had opened her mouth to him, he opened his own. With just that one kiss, her desire flamed like fire.

Her dress was of the same design as the one she had worn in his garden, a round dress with drawstrings, though this one added small buttons up the front of the bodice, giving a better fit to her figure. His fingers fumbled at the buttons at her bodice, and she put her hands on his, unbuttoning for him. When she'd finished, he kissed each fingertip, and her heart brimmed at the tenderness of the gesture.

She wished to lose herself in sensation, in the moment, forgetting obligation, forgetting the danger that surrounded her. She wanted only to love him once more. Releasing the fabric over her chest and pushing it aside, she felt the warmth of his hand as he cupped her breast, then bowing his hand to her chest, he kissed her tenderly, rolling her nipple between his lips. She felt the tension in her body tighten, until she could no longer hold back her moans of pleasure. Smiling, he moved back to kiss her mouth as his hands loosened the drawstring. She helped him slip her arms free of the material, then felt exposed and aroused as he folded the dress down to her waist.

Her hands, through the banyan's silk, caressed the plains of his chest. She let the sensations overwhelm her, until every cell of her body coveted his touch. "More," she whispered, and he stilled, as she greedily unbuttoned his waistband, and pushed his banyan open, revealing a line of bare flesh from his chest to his waist. She let her fingers explore the plains of his body, the breadth of his shoulders, the strength of his upper chest, the narrowing of his waist, the cords of his hips. His skin felt like silk over iron, soft and hard at once. Growling at her touch, he pulled her close, pressing her now sensitive breasts against the plains of his chest, skin to skin. She opened her mouth to him, let his lips tease hers and his tongue invade her mouth once more. She felt demanding, wanting him again, no matter the consequences.

Next he touched her lips with his fingers, then kissed her lips. It was a teasing sort of game, her never knowing where his fingers would take his lips next. Her jaw, then down her neck, between her breasts, the fire of her passion following his fingers, until all the fires united in the middle of her belly. There she felt him release her dress fully until it fell in a circle around her feet. As the fabric fell, she watched the passion flare in Aidan's eyes and on his face. His beautiful face.

Aidan lifted Sophia from the circle of her clothes and set her on the edge of the bed. He drank in her beauty, the rise of her breasts, the curve of her ribs, the gentle smoothness of her belly, the down that led to the seat of her passion. He placed his hand on her belly, below her ribs, and felt her breath come and go. He trailed his fingertips between her breasts, to her collarbone, to the crease where her neck met her shoulder. He opened her legs and stepped between them, felt the pressure of her hands, pulling him close, her lips kissing his neck and chest, nibbling at his breasts.

"Not enough," she demanded, and with both hands, she pushed the banyan fully from his chest. Aidan allowed it to fall behind him as he pushed her back onto the bed and climbed over her. With her lying before him, he began to trace the lines of her body, gently with just the tips of his fingers. And with each caress, he felt like he had returned home.

He slid his hand between her thighs, caressing until she moaned softly, deeply. He kissed her again, more deeply, more firmly, until she returned the kiss more passionately than before, and her legs parted for him. He kissed her chin, her neck, her chest, moving slowly, carefully, down her body.

She clutched his hair with her left hand, almost as if she intended to slow the line of his kisses down her belly. But he persisted, kissing her, offering light flicks of his tongue, until she relented. He felt the exquisite torture of her fingers stroking his back, of her running her hands over his shoulder blades, then back up to his head. She lingered stroking his hair, then clutching it with her fingers. Then she stroked his back once more. Everywhere that her hands touched him, his pleasure bloomed.

He kissed her belly, then her hip, and the fold where her leg joined her body, delighting in the sight of her. He brushed the soft flesh of her thigh with his cheek. Then, surprising her, he moved his mouth to the warm lips of her sex, reveling in her gasps and sighs. He tasted her, teasing her flesh with his tongue. When she pressed herself against his groin, his passion grew. His control weakened in the pleasure of her response.

He wanted to possess her, all at once, all of her. He explored her sensitive skin with his mouth, while his hand stroked her stomach, her breasts, her cheek. With his other hand, he kneaded her thigh, her calf, her foot. As his hands moved across her body, he realized that the difference between this joining and that in his dreams was Sophia's pleasure: her soft moans, her tensed muscles, her eyes searching his. He had thought the dreams just replayed their lovemaking. But he had been wrong. Sophia's responses were the treasure the dreams had lacked. And he wanted nothing more than to give her pleasure again and again.

As her body moved beneath him, he brought both his hands up her sides until he could cup both her breasts. Softly kissing her as he rose, he caressed once more down her shoulders and her arms. When his hands reached hers, she grasped them, and pulled him upward, toward her mouth. His body rested fully on her now, firm between her legs. Their limbs entangled and entwined.

"We have to be wise. If we were to create a child . . ."

He took her hand and guided it to between her legs, leading her fingers to feel the smooth skin of a French condom.

"Neither of us wishes for a child—just pleasure, just passion." He kissed her neck in a line to her cheek, back to her mouth.

"Now. I want you. Now," Sophia demanded, and he met

her demands, joining her in passion, giving her his heat, as she gave him hers.

Sophia felt their need for one another stronger than it had been in their youth, the ache of passion more insistent. They moved together slowly, gently at first, and Sophia matched his rhythm. Again and again she pressed herself against him, heightening both of their pleasures. His arms held her firmly. She felt his breath on her neck, his lips grazing her face. She was lost in time, floating, yet aware of her body, of the heat, of their passion.

It felt like they had never been apart, like the years separating them had collapsed into a breath. His hands knew her body as hers knew his. His shoulders were broader, his chest fuller, but it was still the Aidan she had loved. Her body had not forgotten his.

As the passion rose between them, she felt the years, the decade of separation, melt away. She looked in Aidan's eyes, saw the young man she'd loved, the young man she'd intended to marry, to live with, to love. His older face melted into her memory of him. And she believed it was the same for him. His eyes told her that he was seeing her as she had been then and as she was now.

At that moment, her body moved faster and stronger against his. Her back arched her into him, until there was no space between them.

Together they were lost in the rapture of waves of pleasure. She moved against him, pulling him even closer. She wrapped her legs around him, holding him, willing them to remain in the moment. As his body stiffened, hers relaxed. They both crumpled together into the sheets, holding one another in an embrace so close that they appeared of one flesh.

She drifted to sleep, sated, Aidan's arms holding her, his hands still caressing her body.

* * *

Hours later, Aidan lay awake, Sophia sleeping curled into his side. He listened to her soft breathing. Somehow, despite all the lies and misunderstandings, they had found a place of trust and reconciliation. They'd accepted their past; now it was time to create a present together—and a future. Aidan imagined all the things at his childhood home that he wished to share with Sophia, the pond he'd loved as a boy, his favorite views. But most of all, it would be a new start.

First, though, he imagined another day together. The tasks that Seth had left him had given him more insight into the things she valued. She and Tom had forged a companionate marriage, and he found he wanted to know her mind as well as he already knew her body. He wanted to have things over which they would argue as intellectual equals. He had avoided marriage, he realized, not because of her betrayal, but because none of the women he'd met could read Greek or Latin, knew all the plants and their properties, or could debate the advantages of the various systems of draining lands. He hadn't married because none of the women were Sophia.

She stirred, awaking, and he nuzzled her neck with his cheek.

"I have a very important question."

"And it is?"

"What was your favorite part of Italy?"

She laughed, arching her neck to allow him to turn his caresses to kisses. "That's impossible to answer. It's like asking what flower is my favorite to paint."

"Then what do you miss?" He blew softly on her neck, then kissed her again.

She grew silent. He paused, waiting for her response.

"I had a salon. It drew from all quarters: the tourists and expatriates; women of the old Neapolitan families and some whose husbands were in the Austrian government. We discussed art, literature, music, agriculture, medicine, science, and politics sometimes, depending on which factions were present at the time. But we also helped each other when help was needed. When Tom grew too frail for guests, I had to let it go. I'd forgotten how much I loved those conversations." She leaned her head back onto his shoulder.

"Why don't you start anew in London? It would not be hard to attract a congenial circle. You already know Judith, Audrey, and Tom's sisters. I could introduce you—if you would like—to some bluestockings." He trailed a finger down the middle of her chest.

"None of your friends in the demimonde?" She turned her body to allow him more freedom.

He smiled. "I know well enough not to answer that. What will you call it?" His hand moved down to the plains of her stomach.

"Call what?"

"The salon." He started doing something tantalizing with his fingers.

"Why would I need to call it anything? It's simply a salon."

"It needs a name." To accompany the movement of his hand, he blew hot breaths in her ear, then followed the line of her jaw with kisses.

For a moment she couldn't think, her passion rising. Then she remembered Tom's teasing name. "Muses. We would inspire each other. The Muses' Salon."

"Would you allow men?" He leaned farther and kissed a line from her ear down her neck.

"Only if they are as clever as you." She felt the need for him strong once more.

"At what?" He stopped all kisses and touches at once.

"I'll let you know." And she kissed him back with a fervor that matched his.

Sophia was trapped in tormented dreams, a scream unvoiced in her throat.

Ian was missing. He wasn't in the nursery or in the kitchen. In the dream her anxiety grew, until she met Tom in the garden. An unfamiliar garden with hedges where there should have been beds. In the half-light of shadows, Tom pointed down an avenue. She ran into the hedged walk, toward the center. There Ian floated lifeless in the pool; his hair—dark and curling—waved in the water as his body bobbed face down. She ran forward, but arms pulled her back. A knife intricately designed flashed against her neck, then she herself was falling to the water, joining her child.

She awoke, panting, feeling her heart still pounding in her chest.

She turned to take solace in Aidan's arms, but he was gone.

But of course he would be gone. She shook her head at her foolishness. Had she expected him to stay and be found in her room by the servants?

She touched her cheek where he had kissed her.

Chapter Twenty-Nine

It had been three days since they had become lovers. Their passion, denied for so long, ran strong. Reclaiming some of the past they had lost, they revisited every place they had made love in their youth and made love there again. And they talked, gingerly at first, of things not likely to endanger their growing trust, then voraciously, on every topic they could imagine, so hungry were they for each other's thoughts. Eventually they would have to travel on to Aidan's estate or return to London. But neither raised the question. It was an interlude, one to talk, and laugh, and learn to love again.

Early that morning, they had walked to Sophia's studio, leading a mare carrying paints, boards, and other supplies, and pausing only to talk with two cottager's children, fishing on the banks of the stream.

"Sit there." Sophia motioned toward a chair in front of the large picture window.

"I wish I had not been so precipitous in having your house-keeper remove the dust and spider webs." Aidan groaned, but obeyed.

"It was a kind and generous act to have my portraits moved to the manor house." Sophia countered gently.

"For which I am now being thoroughly punished." He seated himself, his body all petulance.

"No, sit up straight, shoulders back. Pretend you were once an officer in His Majesty's army." She moved to arrange his body. "Turn your upper body like this. Move your right leg a bit. There."

"Where should my left arm go?" He extended his arm and let his hand hang from the wrist like a marionette.

Ignoring his extended arm, she placed her hands to either side of his head and tilted it just so.

"Do. Not. Move." She looked him in the eyes.

"I can't agree not to move without moving my mouth."

Shaking her head, she began to push the large table toward his side.

"Wait." He started to rise.

"Do. Not. Move." She pushed with her hip once more.

"But I can help."

"Whatever for?" Sophia pulled her shoulders back. "I'm perfectly capable."

"My self-sufficient Sophia."

Her face softened. "I haven't felt sufficient . . . for some time. But I'm starting to again." She maneuvered the table under Aidan's still-outstretched arm and tapped his elbow for him to lower it. "I want your arms bent out from your sides to form a sort of pyramid."

"With my head at the top?"

Sophia pulled a bit of his white shirt cuff past the end of his coat.

"So, *not* with my head on top?" Aidan feigned concern.

Continuing to ignore him, she set a globe behind his shoulder.

"With a *globe* on top?"

She batted his head lightly. "Portugal and Spain will appear obliquely behind you to acknowledge your service in the Peninsular War."

"You seem to know exactly how you wish for me to appear."

"When I was a girl, I collected engravings of famous naturalists. And I always thought you looked a bit like Sir Joseph Banks, as Joshua Reynolds painted him."

"Do you have the picture still?"

"I didn't take the album with me to Italy. . . ." Turning to the bookcases behind her, she flipped through several volumes. "So, perhaps. Brilliant!" She held the engraving out to him.

"I should sit . . . thus?" Aidan mimicked Banks's position.

"Yes. Pretend you are welcoming someone to your study."

"I would never welcome anyone wearing this . . . cravat." He pulled roughly at its lace edges. "It's bad enough we pillaged Seth's closet for the waistcoat, but you have made me look like a dandy! Barlow will be mortified."

"You claimed the coat was originally yours, borrowed for a ball and never returned. As to the cravat, I need a sense of its folds." Sophia pushed his hand away as she reshaped the knot. "Hold still, or I'll paint you strangled by it. You fidget more than Ian."

"If you wish for me not to fidget, then you must entertain me." He shifted his hips in the chair without moving his upper body.

"How can I entertain you while I paint? Is it sufficient to describe what I do as I paint or must I do something else?" She set his hand sideways across the end of the armrest.

"I want you to describe what you are doing *and* something else. A story from your life, perhaps?"

She looked to the sky in supplication. "In the last three days, we've discussed everything." At her easel, she perched on a tall stool. "Or do you not remember?"

"I remember. In Italy you became fluent enough to read the dramatists Goldoni, Alfieri, and Metastasio and the poet Parini in the original language." The surprise in her eyes pleased him.

"While I block in your outline, should I test you on the rest of our conversations?"

"Oh no, I am happy to volunteer it. Both of us have little use for magazines. I find *Gentleman's Magazine* pompous; you find *Lady's Magazine* vapid. Our only exceptions are the *Monthly Review* for advice on new books and the *Edinburgh Magazine* for politics and science." He smiled broadly. "I can summarize all our conversations in equal detail. Would you like me to start?"

She set the crayon down and looked carefully at him, but not—he suspected—to determine how to sketch him. "No, I concede; you have listened—and carefully. Which begs the question: what else can you possibly wish to know?"

"Everything. Who you became when we were apart. The shape of your mind."

"I've never thought of my mind as having a shape." Her eyes lit with humor. "Hmmm. I choose a quatrefoil."

Aidan groaned. "Never ask an artist about shapes. What is a quatrefoil?"

"Four overlapping circles sharing a big middle." In the air, Sophia drew a sort of four-leaved clover. "You see it in heraldry and architecture."

Aidan stuck out his tongue. "I wished to know your mind, not its geometry."

"No, I answered fairly." Sophia sketched his outline in broad strokes. "If your mind had a shape, what would it be?"

"A rectangle: orderly, predictable, clean edges. Like a square, but more interesting."

"No, Tom's mind would have been a rectangle . . . or perhaps a cube because he was a man of depth." Sophia used her charcoal as a gauge. "But you didn't answer fairly. Your mind is nothing like a square, and you know it, so you have to choose another shape."

Her marriage to Tom was a subject they had avoided since

they had become lovers. Now was the time for that to change. "What was the shape of your life with Tom?"

She answered without pause. "An octagon. I expanded his rectangle; he structured my quatrefoil. He was perhaps the kindest man I have ever known . . . and certainly the most stubborn." Her charcoal settled in her lap as she spoke. "We had the best conversations, and on everything—politics, art, science, music, rearing Ian, propagating plants." Her voice wavered, and she brushed her eyes with the back of one hand. She began to sketch again, and when she spoke again, her voice was firm. "We were friends and partners. A marriage of minds, Tom always called it. I miss that, him."

She did not mention passion. Aidan wondered again about Tom's mistress and whether Sophia had known. But he was happy she had felt valued. "Someday—not today—I would like to know about his illness, his death."

"Of course. Up to the day of his death, he spoke of you, your friendship, with great fondness." From two porcelain pots of pigment, she dabbed a white and a very deep brown on her palette. "Now, over my charcoal sketch, I will paint a wash of lights and darks to create depth."

"Can I move?"

"Arms and legs, but not your head." She mixed pools of color across her palette. "I know it is foolish, but sometimes I feel like Tom still watches over us. For the last year, I dreamed scenes of our life together, but since the opera, I often dream he's warning me about some danger."

Aidan stiffened, but kept his voice level. "Danger?"

She dipped her brush in the darkest colors. "When I wake, I never can remember what it is. But Tom was always so protective, and I have been anxious. It makes sense I would dream of him."

Aidan stared at a place on the floor beyond his boot and kneaded his outer leg with his hand. "Do you not dream things that come true? After I returned from the wars, I dreamt repeatedly of Benjamin, wounded and separated from his men, and of Colin, searching the battlefields, but always missing the cave where Benjamin lay broken. I wrote letters, warning Benjamin and Colin, but the letters arrived weeks too late." Without thinking, he stood up and walked to the fireplace. Throat tight, he kept his back to Sophia, not wishing to see the disbelief or pity on her face. A heavy knot of grief filled his belly.

"It isn't your fault." She leaned against his back, slipping one hand around his waist to his chest. With the other hand, she caressed his back in slow soothing strokes. "When your father called you both home, Benjamin refused to return. And you don't know if he were in some cave alone. You only know that is how you dreamed it. It's what you fear happened."

Without turning, he forced himself to tell her the rest. "But now I dream he is alive, watching me from the shadows, but refusing to come home . . . as if I failed him somehow." The truth, finally spoken, eased a bit of the grief.

"Oh, Aidan, my love." She turned his body toward hers, and he buried his face in the curve of her neck. She stroked his hair. "Benjamin would never have thought you failed him. He was always so proud of you. The 'best duke among us,' he wrote Tom time and again. The letters are in one of the remaining trunks. I'll give them to you."

His stomach still tight, Aidan pulled her against his body. "I resented Benjamin for sending me home. He was the heir after Aaron, not me. Then when I discovered how badly overspent the estate accounts were, I resented him more. I had even planned the drumming I would give him on his return. Then he didn't come home. It took me years to return the estate to sound footing."

"But your brothers never said anything about the estate being troubled." She brushed his hair back and searched his face, still wet with tears. "Because you didn't tell them.

You took up the responsibility before it was yours. And you told no one."

"Not no one. Judith made me tell her. Then she helped me repair the damage. For years we met each month, reviewing the accounts, making whatever changes we could, until the estate began to flourish." As he spoke, Sophia looked past his shoulder, her eyes focusing far away. "Benjamin was wrong; Judith's the best duke of us."

But Sophia appeared to no longer be listening. He watched her expression grow speculative, some awareness spreading across her face.

"Aidan." She raised her arm, pointing out the window. In the near distance, between the folly and the two manor houses beyond, a column of black smoke grew and thickened. "Fire."

She moved out of his arms. "Look at the trees. There's a strong wind—across my uncle's lands toward Tom's manor. It's been a dry season. If the hay meadows catch fire . . . Take the horse. Warn them."

"Ride behind me." Taking her hand, he pulled her toward the door.

"The mare can't carry us both and run with any speed." She squeezed his hand. "Go. The servants will need your skill at marshaling troops. I'll follow on foot." She pulled him into a hard kiss.

"We are upwind. It's safe here." He looked hard into her eyes, then smiled tightly. "Do. Not. Move."

Sophia watched Aidan ride toward the manor house. The column of smoke grew broader, then it seemed to slow and stand. The trees, however, still rustled in the breeze. She squinted to see the direction of the leaves. No, the wind had shifted toward the land between the folly and the manor. If it shifted a bit farther, the folly would be caught in the fire's widening path. And if the fire caught the hay meadow before she was across . . .

From living below Vesuvius, she knew the dangers of breathing the hot air, filled with ash and debris. She pulled her fichu over her head for protection, covering her mouth and nose. Then she ran for the footbridge.

After a hundred yards, she looked over her shoulder. Behind the folly rose a wall of smoke. She could see nothing else. The fire was moving too fast. She ran faster, stumbling, tripping, falling to the ground. Her knees and palms hit hard. The fire crackled behind her, breathing heat. It wasn't sweltering, not yet. But it would be, and soon.

The thickening smoke, like fog, enveloped her. Feeling suffocated, she stooped to see below it. Over the last several days, they had tamped down the grass from the stream to the folly. As long as she could see her feet and the ground below, she should be able to follow the path to the bridge and safety on the other side.

With no landmarks but the flattened grass below her feet, she had no idea how far away the stream still was. She walked, half hunched over, knees bent low. If the smoke thickened nearer her feet, she might have to crawl to find her way, and if she crawled, she might run out of time. Her legs and back cramping, she heard the gentle rush of the stream. And the sound of crying.

Her eyes burning above her fichu, she continued toward the sound of the crying, still following the trail of beaten-down grass. She remembered the cottager's children and prayed they had remained on the bridge. The smoke grew thicker with each minute. She would never find the path again if she had to leave it to find the children.

The children or the bridge? Their lives or hers. She pushed the thought away. She had to find them, whether they were near the bridge or not, even if it meant that she left Ian an orphan. She closed her eyes against the smoke and her tears.

It would be easier to find them if she could call their names. Aidan had given them a half-pence each in exchange for their names and ages. And they had been delighted to tell him. One—the girl—was four, the boy six. She remembered that clearly. *Think, Sophia, think.* Margaret? The child's pronunciation had been inflected with the lilt of her Welsh heritage. Margaret wasn't quite right, but it was close. Perhaps close enough that the child would respond? "Margaret? It's Lady Wilmot. I gave you and your brother apples this morning. Margaret? Answer me, and I'll come find you."

Nothing. Sophia's back and legs ached. To relax them somewhat, she closed her eyes and held her breath, then she stood up straight into the thick smoke. Then, hunching back down once more, she inched forward. Another few feet of slow movement and she heard it, a child's voice, too faint to position easily. But a voice.

"Aye." Then coughing, loud enough to follow.

She pushed forward another ten feet, the ground descending sharply. The bridge. She had made it. Relief felt like a drug. The stream was, thankfully, in a small declivity, and the smoke had not descended as low near its banks. But even so, she could not see past the landing of the bridge.

She stepped forward and found Margaret huddled in the bridge's middle. Alone. The child flung herself at Sophia's knees weeping. And Sophia knelt beside her, wrapping her arms around the thin child. "I'm here, Margaret. Where's your brother?"

Wide-eyed, the child pointed toward the bank Sophia had just left.

"Which way did he go?"

Margaret pointed down the stream.

"Did he go to get help?"

The child nodded.

"Did he tell you to stay here?"

The child nodded.

"Let's go find him. And take you home."

The child held out her arms to be carried. Sophia's legs and back ached at the thought of carrying the child while hunched over. But she couldn't risk the boy's having been overcome by the smoke somewhere, perhaps only a few feet away. She looked at the water flowing below, its cold keeping the thick hot air from descending too low. If she went to the deepest part of the stream, she might have enough visibility to walk upright.

She knew roughly where the fire had started, and from her youth, she remembered something of the river's course. In parts it was quite deep. At some point below her studio, the stream turned, leading away from Tom's and her uncle's estates and away from where she thought the fire had begun. But she couldn't be sure. If she were wrong about where the fire had begun, she might be walking into the fire, not away from it. But it didn't matter. That was the direction the boy had taken.

Removing the fichu from her head, she soaked it in the water, then wrapped it around Margaret's small head, pulling the edge over her face to protect her eyes from the smoke. Then ripping a strip from her own shift, she did the same for herself, wrapping it around her nose and mouth, but leaving her vision unimpeded.

On the edge of the bridge, she sat, her legs dangling over the water. "Climb on my back."

Margaret sat down behind her, extending her legs on either side of Sophia's hips and wrapping her arms around Sophia's neck. The girl tucked her head trustingly into the curve at the back of Sophia's neck. "What's your brother's name?"

"Hugh," Margaret whispered.

Sophia lowered herself into the water, feeling the cold rise over her waist. Once she had her footing, she waded as close to the fire-side bank as she could to watch for the boy.

Treading forward, Sophia called Hugh's name and watched for him on the four or so feet of bank she could still see. She prayed he was no farther up, lost to her in the smoke.

The smoke bore down closer to the water's surface, and she lowered her body to the pits of her arms. With the water supporting her body, it was easier to walk with bended knees. Soon she couldn't see the bank at all, just the line of water in front of her. She moved farther into the center of the stream, praying that she would get past the fire, praying that the fire didn't change its course to pursue her down the stream. Every few steps she would call out Hugh's name and listen. There was never any response. She hoped the boy had made it home safely, just as she hoped none of the cottagers were risking their lives to save Margaret or her.

Carrying the child on her back made her think of Ian. If she were to die, Aidan would protect him, Aidan, who she had finally been able to love. Tears ran down her cheeks, but she was strangely grateful. She would leave them each other.

She tried to imagine the distance she'd traveled, but she could see only smoke and water. After a seeming eternity, the stream curved slowly. But at her next step, the depth of the creek increased precipitously. She sank up to her chin. Margaret cried out in fear, until Sophia cooed reassurances. Sophia was already exhausted, muscles fatigued, body shivering. Though the deeper water lifted more of the child's weight, Sophia had to fight harder to pull her body forward. Freezing below the water, heat burning her face above it, she estimated how much longer she could keep moving. Ten minutes, maybe less.

After the curve, the water shallowed incrementally, and she began a slow climb up. Soon the water reached only level with her waist. As the water receded, Sophia had to bear more of Margaret's weight, but before her, trees appeared in ghostly outlines. Sophia's heart lifted. She was past the fire, and it hadn't turned to pursue her. She looked where she had been. There, the smoke still lay thick, obscuring all reference points.

Progressing another twenty feet, she could see the bank and a bit beyond. Another twenty feet beyond that, she could see most of the banks on both sides. She set Margaret onto the grass, then pulled herself up onto the bank, and collapsed, spent.

She lay breathing hard, until Margaret took her hand and pulled it. "Yes, dear, you are right. We need to get you home. Can you hold my hand to walk?"

The child nodded. Sophia wet their facecloths once more, then they began to walk hand in hand along the bank.

Within another ten minutes, they had reached an area almost without smoke, though the burnt smell remained heavy. At another turn in the stream, Margaret tugged Sophia away from the stream, and Sophia allowed herself to be led.

With Aidan's warning, the cottagers and the manor staff had been able to beat the fire back with few losses to the estate. Even so, it had been several hours before the danger was fully past and all the arms of the fire extinguished. Some of the cottagers had lost their homes, but Aidan knew Sophia would not allow them to suffer.

Standing outside the manor house, he listened as the housekeeper outlined what temporary quarters could be arranged above the stables and in the servants' quarters. As the two conferred, Sophia's Uncle Lawrence arrived, clothes covered in soot and grime.

"We beat it, son. But we might not have, had you not brought the warning in time." Lawrence clapped Aidan to his breast. "Now, where's my Sophia? In the house? I imagine you had some difficulty keeping her from shoveling dirt with the tenants."

"We saw the fire from the folly, and I left her there for safe-keeping. I was about to take some horses and retrieve her."

Sophia's uncle paled and swayed. Placed his hand on the wall of the house for balance. "The folly? But . . . we turned the fire into the hay meadow to keep it from the houses. The folly's burned to the ground, nothing left. If she stayed in the folly . . ." Lawrence turned his face to the wall and wept.

Aidan felt gutted, like the inside of his backbone had been scraped clean with a very sharp knife. Somehow he kept finding and losing Sophia, just as in his dreams. But what good were dreams, if having them never changed anything? Benjamin was dead, and Tom, and now Sophia. Just a week ago, she had confessed that she loved him, and though he had held her in his arms, he had refused her the words. And why? What did it gain him? If she were still alive, would he refuse them to her still?

In the past weeks, he'd learned her secrets, learned why she had married Tom, learned, above all else, that he could trust her. He had even spent much of the last week seeing exactly the kind of life they might have together: a marriage of minds *and* bodies. A union of intellect and passion.

Aidan put his hand on her uncle's shoulder and led him into the house. Neither man wanted to speak—not yet. There would be time enough to plan for the services, to sort out the various legal circumstances, to tell her kin. At the thought of Ian, Aidan felt a heavy weight on his chest.

Aidan poured two deep glasses of whiskey and drank both. Then he poured another two and held one out to her uncle. The two men sat without speaking, dirty, exhausted, and heartbroken, drinking until the bottle was almost dry.

"Your grace, one of the cottagers wishes to see you." The butler had rapped twice to no answer, then entered without being called.

Aidan didn't look up from his glass. "Send him away."

The butler came closer. "It seems to be important, sir, but frankly, I can't understand his accent. He's one of the Welsh craftsmen her ladyship hired to repair woodwork. And he's becoming agitated."

"I'll come to the hall. And call for the footmen in the event he needs to be removed. I find myself unsympathetic to other people's ills." Aidan rose and placed his hand on Lawrence's shoulder as he passed by. "I'll return in a moment, and we can decide how to proceed."

Lawrence nodded and lifted the bottle to see one small drop at its bottom. He lifted it to his lips and waited for the drop to roll slowly down the bottle's neck onto his tongue. He returned the bottle to the table, resisting the urge to throw it against the wall.

The door opened, and Aidan yelled into the room. "Come along, Lawrence. She's alive."

A wagon and two horses were ready to leave by the time that Aidan, Lawrence, and the Welshman Dayffd Morgan entered the yard.

"A wagon?" Lawrence asked. "You've three perfectly fine carriages in the mews."

"Sophia sent for a wagon. Apparently she wishes to move Mr. Morgan's family to the manor house. We can ride beside."

Morgan swung onto the wagon seat easily, followed by one of the stablemen, and led them out.

At the cottage, the young boy Aidan recognized from the bridge stood watching the road, then ran inside. The cottage was dreary, no curtains on the windows, no flowers in the yard. The boy returned to the door, holding his sister by the hand, while his sister clutched a skinny kitten to her chest. Morgan pulled up the team and called out instructions in Welsh. The children disappeared into the house. Aidan had understood Morgan's Welsh easily, having learned it from his nurse as a child, but having hidden the fact from his father who held all the English prejudices. Morgan was not the children's father, as Aidan had assumed, but their elder brother, all three being orphans.

A moment later, the children appeared with Sophia, the girl clutching Sophia's skirt and the cat, the boy holding his sister's hand.

Aidan's heart fell into his stomach with relief. Her hair was loose and tangled, her dress torn and streaked with mud and moss and soot. And she was the most beautiful woman he had ever seen. He leapt from the horse mid-stride and ran to embrace her.

Chapter Thirty

When Sophia awoke, Aidan was beside her, the sunlight bright in the space between the heavy curtains. "I told the servants to let you sleep until you woke on your own."

He was lying on his back, his hands behind his head, his eyes focused on the pattern of the bed curtains. She curved into his side, traced his cheek with her fingers. He caught her hand in his hand and held both over his heart.

"This might be a good time to travel on to my estate in Monmouthshire. Malcolm and Audrey can bring Ian there on their way back to London."

"When do they return?"

"Whenever we send for them."

"I thought their trip was for a fortnight."

"They agreed to take as long as was needed to keep Ian safe."

"Ah." She lay her head on his shoulder. "Then it would be nice to see your estate."

"Seth has stolen most of my innovations." He shifted to pull her on top of him.

"Has he now?" She settled her legs on either side of his hips and ran her hands across his chest.

"Yes, that new drain system . . ." He caressed her body

from hips to breasts and down again, then back to cup her breasts against her chest.

She pressed her hands against his breasts in return. "You mean the one I adapted from the description in the Royal Society papers and sent to Seth in detailed drawings?"

"Yes, that one." He moved his hands to her hips and settled her on his firmness. "I think you should inspect my version to compare it to yours."

"I'll instruct Cook to make us a basket. We can leave in the hour." She rocked gently, arousing them both more.

Two hours later, Sophia entered the morning room to find mail from London. She didn't want to look through the pile. She didn't want her time with Aidan to end. Perhaps there would be nothing of note.

She sorted the pile into smaller ones. Three letters addressed to Seth personally, not as estate manager, would be sent on to Judith's manor. A letter for Aidan, surprisingly, from Lord Walgrave, and a package with no return address, but addressed in Walgrave's hand. Sophia knew Walgrave; he was one of Tom's friends from Cambridge. Odd.

A single letter for her, from Luca, sent from London.

She slipped a penknife under the wax, releasing the seal, and unfolded the letter to read it. Luca and his sister had arrived from Italy. She remembered her dream, the dark-haired child floating in the water. It was time to return to London.

But how to tell Aidan? Over the last week, she'd watched the lines of his face soften, the set of his shoulders loosen, his eyes grow less guarded. Several times, often when they were in bed, he had looked on her with real affection. Not love, though. They were old friends and lovers. Perhaps if they had been able to go to his estate, to have more quiet days, perhaps then he would have remembered what it felt like to love her. She already knew too well what it felt like to love him.

She turned back to the letter, its single sheet heavy in her hand. Luca's return complicated things, but whether now or later, they would be complicated anyway. If she told Aidan why she'd encouraged the Brunis to come to England, she would have to explain everything. But to do that, she needed the papers, and the papers were in London.

Before she had decided how to broach the subject, Aidan arrived in the morning room, face freshly washed, his hair wet and mussed. The butler offered him chocolate from a service on the buffet, then withdrew. Aidan watched the butler go, then, sipping his chocolate, smiled provocatively over his cup at Sophia.

She touched his hand and pointed at the pile of letters. "Unfortunately, our lives have caught up with us."

Picking up Walgrave's letter, he broke the seal and read. The muscles in the corner of his mouth tensed, and he picked up the packet, cutting its twine with the knife but not opening it. "I have some business that needs attention."

She wondered why he could not examine the packet in her presence, but she shrugged it away. Like Aidan, she had her own business to attend to, and she began a list of items to discuss with the housekeeper before they left.

Aidan returned to the library twenty minutes later, carrying a folded newspaper under his arm. His chocolate had grown cold, but he paid it no mind, drinking from it as if he needed a distraction. His manner had grown cold as well, surprising given his playful sweetness since the fire.

Sophia broached the change of plan carefully. "I know it's not what we had hoped to do, but I need to return to London. Some matters have arisen. . . ."

"And you consistently choose to put yourself in situations where you are at risk of harm." His voice was hard.

It wasn't a question, so she didn't answer.

"What can be so important that you'd return to London where we know a man wishes you harm?" His voice was level and calm, but even harder than before.

She looked away. "I can't tell you. It's a confidence I've promised to keep."

"What will it take for you to trust me? Is it that you can't tell me or you won't?" His shoulders stiffened into an almost military stance.

"Both." She would not be harangued to answer more. "I would prefer to discuss something else."

"Then tell me about Tom's death."

Sophia sensed the edge to his voice, an exertion of control that made her wary. He sounded as if he were about to interrogate a prisoner.

She bristled. "I'd rather not. Those were painful years; I'd rather not relive them for your amusement." She let him hear the irritation in her voice.

"I will not be amused."

She was tired of the lies Tom had trusted her to maintain. Only half an hour ago, she had decided to let Aidan know everything and bear the consequences. But this was not that Aidan. No, they were back to their London détente, and her previous path was best: tell him only what was essential. The rest could wait until she was sure where they stood.

"What do you want to know?"

"I don't know yet. Let's start with when he got sick."

She gestured uncertainty. "I don't know. I first realized something was wrong when Ian was five. The night was stormy, and Tom and I were working in the library; Ian had been scared and wished to stay with us rather than go up to his nursery. He fell asleep on the rug in front of the fire, and Tom decided not to call for the footman, but to carry Ian up to the nursery himself. When carrying Ian up the stairs fatigued him, I realized how pale and thin he'd become. After that, I watched him more carefully. If he took cold, it took him longer to recover, and he took cold more often. Chills, fevers. His bones ached."

Aidan listened carefully. Her story matched the one Ophelia had told him after Tom's death. "Did you consult a physician?"

She shrugged. "Tom was a scientist. He knew his symptoms, so he read widely. He found a description of cases like his in Hewson's *Inquiry into the Properties of the Blood*. So he asked an Italian at the Academy of Sciences to examine his blood. Like those Hewson described, Tom's blood, when left to sit, appeared white like milk. The treatises tied that to poor digestion. Since Tom's stomach was frequently unsettled after eating, he tried to choose foods that were more mild."

"Did that work?"

She shook her head. "Had it been his digestion, a change in regimen would have helped. But it didn't."

"Tell me about the day he died." Aidan's voice offered no more inflection than if he were asking about the weather or a new barn cat.

"The day he died or his death."

"Both."

"The day he died was ordinary. We worked in the library on his book, and he wrapped up some chapters and correspondence for his publisher. I remember because Tom seemed more relieved than usual to have that task out of the way and because I found the package unsent after his death. Ian had exhausted himself playing at the house of a friend, so he took dinner with his governess in the nursery. After dinner, I took my leave of Tom and returned to my rooms. In the morning he was still in the library, lying on a couch. Luca called me, but Tom was already cold. He looked like he had fallen asleep; his arm was hanging off the edge of the couch, the book he had been reading on the floor."

"What book?"

She looked startled. "Charlotte Smith's *Elegiac Sonnets*."

"Was that a typical book for Tom to read?"

"No, actually, it was one of mine. Tom usually fell asleep to something more weighty."

"Is it here?"

"It might be in the box of books we took from the trunks."

"Can you remember anything else?"

She could remember every detail. Sending Luca for Tom's doctor, asking a footman to tell the governess to keep Ian in his rooms until Sophia had a chance to talk with him. The faces of the magistrates as they expressed their condolences. The wailing of the Italian servants. Ian's pale frightened face. Holding herself tightly under control until she could escape to her room. The color of the pansies outside the door in the garden. "No; that's all."

"I've just received this from London." He took the folded newspaper from under his arm. "Read this." He held his finger at a point circled in pencil midway down the page. It was one of the scandal sheets Ophelia loved reading.

> *"Last year Lord W died in Naples after a long illness. But some say Lord W's lips smelled of bitter almonds. Did Lady W poison her loving husband's wine? Or did Lord W commit suicide to avoid discovery as a traitor?"*

She sat frozen on the chaise longue, turning pale. For a moment, Aidan feared that the paper might include some truth.

She slowly shook her head. "Treason? No one was more English than Tom, all king and country. We stayed abroad so long only because I wished it. Tom would have come home years ago. Then later, he was sick." Her voice drifted off. "Why would someone kill a dying man? It makes no sense. And I . . . I never would have harmed Tom."

Suddenly all her stoic reserve felt a fragile wall. Her shoulders began to tremble as if she had just come in from a cold night. Aidan placed his hand on her shoulder, its weight and warmth offering her some calm. But the touch was too much, and the contact set her weeping.

"I'm sorry, Sophia. When I opened the packet and saw the paper, I didn't know what to think. . . ." He sat beside her, pulling her into his chest, letting her weep, and brushing her hair softly with his hand. "I believe you. But you are right: it's time to return to London. We'll leave in the morning, and when we arrive, I'll set Aldine to investigate who might be spreading such malicious gossip."

Chapter Thirty-One

Charters scanned the bar. Mostly old seamen and soldiers, hungry by the look of them. Now that the wars were over, too many wounded soldiers languished without employment or family. He didn't see the man he'd come to meet, one of the proprietors of a gambling hell with extensive connections. Charters had been wary when the meeting had been set for outside the hell, wondering if it were an ambush.

"You might want to sit down, sir. . . ."

Charters stopped and turned. A light-haired man in his forties, one arm bandaged, sat at a three-legged table, the ground around him covered with wood shavings. The man picked up a new piece of wood, and Charters watched a shape emerge.

"I beg your pardon," Charters stated.

"I been watching you. Wasn't sure I knew you before tonight. But now I'm sure. We served together in the wars." The soldier's hands were steady, despite the appearance of a damaged arm.

"I didn't serve in the wars." Charters watched the wood turn. A round body with a long neck appeared, then two sharp cuts gave the head a beak.

"Depends on how you define service. Maybe you didn't do service to crown or country. But you served a cause, all the same." The soldier never looked up from his carving.

Charters wished he could see the color of the thin man's eyes or his expression. Two long legs began to emerge from the wood. A heron, Charters realized. He might well know this man. He pulled out a chair. "I'm sitting. And I'm listening."

The man laughed. "It's as I expected. You were always a cold one. Waiting until you had enough information before you acted." He turned the bird to smooth the edges.

"I'm not sure I have enough information yet. Who do you think I am?" Charters picked up a piece of whittling from the table and took a penknife from his pocket. He began to carve as well.

"You saved my life once. I expect I'll be saving yours tonight." The man's hands were still calloused and worn, but his movements with the knife created delicate lines.

He'd been a big man, strong. Charters tried to imagine him hale and hearty, instead of wiry and thin.

"I suppose I should buy us dinner. I'd hate to have an empty stomach." Charters lifted his hand to the barmaid and indicated two dinners. He wouldn't eat, but the soldier might want both.

The men fell into silence. The wood was soft, easy to carve. Charters made a fat ship, with a raised deck at the front and rear. Then he scored the boat's sides to signify cannon bays and windows.

The dinners came. Charters saw part of a naval tattoo on the lower part of the man's arm when he raised bread to his mouth. Though it was clear he was hungry, he didn't fall on his food. Instead, he ate slowly, watching the room.

"A man's sitting in the back corner across from the bar." The seaman didn't look up when he spoke.

"I saw him when I came in." Charters focused on his design, the line of the stern, the lift of the prow.

"He's been asking after you. Seems you have some dealings he doesn't like." The man tested the base of his bird, seeing if it would stand on its own.

"I don't know your name." Charters turned to a second scrap of wood, made a mast with a small sail attached.

"My friends call me Flute." The man brushed his mouth, not with his sleeve but with a handkerchief from his pocket.

"What should I call you?" Charters twisted a hole in the wood and set the mast.

Flute watched Charters's carving take shape. "I knew you'd remember me."

"Hard to forget dragging a man out of the ocean, then having him curse you for its being too cold." Charters pushed his plate across the table.

"It was a nice fire you built, though," Flute offered. He began to eat the second meal.

"I'm still not sure why I did it," Charters acknowledged.

"I wasn't sure at the time, but I was real grateful. Didn't much want to drown that day." Flute trimmed just a bit more off the bird's base and pushed it toward Charters. "A memento for you of a good ship."

"A good ship," Charters repeated, surprised that he found conversation so easy with the former midshipman. He pushed the carved ship across the table to Flute. "I find I'm in need of an assistant; the pay may not be much at first, but I reward loyalty."

"I've been listening to that man's complaints for most of the last week. If half of what he's saying is true, you need discretion as much as loyalty." Flute smiled. "As for loyalty, I came home to a country that has already forgotten I served her; I serve myself now."

"That's the words of a revolutionary," Charters said. "That kind of talk can get you transported, or worse."

"Then call me a revolutionary," Flute said, his expression turning hard. "I serve no king."

"Then we'll serve no king together. Now, how do we get out of here without either of us getting killed?" Charters asked, slipping the heron into his pocket.

"I've already worked that out." Flute picked up the carved ship and smiled.

Chapter Thirty-Two

That night Sophia slept fitfully, her dreams only incoherent flashes. Tom in their library in Italy was showing her the pages of his manuscript. He pointed at the titles of the plants in her illustrations, but when she tried to read the words, they shifted to gibberish. The plants held a message. If she could only read the words or recognize the plants themselves, she was sure she would know something important.

The dream shifted: images of Aidan angry, the lines of his face hard, pushing her away. Flashes of Tom searching for Ian, but not finding him. The body of a dark-haired child floating in a pond, and Tom's voice calling out to her.

She awoke, her pillow wet with tears.

Aidan rode outside the carriage. To keep watch, he said. But with the slanderous accusations in the newspapers, something subtle had shifted between them.

He'd worn so many faces in the past weeks, the solicitous old friend, the protective duke, the concerned elder brother, the attentive lover, and even, for some fleeting moments, a man she didn't yet know, one who was all of those things, but somehow new. She'd first glimpsed that man in the folly when he'd looked on his own portrait.

Yet with the renewed threats, he had reverted to his role as the detached former officer planning some strategy. She wondered which man—if any—would come back to her in the end.

The countryside passed beyond the carriage window, the rolling hills, the thick green of the hedgerows of the enclosed land, the glimpses of open pasture beyond the stands of trees. She realized she had missed the English countryside, the way the light suffused a scene rather than shining directly on it. She'd loved the Italian sun, its warmth, its angles, but she'd missed the soft rain of an English morning, the gentle breeze of the afternoon, the smell of wet hay. She closed her eyes and listened to what seemed like purely English sounds: wood pigeons, collared doves, thrushes, jackdaws, the bleating of the goats at the crossroad.

She had believed that she could live to old age without coming back to England. But in truth, she had needed to come home.

When they finally reached London, Aidan escorted her into her hall. He consulted briefly with Dodsley, then took his leave, claiming an important meeting. He had showed her the newspaper, but not the letter from Walgrave that accompanied it.

Once Aidan left, she climbed the stairs to the family wing and Luca's bedroom. Luca answered at the first tap, and a lithe child with thick black curls ran past him to embrace her. "Sophie, Sophie, Sophie!" Liliana hugged Sophia through her skirts, then hid in them as a game, making Sophia turn and turn to "find" her.

"Luca almost made me go to bed, but I knew you'd come today. He wrote you day before yesterday, so I knew you'd come today."

Sophia picked the child up and hugged her to her chest,

kissing her forehead. "I had to come. My sweet Lily was waiting for me. But it's long past time for you to be sleeping." She carried the child to the bed. "I see your brother has given up his room for you."

"I'd rather be in the nursery with Ian. Where's Ian?" Sophia tucked the coverlet under Lily's chin and made her giggle.

Sophia considered her words, then decided Lily had seen enough to be told the truth. "There's a man who knew your father, but didn't like him. I was afraid he might steal Ian away, so I hid Ian with my cousins. So, I want you to stay very close to Luca or Dodsley, so the man can't steal you either."

"What about you, Sophie? Can I stay close to you?"

"Yes, my darling, you may. But for now—just for a little while—I want you to be very careful. Don't talk to anyone that I haven't introduced you to . . . and if someone tries to talk to you . . ."

"I'm to run and tell you or Luca."

"Yes."

"Luca already told me, and Mama told me I had to mind whatever you tell me to do. Do you like my English, Sophie? Luca has made me practice every day. No Italian."

"Your English is beautiful." Sophia remembered her determination to rear Lily as her mother had her. "Ian has a tutor, Mr. Grange; would you like me to ask Mr. Grange to teach you too?"

"Just like Ian?"

"Just like Ian."

"Molto buono." Lily grimaced and corrected herself. "I'd like that."

"Then I'll write and see if we can begin tomorrow. Sleep now." Sophia brushed the child's hair back from her face. Within moments Lily was asleep.

Luca understood the dangers. Whenever possible, they were to stay out of sight—the fewer people who knew he had returned the safer. Luca, devoted to his niece, proclaimed with honest fervor that he would not leave her side. He would play with her in the nursery unless Mr. Grange was available to tutor her.

Before she retired to bed, Sophia reviewed the mail Dodsley had stored in the study. A pile of invitations. She opened each one quickly, making two piles, future regrets and past apologies. Until the blackmailer was discovered, she would not be making social calls.

Before she retired, she wrote Mr. Grange a lucrative proposal, asking if he would be interested in educating her ward Lily as if she were a boy.

Walgrave's letter had warned that new information might implicate her ladyship and had summoned Aidan to a secret meeting at his home. Aidan assumed that the new information was more than just society-page gossip.

Walgrave's study was darkened when Aidan arrived. A low fire burned on the grate; a single lamp was placed next to an empty chair. Aidan paused, letting his eyes adjust to the half-light. From his armed chair, Walgrave motioned Aidan to sit. From the position of the lamp, Aidan would be illuminated, but would be unable to see past its light.

Walgrave stood and tapped on the butler's entrance. A moment later, the door opened, and a figure entered the room. It moved deliberately but slowly to a chair set well in the dark. Aidan listened as he watched: the thump of a cane, the twist of the body as a foot dragged behind. A veteran, he thought, and then wondered, of what battles?

He acknowledged the wisdom of the man's entrance: had he been in the room when Aidan arrived, the light from the door or the lamp between them might have revealed more to Aidan's view than this method did.

As soon as the third man was seated, Walgrave spoke. "If anyone ever asks, you and I met alone."

"Understood."

"Someone in the Home Office owes you a favor. He has asked for me to convey a warning."

"That could be many people. Anyone in particular?"

"I'm only at liberty to divulge that promptly at eight a.m. two officers of the court will arrive at Lady Wilmot's house to search for documents tying her husband to instances of treason abroad. In particular they will be looking for evidence Lord Wilmot was involved in the death of a British courier in Naples."

"What am I expected to do with this information?"

"They have it on good authority that the papers will be found in Lord Wilmot's library. In fact, the informant is so trusted that a warrant has already been issued for Lady Wilmot's arrest."

"I've already reported there's nothing there."

"That's why you are receiving this warning. You have a little more than eight hours. I suggest you find those papers before the officers arrive at Lady Wilmot's door."

"Is there no way to stop this search?"

"People aren't sympathetic to traitors, particularly aristocratic ones. If you use your influence to keep Lady Wilmot's house from being searched, and her enemy decides to place other advertisements in the daily post indicating your interference, she will appear guilty of something. With the times as they are, she will become a target for the discontented."

"She won't like this."

"I'll come with you. I visited the Wilmots in Naples. She won't believe me in collusion with whatever ill designs you have on her."

"Ill designs?" Aidan shook his head in exasperation. First Malcolm, now Walgrave.

"We can discuss that later. Her enemy is clever enough to

gain the assent of someone high enough in government to approve the search of the home of a peer. She's in trouble."

Aidan nodded. "We should be going then; we have little time."

"I'll meet you in the hall," Walgrave replied.

After Aidan shut the door behind him, Walgrave turned to the man in the dark. "Are you sure meeting with him was a good idea, sir?"

"I wanted to see him again. Besides, once you are dead, no one expects you to be alive. With this broken body, I could pass him on the street, and he would never give me a glance."

"Won't he wonder why someone in the Home Office is watching out for him?"

"He was a good agent; he has many friends. He will assume that I can't reveal myself for other reasons."

"Wouldn't he prefer to know you are alive?"

"Perhaps. But if he knew I were alive, he'd feel compelled to step aside, to relinquish the dukedom in my favor. That's the last responsibility I want."

"But it is your right."

"The king accepts my desire to live in shadows. He gives me an ample stipend, and I have no interest in being on display. As far as anyone will ever know, Benjamin Somerville died at Waterloo."

Aidan and Walgrave arrived at Sophia's house shortly after midnight. The curtains had been drawn in all the downstairs rooms, including the library. It was unlikely anyone would be watching the back of Lady Wilmot's house, but Aidan wished to be cautious, and Walgrave concurred. They took the entrance from the side yard directly into the kitchen. There waking Dodsley, Aidan instructed the butler to keep watch at Lady Wilmot's bedroom, and if she woke, to call for him.

An hour later, Walgrave opened a book supportive of the radical revolutionaries in Italy and found in it a small packet of pages carrying the broken seal of the British consul in Naples.

"I've found them." Walgrave held out the papers. Dark rust-colored stains had caused the ink to run until the words were illegible.

"Blood?"

"The courier was stabbed several times in the chest before his body was cast in the river. He must have been carrying the papers close to his heart, and the blood . . ."

". . . has made them unreadable." Aidan placed a second set of papers on the desk. "I've found something as well. Bank notes. Forged."

Walgrave picked up a one-pound note and held it to the light. "If it's a forgery, it's a very good one. How do you know?"

"Neither these notes nor those papers were here when last I searched."

"So if we hadn't found them first, she'd be a traitor and a forger. The officers could allow her to remain at home with the courier's papers alone, but the forged notes would require her to be committed to jail until a hearing." Walgrave ran his hand through his hair in consternation. "Whoever has crafted this net wishes to destroy her quite thoroughly."

Aidan suppressed a desire to curse. "I think it's time to talk to Lady Wilmot."

When Sophia came downstairs, she took in the mess in the library in one sweeping look. Her resentment at the destruction and the invasion was palpable. This was fully the Sophia he knew in their youth, alive with ire and passion.

She looked at Aidan with barely concealed fury. "To what"—she clipped her words—"do I owe the pleasure of your company? If you wished some reading material, Dodsley could have delivered anything you wished to your homes."

"My lady, I think . . ." Walgrave started forward to appease her, but Aidan held him back with his hand.

She turned on him. "You already knew what was in this library. We searched it together. If you believed there was something more to be found, why did you not call for me to help?"

"You couldn't be here when we searched," Aidan explained. "Someone claimed you had the papers, proving you were a spy. We were only making sure they weren't here."

"And they weren't." Sophia glared. "So why are you here?"

"Actually, Lady Wilmot," Walgrave offered, "we have them; we found them quite easily." He held out the papers, and Aidan searched her face for signs of recognition.

She moved forward and looked at the papers without touching. "That red . . . Is it?"

"Yes." Aidan watched her face pale. "These cannot be found here. Walgrave will take them to the Home Office."

Walgrave placed the papers in his inner coat pocket.

Sophia turned to Walgrave. "Forster can attest that those papers were not here as recently as last month. I can also prove they were not in my husband's possession . . . at least not in those possessions we sent home from Italy."

"How?" Walgrave stepped forward. "We may need to know."

"May I see them?" Sophia motioned at the papers.

Walgrave took the papers from his pocket, and held them out, one sheet in each hand.

"I would prefer not to touch them. Can you turn them over for me?" Sophia examined the upper margins.

Walgrave held the backs of the sheets out for her inspection.

"Before we returned, I numbered each piece of Tom's papers and recorded them in a ledger, so that if a trunk went missing at least we would know what was lost. These aren't numbered."

"Can we see the ledger?" Walgrave folded the papers and returned them to his pocket.

"Certainly. It's in the locking cabinet." Sophia pointed to the corner behind the desk.

Aidan unfolded the bank notes and slid them forward for her examination. "What do you know of these?"

"I know nothing of those." Sophia looked bewildered. "I pay my staff and make my smaller expenditures in coin. Any larger bills I forward to Aldine to draw against my accounts."

Aidan exchanged a glance with Walgrave. "Are you aware that simply having forged notes in your possession is as much a crime as making or using them? The officers, finding these, would have taken you directly to the Tower."

Aidan folded the bills and handed them to Walgrave. "You know what to do with those?"

Walgrave nodded.

Aidan turned his attention back to Sophia. "Think carefully. Are there any papers here that you would not wish to be discovered?"

She looked to the desk and put her hand to her breast. Aidan could see the faintest hint of a ribbon. Aidan glanced at Walgrave to see he had also noticed. Walgrave nodded in acknowledgment.

"Show us what you have and where they are hidden. We can't risk that something else has been hidden there as well." Aidan felt the same anxiety he'd felt when they'd entered. What if they failed? What would happen to Sophia if they didn't find all the evidence planted against her? Would he lose her just as he'd found her again?

"There are some papers. But I . . ." She turned slightly away from him and instead looked imploringly at Walgrave. Aidan felt his blood rise as anxiety turned to anger. She should have looked to him. What was she hiding?

"Damn it, woman. We have little time." Aidan stalked to the desk, barely containing his growing fury. Ignoring Sophia's side of the partner desk, he sat on Tom's side. His eyes followed each curve of the carved design, examined each panel until he saw a slight bump near the corner. He felt the molding, exerting pressure with his fingers as he moved his hand along the frame. He felt a click, and a panel opened. Behind it was a keyhole.

He turned to Sophia. "The key." He held out his hand.

She didn't move.

"Sophia, any agent of the Home Office will find this compartment in no more time than it took me. Give me the key. I can pick the lock, but I might damage it."

She still didn't move. He remembered again the press of her lips against his, the crush of her body moving in passion against him, his own passion sated in her sighs. A week in his bed and his company, and she still didn't trust him. He'd been betrayed again, by her and by his own desires. To think he had changed his mind about her and her motives—to think he had almost confessed he loved her.

"Fine." He pulled a penknife from his boot and reached toward the lock.

"No. Don't destroy it; it would be obvious." She lifted the ribbon from her neck and handed him the key. "Would you trust me if I told you the papers are only of the most personal nature?"

"What, Sophia? Letters from a lover?" Aidan growled.

"In a sense." Her voice was almost a whisper.

That was the wrong answer. He resisted jamming the key in the lock. He had to get himself under control. He had been searching the library, frightened they wouldn't find whatever had been hidden there in time. And she had been hiding papers all along, even through the night they had searched together. Papers of a "most personal nature."

He heard the lock click open and pulled gently on the key as if it were a handle. The door swung free.

"Is the hair still there?"

"Hair?"

"I placed a hair over the stack, so that I would know if the letters had been disturbed."

"Look for yourself."

He pulled away from the space so that she could lean in to see. The plait of her hair in a loose braid down her back brushed his shoulder. Without wanting to, he desired her. She began to reach in, but he stopped her. "That's enough. Step away."

Her hand hesitated, then withdrew. She obeyed with reticence. "I would prefer for Walgrave to examine the papers."

He ignored her and took the papers out. There were several documents. Two were folded in half then in an accordion, the outside of the document labeled. His Italian was sufficient to see they were both certifications of birth. The third was a letter, seal intact, addressed in Tom's hand . . . to him.

He began to break open the seal.

"Aidan, wait. Let me explain."

"This letter is addressed to me. You have had weeks to explain whatever it reveals."

She looked crushed, and Walgrave went to stand by her, placing his arm around her shoulders in comfort. She looked up at him pleadingly. "It's not the time. Please, stop him. I promise I'll explain later."

Aidan glared at Walgrave, who shrugged. He placed the letter addressed to him to the side and focused on the birth papers.

The first birth certificate was six years old, and recorded the birth of a Liliana Gardiner; mother, Francesca Bruni, father, Thomas Gardiner, Lord Wilmot. Tom had fathered and acknowledged a child, while married to Sophia. So she did know of the mistress.

The second was a birth certificate for Ian, mother Sophia, father Tom, but the date of birth was wrong, making Ian older, almost ten. If that were the case, then Sophia had been pregnant when she married Tom. That didn't fit with her story of a marriage forged by her aunt's machinations, but her aunt had offered the story herself, and Sophia's dislike of her aunt had been palpable. Something didn't fit, but he would think on it later; he was still too angry to think clearly. He reached for the letter.

"Aidan, Tom left that letter in my care; I was to choose the best time for you to read it. Trust me: this is not it." She was pleading. And through his anger, he saw the moment of his revenge come into focus, if he still wished for it. She was in his power. The passion of the past week had given him the hold he wanted, but the softness of her body had stripped him of his resolve. There was only one truth he knew: whatever was in the letter, she wished for him not to know. And he had thought she had trusted him with all her secrets. Had he been less angry, he might have admitted that he still had secrets of his own. But he felt frustrated, hurt, and betrayed. Again.

He pushed the letter into his boot. "Then I will read it later. But this one tells me a great deal." He held out Liliana's birth certificate. "Tom fathered a bastard."

"No. Tom acknowledged Liliana as his child; I agreed. In part, the letter to you asks for you to serve as Liliana's guardian. Tom knew Lily would need a powerful ally to ensure she is never deprived of her settlement as his daughter."

"Francesca . . ." He looked back at the name of Tom's mistress, then remembered the woven blanket in Tom's case in the attic, the perfume of bergamot. "The Francesca who lived at your villa?"

Walgrave interjected. "Aidan, there is no time for this. We still haven't found Tom's code key. And we have to repair the room before the magistrates arrive." He turned to Sophia, apology on his face and in his voice. "Forster has to read his letter now. It might offer something of value to us in understanding Tom's code."

She watched with dread as Aidan pulled the letter out and turned it over. "Stop! If you must read it, we should be alone. Walgrave, could you remain here and repair this mess? I'll call Dodsley. We'll be . . . only a little while." Once more in control, she motioned toward the door. "Please."

Aidan leaned forward, shutting the door on the now-empty compartment, relocking the door, and resetting the panel that hid it all from view. He placed the key with the ribbon in the top desk drawer for the officials to find and use. Then, standing, he picked up the birth certificates and his letter. He offered with false gallantry, "After you, my lady."

She led him, not to the study, but up the stairs to her dressing room, which was brightly lit.

"Are you thinking to seduce me, madam, to regain those papers? Because I'm sure we have time for such entertainment." He pulled her to him, kissed her deeply, pressing his firmness into her belly. She pushed him away.

"I need to change into more suitable clothes if I'm going to be surprised by the police. I assumed you would want to search my private rooms."

"No, I've already done that. Weeks ago."

She looked startled, confused. This was his opportunity. To watch her face change from trust to realization.

"You've been spying on me?" Her tone held startled disbelief. "Why?"

"It was a request of the Home Office, nothing more."

"If it were nothing more, then you wouldn't have agreed. What was it that made you agree? It couldn't have been something I'd done. . . . We hadn't seen each other in years. All this time, I thought you were being kind to me. To Ian."

Tears filled her eyes, and the pain in them clutched at his heart, but only for a moment. She turned away from him, and he watched her back as she stood quietly. She took a linen handkerchief from a pocket in her dress and wiped her eyes. He watched her back stiffen before she turned back to him. When she did face him once more, his Sophia of the past week was fully gone. "But you weren't, were you?"

The flat emotionless tone was back in her voice, and like Shakespeare's Hermione, Sophia had turned back into a statue.

He began to speak, but she held up her hand, pressed it lightly to his lips, a motion that had she done it only an hour ago would have been the touch of a lover. But now she was cold. "No, don't speak, at least not of this."

"Why didn't you tell me you were increasing before you married?" He sat on the stool in front of her toilette. The scent of lavender water almost made him relent.

She stiffened. "You didn't ask. But Tom's letter will explain."

"I'm not interested in Tom's letter at this moment." To emphasize his words, he placed the letter on her dressing table. He watched her look at the letter. "I'm interested in how quickly my fiancée threw me over to marry my best friend. I was gone less than two weeks before my father wrote with the news that you and Tom were engaged." This was his moment to turn the knife. He stretched as if completely at ease. "Given Ian's birthday, you must have fallen into Tom's bed almost as soon as I left."

He watched her eyes widen, and her face turn pale. The knuckles in her hand whitened as she grasped the back of a chair.

"You got the letters in time, before the wedding." She spoke slowly, parsing out the words. "You knew we sent for you, but you hid from us. From me."

He nodded, offering his most charming smile, and shrugged. "I was ready to go abroad, to make my fortune, and you had chosen a more lucrative arrangement." He had it: his revenge, there in the way her shoulders collapsed just slightly, the downward turn of her head, the tightening of her hand into a fist that she pressed to her mouth to catch the sob.

"So, let's read this letter. Perhaps I can ignore it as well," he quipped. She said nothing, staring at him inscrutably.

He began to read. Tom began with the same narrative of how they had been forced into an engagement by the machinations of her aunt. Aidan could hear his old friend's voice, and he pitied Tom for falling for the siren he now knew too clearly Sophia had been . . . and remained.

"By now Sophia has confided in you the reasons for our marriage. The night of the ball I had been coming to find you, so that you and she could elope. But her aunt's scheme complicated everything; the man was cruel and a rogue, and I feared what he would have done to her—or your child—if she had been forced to marry him."

The words "your child" struck home. Aidan's head reeled. Suddenly, he saw all the details he'd ignored come together in a clear picture: Tom's insistence that Aidan be Ian's guardian; Sophia's face when she'd told him Ian's age; Ian's ability to strategize; and Malcolm's persistent intuition that there was something to the story they didn't know. Aidan's stomach turned at the realization that Barlow had been right: Aidan had let his irrational pursuit of Sophia's guilt cloud his judgment, and now, he had destroyed his own happiness as much as he had destroyed hers. He needed time to take it all in, to see the true shape of the story. But this much was clear: whatever Sophia had believed before, she knew now that he had chosen to abandon her.

The sound of Sophia talking brought him back to the present.

"All these years I thought you hadn't gotten my letter, that if you had, you would have returned, that it was my fault, all of it, for loving you too much, for putting Tom in the position to save my reputation, for making it so that Tom couldn't marry the woman he loved when he found her. All those years

I wondered how my life, Tom's life, all of our lives, would have been different if you had received just one of those letters, if you had come back. All these years I felt that we cheated you somehow of your child, of your right to see him grow up. But you *chose* not to come back. I never considered that: that you would choose to stay away."

"Sophia . . . I believed you had chosen Tom."

She shook her head, refusing him the explanation, and her belief. "You told me to send for you if I needed you, and I did. I trusted you. Trusted that you loved me. But you didn't trust me. Or Tom. And you never wondered, not for one instant, what might have happened for us to call you back."

She turned toward the fireplace, speaking to herself, not to him. "I never let myself believe that Tom was the better man. I always loved him for the man he was, and for all he did for me and Ian. But I never let him replace you in my heart. Yet he was faithful to you all along, giving up his own freedom because you and I were reckless. Because he loved you . . . and me."

Aidan watched her in the mirror beside the fireplace, and he waited for her anger. There should have been anger; he had been the faithless one, not her. He had chosen to believe her a flirt and a jilt, less interested in his love than in Tom's money. Without realizing how much he had imbibed his father's and Aaron's values, Aidan had believed himself to have so little value that he had been unable to believe that Sophia loved him. The words had come so easily to her; they couldn't be true. Though all his work for the Home Office during the wars had relied on his ability to see past appearances to the truth of things, in his own affairs, he had failed to exercise even the most basic curiosity. He had failed to ask *why*, because doing so would have revealed his own failings and his own culpability. He turned his attention back to Sophia—the woman he now realized he had wronged deeply and repeatedly.

"One thing I have to know." She did not look at him as she spoke, but kept her gaze on the image of her husband. "Tom knew you had chosen not to come back, didn't he?"

Aidan felt more ashamed than he had at any other moment in his life. But she deserved to know the extent to which he had failed her. He owed her that, even if it meant she would hate him.

"I sent Tom a message telling him where I was and offering to give up my commission if he would break the engagement and travel the Continent with me." He forced himself to speak firmly. But he wished she would turn to him, let him make his confession face-to-face.

She nodded in thought. "That makes sense. The day before the wedding Tom gave me a choice. He told me he believed you were in Dover. He and I could pretend to elope, find you, then—with Tom as our witness—you and I could go to Gretna Green. Or—he even knelt before me and took my hand," she said, and smiled sadly at the memory, "he and I could marry the next morning in the church surrounded by all my cousins and his sisters, and he would cherish me and our child until the day he died." Her smile faded, and she grew silent.

In her silence, Aidan heard all his hopes for a life together disappear. Just when Aidan thought Sophia would not speak again, she turned. "And Tom did. He did cherish us. Tom never broke a promise to me or to Ian. And I loved him for it. Not the kind of love I have, had"—she corrected herself—"for you, all passion and emotion. But a rational love as true as my love for you was strong. So you are right: in a way I did choose Tom. I chose his kindness, his dependability, his truth, even his idealism. When he fell in love with Francesca, he realized what possibilities he had given up in marrying me. But he gave me a choice again: I was his wife; he would be faithful. But Francesca loved him, and I told Tom to love her, as I had loved you."

He heard the slight emphasis on the word *had*. It had all fallen apart, as Malcolm had predicted. Having gained his revenge, Aidan was left only with the knowledge that he was the betrayer, of her, of Tom, of his son. Worse, he had loved her all along. And he'd lost her twice because he was a fool.

She turned back to face him, the portrait of Tom behind her. Both of them looked at him, disappointment in their eyes. "Ophelia assured me you never reveal your affairs. I hope you will be discreet about ours, if only for the sake of your ward. Ian should not suffer for my sins. Of course I've put myself at your mercy, haven't I? I suppose it was your plan all along. You must have hated me a great deal."

"Sophia . . ."

She raised her hand to silence him. "It's growing late—or rather early. Your magistrates will be here soon. I would like for you to return to the library to help Walgrave and Dodsley. But by the time I come downstairs, I wish for you to be gone. We can arrange for Ian's care through Aldine from this point forward."

She held out her hand, and he hoped for a moment she would touch him one last time. "My children's birth certificates, please. I will send them to Aldine. You may, of course, keep Tom's letter. I trust you will keep its contents a secret."

There was nothing he could do but return them. He held them out, and she took the certificates without touching him. She crossed the dressing room to the door leading to her bedchamber.

She turned back toward him before leaving the room, her eyes sad. "Tom sacrificed a great deal to protect your son. He gave Ian a legitimate name and a title. As Tom's sisters can tell you from their various settlements, Tom went to great lengths to ensure that no one would ever challenge Ian's rights. You can marry and have other sons. Tom had only Ian. For his sake and for Ian's, never reveal the truth."

She shut the door to her bedchamber, leaving Aidan in her dressing room, the light of the candles still bright. He heard the turn of the key in the lock behind her. He listened, hoping to hear weeping. . . . Tears would mean he had a chance to make amends. But there was nothing, no sound at all.

Everything he had believed for the past decade had turned out to be a torment he had created for himself. He hadn't told her, but his father's letter had set the stage, in its sneering announcement that his "fool friend" had gotten his "wings clipped" by some "country trollope" who'd likely "turned her heels up for a dozen men" before she found one with a title to marry.

Marrying her would have been difficult, but her uncle had liked him. Why had he not considered whether they could live on her settlement? Why had he left her, expecting her to wait? Why had he not wondered why she and Tom had called him back? Had he really been so young, so inexperienced, that he hadn't considered she could be increasing? What sort of fool had he been? And more significantly, what sort of fool had he remained? Had he not been proud, he could have been married to Sophia and watched his heir grow from infancy. Had he not been intent on revenge, he would have realized Tom had offered him a great gift in the guardianship.

Sophia leaned back against the door, then turned the key in the lock. She would not cry. There would be time for tears later. She would not give him the satisfaction of hearing her weep.

She should not have been surprised at his revelation. She'd known who he was . . . or rather who he had the potential to be. She'd seen it in his brother Aaron. It was the reason she'd stayed in Italy so long.

But somehow with Aidan these last weeks, she'd allowed herself to forget. And now she was in his power. Now that he knew Ian was his son, he would never let her keep him all the year round. No, he would expect Ian to live at his estate . . . and to go away to school sooner.

She'd trusted Aidan again, and he'd again betrayed her. She should have grown wise before she'd grown old.

But even now, feeling the sting of his betrayal, she loved him. She would never admit it, never acknowledge it again, but her heart still pined for the sound of his voice, the touch of his hands, his lips.

But she would survive. She had done so once; she would do so again. She simply could never have any expectations, except that he would—if she allowed him the chance—fail her again.

Aidan was still with the officers in the library when Sophia was called from her room, suitably dressed in her morning clothes, three hours later. She looked past him as if he meant no more to her than one of the officers themselves. Regardless of what she now thought, he would not abandon her again. . . . Even if she never knew, he would watch over her.

That night the dream came again, but without any trace of Sophia. Tom stood half in darkness, one hand on the top of a gold-handled cane, and the other extended toward a pool where the dark-haired child floated facedown in the waters. There was nothing else, just the floating child, and the sorrow on Tom's face.

Chapter Thirty-Three

The night had a chill, and Aidan pulled the blanket tighter around his body. The crawlspace above the stables provided little room for movement. But it gave a vantage point over the wall of the garden where he could watch to see if anyone approached the house from the back. He had pulled a board loose to improve his range of vision. But having lain flat on his stomach for several hours, he'd begun to feel the position in his neck and shoulders.

He had intended to slip into the house and guard over Sophia as he had in the nights before Seth was injured. But he found the gate at the bottom of the garden repaired with a new and sturdy lock. When he walked through the mews to her stables and tried to get in through the kitchen, he found Cook, holding out what was left of a bag of pistachios. She'd seemed relieved when he refused to take them, but the message was clear: he was no longer welcome. When he'd asked to speak with Dodsley, the butler had appeared immediately, but refused him entrance, stepping into the yard to talk with him and reminding him that his loyalties were with her ladyship.

None of her servants seemed to understand that Aidan only wanted to keep her safe. Dodsley had finally agreed to allow the additional four servants to return under three conditions: that they answered to Dodsley and not to the duke; that the duke continued to pay their wages; and finally that her ladyship didn't object to their presence. As a concession, Dodsley had agreed not to raise the issue of the servants with her ladyship, lest she object. But that was solely because Dodsley cared for her safety.

Dodsley had also agreed, and Aidan was sure it was intended as a punishment, that if his grace insisted on staying on the grounds, he could take the crawlspace above the stable that her ladyship thought not fit for the groom. That was how Aidan had arrived here, cold, flea-bitten, and stiff.

Sophia knew that her blackmailer had not been found, that she needed protection, but she refused Aidan's help, saying she had other relations on whom she could rely. But affable Hal and the twins had no experience with the kind of enemy she faced, and they were more likely to get themselves hurt than do any real good at protecting her. No, she was only making it harder for Aidan to keep her safe. But knowing Sophia, she would tell him she had managed to take care of herself for years without his help. And she had. Still, what else could he do? He owed her too much for his past inconstancy to fail to be faithful now. He wanted somehow to make amends, and he still held a very slender hope that someday—if he were constant and patient enough—she might give him another chance.

During the day, he would return home to sleep, trusting his men and her relatives to guard her in the daylight. Then each evening, he would spend his time in the alleys and mews behind her house and after sunset in his stable loft, waiting and watching.

On returning to town, he'd immediately put Aldine on the task of tracing who had placed the scandalous advertisement. The information Aldine had uncovered was disturbing. The man who had placed the advertisement had paid in advance to insert one advertisement each week for a month;

he'd paid for all four weeks in advance in bank notes, not coin. The newspaper had inserted the first week's notice immediately, but when the bank notes had proved to be forgeries, the firm had thrown away the text for the later insertions. It was regrettable; the text might have given some hint to their adversary's plan.

The description of the man who had bought the advertisements matched that of Aldine's temporary clerk, Charters, now missing. Charters had disappeared about the time that news began to circulate that the body of the clerk he'd replaced, a country boy who had resigned by way of a note about returning home, had been pulled from the river. Aldine now suspected the clerk's resignation note had simply been a ruse, and he was displeased he had believed it without further investigation. Both Aidan and Aldine had decided to see if Charters could be found, but when they had gone to the address he had provided, they'd found a blacksmith's shop with no lodgings. Another indication that Charters was somehow connected to the man they sought.

Sophia's garden was dark. He watched her movements, or rather the light from the lantern she carried, as it traveled from her library, up the stairs, to her bedroom, then blink out. Across the park, another lantern burned, in a house perpendicular to Sophia's; a figure stood before a window briefly, then moved away from it, and Aidan decided to investigate the house later to see if it might provide him with a better—and more comfortable—vantage point.

He stretched. Cold, hungry, tired, and uncomfortable. If this was his penance, it was well deserved.

Sophia carried a cold collation into the library, feeling the quiet of the house as an empty grave. Cook and Sally had gone to the market and wouldn't return until late in the evening. Perkins had left that morning, called back to the estate by the housekeeper who had written earlier that week complaining about the size of the rabbits in the kitchen garden. Ian was still in the Lakes with the Hucknalls, and Aidan . . . Well, he knew better than to call.

Her anger had cooled, but not her deep sense of betrayal. Somehow she could forgive his youthful foolishness more than a decade ago, but she could not accept—not yet at least—the cruel intentionality behind his more recent behavior. She could think of nothing he could do to redeem himself. But perhaps over time she would come to feel more generously toward him. Strangely, she realized, he had behaved no worse than she had imagined he would all those years in Italy. But that was cold comfort.

At the same time, Sophia reminded herself, she was not completely alone. Dodsley and the Brunis remained with her, and Aidan's various servants still lurked about in her halls and gardens. As long as he paid their wages, she cared little whether they stayed or went. Perhaps a visit to the nursery later to see how Lily was enjoying her studies would alleviate some of the plaintive loneliness that surprised Sophia at some point each day.

With Aidan gone, she had been able to accomplish the tasks she'd let languish for the last several months. She'd read the corrected proofs for volume two of Tom's book, making sure all the corrections had been made and that no new errors had been created in the process, and she'd ensured that the image of the agave had been replaced by a rose. She'd watercolored a set of the engravings in Tom's book to show the women employed to paint the pictures exactly what each color should be. And she'd finally finished her own book, *A Girl's Botany*, which she had written under the pseudonym, Mrs. Teachwell.

The engravings for her book were not as meticulous as those for Tom's or as large. But in each one she freed herself from the conventions of botanical illustration to show something of the plant's personality, combining groups of flowers into pleasing bouquets by season. She'd even included instructions on how each part of each plant should be colored, allowing her girl readers to learn the characteristics of each plant while coloring them.

But all that work had been completed days ago, leaving her unable to ignore the emptiness that the break with Aidan had left.

In the early afternoon, having started and discarded a dozen sketches, Sophia was grateful to be interrupted by Dodsley's bringing her a note.

"A note, your ladyship, delivered by special messenger." Dodsley held out an unmarked envelope with no address and no seal. "The messenger is a boy no older than five or six, but he's been told a guinea will be his reward if he waits for your reply."

"A guinea? Perhaps you should wait."

"Yes, your ladyship. Of course." Dodsley watched as she opened the note cautiously. A lock of dark hair, curled in ringlets and scented with orange bergamot, fell into her hand. Sophia gasped.

"I will check Miss Lily's room." Dodsley, suddenly pale, left without waiting for her answer.

Sophia's heart pounded hard, until she could hear the rush of blood in her ears. Shaking, she lowered herself slowly into the chair behind her desk, holding the letter still half closed in her hand. The lock was Lily's. She and Dodsley had both known it immediately. Only in the last few days had the child taken to wearing a touch of bergamot oil on her neck in a sweet remembrance of her mother's perfume.

Sophia didn't want to open the letter any further, didn't want to find that the blackmailer had made good on his threat to take away something she loved. She didn't wish to discover that Lily was already dead. But she had no choice.

Refusing to give in to the panic rising in her gut, Sophia placed Lily's curl gently on the table. Then, taking a long deep breath, Sophia began to read.

The letter offered her an easy trade—the child for the papers—on two conditions, written in all caps and underlined twice. COME ALONE and TELL NO ONE. Relief and hope warred with suspicion and reservation. The rest of the letter provided a riddle she had to solve to discover the time and the place of their meeting.

The riddle wasn't hard; Sophia worked it out in a matter of moments. But then it wasn't supposed to be hard; it was supposed to be an assertion of her adversary's power. By giving her a riddle, he made her into a sort of circus animal performing tricks for his amusement. At the same time, the riddle offered a threat. By tying her destination to a place she could see from her bedroom window, the letter intimated that someone had been in her house and in her bedroom. And by extension, it intimated that someone in her household was watching her to see if she followed instructions.

Like a perverse invitation, the blackmailer requested a reply to his letter, giving his name as Nick Mephisto and his address as the Fallen Angel Tavern. She found the allusion more pretentious than frightening. She'd already faced the Devil that week.

Certain that Dodsley would tell her Lily was missing, Sophia began to consider her reply. Laughing to herself darkly, she took a play from Aidan's book. Taking out a piece of her best, largest notepaper, she wrote two words—"I accept"—confidently in the middle of the sheet.

Dodsley came to the doorway, looking ill. "Miss Lily is not in her room or the nursery, nor is Luca. I have set the servants to search from attic to cellar."

She met him at the door to the library, holding out the letter. "Will you give this to the messenger?"

Dodsley looked a question, but he didn't ask it. He merely took the letter and disappeared.

Requiring an immediate response was a brilliant ploy, she had to acknowledge, as was choosing a child to deliver the message. It had given her no time to set someone to follow the messenger or to intercept the message at its destination. At the same time, she doubted if the Fallen Angel Tavern even existed.

Though she was afraid—for Lily, for herself—she also felt a kind of relief; she no longer had to wonder when the blackmailer would attack. And in that, she found a sort of calm resolve. She would not panic. First, she would save Lily; then, when Sophia was back at home safe with her children and her friends, she would acknowledge how utterly foolish she had been to even attempt the rescue on her own.

Sophia returned to the desk. She had to consider that she might only be able to save the girl, and if that were the case, Sophia needed to make arrangements for Lily's future. She took out four pieces of notepaper.

Her first note was to Aldine, enclosing Ian's and Lily's birth certificates, and instructing him to open a sealed packet sent to him some months before Tom's death, which contained guardianship papers for Lily, bearing all the necessary signatures—hers, Luca's, Tom's, and Francesca's, and those of witnesses. In the event of her death, Sophia appointed Ophelia Mason to act in her place, and in the event of Aidan's refusal, Malcolm. Luca would always have the final word in the rearing of his niece, but she and Tom had given him strong English allies. The second and third notes were to Ophelia and to Malcolm, and Aldine would distribute these last, if the need arose.

She had just finished tying all the materials into a single packet when Dodsley returned.

"Neither of the Brunis are on the grounds, nor can we find Mr. Grange who had been tutoring Lily this morning. I've sent the men out in widening circles to see if somehow any of the three are close by."

"I need for you to carry some documents to Mr. Aldine at his offices."

"Now, my lady?" Dodsley looked suspicious and concerned.

"Yes, now." She pressed money for a hackney into his hand. "Return as quickly as you can."

Though clearly unhappy with her direction, Dodsley took the package and left. Sophia watched him go with regret and resolve. Certainly she could have kept Dodsley with her, but what good would the aging butler be against an adversary who was already a murderer?

No, however her adversary had managed it, she had been left alone.

With Dodsley gone, she turned to her last note, one to Mr. Murray, including with it a warm dedication to her beloved son, Ian, to be placed at the front of her book. She placed the letter on the mantel, below Tom's portrait, ready to be delivered. Though she'd missed Ian sorely, Sophia was grateful that he was safely ensconced in the Lake District, and that he had a powerful guardian in Aidan who would not abandon him, especially not now that Aidan knew Ian was his son.

Strangely, even after all that had happened, she wished she could call on Aidan. But she couldn't risk disobeying the blackmailer's instructions. But there might be a way. She cleared her desk of all other papers and set the blackmailer's note open, next to the lock of Lily's hair, in the middle of her desk.

She wiped away her tears brusquely. She was left to her own resources, and she prayed, for Lily's sake, they would be sufficient.

* * *

Aidan was sleeping. The heavy curtains of his bedroom windows were pulled to block the afternoon light. But his sleep was disturbed. In the dream, disaster was looming, and he was running to avert it. Running, but not fast enough. Never fast enough.

He heard Tom calling his name, calling for help, heard him beating his dragon-headed cane against a door. But the door wasn't one Aidan knew: framed in metal, it was surrounded by glass, and beyond it Aidan could see a pond, filled with water and lilies. Half-buried in the mud, Aidan found a toy soldier, the banner-bearer. He picked it up, but it was crushed, and the pieces fell apart in his hand.

The sound of the beating grew louder, louder, mirroring the pounding of his heart. Tom's voice calling his name over and over. And the dragon-headed cane pointed toward the pond.

He awoke to Barlow's beating on the locked bedroom door, calling his name. But he knew already. Sophia was in danger. Aidan hoped this time he wouldn't be too late.

Sophia examined herself in the mirror. She'd taken a shirt and a pair of trousers from the back of her wardrobe. Both had been Tom's, and she used them sometimes to work in the garden. Well worn, but still serviceable, they would give her an advantage: The blackmailer would expect her to be encumbered by skirts and petticoats. He wouldn't expect a woman in pants.

From Luca's room, she'd retrieved an old Scottish dagger given to him by Tom; why, she'd never known. She held it, felt its weight, tossed it in her hand to gauge its balance. It had been years since she had sparred with her cousins in the portrait gallery, her aunt Clara watching and applauding their efforts as if they'd been in a play. Perhaps that had been Clara's contribution to Sophia's education, adding skills of the body to skills of the mind. Funny how she'd never valued that before, but if she and Lily lived, Sophia would add fencing and boxing to Lily's curriculum.

The dagger had a sheath and a leather strap she could use to tie it to her waist, but she had no wish to be subtle. No, she would meet her adversary, dagger in hand, like the old engravings of Shakespeare's Imogen going into the cave.

If her adversary had wished to unleash a Fury, he could have found no better way than to threaten her children. For the first time, she understood exactly how her mother had felt, spurred by injustice to act, and to act regardless of any personal consequences.

Sophia was ready. But there were one or two items she still needed before her meeting, and she would find them in the garden.

Barlow was accompanied by Dodsley and the Italian, Luca. Barlow must have found their urgency convincing to have allowed them to accompany him to Aidan's bedroom door.

Aidan was only half-undressed. They told him their stories as he pulled on the rest of his clothes.

Luca had been drawn from the house by a forged letter from Aidan, asking for his help and secrecy. The meeting place was a tavern in the City, but even before the time of their meeting had come and gone, Luca had realized he'd been duped.

Dodsley had returned from Aldine's office to find Sophia gone from the library, and the note from the blackmailer open on the desk. He'd returned to the front of the house to find Mr. Grange beaten and bleeding, stumbling up the porch. Grange confirmed what they had already come to fear: in the park, four men had stolen Liliana. Dodsley had determined Aidan was their best help, and, on his way to Aidan's house, he'd met Luca on the street, with the same destination.

Aidan read the blackmailer's doggerel, feeling the black-mailer's injunction that Sophia could ask no one for help as a stab in the gut:

> From your bedroom window's line,
> A reflection to the north, you'll find.
> A monument in iron and glass,
> A trial for betrayed love to pass.
> When the compass in your garden's run,
> All supplicants to Flora come.
> Alone, alone, the sad doves call
> To save the child from danger's thrall.

Aidan didn't know where Sophia had been told to go, but she had clearly understood. The rhyme made clear that the starting point was her bedroom. He shoved the letter in his pocket and ran to his shortcut through the mews.

In the distance, he saw a young man leave the Wilmot garden with a sack over his shoulder. Perhaps a thief, perhaps something else. The young man turned in the opposite direction from Aidan and began walking swiftly away from the Wilmot house.

The young man was important. Somehow Aidan knew it. Aidan shoved the riddle in Dodsley's hand. "You, solve it." Then he turned to Luca. "You, find my men."

Aidan had only looked away for an instant, but the young man was already out of sight. He ran. Barlow followed, ready to convey a call for help back to Luca and Dodsley and Aidan's men.

Sophia's house was the second from the corner, and

shortly down from the Wilmot yard, the alley turned a sharp right, to parallel the street. On the left were the walls enclosing the yards of the houses, interrupted intermittently by doors. Aidan counted twelve doors. On the right were various entrances to different stables. He could see to the end of the long block, too far away for the young man to have reached it and exited onto the street already. But through which of the garden doors or openings to the mews had he gone?

If Aidan had to, he would break into each yard, and have his men search, but that would likely take too much time.

He'd been too complacent; he'd thought to wait patiently, to let her see that he could be everything he had not been before. But he still didn't know who was threatening her. Now he prayed he wasn't also too late.

The riddle had told Sophia to look north from her bedroom window, and when she saw a monument in glass and iron, she would know her destination. It was the third house to her left, the first after the turn of the corner. Attached to the back of the house was a conservatory, and at the top of the plated glass and iron was a statue of Flora, goddess of flowers. That much she could see from her bedroom.

The garden door facing the alley was unlocked and recently greased. It pushed forward easily. She had anticipated someone might be standing behind the door, but no one was. The garden was green with the recent rain, and the open spaces were heavily overgrown with weeds. A path to the conservatory door had recently been beaten down. It would be easy to watch her approach from the upper walks of the conservatory. And just as easy to intercept or harm her.

But under the trees where little or no light fell, there was little undergrowth. She turned away from the obvious path to skirt the edges of the garden nearest her own garden wall. When she had visited Mr. Anderson at the Apothecaries' Garden and told him where she lived, he'd exclaimed with delight that she must visit a prototype of a new kind of conservatory not three doors down from her. He'd shown her the plans, and she recalled a side entrance, concealed by the stoves that heated the space. It was her one advantage.

The side door was ajar, but from the debris between the door and its jamb, it had been standing so for some time. Not a trap. She slipped through easily. From behind the large stoves she could hear two men's voices, arguing. One sounded especially familiar.

"You didn't have to hit me so hard."

"You wanted them not to suspect you; now they don't."

"I want my money. I've done everything you wanted, drugged the child, made sure her uncle got the letter, everything. Pay me."

"A little longer. If you are patient, you could be richer than you ever imagined."

"All I want is the money we agreed upon. Pay me . . . or else."

"Else what?"

"I'll return the child to her home. You have nothing to bargain with without the child."

The voice that wanted money was agitated, the other almost preternaturally calm. Sophia thought the agitated one should be more careful; he was in danger.

"I've given up a great deal. Even if she believes I was attacked, I still lost her ward. It's unlikely Lady Wilmot will write me a recommendation after that. Pay me my money, and I'll disappear."

Mr. Grange. *The traitor.*

She peeked between the pipes of the stove. Between her and the kidnappers was a deep, large pond, meant for water lilies, but the plants had either died or been removed. Liliana had been placed, bound and unmoving, on the stone edge of the pond. All her adversary had to do was push Lily over the edge into the pond, and, if Sophia were delayed at all, Lily would drown before Sophia could reach her.

The men continued to argue. Grange foolishly recounted everything he knew: the location of a barn filled with something valuable, the names of several associates he would convey to the police. But she paid little attention; she was trying to imagine a way to save Lily and herself.

She heard a shot and looked toward the noise. Grange fell to the floor, moaning, and the calm one—he must be the one who had threatened her in the opera box—moved to stand behind Lily. "I know you are there, Lady Wilmot. You should show yourself before I end this game with a swimming lesson."

If she revealed her position, she had no advantage.

If she didn't, Lily would die.

Aidan heard the shot of a pistol. Concentrating on his memory of the sound, he chose the garden door he had just walked past. He didn't let himself imagine who had been shot. He didn't let himself consider what might have happened if he'd been farther down the alley when the shot rang out, knowing Sophia was in danger and unable to choose the right door. At least this way he knew he had the right garden.

The path was well trodden, and, Aidan, caring little for surprise in his fear for Sophia, ran up to the open door of a glass conservatory. The blackmailer was positioned on the other side of a large, deep pond, a bound child before him on the water's ledge, her feet tied to a large rock. He'd clearly chosen his position both to be visible from the entrance and inaccessible behind the pond.

Aidan couldn't see much of the body lying on the ground,

but he could see trousers and hear groaning. A man's voice. Not Sophia. He still had time to tell her he loved her.

The blackmailer looked up from the injured man, turning the second in his pair of pistols in Aidan's direction.

"Well, Forster, I didn't expect you. Lady Wilmot made her dislike of your company quite obvious this week, or so my colleague here has told me. I'd also expected her to abide by our little agreement. She promised not to tell you and to come alone."

"Where is she?"

The man shrugged. "I didn't anticipate that she'd let her husband's by-blow die a watery death. Wilmot thought she was devoted enough to him that he could force her to raise his bastard. Apparently he was wrong. Perhaps I've offered her a solution. I must admit I like her the better for it."

Sophia set her bag on the ground, hoping that between her tools and Aidan, she would have enough to save Lily. She laid the croquet mallet and the three croquet balls on the floor before her. She picked up one ball and bowled it to hit a large planter several feet away and to her adversary's right. A distraction.

"Ah, so Lady Wilmot has joined us. Come out, your ladyship, where I can see you." Her adversary kept his gun aimed at Aidan, but he spoke in the direction of the planter she had hit. "If you don't come out, next time you move, I'll shoot you or Forster."

She needed to distract the blackmailer enough for either her or Aidan to get close enough to save Lily, or to gain enough time for others to come to their aid. Aidan, she expected, would not have come alone.

She needed the next ball to go farther, to sound as if she were moving closer to the blackmailer. She bowled again. The ball at first appeared to be falling short of her goal, slowing almost to a halt. She caught her breath. But then the ball quickened as if going downhill and hit her mark. Sophia caught the barest hint of orange bergamot. Half expecting to see Francesca behind her, she turned. There was no one there, and no oranges on the trees.

Her adversary fired his pistol into the avenue nearest where her second ball had struck. "Still alive, Lady Wilmot?"

Aidan listened for the fall of a body or a rustling of plants that would indicate Sophia was hit. But to his relief he heard nothing.

The kidnapper had used both of his shots. Aidan inched slowly around the edge of the pond. If he could get far enough, he would try to run the blackmailer down. If Sophia was still alive—God, Aidan's heart stopped at the idea that she might be wounded or dead—then she might be able to run for Lily before the child was pushed into the water and drowned.

"Stop there, Forster. You cannot reach the girl in time if I push her in. The pond is deep; I've weighted her with rocks; and she's had just a bit of laudanum, so she won't know to hold her breath. Have you brought me my papers?"

"We've never found any papers. But whatever and wherever the papers are, I'm sure they are not yours."

"But you did find the papers I left for her ladyship. It was very disappointing to hear that the officers found nothing." The blackmailer laughed.

"How many have you killed for those papers: Aldine's clerk, the courier, Wilmot?"

"Wilmot was a dying man; I did little more than help him along."

Sophia gasped.

"Ah, Lady Wilmot, not dead yet? Come out, or I'll kill your ward."

Sophia had no choice, but he had used up the shot in his pistols. Now the only worry was his knife and how good he was at throwing it.

She picked up Tom's dagger and tucked the last of the

croquet balls under her arm, concealing it in the folds of her oversized shirt.

"Lady Wilmot . . . I'm growing tired of waiting."

She stepped from behind the wall that hid the stoves, holding the dagger defensively in front of her.

Aidan was praying that she wouldn't step forward. But he knew she would; she'd been brave as a girl, and she'd become brave again.

When she moved, he would have a chance to get closer. He needed to resist his natural inclination to look at Sophia when she stepped forward. He had to watch the blackmailer, watch for his chance. He heard a movement to Charters's left and saw the man recoil.

"It can't be you, Wilmot. You're dead." The blackmailer, focused on the trousered figure before him, held up his knife. "Must I kill you again?"

Sophia heard the threat and held her dagger up before her in protection. She took another step, watching for her opportunity. Her adversary had put down his pistols, but not his knife. She paused.

Aidan moved around the side of the pond, close enough that he could save Lily or Sophia, but still not both. But when he rounded the edge closest to Lily, he stopped. It wasn't Sophia who had stepped from behind the wall, but a man—a man who looked like Tom.

In the slanting light of the conservatory, with the lowering sun reflecting off the various angles of glass in the roof, the figure held out his hand to Aidan, toward the child. And Aidan knew who to save.

Sophia could see Aidan moving toward Lily, so she focused on the man before her. She smelled sandalwood, Tom's scent, and she took courage in the memory. She held out her hand with the dagger and stepped even farther forward.

The man blinked, but the look of fear remained on his face.

"I killed you. Stay away." The blackmailer, so preternaturally calm before, now seemed agitated, even frightened.

She stepped further into the slanting light, close enough to see the body of the tutor, Grange, stretched out on the floor, blood pooling under him. The smell of sandalwood intensified. She stopped, watching Aidan move almost close enough to save Lily.

But at that moment, the blackmailer made a decision. "You can't harm me, Wilmot. Save your child." In one motion, he pushed Lily into the water and lunged toward Sophia. She saw Lily sink. Aidan, running, leapt into the pool.

While the blackmailer had been focused on Lily, he hadn't seen the croquet ball she'd held slightly behind her. Now she bowled it, aiming at his feet, hoping to trip him. The ball bounced, hitting him slightly below the knee, enough to surprise and hurt, but not stop him. He howled and looked down, allowing Sophia to move out of his grasp.

She held up her dagger defensively, hoping to dissuade the blackmailer from further attack. The man stared at her, his own dagger raised. In the distance she could hear people running, calling her name and Aidan's. The man stopped, and with one last look of horror and fear, ran.

In the corner of her eye, she saw Aidan raise Lily's body. Not caring if the blackmailer escaped, she ran to Aidan.

Together, they put the child on the tiled floor, cut the gag and blindfold. Sophia cut the ropes binding Lily's hands and feet. Aidan turned Lily over and beat her back. Nothing. Sophia's heart sank. Aidan continued beating Lily's back. Three, four, five times. Tears welled in Sophia's eyes as she looked away.

"Lily! Lily! Breathe." Aidan pressed the girl's chest.

Sophia put her hand on his arm, to stop him. But just then, Lily took a breath and began to cough.

The men were there now. Aidan was giving orders, some of his men running after the blackmailer. An older man she knew as Aidan's valet was kneeling beside the tutor, who was not yet dead.

She rocked Lily's body against hers, caressing her hair. Somehow Lily was safe, and Sophia was still alive.

Aidan knelt beside her, rubbing the child's arms and legs to bring warmth back into them, wrapping both Sophia and Lily in his cloak. Then Luca was with Sophia, and they were crying. She handed Lily to her uncle and picked herself up. She looked around.

Aidan was gone.

But he had come. He had come, and Lily was alive.

By the time Aidan told his men to give up the hunt, Sophia and Lily had gone home. Barlow moved the wounded tutor to Aidan's house where he could be doctored . . . and watched. Luca had returned to report that the doctor said Lily would be fine. Apparently the tutor had dosed her tea with laudanum, and she remembered little between going to the park and coming awake wet with cold in Aidan's arms. She would not have bad dreams of being kidnapped.

Aidan wanted to see Sophia, see she was safe, hold her in his arms. But he didn't want to go to her half wet from the pond. Saving Lily had not balanced the scales between them, though perhaps now Sophia knew he would not abandon her.

He also had to consider what he had seen in the conservatory: a figure that had been Tom. Aidan was sure of it.

Tomorrow. He would call on her tomorrow.

* * *

Sophia took a long bath, wondering if Aidan would try to see her, and what she would say to him. She'd hoped he would come to her house after searching for the blackmailer, but he hadn't. At least he had sent her a message through Dodsley, saying the blackmailer had escaped, and Aidan's men would be watchful. He believed the blackmailer would no longer try to harm her or her children, and she agreed. Something in the look of unalloyed fear she'd seen on the man's face suggested it was over.

She thought of the sandalwood she'd smelled in the conservatory, and she determined to make inquiries about how she might acquire the tree. If the sandalwood were still sufficiently small, she could have it moved to her own garden. The scent had made her feel that Tom was by her side, supporting and caring for her, as he'd always done. She had had a good life with Tom, a kind, quiet, gentle life. Now that her grief had subsided, she could look with joy on their time together.

She remembered the last time they had played bocce. It had been one of those perfect Neapolitan days, the air cool from the ocean, the sky clear. The sun had slanted across the flat of their Italian lawn, and they had made a picnic. Lily had chased Ian, stumbling over her chubby infant feet, and Ian had laughed. When Lily fell down and started to cry, Ian had shared a piece of hard candy, and Lily had happily grown sticky, the sugar on her hands and face. Francesca had been sitting on the blanket with Tom, clearly in love, but in a way that had made Sophia feel grateful that Tom, whom she adored as she would a kind older brother, had found a woman to share his heart. Sophia and Luca had played bocce, and she'd beaten him roundly for the first time. It had been the six of them, the Brunis and the Wilmots, and their strangely contented family. And she wondered how it would look in a painting.

Curling up in a thick dressing gown with her pad and

crayons, she began to sketch, but each time, she found her pencil tracing Aidan's face. She no longer dreaded seeing him, no longer hated him. Though she still felt the ache in her heart that only his face could fill, she understood that they might never find a way to love one another as they had once. In their days at Tom's estate, they had come to understand each other's stories. Those allowed her to let go of the past. And in saving Lily, he'd balanced the scales for abandoning Sophia before.

Aidan slept that night without dreams. But he'd expected it to be so. For a moment in the conservatory he too had seen what terrified the blackmailer. Tom. Not Sophia wearing Tom's clothes. Not a trick of light. But the ghost of his old friend intervening to save them. Later, when Aidan had returned to the quiet of the conservatory intending in some way to say good-bye, he'd found Tom's dragon-headed cane near the pool. And Aidan had spent the evening sitting in front of his fire, watching the gem in the eye of the dragon catch the light, considering everything that had happened.

By special rider, he sent letters calling Malcolm and his family home. They had spent more time than planned away and would, Aidan was sure, be glad to return. And he wished to see his son, the son he could never acknowledge, but whom he'd grown to love. He smiled at the memory of Ian's playing soldier, of his delight in the game, of the thoughtful Tom-like turn of Ian's head and mind. Aidan realized now why his own name had not been on Tom's list of bequests: Aidan's gift was Ian, nurtured and loved by the man Aidan could once again call brother. He had a great debt to repay, and the rest of his life to pay it.

Chapter Thirty-Four

Sophia expected Aidan to call the next morning, but he didn't. And not the next day or the day after. But her drawing room was rarely empty, filled with her Elliot cousins, Tom's sisters, and Aidan's brothers, as well as an ever-increasing circle of friends. She accepted the change, and not just for Ian's sake. Tom had been right all along: she needed to return to society, but for her that meant a society of her friends and relatives.

She'd also begun to paint, every day, as she hadn't since her girlhood. She started with the scene she couldn't—and had no wish to—put out of her mind: the picnic on the lawn in Italy surrounded by the people she loved. She wanted to preserve it for her children: Ian, Lily, and Luca. But she had also begun a portrait of Aidan that she wished to finish—and when it was done, she would decide her next steps, whether to try to reconcile or to let him go.

That morning, the Hucknalls had left their sons to play with Ian at soldiers while they stole away alone to shop on Bond Street. She had just escaped from the drawing room to her library to paint when Dodsley announced the Hucknalls had returned to retrieve their boys.

"Malcolm, Audrey." She kissed them both on the cheek.

"I still feel that I haven't thanked you sufficiently for caring for Ian so well."

"Ian can travel with us anytime. Our boys never quarreled once with him present," Audrey offered. "And I must confess: traveling in the ducal carriage has ruined me for regular hackneys."

Though Sophia tried to hide her fleeting sadness at the allusion to Aidan, Malcolm caught her up in his arms, lifting her off her feet. "In the states we call that a 'bear's hug,' cousin. We have a surprise for you, and we've come to celebrate!"

When he put her down, Sophia shook her head in mock dismay. "You grow more colonial each day."

Audrey laughed. "He's been teaching the boys all his tricks and sayings. Wait until you hear all the Americanisms Ian learned on our trip."

Malcolm ignored the women's jibes and held out a broadsheet flyer. "We thought you might like a copy of this."

Sophia held the broadsheet up to read it aloud. "Mr. Murray is happy to announce the publication this coming Monday of the late Thomas Gardiner, Lord Wilmot's greatest work, *Botanical Specimens of the Mediterranean Best Suited to the Climate of England*." She felt her eyes grow moist, and Audrey handed her a handkerchief. "Thank you— I will have to show Ian. I had no idea the books would be available so soon."

"Well, from the looks of the reservation list on Murray's counter, Tom's book will be a great success." Audrey grinned. "In fact, Murray showed us the colored engravings for the illustrated color edition. They are stunning."

"You must be proud of the work you've done." Malcolm took her hand. "I know Tom would be pleased."

Audrey grinned and held out a second broadsheet announcement. "Murray also suggested we look at another book he has coming out next week: *A Girl's Botany*, by

Mrs. Teachwell, the illustrator of Lord Wilmot's *Botanical Specimens*. We had no idea you were an author as well!"

Sophia felt her cheeks grow hot. "Oh dear. I knew the books were coming out together, but I hadn't realized he would make the connection between them so explicit. I certainly don't wish to detract from Tom's debut."

"I think it's lovely—and not a distraction at all." Audrey curled up on the chaise longue. "Lord and Lady Wilmot's books published together in the same week. A lovely coda to a fruitful partnership of like minds."

At that moment, Audrey's boys ran into the room, clamoring for their mother's attention.

Malcolm brought the broadsheets back to Sophia, and spoke softly so that only she could hear. "Have you heard from the great coward yet?"

She shook her head no. "But I made a contented life with Tom, and I will make a contented life again—with or without Aidan in it."

Chapter Thirty-Five

It had been two weeks. Each day Aidan rose intending to visit Sophia, and each night he retired to bed, telling himself "tomorrow." Life was short, and they had lost so much time already, but he was afraid—afraid of seeing her face and knowing she no longer loved him. So much easier to live with the hope that when he did see her, her face would soften with forgiveness.

Ian had returned to his mother lighthearted, with two bosom friends in Jack and Toby, a threesome that reminded Aidan of himself, Tom, and Malcolm at that age. Two or three afternoons each week, Ian came to his house, often with Liliana and Luca, and the four explored the sights of London. Aidan had never known the city as he did in showing it to Ian and Lily. Last week they'd taken the river to Hampton Court and remained until the change of the tide. Aidan had quickly discovered the depth of affection between the three, all in some way Tom's children.

Neither Aidan nor Ian brought up the subject of his mother. Where before Aidan had seen Tom in Ian's features, now he saw only Sophia, calling him to a hell of his own making. Sometimes the boy looked at him with serious eyes, and Aidan wondered what sober thought troubled Ian. But whatever the boy was pondering, Aidan did not ask, and Ian didn't offer.

The Home Office had notified Aidan that his services in watching Lady Wilmot were no longer required. Though they still had no idea who Charters was, they had intercepted a large stash of forged bills from various London gangs, and they had seized some printing plates, along with a small amount of fine paper, from an abandoned barn on the outskirts of London. They were sure that Tom's fair copy contained the coded information, but the agave engraving had offered no words that proved to be the code key. Without it, they could not decipher Tom's last message.

And Aidan had the new papers he'd requested from Aldine, signed and witnessed, but still undelivered.

He opened a bottle of Kentucky whiskey, a new import brought home from America by his cousin George Heywood. Then Aidan changed his mind. Not tomorrow. Today.

He called Barlow to help him dress. He wouldn't send her a note, wouldn't risk her refusing him. No, he would show up in his finest clothing, with the ring all the heads of the family gave their betrotheds. But he would expect nothing.

He'd rounded the corner between his house and Sophia's when he saw Sally bringing Liliana and Ian home from the park. He realized—if he quickened his steps just slightly—they would arrive at the same time, making his entry into the house easier.

In front of the house, Liliana threw herself into his arms, and he picked her up, intending to carry her into the house. But Luca opened the door and—clearly upset—stepped outside to meet them.

"I think it would be best if I took Liliana and Ian back to the park, your grace." Luca reached out for Lily, and Aidan's heart fell. "Perhaps her ladyship would welcome your support."

Aidan stepped gratefully into the house. The sound of angry voices led him back to the library. The door to the library stood open only an inch, and Dodsley was standing outside it, listening and occasionally peeking inside. The silver-haired butler stepped aside in gratitude. "I believe her ladyship needs her brother removed from the premises," he whispered.

Aidan smiled. He'd worried if he would have the support of her staff, and now he knew. He pitched his voice low. "She sounds like she's managing quite well."

Dodsley smiled in return. "Actually, your grace, I'm expecting her to throw the tea service at him any moment now."

"Should we wait?"

"Why not?"

The two men turned back to listen, taking turns watching through the slightly open door.

"You cannot imagine my horror." Phineas fisted his hands at his sides.

"I do not need to imagine it. You are enacting it quite successfully in my drawing room." Sophia's voice was firm, unmoving, the tone one would use with a petulant child.

"You can't really intend to keep that child here, Sophia." Phineas's voice was shrill.

Sophia stood, her back to the fireplace beneath the portrait of Tom.

"Have you no idea how inappropriate this is? Send the child back to Italy, to a boarding school in Wales, hire a nurse and send her to the country, but she cannot remain in this house."

"Liliana is Tom's daughter, acknowledged by him and his heir in her own right. I will not send her into the country or out of it for that matter. She belongs here with her brother."

"Brother?" Phineas sputtered, and Aidan almost stepped into the room. But he waited to see if Phineas had discovered Ian's true paternity. "Half brother! He will only have family feeling for her if she is reared in the same house. They must be separated!"

Sophia grimaced at the idea that living in the same house ensured family feeling. Phineas had never held any for her.

"It's a disgrace, Sophia, your allowing—no, welcoming—Tom's by-blow into your home."

"Phineas, this is no business of yours."

"I'm your brother, Sophia. When there is gossip about you, I must hear it. And this, this is certain to cause talk. It's scandalous."

Phineas, never a handsome man, was far less handsome when angry. The red of his face extended past the weakness of his chin to contrast strongly with the pink of his cravat. Phineas, Aidan thought, couldn't have chosen a more unfortunate color for his visit.

"Sophia, are you even listening to me? The fact of the child is scandal enough, but your taking her into your home . . . calling her Liliana Gardiner . . ."

"That is her given name, Phineas. The name the legal papers give her."

"But it's an embarrassment."

"To whom? Would it be better, Phineas, for me to refuse to acknowledge a child that Tom himself acknowledged? Would it be better for me to pretend that such a child doesn't exist, because someone might think less of me as a woman or a wife? There are plenty of by-blows in the world—and plenty of starving children sired by men 'of quality.' Tom did not leave his children destitute."

"But your reputation, Sophia. I simply can't allow this."

"It's not your choice to allow or disallow. My money is my own; my home is my own; my reputation is my own. Tom made sure of that. If as a widow, I choose to make myself scandalous, I have no one to please but myself. And it pleases me to rear Tom's child as my daughter."

Phineas blustered, taking up his hat and coat. "For a while after you had returned, Sophia, I believed you had finally become a proper lady, but bad breeding will out. I cannot allow my girls to visit you. They cannot be seen to enter such an . . . an . . . establishment as this, where a wife openly accepts such behavior on the part of her husband. No respectable woman or man will likely visit you either. You will be ostracized for such behavior. I will be taking up this matter with the duke; Lord Wilmot cannot be raised in an environment of such depravity."

"What matter, Phineas?" Aidan stepped into the room.

Carried on by his indignation, Phineas recklessly continued. "Your grace, you must remove my nephew from this house at once. We can place him at the boarding school I sponsor near my estate, but he cannot be allowed to live in a home where his mother welcomes bastard children. She makes no distinction between the girl and Lord Wilmot, treating them . . ."

"Both as Tom's children," Sophia intervened.

Phineas had no idea, Aidan thought, which meant their secret was safe.

"I must stand with her ladyship, Phineas. I've reviewed the legal papers: Lily is undeniably Tom's daughter. Of course one doesn't really need legal papers to see that. Look at how much she resembles her brother; no one could believe she wasn't Tom's." Aidan enjoyed offering that last tidbit, a useful lie that he hoped would spread.

Phineas howled in outrage, then rushed from the room, where his exit was aided by the ever-efficient Dodsley. Aidan would deal with any threats later. But for now, he was in Sophia's library.

"I see your brother is more agitated than usual by . . ."

"My behavior." The image of Sophia as an avenging angel remained. "Today, I'm a bad wife to a bad, though dead, husband. How much did you hear?"

"Enough."

She collapsed into a chair in front of her tea service and began to laugh. He stood silently, glorying in the sound of her rich, full laughter. She pointed him to a chair, then her laughter turned to giggles as she pointed at the tea service, where several tea cakes sat wrapped in her table linen. "He never forgets his cakes. Do you think he'll come back just for them?" She laughed some more.

He smiled at her amusement and found himself sharing a moment of delight with her. She was not afraid, or grieving, or a statue any longer, just a vibrant, clever, beautiful, brave woman. And he loved her.

"Now to your business, your grace." The use of the honorific would have made his heart fall had she not still been smiling.

"I was coming to wish you adieu. I leave for my estate at the end of the week."

"And you intend to take Ian with you." Her voice shifted from joyful to resignation.

"No. I was going to leave some papers for you. But since we are both here, I thought I could deliver them myself." He pulled a packet from his overcoat, divided the papers into two sets, and handed the first one to her. The name of Aldine's firm was neatly lettered on the outside.

"I'm giving up the guardianship, Sophia. Or at least I've changed the rules by which the guardianship works. You make the decisions. Ian's your son, and Tom's. I wish he had been mine, but I was foolish, unable to believe that someone so lovely as you could love me. I remain his guardian on the paperwork only to protect Ian if you are incapacitated or you need a threat to control your brother. I would like to see Ian when I am in town, but I'm here rarely, and now that you and I . . . Well, no matter."

He waited for her to read, then gave her the second set. "These papers extend the guardianship to Lily as Tom wished. Again, I will be guardian in name only, leaving the decisions to Luca . . . and to you."

She read the papers, then folded them. He couldn't read her expression, but he could feel his heart tightening in his chest.

"I also have a gift of sorts." He held out a card with a name and an address on it. "It's the address of your old governess; she teaches in a girl's school in Cornwall. She did not choose to leave you. There's a story there, but she'd like to tell you herself. I'd be happy to escort you to visit her, were you to wish it."

Silently, Sophia took up the card and the papers, then walked away from him toward her desk.

It was his only chance. He spoke quickly to fill the silence growing between them.

"Tom didn't create the guardianship because he didn't trust your judgment or because he thought Ian needed a male influence. He created the guardianship to give me a chance to make things right . . . to admit I wronged you all those years ago. To tell you I love you, that I've never stopped loving you." The words came in a rush, and were not the ones he'd planned. She stilled, but did not turn toward him. "And I love our son—our son and Tom's."

She placed the papers on the desk and turned toward him, her face inscrutable.

He breathed deeply, fingering the ring in his pocket. "If you ever need me again, Sophia, for anything, this time I won't ignore you. If it takes you another decade to trust me again, then I'll wait. As long as it takes."

Her eyes searched his face, as she took his measure. Then she looked down at her hands.

His hopes faded. Clearly she was looking for words to send him away. To the life he deserved—a life without her. Feeling stabbed in the gut, he let the ring slip into the depths of his pocket. He picked up his overcoat.

"Before you go."

He stilled, his chest tight, hoping, but afraid to hope.

"I was wondering if you would critique a painting I've been working on." She gestured toward the easel.

It wasn't the response he'd expected. But it wasn't a rejection. He remembered the companionable comradery of minds she and Tom had forged. Perhaps this was a chance to start anew.

She'd finished the portrait that morning. Her intention had been to send Aidan a note inviting him to tea. But Phineas had arrived.

It was, she thought, her best work, combining a mature hand with an old love. She hoped that Aidan could see in it the truth of her heart. His reaction would tell her, more than words, whether what was between them had a future.

Aidan looked at the portrait with amazement. In it, he sat in the nursery with Tom and Ian, a green cloth spread out between them on the table. On it, the soldiers stood in battalions, watching as their generals declared an end to their hostilities. In the background, hanging on the wall were Sophia's botanical drawings, and in the best detail was the one that Ian loved, the rose with the hummingbird. Even in miniature, the hummingbird was finely detailed.

Suddenly Aidan knew what the code key was, though this was not the time for it.

Sophia watched as Aidan examined the triple portrait with delight. His eyes focused on the drawings in the background, then his face lit with surprise and revelation. She followed his eye to the image of the rose and suddenly remembered her dream of Tom's showing her the pages of the illustrations.

Sophia's eyes met Aidan's, and they began to laugh. "The

misplaced engraving of the agave—it was supposed to point us to Ian's illustration of the rose. The code key; it was so obvious we missed it."

"Are you sure it's the rose? It could be the bird that was out of place, the one that didn't feed on roses." Aidan pulled her against his side, smelling the lavender in her hair.

"Hmmm. I thought the hummingbird was just a joke between Tom and Ian. So which is it: the hummingbird or the rose?"

He held her tightly against his chest. "What should we do first? Tell the Home Office? They will want to begin testing which word is the key. It should reveal some important information, now that we know where to begin."

"After this long, there is no hurry." She turned her face up to his, kissed him softly. "You offered once to show me your bedroom. But you haven't. Perhaps that was just an insignificant promise."

"None of our promises were insignificant. And they never will be. Does this mean I'm forgiven?"

"Always. Always forgiven." She touched her hand to his face. "I've never stopped loving you."

"Nor I you." He held her to him, and she turned her head to lay her cheek on his chest. "I know a path through the garden; it goes through the mews. I could show it to you."

"I'd like to see it—and my garden; I've been wanting to see how my designs turned out. It will be our new start."

Chapter Thirty-Six

Charters sat in his study, his antiquities arranged as he'd wished. But their quiet history did not calm his mind. Instead, he couldn't forget what he could not have seen in the conservatory. It couldn't have been Tom. It was only an illusion: Lady Wilmot wearing her husband's clothes. But it had been Tom's face, his eyes offering recrimination. Tom protecting his wife. Charters had known the man his whole life. He hadn't made a mistake.

He wouldn't act against Lady Wilmot again. Even if she had the list of peers who had betrayed England, he wouldn't risk it. Besides, he had received another letter from Octavia—this one some twenty names long. His name had not been on it, though he still did not know if it had been on Tom's.

And he had other ventures to pursue. Other possibilities.

He'd raised more than ample funds with his forgeries. He was now a significant shareholder in a shipping firm. The first of his investments were now at sea in good weather. If only half of his ships came back safely, his return would be strong. And he'd made inroads into the criminal gangs.

He even had money left from the banknote robberies. The tutor had been wise not to mention his part in those, though he was still being transported for his part in the blackmail. To mollify the young tutor for shooting him, Charters had given him a substantial portion of cash, but not his full part. It was not kindness. It was forethought. Paying against a time when Charters's enterprises might lead into colonial markets.

Eventually he would have the power he deserved. But for now he was satisfied with the money.

He turned to his companion, who was carving another piece of wood. Flute had filled out over the last month. He was now once more the strong man he'd been when Charters had first known him. And completely loyal.

"Mr. Flute, what do you think about gambling hells?"

"I don't gamble. Or at least not with money."

"Then I think we have a new venture. What do you think of calling it the Blue Heron?"

Chapter Thirty-Seven

Walgrave entered the inner office to give his summary report on the Wilmot affair. But first he'd lost a bet with the men in the division, and it was time to pay.

Benjamin put down his pencil and motioned for Walgrave to take a seat. Joseph, as always, was close at hand.

"I'd prefer to stand, sir. I've been tasked by the men to press an issue of some importance." Walgrave felt more ill at ease than he'd imagined possible.

"Then speak. What's troubling the men?"

"It's the issue of your new name, sir. Eventually one of us will slip up, say your name, and then all your sacrifices will be for naught. Your brother Aidan will step down in your favor. You will have to marry."

Walgrave ignored the glances between Benjamin and Joseph.

"I'm listening."

"Our recent investigations into the Methodist revivalists have led us to consider Biblical names that convey the . . . unique nature . . . of your situation." Walgrave found himself unaccountably nervous.

"Unique?"

"Yes, sir. In a sense you have died and are now raised from

the dead. So, Lazarus would be appropriate, or Jonah—he was trapped in the belly of a whale, sir. . . ."

"I'm familiar with the story."

"Or there's Enoch and Elijah, who never died. Or we could look to other sources: King Arthur is the once and future king. Romeo is believed dead, then isn't. Of course he does die in fairly short order."

"I take your . . . somewhat obvious point."

"Thank you, sir."

"How about James?"

"James, sir?"

"Yes. I'm a version of my former self. Benjamin leads somewhat easily to James. As opposed to the other names you suggest, I might actually answer to it."

"Mr. James," Walgrave repeated. "Very good, sir. I'll inform the men."

"I believe you have a report for me."

Walgrave nodded. "We have been able to trace neither the paper nor the plates. The barn was rented through the mails, and the agent never met the man, a Mr. MacDonald."

"If that's even a real name."

"We think it's unlikely. The tutor indicated that his accomplice never appeared to him without a disguise."

"Then, we'll have to wait. I fear we have a new player on the board. And we have no idea what he might want."

Dear Reader,

If you love history as much as I do, I thought you might like a little more information on the background to Aidan and Sophia's story. Whenever possible, I use period magazines and newspapers for background over current history books. Sometimes with the benefit of hindsight, we understand events differently than a person living at the time would have, and I want to create a nineteenth-century world as the characters—had they been living then—might have experienced it. For the most part, this context comes up in small ways: Aidan is right when he says that the Wilmots in Naples were out of harm's way.

So, for those of you who want to know more about a book's historical events, here are some juicy details.

The Chelsea Physic Garden, botany, and Linnaeus

Still nestled alongside the Thames, the Chelsea Apothecaries' Garden, sometimes called the Physic Garden, was founded in 1673 by the Society of Apothecaries. *Physic* at the time meant "of the natural world," and the apothecaries used the four-acre plot to train their apprentices in the healing properties of plants. The garden gained world renown, receiving plants and seeds from botanists around the world, during the fifty-year curatorship of Philip Miller (1691–1771). Miller also authored *The Gardener's Dictionary,* a comprehensive guide to plants that went through eight editions in his lifetime and quickly became the standard reference work. Sophia inherits Miller's *Dictionary* from her father and uses it to investigate Tom's proofs. William Anderson, the Scottish curator Sophia meets during her visit, is also a real historical figure: Anderson served as the garden's curator from 1815 to 1846. The description of the physic garden's buildings and beds comes from contemporary engravings and other notices.

During Miller's curatorship, a number of botanical classification systems for identifying plants vied for prominence. The one that eventually gained widespread acceptance was Carl Linnaeus's sexual system, which places all living things into hierarchic groups by genus and species. (We use Linnaeus's system when we identify human beings as genus *homo* and species *sapiens*.) Linnaeus even visited the Chelsea Physic Garden several times in the 1730s, and it is his bust that rests above Tom's books.

One well-known follower of Linnaeus's system was the beloved Queen Charlotte, George III's wife, an avid botanist. The queen's interest in the emerging science made it a popular and accepted pastime for girls and young women. As a result, the Regency book market was filled with books on botany geared to every segment of the market: children, students, dabblers, and specialists. Some books like the one that Sophia completes for Tom were hand-watercolored by women specially hired for the purpose (machine-colored illustrations are decades away). Purchasers really could choose how they wished their book to look, from the type of binding to the number and quality of the illustrations—and each option changed the cost of the book itself. The children's botany book Sophia reads—Priscilla Wakefield's—was first published in the late eighteenth century and frequently reprinted throughout the nineteenth as was Philip Miller's *Gardener's Dictionary*.

For Sophia's nom de plume, I've stolen the name Mrs.

Teachwell from Lady Ellenor Fenn, a prolific children's author who wrote from the 1780s to 1809. Contrary to popular belief, works by women writers filled the bookshelves during the late eighteenth and early nineteenth centuries. In fact, more than four-hundred female authors published between 1789 and 1824, though today most people can't name more than a handful of them. (For my list of the hundred best books written by women prior to 1900, check out my website.) In fact, between 1780 and 1830, the cost of novels differed based on the *gender* of the author! Women's novels cost the most, followed by books authored by anonymous authors (by a lady, by a gentleman, etcetera), and finally, books authored by men, which earned the very least.

Words and their uses

I love words—and as much as I can, I use them as they would have been used in the period. So, even though I would have loved to have Aidan *empathize* with Sophia, the best he can do is *sympathize*. Empathy as a concept originated much later in the century with Sigmund Freud. I'm keeping a list of words characters can't use in 1819 on my website . . . for other word-nerds like me.

Having said that, I have chosen clarity over accuracy when I use the word *croquet*. As a game where one strikes a ball through a series of hoops in a particular order, croquet wasn't part of British culture until the 1850s. However, an earlier game similar to croquet called variously Palle-Maille, Pell-Mell, or Pall-Mall was popular in England from at least the seventeenth century. In that game, a hoop is placed at either end of the playing field. But for the purpose of conveying quickly and precisely what sort of game Sophia plays, I decided *croquet* was the word readers would understand best.

I hope you enjoyed Sophia and Aidan's story, and that

you are looking forward to the next installment in Charters's villainy.

I'm always happy to hear from readers; you can e-mail me at rachael@rachaelmiles.com. For more historical notes on JILTING THE DUKE, or to connect with me on social media, go to my website—rachaelmiles.com—which provides links to Twitter, Facebook, etcetera. While you're there, sign up for my mailing list, and I'll send you an announcement when the next book is coming out.

I'm happy to talk to book clubs and community groups. Drop me a line to set something up.

Happy Reading!
Rachael Miles

Loving the Muses' Salon Series?

Keep reading for
a sneak peek at

CHASING THE HEIRESS,

available in June 2016
from Zebra Shout.

Colin Somerville woke, heart pounding, the heavy thud of cannon fire fading with his nightmare. Heavy brocaded curtains hung over the carriage windows to his left. Feeling suffocated, he shoved the curtains apart and breathed in gulps of crisp September air. Beyond the window, the sun fell gently on the green rolling hills of Shropshire. In the near distance, open pastures with grazing sheep gave way to enclosed land growing turnips. He fell back against the seat. He was in England, not Belgium. It was only a dream.

Judging from the position of the sun, they should reach Shrewsbury by dusk. He rubbed his face with his hands, pressing his fingertips into the tight muscles at his forehead and temples. To calm his heart, he used an old trick his brother Benjamin had taught him. He focused on naming the various scents in the air—wool, newly harvested wheat, dirt loosened to pull the turnips, and water. Likely the Severn.

His companion Marietta grew restless in her sleep. He stilled. She curled her hand under her chin and nestled further into the thick, down-filled pallet tucked into the well between the two carriage seats. Colin had bought her the pallet that morning at Wrexham. The gift had cost him more than he could easily afford, but her widening smile had been worth the cost. Since then, she had spent the day sleeping, her back to one seat riser, her swollen belly pressed against the other.

A line of bright sunlight from beneath the window curtains shone above Marietta's head like a nimbus. But unlike the Madonnas he had seen in Rome or Venice, whose faces were lit with an internal glow, Marietta—even in rest—looked weary. The dark hollows in her cheeks, the deep circles under her eyes, the blueish undertone to her lips, all reminded him of the El Grecos he'd seen at Toledo. He thought of his sister Judith's confinements—she had never looked so ill, not with any of her four boys. If the Home Office had sent him to bury another woman . . . He pushed the thought away.

It had taken Colin two days to travel to Holywell, two days in which he had steeled himself to smile and be charming. But ultimately the princess had charmed him. Heiress to a mining magnate, Marietta had caught the eye of a visiting (and impoverished) member of the Habsburg royal family. Though she had been impeccably trained at the best finishing school in Paris, when Colin arrived, he found her teaching the housekeeper's parrot to curse in five European languages. "Don't call me princess," she whispered, casting a grim eye to the housekeeper, hovering at the edge of the terrace. "Or she will raise my rate."

It had taken two more days to separate Marietta's possessions into two groups: those which the carriage could carry and those which would have to be shipped from Liverpool around the coast to London. Most difficult had been determining exactly which clothes she could (and could not) do without for her first week at court. Then, just when he had thought that they might set out, she had grown anxious that her belongings would miscarry, and she had insisted that his coachman Fletcher accompany her trunks across the inlet to ensure they were well stowed for their London journey. All told, he had been gone from London for more than a week before he bundled Marietta, her paints, embroidery, knitting, books, and a handful of magazines into the carriage and set off on their trip. But somehow he had not minded. Marietta was sweet, resilient, and companionable, anticipating the birth of her child with real joy. And Colin was already fond of her, treating her as a sort of younger sister.

Marietta moaned and tried to shift her weight. Why—he berated himself for the fiftieth time—hadn't he borrowed a better carriage to carry her to London? One with ample seats, thick comfortable bolsters, and better springs. Why hadn't the Home Office informed him that his charge was increasing? Had they intentionally withheld the information? Or had they not known?

He forced his attention back to the map. If Marietta gave birth on the road with only him and Fletcher for midwives, Colin would kill someone in the Home Office. He wasn't yet sure who. Perhaps the lot of them, but he would begin by strangling Harrison Walgrave.

The carriage began to slow, the springs creaking into a new rhythm. Colin waited for Fletcher to offer the usual signals: two slow taps for an inn, a fast double-tap for a crossroads, and a heavy heel-kick for danger. But no taps, kicks, yells, or pistol shots alarmed Colin, except perhaps the nagging absence of any warnings.

Colin tapped on the roof and waited. No response.

He shifted one foot, then the other—both numb from inactivity—from the opposite seat to the floor. Colin slid several inches toward the middle of the bench and moved the cushion aside to reveal a built-in pistol cabinet, added by his brother, the Duke of Forster.

The door handle moved slightly as someone tried to open the door. But Colin had bolted it from the inside. Their attacker grew frustrated, pulling against the door handle several times.

Colin wrenched the pistol cabinet door open as the

window glass shattered inward and the curtains were torn away.

Colin tried to stand, needing to place himself between Marietta and the broken window. But his feet found no solid purchase, just a river of down shifting beneath his weight. Losing his balance, he fell backward onto the seat.

Two hands in long leather gloves, each holding a pistol, reached through the window frame into the carriage.

As in battle, everything slowed. Both pistols pointed at a spot in the middle of Colin's chest. At this range, he had no hope of surviving. And he felt more relief than fear.

Colin held out his hands to show he was unarmed. He could see nothing of the highwayman. Only a dark duster and a mask.

The guns didn't fire.

One pistol shifted to the opposite seat. But Marietta wasn't there. Seeing her on the floor, the highwayman repositioned his sights.

Colin moved, flinging himself between Marietta and the barrel. He heard the cock of the trigger, saw the flash of fire, and felt the hit of the ball in his side. Black powder burned his flesh.

Dark smoke filled the cabin, and he choked, coughing.

His ears rang from the boom of the gunshot, but he saw the flash of the second pistol firing, along with a shower of sparks from the side and barrel of the gun. He felt Marietta's scream. He pulled himself up, half-standing, one hand against the carriage roof to steady himself. His side stabbed with pain at each expansion of his lungs.

Marietta tried to rise behind him, choking as well. She pulled against the clothes on his back, but he pushed her hands away. When the smoke cleared, his body would stand between Marietta and their assailant. Marietta beat the backs of his legs. Some of the lit sparks from the pistols had fallen onto the down-filled bed. Colin assessed the dangers automatically. Once the embers ate past the woolen cover and fire caught the feathers, the danger would spread quickly.

Still on the floor, Marietta pushed herself to the opposite door, kicking the smoldering bolsters and pallet away from her. With each kick, she further entangled his feet. He couldn't reach her, at least not easily. And he couldn't reach and load a gun without stepping from his defensive position in front of her. Thick smoke burned his eyes.

With neither sound nor sight to help him, he had to choose: the dangers of the fire, growing with each second, or those of the highwaymen who could be waiting outside to rob or murder them. Tensing, he unbolted the door, pushed it open, and leapt out. His leg hitting wrong, he fell and rolled into the ditch beside the road. He raised himself cautiously. The highwaymen were gone, having attacked, then left. Not robbers then.

He pulled himself to standing. He should worry about Fletcher, but there was no time. Smoke from the feather-stuffed pallet billowed from the coach. He could see Marietta's legs, vigorously kicking the smoldering bed away from her. She was alive, but trapped against the locked door on the opposite side of the carriage.

Ignoring the pain below his ribs, he pulled hard on the pallet, dragging a portion through the coach door. Already, the smoldering feathers were breaking through the wool in patches of open flame. He heaved again, releasing all but a third from the coach. Flames began to dance across the pallet.

If the pallet broke apart before he could remove it, he'd have to sacrifice the carriage, and then he could offer little protection to Marietta. He pulled once more, hard, and the pallet fell onto the verge next to the road. Then, to protect neighboring crops and livestock, he dragged the pallet, flames licking at his hands, into the middle of the road, cursing at each step. Once carriage and countryside were out of danger, he hunched over, hands on his knees, trying to catch his breath without expanding his lower ribcage.

After taking a few minutes to recover his breath, Colin looked up at the carriage. Fletcher remained at his post, his body slumped forward.

Colin climbed the side of the coach, gritting his teeth against the pain. Blood oozed through the hair at the back of the coachman's head. Pressing his fingers to the older man's neck, Colin felt the beat of the artery. Alive.

Listening and watching for trouble, Colin weighed his options.

They needed to move, to get off the open road. But for that, he needed Fletcher conscious. At least he wouldn't have to explain to Cook how her man had been killed on a quiet English road after surviving a dozen campaigns against Boney.

Still unable to hear, he poured water from the flask under the coachman's seat over the back of Fletcher's head. Tenderly cradling the older man's head, Colin washed the blood away. The wound ran in a long gash slantways from the back of Fletcher's ear toward the back of his head. Colin pressed his fingers against the gash. Long but not deep and worst at the curve of Fletcher's head where the weapon had bitten hardest through the skin.

Fletcher moaned.

Colin lifted Fletcher's chin. "Pistol shot. Can't hear." Colin picked up the fallen reins and held them out. "Can you drive?"

Fletcher took the reins in one hand.

Colin's strength suddenly faded. "How far to the next inn?"

Fletcher held up two fingers, then three. Two to three miles.

Colin moved slowly to the open carriage door, calling out in case Marietta's ears had recovered from the pistol shots. "Marietta, there's an inn within the hour."

He stepped in front of the open door. Marietta was seated

on the floor, leaning against the backward-facing seat riser, her legs bent at odd angles. Her eyes closed, she held one hand to her chest; the other cradled her belly. At her shoulder, blood seeped through her fingers, covering her hand and staining the front of her chemise. Blood pooled on the floor below her.

Colin's chest clenched. He swung himself into the carriage, yelling "Fletcher! Drive!" as he pulled the door shut behind him.

He pulled off his cravat and tore it into strips to make a bandage, then crawled beside her.

To stage an attack and steal nothing. . . . Not robbery. Murder. He needed to think. But first he needed to slow Marietta's bleeding.

Lady Arabella Lucia Fairbourne plunged her hands into the wash water, reaching for another dish. By pure luck, she'd found work as a scullery maid at an inn—and with it servant's lodgings. A place to hide. She'd even taken a servant's name: Lucy.

Several times in the last fortnight, the innkeeper's wife, Nell, had offered Lucy the easier work of waiting on guests in the dining hall, but each time she had refused. The dining hall was too public. Someone might recognize her.

She pulled her hands from the water and examined them, first on one side, then the next. Fingers puckered, cuticles split, palms roughened and red. Her hands looked like those of a woman who worked for a living. The hands of a scullery maid doing hard but honest labor. She smiled. She was exhausted, but free.

She preferred useful labor to idle luxury . . . even if that work was washing dishes rather than caring for the wounded in her father's regiment. Others would consider working in a tavern kitchen a reversal of fortune, but then, they had never lived in her cousin's house. She pressed her palm against the seam of her dress on the outside of her leg. She felt the comforting thickness where she had sewn in the letter her great-aunt Aurelia had entrusted to her. "Take this to my old love, Sir Cecil Grandison." Aurelia's frail hand had patted Lucy's gently. "He'll understand what to do."

Lucy dried a silver platter with a soft cloth. From the windows far above her head, a soft light suffused the kitchen. Evening. Her favorite time of day. Guests, servants, and family all fed, the kitchen cleaned for the night, and Alice the cook leaving Lucy alone to finish the washing. Even so late in the day, the autumn sun would be out for another hour or two, allowing her some time in the inn's private garden. Separated from the public yard by a high wall on the courtyard side and thick hedges on all others, the garden made her feel almost as safe as being in the kitchen.

But feeling safe was different from being safe. The roads were still too full of her cousin's men to try another move. Only that afternoon, she'd seen the one called Ox ("Oaf," she thought, would be more appropriate) looking around the stable yard while his horses were changed.

He hadn't seen her. She had been looking out of the window of the attic room she shared with Mary, the cook's helper.

Ox had seemed preoccupied, almost as if he wished not to be noticed, keeping to himself rather than joking with the other stableman as he typically did. Had they given up on finding her? Certainly no one would expect her to be so close. After all this time, she had hoped that they would have moved the search to London by now. She watched until Ox mounted a horse and rode away.

Garrulous Mary noticed all the men in the stable yard, and it was easy to learn anything she noticed. Ox hadn't spoken to any at the inn, save for calling for a new horse.

He hadn't even haggled the price, Mary had added with surprise.

Lucy placed the last dish in the drying rack. She let the water drain from the sink as she wiped her hands on a rag. Perhaps she should stay another week.

From the hook beside the garden door, she lifted a long, black knit shawl Nell had loaned her for her evening walks in the kitchen garden and wrapped it around her shoulders.

Behind her from the dining hall, she could hear raised voices and shouts, then footsteps ran toward the kitchen. Alarmed, she stepped outside, pulling the door quietly shut behind her. She put her ear to the door, hearing muttered curses, and the kitchen being searched. She pulled the shawl over her head and slipped to the side a few feet—into a darkened corner where the garden wall met the house. There a trellis covered with roses climbed the face of the wall, creating a small declivity where she could step out of sight. She had found it weeks ago when she'd examined the house and yard, looking for places to hide should she need them.

The door opened, the light from the kitchen creating a tall shadow on the ground. She remained very still.

"Lucy!" one of Nell's sons called into the garden from inside the house. "Lucy! Alice!"

She did not move or answer. She would not show herself until she knew why she was wanted and by whom.

"What are you doing, boy?" Alice's voice joined Ned's. "Lucy's done for the night. Leave her be."

"B-b-but there's a lord in the yard. His carriage was attacked by highwaymen," Ned stammered. "Ma said to find you and Lucy."

Not Ox or her cousin. Lucy stepped out from beneath the roses and returned to the kitchen, as if responding to Ned's call. If there were wounded, she might be of use.